THE GARDEN OF DARKNESS

GILLIAN MURRAY KENDALL

First published 2014 by Ravenstone
an imprint of Rebellion Publishing Ltd,
Riverside House, Osney Mead,
Oxford, OX2 0ES, UK

www.ravenstone.com

ISBN: 978 1 78108 248 5

10 9 8 7 6 5 4 3 2 1

A CIP catalogue record for this book is available from the British Library.

Designed & typeset by Rebellion Publishing
Cover art by Luke Preece

Printed in the US

Thou shalt not be afraid for the terror by night;
Nor for the arrow that flieth by day;
Nor for the pestilence that walketh in darkness.

Psalm 91

*For Rob
and for Sasha and Gabriel (of course)*

After They Left the City

THE PANDEMIC burned through the population until only a few children remained. The adults died quickly. When SitkaAZ13, which everyone called Pest, first began to bloom, Clare and her father and stepmother, Marie, listened to the experts on the television—those desperately mortal scientists with multiple initials behind their names. And then one by one the experts had dropped away, taken by the pandemic they so eagerly described.

But not before they'd made it clear: while a very few children might prove resistant to the disease until they reached late adolescence, all of the adults were going to die. All of them.

Clare had found it hard to watch her father and Marie, still vital, still healthy, and know that the two of them would soon be dead. She supposed she would be dead too before long. The odds weren't great that she would prove to be one of the few who lived into their late adolescence. Her father and Marie simply tried not to talk about death. Not until her father's words at the very end.

NOW IT WAS over, and Clare, a temporary survivor after all, stood on Sander's Hill looking down at the giant necropolis that stretched out below her—the city of the dead and dying. The city of crows.

Clare was fifteen years old. And it astonished her that she was still alive. Everything that told her who she was—the intricate web of friendships and family that had cradled her—was gone. She could be anyone.

PART ONE

CHAPTER ONE
SCENES FROM A PANDEMIC

CLARE AND HER father and stepmother survived long enough to leave the dying city in their neighbor's small Toyota. The family SUV was too clunky and hard to maneuver, and their neighbor, decaying in his bed, offered no objections when they took his more fuel-efficient car. Their departure was hurried and late in the day—they had spent most of the day waiting for Clare's best friend, Robin, to join them. But Robin never came. They daren't stay any longer; the Cured now ruled the city at night.

Clare knew that once they left the city, there was no possibility she would ever see Robin again. While Clare had loved Michael, still loved Michael, would always love Michael, her friendship with Robin was inviolate. Which was why Clare knew that if Robin could have made the rendezvous, she would have. They might wait a thousand years, but Robin would not come. Clare did not doubt that someone—or something—had gotten her.

On that fresh summer day, as the shadows began to creep out from under the trees, and the strange hooting of the Cured began to fill the night, Clare was under the illusion that she had nothing more to lose. She had, after all, even lost herself—she had been a cheerleader; she had been popular; she had been a nice person. And under that exterior was something more convoluted and complicated, something that made her wakeful and watchful, that made her devour books as the house slept. But none of that mattered anymore. Her cheerleading skills were not needed. And there was nothing to be wakeful about anyway: the monster under the bed had been Pest all along.

*   *   *

THEY WERE TAKING all the supplies they could fit into the car, but they were not taking Clare's parakeet, Chupi. Marie talked about freeing the bird, but Clare knew that Chupi would not last a winter. She knew that Marie knew it, too. When it was almost time to go, Clare got into the Toyota listlessly, fitting her body around backpacks and cartons of food and loads of bedding and enough bandages and bottles of antibiotics to stock a small pharmacy.

Then she got out again. Her father and Marie were arguing heatedly about who was going to drive as she slipped into the house. "No, Paul," Marie said in her patented Marie-tone, "*I'm* a better driver on the freeway."

Clare went straight to Chupi's cage. They had never had a cat or a dog. Marie was allergic to both. That left fish or something avian. It was a choice that wasn't a choice—Clare wasn't about to bond with a guppy or deal with ick—so they bought her a birthday parakeet. And, eventually, Clare found that Chupi charmed her. The parakeet would hop around Clare's books while she studied. Occasionally, he would stop and peck at the margins of the pages until they were an amalgam of little holes, as if Chupi had mapped out an elaborate, unbreakable code in Braille.

Chupi's release was to come right before they left. Her father, Paul, didn't have the heart to wring the bird's neck—Clare knew that Chupi had charmed him, too. Marie's delicate sensibilities made her a non-starter for the task, although Clare thought that, actually, Marie might turn out to be rather good at neck-wringing. They didn't ask Clare.

When Clare got to Chupi's cage, she opened the door and pressed gently on the parakeet's feet so that he would pick up first one foot and then the other until he was perched on her finger. Then she transferred him to a smaller cage. The car was packed tightly, but there was a Robin-size gap in it now, and she had suddenly determined that Chupi, with his bright blue wings and white throat, was coming with her. He was going to be all she had of the old world.

She returned to the car. The argument between Marie and her father had apparently been settled, and her father said nothing when he saw Clare and Chupi. When Marie opened her mouth in protest, he said, "Never mind."

Clare leaned forward to wedge the cage next to a sleeping bag. She wore a low-cut T-shirt and Michael's Varsity jacket, unsnapped, and she looked down for a moment at the pink speckles sprinkled across her chest: the Pest rash. It was like a pointillist tattoo done in red. They all had the Pest rash, but so far they hadn't become ill.

As they began the drive, her father and stepmother scanned the roads for wreckage. Marie had a tire iron in her hand.

"What's that for?" asked Clare.

"Just in case," said Marie.

Clare tried and failed to picture Marie wielding a tire iron against one of the Cured. Marie was a runner.

They were retreating to their house in the rolling countryside.

They drove until they came to a place where the highway was blocked by four cars and a tractor-trailer. When her father left the car to explore the collision, Clare was sure he wouldn't return.

"Be careful, Paul," yelled out Marie, alerting all the Cured in the area. Clare pictured hands reaching out of the wreck and pulling him in like something out of a zombie movie; she pictured faces sagging with Pest leering out of the windows.

But he came back to report that the vehicles were empty. There was a basket of clean laundry in one of the cars, and they rummaged through it and took a blanket from the bottom of the hamper. He had found some pills in the glove compartment of the tractor-trailer. He took those, too.

There was no way to maneuver around the wreckage, so they filled their backpacks with as much food as they could carry and left the car.

"Once we get clear of this mess," said her father, "we'll look for another car."

"I didn't know you could hot-wire cars," said Clare, impressed.

"We're going to look for a car with keys in the ignition."

"Oh." Clare poked holes in a shoebox and, after putting Chupi in it, placed him at the top of her pack. She jammed him solidly between a bunch of fresh bananas and a can of baked beans. It was when they started moving on foot that Clare noticed that her father's face was flushed. She stopped walking, and the cans in her pack pressed against her back as she stared at him. She was suddenly afraid of all that the angry patches on her father's cheeks and forehead might mean. Then—

"We have to go on," he said to her. "No matter what."

They found a car late that afternoon—an abandoned Dodge Avenger with the keys dangling from the ignition.

It took them three long days to get to Fallon. Both Marie and Clare's father were too tired to drive all night, so they stopped and made camp and engaged in the pretense of sleeping. Two would huddle together under the sleeping bags while the third stood watch. Mostly Clare found herself lying awake back-to-back with Marie while her father sat against a tree and stared into the dark. She wondered if the sour damp smell she detected were coming from Marie or from her. She knew that smell. It was fear.

Robin would not have been afraid. Clare knew that, back in the city, when the time had come, Robin would have faced whatever it was that took her down. Pest; an End-of-the-Worlder; a Cured; someone hungry.

When they reached Fallon, they were only two miles from their little country house. By then her father's face was a strange and deep crimson. His cheeks and lips and eyes were slightly swollen, and his smile, when he tried to be encouraging, was lop-sided and forced. His lower lip was grayish and sagged on the left side. He had allowed Marie to drive the last stretch, which Clare did not take as a good sign.

Marie wanted him to rest for a while in Fallon.

"You gave me a scare, Paul," Marie said. "But now you look better." Clare looked at Marie, astonished by the magnitude of the lie.

It was Clare's father who wanted to push on, but Clare knew that it didn't make any difference anymore. Not for him. She loved her father dearly, and she would have loved to sink back into the comfort of denial. But Marie had already taken that route, and somebody needed to be vigilant and to cook the food and to try and keep the living alive. And, of course, to be prepared for the Cured, if any had left the rich scavenging of the city. Marie was not up to those things.

In the end, they spent the early afternoon in Fallon rather than moving on to their country house. Clare put together the kind of lunch she thought her father could stomach, while Chupi, on her shoulder, occasionally tugged at her hair. She was glad she had brought him.

"The two of you will come back to Fallon and search for supplies once we've settled in," said her father. "I want to get to the house. We can rest there. There shouldn't be any Cured this far from the city." The words came out with effort.

"Daddy," said Clare. She hadn't called him Daddy in years.

He looked at her steadily. "I'm afraid I'm going to have to duck out on you, Clare," he said. "I'm sorry."

"That's nonsense," said Marie. "You'll be fine."

They walked. By the time they reached the house, even Marie didn't try to deny the facts.

Her father had Pest. There was no mistaking it; his eyes were swollen almost shut, and he was flushed with fever. His Pest rash had bubbled up into ridges of blisters, and there was blood in the corner of his mouth. Marie quickly made up the double bed so that he could lie down.

"He can be all right if we're careful," said Marie when he was settled in the bedroom, and she and Clare had gone to the living room to talk.

"But there's nothing we can do," said Clare.

"Rest, liquids, aspirin. That's what he needs," her stepmother said.

"And then he'll die anyway." Clare wanted to shake Marie.

"Don't you say that," said Marie. "Just don't you say that."

"They all die," said Clare flatly.

Marie slapped her.

"There's always been a hard streak in you," Marie said. With the slap, Chupi had flown across the room. Now he returned to Clare's shoulder. The slap stung, but it occurred to Clare that time might reveal something rather different inside her. Not a hard streak. Not a hard streak at all.

"I would love to wring that bird's neck," said Marie.

"You don't have the guts," said Clare.

On the second day that he had full-blown Pest, her father managed to get out of bed and walk to a chair. Marie looked almost cheerful at that, but, as he leaned on Marie's shoulder and staggered towards the chair, Clare saw that her father's face was a welter of ropy lines, a perverse road map towards death.

Clare remembered when they had all been hopeful, when, encouraged by television and radio broadcasts, they had been invited to believe that a cure for Pest existed. It had been early days then. It wasn't long before everyone knew that the Cure didn't work. Most who received it died anyway, and even when the Cure did arrest the progress of Pest, it turned humans into something monstrous. The Cure drove them mad.

The Emergency Broadcasting System didn't mention monsters when the word went out not to take the Cure. The Emergency Broadcasting System referred to 'unfortunate side effects' and 'possible instability.' By then, Clare and her best friend Robin knew the truth: the Cured were violently insane. They would kill the living and eat the dead. Despite a certain amount of exaggeration, by the time all the texting and Tweeting and Skyping and Facebooking and YouTubing came to a halt, everyone was pretty well informed.

Once he was in his chair, Clare's father looked up at her. The skin around his eyes and mouth still looked swollen, but the flush of fever was gone.

"I feel better," he said. And Clare thought that maybe it really would turn out all right. Maybe he would be the one person in the whole world to beat Pest. Then he pulled her close.

"I think that maybe you're going to be the one to make it," he said to Clare. "Get supplies. Dig in when winter comes."

"What about me?" asked Marie.

"I'm sorry, honey," he said. "But Clare will care for you at the end."

It was clear from Marie's face that this was not what she had expected.

"What a thing to say," she said. Clare wondered which part had offended Marie. She also realized that it was true—if it came to it, she would care for her stepmother.

An hour later, her father collapsed. Supported by Marie, he staggered to his bed. His skin looked papery and febrile; he began raving in a low and desperate tone. Marie stood and stared. It was Clare who pulled up the covers and put a cool wet compress on her father's head.

Clare was struck by the colossal indifference of the disease. Pest didn't care that her father was a famous writer. Clare remembered that he used to joke that being famous meant that he could, finally, put a comma anywhere he damn well pleased. But commas didn't matter anymore. And Clare thought it would probably be a long time before she read a new book.

Her father never got up again; he was too weak to move.

Sometime during the afternoon the pustules from the Pest rash burst, and Clare mopped up the red and yellow fluid without saying anything. Near the end, Clare tried to spoon a little chicken bouillon between her father's chapped lips. He gave her a wrecked smile. Then he died.

Marie stood in the doorway, weeping, which annoyed Clare.

"We should bury him," Clare said, but she doubted they had the strength. And when Clare looked up at her stepmother, she noticed the beginning of a rosy glow on her face.

"We'll cope," said Marie. "We'll get through this. Right, Clare?" As she spoke, Clare saw swollen lips and eyelids. The Pest rash had crept up Marie's neck and deepened to an angry red. There were blisters on her throat.

They weren't going to be able to cope at all. Clare knew better. Marie probably had no more than three days. People generally didn't last longer than that.

Her father's body remained on the bed; a fetid smell filled the room, but Clare didn't have the strength or the time to do anything about it—open the windows, try to move the body. Marie needed her right away. Clare unfolded the sofa bed in the living room, covered it with the only clean sheet she could find—one with a pattern of bluebells and roses—and helped her stepmother lie down. The cheerful sheet seemed to mock them both.

Clare tended her stepmother as best she knew how, as if her ministrations could make up for all the dull anger she had felt towards Marie after the marriage to her father. She put wet washcloths on Marie's wrists and neck; she brought her stepmother water and aspirin and more water and more aspirin. Lesions began to streak Marie's face and more pustules began to form on her neck. At the end of the second day she got up and, without a word, lurched into the bedroom where Clare's father lay. Marie lay down next to her husband, oblivious to the smell in the room, and so Clare tended her there. Unlike her husband, Marie was never entirely lucid again.

On the evening of the third day, she died.

She died with her eyes wide open. Clare tried to shut those staring eyes by passing her hand over Marie's face the way people did in movies, but it didn't work.

Then Clare curled up at the foot of their bed; she waited in the bedroom for a long time for someone to come. Because that's what happened when you were a kid—even when you were a fifteen-year-old kid. When your parents died, someone came.

Later, on Sander's Hill, Clare blinked in the strong light as Chupi pecked at the ground around her. She wondered if there was a lot of dying going on in the city that day. Clare knew that she was infected with Pest—the rash was enough to prove that. She knew that she was going to die of it, too. Eventually. She might even have a couple of years left, but, according to the scientists, she wasn't going to live to adulthood. That's what they had all said, all those scientists who were now dead. Those scientists had called delayed-onset of the disease the 'Pest Syndrome.' Syndrome. On a triple word score in Scrabble, it was seriously useful vocabulary.

In its own weird way, Clare thought the link between Pest and adolescence sounded logical. Adolescence had always been a bag of goodies: complexion problems, mood swings, unrequited love and now, Pest.

Her thoughts came back to the problems at hand. It was high summer. Not a good time to keep dead bodies above ground.

And if Clare couldn't bury them—and she was sure the task was beyond her—she was going to have to go elsewhere. She was going to have to leave her father and Marie to the forces of time and nature, both of which, it seemed, were sublimely indifferent to Clare's emotional state.

But it seemed to Clare now that she could deal with the grandeur of indifference, the blind workings of the universe. This was not the time for petty gods or the Thunder-roarer; death was insidious, irrational, arbitrary; now was the time of the beetle and the worm. And, for better or for worse, because there was no one else, it was her time too.

PEDIATRICS

IN THOSE LAST days, before it all broke down, he left his lab to work in the wards. They all thought he was a great humanitarian, but the truth was, he enjoyed watching SitkaAZ13 close-up. The disease, under a microscope, looked plump and innocent—right before it would enter a red blood cell and, in the metaphor his mind constructed, scatter the cell's constituent limbs while feeding off its bloody heart.

So elegant. He wished he had developed it himself—the virus was a wonderful world-cleanser. He wondered if someone really had spliced it together, or if the virus were just a natural consequence of too many species sharing the same niches. A vampire bat sucked on a monkey and then shat on a coca fruit that was picked by a farmer. Or maybe it had gone down some other way. But it most certainly had gone down.

The patients came in a steady stream now, and most of the pediatric patients were referred to him. He liked to look at the nurses looking at him as he developed a rapport with his soon-to-be-dead young patients. His manner was perfect; he gained the children's confidence and then he watched them die.

Some of them had lovely eyes.

The waste.

He had read the articles (and many of the articles he had written himself), and although the journals were now largely defunct, shut down by the pandemic, he knew a great deal about SitkaAZ13. Out there were pediatric patients who, although they had the Pest rash, resisted the onset of the full-blown disease. He wanted to find them. The world would soon be almost empty; it would be ripe for a new creation; that creation would come from those resistant child-patients.

He faced a girl called Jenny. She was obviously not resistant; lesions marked her throat and face.

"Hello, Jenny," he said. "I don't need to look at your file. I can see you're a good girl, a caring daughter, just by looking in your eyes. I bet your parents are proud of you."

"They're dead." Her voice was dull, flat. "My brothers too. I had to leave them in the house—no-one answered when I called for help. They're turning more and more dead."

"Admit her," he said to a nurse. Then he turned to Jenny again. "We'll see your parents and brothers are taken care of, but right now, we're taking care of you. All right, honey? You're not going to need to worry any more."

She looked up at him with eyes of infinite trust. He was, after all, the doctor.

"Yes," she said. "Thank you."

The nurse was watching him closely, and he knew word about his humanitarian bedside manner would spread. Why not? All the more pediatric cases would be sent his way. And he would rifle through their folders looking for resistant ones. And among them there would be resistant ones with the elusive double recessive genes he was seeking.

His cause was scientific. Not, perhaps, in the sense that the old world understood science. But he would build a new world. He had already purchased the place he would take all the suitable survivors he could find.

Land was going cheap.

When the folders came in, however, and when he looked them over, he realized he might not be able to be picky: so far, there were no resistant children at all, not at his hospital. The world was engaged in a massive dying.

He took precautions against SitkaAZ13. He would need to be

careful. They were saying now that his cure didn't work, that the side-effects were overwhelming, but when he applied the cure to himself, he didn't feel any side-effects at all. Odd. Maybe the side-effects were already part of his constitution.

The hospital stopped admitting patients. As he went to the pediatric ward, he had to step around gurneys with patients strapped to them. They were in the hallways, and when he went to the cafeteria for something to sustain him, he saw that it, too, had become a staging area for SitkaAZ13 patients. He went to the vending machine for a candy bar, and there were gurneys there too. Pressed right up against the place he wanted to insert his dollar bill.

He moved the gurney.

"Please," said one of the patients. "Can you get me some water?"

He was trying to squash a George Washington into the machine's bill receptor, and finally, after several tries, he got the machine to take it.

"Of course," he said.

He picked up his Diet Coke and went back to the pediatric ward.

He examined child patients wherever he found them, and when he was done, really no matter how sick they were, he gave them a lollipop. Most of them smiled, even if they were too sick to enjoy the candy; it was a comforting gesture, one reminiscent of the pre-SitkaAZ13 world. Like giving Scooby-Doo bandaids to little ones.

Soon other doctors fled. As he indefatigably and patiently made his rounds, he became hospital legend.

And, again, why not?

Meanwhile, somewhere out there were the resistant ones. And surely among them—he tried not to be excited, but it was a thrilling thought—were his little blue-eyed girls.

CHAPTER TWO
THE OLD WORLD DIES

LOOKING BACK, IT seemed to Clare that the breakdown of high-tech devices should have given her the biggest clue that nothing was ever going to be the same again. Take away electricity, and one could light candles and, eventually, get a generator going. Take away Google, take away the contributors to Wikipedia, take away all that, and one was taking away the world as Clare knew it.

WHEN THEIR NEIGHBORS, *the Cormans, boarded up their house and left, Clare, worried, texted Michael, even though he was supposed to be on a camping trip and out of reach of cell service. He didn't answer. Next she texted Robin, who seemed distracted and upset. There was alarming news on the television about overloaded hospitals and overworked doctors.*

One day later, Clare's friends slowly ceased to answer her texts—except for Robin. Two days later Clare's phone was refusing to send texts at all, and the landlines were down. Robin bicycled over to Clare's house since her learner's permit didn't allow her to drive alone.

At the time, those things still seemed to matter.

"My parents are in the hospital," she told Clare. "Can I stay with you?" There were dark circles under her eyes, and she looked drawn and grey.

Clare's father and Marie welcomed her. Robin had spent half her life sleeping over at the house anyway. And, unlike Clare, Robin got along all right with Marie.

"*Mom and Pop went to the hospital to get the Cure*," said Robin. "*But now people are saying that it isn't working right. The doctors wouldn't let me stay.*"

In the morning, Clare's father drove Robin back to the hospital. When they returned, before either of them even spoke, Clare knew that something was very wrong.

"*They died in the night,*" said Robin.

"*Robin.*" Clare didn't know what else to say. She had known Robin's parents her whole life.

"*I should have stayed,*" said Robin.

"*We're not going back,*" said Clare's father. "*Robin will stay with us for the time being.*"

"*They're not releasing their bodies,*" Robin said "*They said there was too much chance of spreading Pest. There're lots of dead people in the hospital now: in the corridors, on stretchers by the vending machines.*"

"*It's a nest of contagion,*" said Clare's father.

That night they all crouched around the television. They tuned in to Natalie Burton, science analyst for Channel 22—Clare's favorite channel because of its Law & Order re-runs.

"*What was early this week thought to be a cure,*" said Natalie, "*has proven deadly: most who receive it die; those who do not, become gravely changed; they become what at least one researcher has called 'inhuman.' These so-called 'Cured' are to be avoided at all cost.*

"*While mortality rates have been reported to be high, a tiny percentage of children under the age of eighteen show no signs of the full-blown virus—although they carry the Pest rash. When this scourge ends...*" (Clare could tell that good old Natalie was winding up to her conclusion) "*...they may be left orphaned and alone.*" Clare's father turned off the television.

And so it seemed that she and Robin were among the resilient. Robin showed no signs of Pest; Clare felt perfectly healthy. Only the Pest rash showed that they were infected, too.

*   *   *

WHEN CLARE GOT back to the house from Sander's Hill, she went into the bedroom where the bodies were. Her father and Marie had been dead for two days. In death, her father stared sightlessly towards the ceiling. Her stepmother lay beside him. Clare wondered how long she could stand to stay in the house with the dead: they didn't seem like her parents anymore now that they lay there, unmoving, flies taking advantage.

Clare suddenly crossed the room and opened the window, overcome by the smell. She wanted to vomit, and she bent over the sill but then realized that she was leaning out over the flower garden. The zinnias were in full bloom, a vibrant riot of reds and blues, and Clare realized that she didn't really want to throw up on them.

Her stomach began to settle as she breathed the cooler air of twilight. Night was drawing in, and now the scent of the moonflowers was in the air. The evening light muted the color of the zinnias, but even in the growing darkness, Clare was aware of the garden spread out below her.

The garden wouldn't last; she couldn't tend it; the weeds would overcome the flowers.

It was a long time before she turned away.

CHAPTER THREE
PICKING UP PIECES

BEFORE THEIR DEPARTURE to Fallon, the electricity had gone off. No phone. The toilet only flushed if the tank were hand-filled with water, and no water was coming out of the tap. But, Clare remembered, she and Robin had been curiously unafraid.

DEEP IN THE *night, after Robin had come to stay, Robin and Clare—long after Clare's father and Marie were asleep—took to their bicycles. They wore dark clothing and no helmets. Had there been cars on the road, they might have been in danger, but there were no cars.*

They coasted down the road. Across the street from the hospital, Robin started to slow down, and Clare almost crashed into her.

"Look at that," whispered Robin. They left their bicycles and crept as close to the hospital as they could without risking being seen.

Gurneys spilled out of the emergency room and into the parking lot, and figures in surgical scrubs moved among them. Enormous lights painted the night blue-white. Even at that distance, Clare could see the faces of the patients. And she heard a sound like the gentle lowing of cattle. It took her a moment to realize that she was hearing the groans of the sick.

By the time Clare and Robin got back to the house, the sky was getting light, and the stars were gone. Only Venus hung low in the pallid grey of morning.

Later that day, Clare and Robin watched from the peephole of the door when they heard Mrs. Hennie crash out of her house, taking down the screen door with her. Mrs. Hennie went into the street, staggered for a while, and lay down. She didn't move.

"What do we do?" asked Robin.

"Nothing," said Clare. "There's nothing we can do. She looks dead."

Clare wondered if Mrs. Hennie's son, Chris, were still alive. Maybe he was watching the same scene from inside his house.

"We should see if Chris is all right," Clare told her stepmother.

Marie was silent, and then she turned away from them.

THE HOUSE IN the rolling countryside was silent now and filled with death. Clare slept in the closet of her room that night. She hung Chupi's cage from the hanger rack and filled his feeder with seed and checked his water. Then she rolled herself up in her old blue comforter.

She considered her situation.

She really couldn't bury the bodies. Not only was she too small, but the very idea of leaving her father and Marie open to the ravages of strange voracious underground things made her faintly sick.

She couldn't move them. So she would have to go somewhere else.

Elementary.

THE DAY THEY decided they would have to leave the city, the army arrived. Clare and Robin watched as soldiers came through the streets in enormous trucks. A few tanks rumbled by. All of the soldiers carried guns.

They left leaflets everywhere. When the street was clear, Robin and Clare ran out and gathered an armful.

The cover of the leaflets showed a woman wearing a surgical mask. From the crinkles around her eyes, it looked as if she were smiling.

The text was all about entering quarantine centers and being under martial law and covering your mouth if you sneezed. And watching out for the Cured. That part was in big letters.

Marie took one of the leaflets from them and crumpled it up.

"The army won't be here long," she said.

The army wasn't. By the evening, Pest was among them. Perhaps it had already been among them. There were gunshots in the night. No more leaflets were distributed.

CLARE ATE A can of peas. Then she made piles of all the non-perishable foods in the house. And after that, leaving Chupi as house guardian, she set out for the nearby cabin that belonged to the Loskeys. She had thought of going there before to find help, but she had been afraid of what she might find there. More sick people. More responsibilities. Bodies.

But when she got there, she found that the cabin was boarded up snugly. It appeared that the Loskeys hadn't even been up there this summer. They were probably back in the city, and they were probably dead.

CLARE AND ROBIN stood by while Clare's parents tried to find the BBC World Service on the radio—the television stations were all off the air, but Clare's father had faith in the BBC. He loved the English. Finally, while he was still fiddling with the tuning, Clare and Robin went to bed. They slept late. Clare's father woke them to say that he had finally found a news channel. The Cured were becoming more vicious. And that's when Clare heard for the first time that all the adults who got Pest were going to die. All of them.

"You need to prepare yourself," Clare's father said. But Clare wasn't sure what that meant, and she was pretty sure that her father didn't, either.

*　　*　　*

CLARE FORCED HER way into the cabin and investigated. There was a bedroom and a kitchen with a well-stocked larder. Outside, there was a tool shed, and in it she found a little wagon with four wheels. It was time to make the move from the family's summer house to the Loskey's cabin.

Chupi's cage was perched on top of the first load, and he flapped against the bars as if protesting against his status as luggage. Clare used the wagon to transport clothes and blankets and matches and food and candles and whatever else came to hand. In her parents' house, the smell of decomposition seemed to taint all their belongings. And the house was growing dark as the day became more overcast. She almost expected to see the darkness clinging to the clothing and bedding and goods when she brought them out into the air.

CHRIS HENNIE OUTLIVED *his parents. He came to the door right before Clare, her father and stepmother left, but there was no question of his coming with them—his face was flushed, and his lips were drooping. Pest.*

They wouldn't let Chris in.

"Do you want to sing?" Chris called out in a strange voice. "Do you want to sing a song with me?"

WHEN SHE NEXT reached the summer house, trundling the wagon behind her, the marigolds in Marie's garden were beginning to close. It was time to hurry; night was coming, and Clare realized that she was going to need the power flashlight. It provided a brilliant beam of light; it was heavy; it was a potential weapon. The flashlight was in the closet near the front door, and Clare had to stand on a chair to get it. For a moment the chair teetered, and

Clare realized that, if she fell and broke something, that would probably be the end.

When she got back to the Loskey place, Clare sat for a moment while Chupi hopped about in his cage. She opened her shirt and looked down at her Pest rash. She was infected, and yet her father had bet on her survival.

She went to the kitchen and opened a jar of pickles and chewed, thoughtfully.

AN HOUR BEFORE *the electricity cut out, a single broadcast came though on the television. Robin and Clare couldn't know it, but this was the last television broadcast they were ever to see.*

"I am master of the situation," a man in a white lab coat said. "All the adults are going to die except me. But if you're alive, then you're probably a child, and I can help you. You don't have to be taken by Pest, now or ever. I can cure you. Once all the sick are dead, I'll reveal my location. Tune in to your radio."

"What do you think?" asked Robin.

"You can't possibly believe him," said Clare.

"He's still alive," said Robin. "Why not believe him? What else do we have to believe?"

"We could believe that some adults are going to survive."

"Everyone says all the adults are going to die, Clare," said Robin. "My parents died. Example A."

"My parents are fine," said Clare.

Robin looked at Clare contemplatively.

"I think this master-of-the-situation should be part of our plan," she said.

"We don't have a plan," said Clare. "Our plan is my father and Marie."

"I just meant that he could be Plan B," said Robin.

*   *   *

CLARE RAN HER hand lightly over her rash.

Plan B.

That night, the Loskey's double bed looked too big and exposed. Clare slept in the closet, curled in Michael's letter jacket, Chupi's cage above her.

At first Clare couldn't sleep. She realized that she would have to learn to be alone. Clare, not for the first time, missed Robin terribly. And she also knew with certainty that she was never, in the course of her life, going to find out what had happened to her.

As Clare finally began to doze, she wondered if all the wild animals had died, too. But the next morning, when she left the Loskey place for another trip back to the house of the dead, Clare saw, brilliant in the sunshine, an enormous stag browsing in the cabbage patch. He raised his head and seemed to look right through her, as if she weren't there, as if she were no more than a ghost of the past.

CHAPTER FOUR
AND THE OLD WORLD WAS GONE

CLARE SLEPT FOR twelve hours, this time in the double bed, and when she woke, the covers were sweat-soaked and tangled around her. Her dreams had been terrifying, and she rubbed her face hard, checking to see if the marks of Pest had begun to manifest. They had not. She had to pee and discovered, much to her disgust, that there was a blockage in the toilet. The plunger was useless. She tried pouring a bucket of water into the tank and then flushing, but the toilet immediately overflowed. Clare fled the bathroom.

She went to the kitchen and ate a can of tuna fish. When she filled Chupi's feed bowl, she noted that he looked listless. She took him out of the cage and put him on her shoulder, and he perked up a bit and pecked at her earring and then pulled at her hair. When she put him back, he immediately tucked his head under his wing. Chupi didn't like change; Clare wished she could block out the world as easily. She sat at the rough table and started making lists of things to do. Lists kept her mind from the still forms under the bedclothes in the other house. And from the emptiness that was Robin's absence. And from the thought of Michael dead. She wrote:

Food

Water

Things for winter

Fix toilet or

Dig Latrine

Then, with a sigh, she added 'Tampons.' And, after that, she added 'Tylenol.'

That afternoon, Clare went to Sander's Hill, the one place from which the city was clearly visible. She had taken *Jane Eyre*, and she also took Chupi, who liked to peck at the margins of the book, leaving behind holes that seemed full of meaning.

The city below her was rotting, but it wouldn't rot forever. Clare pictured the days and weeks and months to come. She envisioned nature creeping through the streets and covering the buildings like a blanket.

When she got back to the Loskey's, Clare left the door of the cage open, so Chupi could fly around the house if he chose.

Two days passed and Clare retrieved her list of things to do from behind some sour-smelling cans in the kitchen. Clare read it and put it back behind the cans.

She opened a jar of brown stuff that smelled nutritious but had lost its label and spread it on a stale cracker. Then Clare had a few spoonfuls of grape jelly from the preserves she found in the root cellar. She washed it down with two Cokes and went outside. The air around the shack was becoming rank, faintly skunky, and it occurred to Clare, as she went back inside, feeling slightly sick, that there were diseases other than Pest.

Her stepmother would have kept the cabin clean; her father would have dug a latrine right away. And it occurred to her that, perhaps, she had been a little spoiled in the life before Pest came.

Things had come easily to her. Clare had been hugely popular in high school—so popular that no one cared that she hung out with an oddball like Robin. They didn't know that, really, she was an oddball too. She just knew how to play the game, and she played it because it was easier than walking around exposing what was within. She had been on the cheerleading squad; she had known what to wear and how to do her hair. Only Laura Sparks, beautiful and mean, was more popular. Now Clare was alone, and all her charm and her ability to do breathtaking back flips could do nothing to help her. Nor, she thought, could her steady habit of reading. Defoe's *A Journal of the Plague Year* was like a joke in the face of Pest.

Clare found her list again and underlined 'Dig Latrine,' but she knew that underlining accomplished nothing. As the evening became chilly, she pulled Michael's Varsity jacket tightly around her. Chupi seemed restless, and Clare thought that his new life must seem as strange to him as hers was to her.

As the light began to fade, she finally let herself think about Michael.

"WE COULD BIKE over to Michael's and see if he's back," said Clare one evening.

"We could."

Clare and Robin left the house at three in the morning. And it was like going out into Hell.

Fires burned in the street, and they heard howling and shrieking from somewhere in the city.

By the time they reached Michael's, clouds covered the moon; a light drizzle had begun, and the bikes gleamed when Clare turned on her flashlight.

Michael's house was dark. The door was open and hung at an angle. When they went inside, Robin just pointed. The body of Michael's dog, Hammer, lay on the rug.

They found Michael in his room lying on his back, dead. Michael's Varsity jacket was on the bed. Mindlessly, Clare picked it up and put it on.

"I don't know what to do," she said, blankly. "He and I were best friends."

"You and I are best friends," said Robin. "You and Michael were something else."

Clare said nothing but pulled a sheet off Michael's bed and covered his body. She wanted to embrace him, but Robin held her back.

"I'm always going to love him," Clare said.

"Yeah," said Robin. "But no hugs. He's decaying. It's like that story we read in English."

"'A Rose for Emily.'"

"Yeah. That."

And at that moment, in the stinking apartment, with Michael dead in front of her, Clare had one of what Robin called her pretty-good-guesses (because neither of them believed in prescience). She saw herself in a garden, alone under a full moon, and someone was walking towards her.

CLARE THOUGHT OF the people behind boarded up windows, in the alleyways, in beds and on floors, lost to delirium in cars, all still engaged in the process of dying. By the time she had walked back to the cabin, it was dark. She hadn't seen any Cured, but she locked down the cabin every night anyway.

It occurred to Clare that she could give up trying to make a life of it here: she could move from house to house, fouling them and then leaving when she had exhausted their larders. There was no one to care, no one to tell her to pull herself together.

She really needed to pull herself together.

Abruptly, Clare thought of her friend Mary. She, Robin and Mary had been close before Mary had moved to Canada. Clare wondered if perhaps Mary had lived, too. There was no reason in the world for Clare to think that she was the only one to have delayed-onset Pest. Maybe Mary was out there somewhere trying to get by, trying to survive.

Or maybe Mary had lived through Pest only to kill herself.

What an odd thought to have.

THE NIGHT BEFORE they were all to leave for the country, Robin and Clare saw a lone woman walking the street in a long ball gown. She wore necklaces and bracelets and earrings that jangled and glittered in the moonlight. They watched her until she was gone.

Then the woman's place was taken by people with lesions on their faces, parading through the streets in a macabre farewell to the world.

"It's more than time to go," Clare's father said as they watched. Shortly after that, the streets were curiously empty. It was as if, in the face of disease, people had finally retreated into their houses, to hide out until they died.

FINALLY CLARE DID dig a latrine, but she did so only to then realize that she was eventually going to run out of food. When she had found the cans and preserves in the root cellar she had thought she could never run out. She had also found gardening tools, packets of seed, bags of dry corn, gallons of water, a bow and some arrows. The bow must have been Mr. Loskey's; it was too taut for her to pull back.

It was as if the Loskeys had been preparing for some kind of apocalypse (and when it had come they had missed it). Clare, on the other hand, had survived the initial onslaught of Pest and now she had a choice: scavenge, clean up, shape up and brush her teeth. Or give up on life and just go to bed and die.

But her death would mean the death of Chupi, too, which didn't seem fair. She went to change Chupi's water, and she saw he wasn't in his cage. He didn't seem to be in the house, either. She opened the front door, just in case he had somehow flown to the porch as she had left for Sander's Hill. As she stood in the doorway, he flew out of the living room and over her head. He perched on the tree in front of the cabin. He had been inside the whole time.

"Chupi."

She went to the tree.

"Chupi."

He behaved as if he couldn't hear her. He flew to the copse of trees by the driveway. She followed, calling him, until he flew well beyond her. And then she simply stood and called and watched as Chupi flew from tree to tree until finally she stopped calling, and then she could no longer see him, and he was just something more that had moved beyond her horizon. And so the old world was gone.

CHAPTER FIVE
ON THE PASSENGER PIGEON

SOMETIMES CLARE SAT on the porch with a pair of binoculars and scanned the trees for Chupi. She didn't expect to see him; it was just comforting to look. Clare thought she was learning an essential lesson about life: post-Pest, one's world just got smaller and smaller. Everything one loved went away.

At least she had the garden. In the garden where she had seen the stag, there were pumpkins the size of basketballs, monstrous zucchini and magic wands of summer squash. There were cornstalks and cabbages, a yellowing vine of cherry tomatoes and a batch of sprawling cucumbers. Every day she did a little work in the garden, and it was the only time she came close to feeling fine. She wasn't sick. She wasn't well. But at least the Pest rash wasn't spreading.

Clare was weeding the garden when she first heard the noise. It was a low sound, a snuffling sound, a growling sound. The kind of sound a large animal might make. The absurd thought that it was Pest itself, somehow embodied, took hold of her. She was overcome with terror.

The thing making the sound was big, that was certain. Very big.

The sound was coming from the area of the garden where the cabbages were starting to go to seed. She started to relax. *The stag*, she thought. *It's a deer*. Deer liked cabbages.

That's when she saw the dog—a dog big as a bear, steel blue, almost black, like the color of the gun her father had kept in his safe. For just a moment, they stared at each other across the wide expanse of green. Clare realized that, given the size of the dog, it made absolutely no difference that it was on the other side of the garden. She would never be able to outrun it.

It never even occurred to her to placate the animal by saying something like, "Good doggie! Good doggie!" The animal's face was running with pus or foam, and it looked like it had never had an owner's care in its life. It didn't have a collar.

Clare knew the dog would kill her. She wondered, for a moment, how much it would hurt.

Clare ran.

She had once been on a nature hike with her cheerleading friends and a shy naturalist who explained with great seriousness that one should never run from a bear. Clare now strongly suspected the same thing applied to dogs, but it made absolutely no difference, and, besides, she almost made it to the cabin. But Clare made the mistake of slowing enough to turn and look over her shoulder. The dog was as enormous as she had thought and was coming for her with teeth bared.

Clare kept running. She was almost to the door.

Then she fell, heavily.

The dog pulled itself up, as if in surprise. Then it came on. The animal was heavier and bigger than she was—there was no chance that she would be able to overpower it. Clare was just starting to put a hand up to defend herself when it leapt at her. Its breath was rank, as if it had fed on corpses, and she felt teeth closing on her arm.

She stared up into the dog's yellow eyes, eyes running with mucus, and at that moment she found herself thinking—strange as it was—about the stag she had seen in the honey light of a morning that now seemed long ago.

Without thinking, she blew into the dog's nostrils.

"Bad dog," she said.

One of her arms was trapped under the dog while its teeth were buried in the flesh of the arm that covered her throat. She had blown all the air out of her lungs with those two words, and now she couldn't breathe in.

She felt the animal pause. Clare managed to free her pinned arm, and she used it to beat the dog on the side of the head. The dog shifted his weight, and suddenly she could take a breath.

"Bad dog," she said again.

For a moment, Clare could feel the dog's anger and hunger, and then, as if he felt her thoughts tangling up with his, the anger began to dissipate into confusion.

They stared into each other's eyes. The dog lowered his eyes first. Then it slowly crept back off of Clare's chest, whining. She gasped, gulping up air, and sat up.

"Dog," she said. "I'm the boss of you." It didn't seem to matter that they were kindergarten words. She gave him a final cuff. The giant animal sat back on its haunches and then leaned forward and began to lick the wounds it had inflicted on her arm.

She was no longer afraid. She wanted to put her arms around his neck, but she knew it wasn't time for that yet. Right now they were busy determining what their relationship would be now and forever.

Clare started to get to her feet, but the dog, with gentle enthusiasm, knocked her over in order to lick her hurt arm more thoroughly. Clare found herself wiping away the mucus from its eyes and mouth. The mouth that a moment before had been about to take her throat out. She was, suddenly, surprisingly, overcome by tenderness.

And she realized that it wasn't just that she had found something instead of losing something more; she had done one better than that. She had been found.

CLARE AND ROBIN, *in preparation for the trip to the country house, put freeze-dried food and other essentials in four knapsacks. If something happened to the car, they wanted to be able to keep on the move.*

But sometime in the night, while Clare slept, Robin disappeared. In the morning, she was simply gone. Long after it was time to go, they waited for her, helplessly. Around them, the city seemed to be asleep; old newspapers and litter blew across their yard. Mrs. Hennie's body still lay in the street.

But Clare knew, after the first hour, that Robin must be dead.

Later Clare was to think that she should have done or said something more as they left without Robin. Certainly she should have somehow known that the last seconds of her childhood were coming to an end, and that she would spend the rest of her life making up for her desertion.

A STRING OF saliva fell from the dog's mouth onto Clare's forehead.

"Yuck," she said, as he drooled on her some more. "I thought you were rabid, but you're just a mess." She wondered where the dog had come from. Certainly it was larger than any city dog had a right to be. Perhaps his owners had lived in Fallon. The giant dog nosed at her again and then lay back to expose his belly.

"You're like a bear," she said. And that's what she called him: *Bear*. She looked into his yellow diamond eyes, and she realized that he was going to be there for her at the end—though of what, she couldn't yet say.

She walked from the garden back to the cabin with her hand on Bear's neck. He had dog breath, she decided. Not corpse breath. After giving him a can of Spam, which he ate dubiously, she pulled all the burrs and briars and ticks out of his fur. He almost purred with pleasure. And she realized that she couldn't help it— she loved this killer dog. More than that, something had passed between them. This killer dog loved her.

Then she thought of all those people who were probably dead. Robin. Mrs. Scherer, her piano teacher. Caroline and Maggie and Heather. Miss Hill, the most popular teacher in school, whose husband had died in the Vietnam war. Gail, at the art gallery.

Larry Garr, her father's editor. Mr. Highfil, the biology teacher, who went on and on about the importance of hand washing.

Hand washing had done nothing to stop Pest.

She thought about Michael. He had confided in her about everything. He was proud of her gymnastic abilities as a cheerleader. He was even proud of her straight A report card, which he seemed to find inexplicable.

But he hadn't been in love with her. He had loved Laura Sparks, with her Angelina Jolie lips and her C+ report card and her Cliff Notes and her pep, which was always on tap.

Clare looked at Bear, who was dozing at her feet, and she thought about Robin's Plan B. The man on the television. A master of the situation. A man with a real cure.

It might be worth living, if there were a real cure.

How many people needed to be left for there to be an actual human race anymore?

Clare had read in school about passenger pigeons, about the way they had darkened the sky for days at a time and made slick the earth with their guano. There had been billions of them. Billions. Then, when their populations had declined beyond the tipping point (and that was when there were still millions of them), Clare read that their numbers had simply dwindled until they had become extinct. She supposed it was like that with humans, too. Pest might have tipped them over the edge. There might be others like her, but there would be no more cities or schools, or, finally, people to think thoughts about passenger pigeons. The world would pass into another age.

Clare felt she should write some things down, maybe just because, as her father used to say, that's what human beings did. So, with Bear walking beside her like an enormous mythical creature, she went slowly back to her own house where the paper was, where the pens were, where her father's study waited.

Along the way, she picked some flowers.

When she got to the house, the stench wasn't as bad as she had thought it would be. She left the flowers in front of her parents' closed bedroom door. In her father's study, she found a block of paper and a pen. Bear lay at her feet, and she rested her toes on him. Clare looked at her father's prizes and degrees—he had always kept them in the country house and not in the city, although she wasn't sure why. And then, with all her father's diplomas hanging on the walls around her, with his Pulitzer Prize gleaming at her from his desk, she tried to write. About the Cured. About the stink that rose from the dead city. About the pandemic—she liked the word 'pandemic'—that had thrown her into adulthood. Then she scratched everything out and started again.

She knew that whatever she wrote would be inadequate for the occasion, but she also knew that, anyway, there wouldn't be any more Pulitzer Prizes given out anytime soon. So she just wrote what had been on her mind. She wrote in small print letters:

THE LAST PASSENGER PIGEON WAS NAMED MARTHA. SHE DIED IN THE CINCINNATI ZOO IN 1914, AND, AFTER THAT, THERE WEREN'T ANY PASSENGER PIGEONS EVER AGAIN.

CHAPTER SIX
THE MOMENT THAT DETERMINED

THE NIGHTS WERE getting colder. She and Bear sat on Sander's Hill companionably, her arm around the great dog. She opened a new block of paper and started a fresh page with the heading, 'Getting Ready For Winter.' She was preparing to go into Fallon, but she wanted the trip to be as fast and efficient as possible. "A surgical strike," Michael would have called it. A few leaves drifted into her hair as she prepared to write 'gloves,' but the pen remained poised above the page. She was deeply uninterested in gloves, or scarves, or boots, or going into Fallon. A few rogue leaves might have been falling, but winter still seemed far away. Maybe she was fooling herself, but it was hard to think ahead. The light was a syrupy golden morning glow that highlighted Bear's black fur. In the long grass, blue cornflowers and tattered Queen Anne's Lace still held sway. Instead of writing 'gloves,' she started to doodle.

She found herself writing Michael's name, and soon it curled down the margin, dark and important, underlined, shaded. Delicate tendrils of climbing vines wound up onto the page from the 'h' and the 'l,' while Clare pictured Michael going ahead of her into the darkness, scouting out the black territories, finding a final haven where it would matter how much she had loved him. Where they could be together forever. Together Forever. And then she found she couldn't really invest much in the fantasy. It was too much like Barbie and Ken in heaven.

Besides, her father had taught her that there was no afterlife, an idea he had tried to dress up by talking about becoming one with the universe and scattering one's atoms back into primal matter. But Clare had seen a lot of rotting bodies since Pest had taken over, and she now recognized that he had been a romantic. Scattering atoms back into primal matter was a nasty business.

She remembered her father at his computer, writing *Bridge Out Ahead*. She remembered pizza night for the cheerleading squad. Reading *Mrs. Dalloway* at two in the morning. Michael, slightly drunk, kissing her after the Spring Dance—where she had been elected Princess by those who probably didn't realize such things usually went by blood. The kiss had surprised her. The Princess status had not. She was, after all, the only cheerleader who could do decent back flips. And when she did enough of them, she could, finally, stop thinking—as the blood roared in her ears, as she became nothing more than her body.

She thought of Michael and Robin and Chupi and of Mrs. Hennie, lying dead in the street. And then she thought of Plan B— of the man who had called himself the master-of-the-situation.

Whoever he was, he had made big promises.

Clare watched the mists rising from the city below until Bear nuzzled her, asking for more attention. She stroked him for a while and then stood up and carefully folded the piece of paper with Michael's name on it.

"Let's go," she said to Bear. She wanted to go into Fallon to look for supplies and then get back to the cabin before nightfall—even if the night were probably still safe. Her father had thought the Cured would stay in the cities for a long time.

Clare had already broken into some of the other places near the cabin to look for supplies, and she had found some food, a couple of hurricane lamps, more candles, a camping stove. But she also found, inevitably, bodies. In one small house, a body had decayed into the bed it lay on; fluids leaked into the sheets leaving a grisly outline. In another house, two bodies on a sofa clutched each other, while another, almost skeletonized, lay on the floor.

And everything stank.

Every time she emerged from a Pest house, she felt darkness and stench clinging to her, penetrating her clothes, infecting her breath with death.

The houses in Fallon belonged largely to people who came to the hills only for the summer. Clare hoped that these houses might be empty of bodies and full of stored food. And Fallon had a grocery store, a gas station, and a general store that stocked everything from toys to linens to camping equipment. It also had a yarn store and a basket outlet. Even before Pest, Clare had never understood the phenomenon of the basket outlet. But the other places—even the Yarn Barn—had potential.

There were animals everywhere in that sunlit morning. Clare thought that maybe there had never been so many wild animals in the world, or that soon enough that would be true. There were rustlings in the unmown lawns, and she startled three deer that were lying in the grass nearby—they bounded away, white tails held high like absurd semaphores. Bear left her side to pursue the deer, and, although she called him, although he stopped and looked back at her for a moment, a second later he was crashing through the fields after them. A startled fox ran in front of her and a covey of partridges burst into the sky. And everywhere there were rabbits—nibbling at the verge of a meadow, lying in the shade of the bushes. They would freeze until she was almost on them and then lollop, casually, into the deeper grass.

The world was thriving. And she felt pretty good. Not great. But pretty good.

She pulled her little wagon around the turn that led into the road that went into Fallon, that, she thought, stretched back and back until it joined the road to the city and back some more until it reached the place where they had abandoned the Toyota and taken the Dodge Avenger (what a stupid name) and even farther back into the doomed city itself.

She felt her mood darken; she had reached the entrance to the town, and there was a body in the middle of the road. She wished the person hadn't died in the road. The smell, even outdoors, made her think of meat gone bad in a closed and broken freezer. The lips had drawn back from the corpse's teeth, and the eyes were gone. She supposed the birds had plucked them out.

She wished Bear would return from chasing deer.

Once she had passed the body, she was on the main street of Fallon. Old newspapers scudded down the street. Clare dropped the handle of the wagon and caught one. It was wrinkled with water and stained with rusty blotches. The headline was 'SitkaAZ13: The Disease and the Cured.' The article was short, as if the reporter had been working against a demanding deadline, and it occurred to her that he had probably been working against the most demanding deadline of all. The piece mentioned the violence of the Cured. Clare looked down to the bottom of the article to see if this reporter had anything new to say, and, indeed, the very last line was the most telling of all:

Please come and get my baby daughter, Gwennie. I'm dying, but she only has the rash from SitkaAZ13. *1123 West Spring Street.*

Clare looked at the date.

If no one had gone to find Gwennie, then Gwennie was dead.

Obviously, it had not been business-as-usual at the paper. It had not been business-as-usual anywhere. Clare noticed typographical errors, and she saw that the paper was blank on the other side. No mention of the man she had begun thinking of as the master-of-the-situation.

Perhaps the reporter alone had written and printed the last, the final, the evening edition.

In front of her, a few crows squabbled over carrion. One pecked at something ropy in the street; the other birds jockeyed with each other, waiting for their chance to get at what looked like a long string of rotting meat. Abruptly, the first bird swallowed the dangling lump. There was excited cawing, and then the birds flew off.

Everything was silent. After the noises of the brush and the hay field, the silence was oppressive. Clare wasted no time—she went into the grocery store, which, for the most part, had been stripped.

After a careful search, she loaded up the little wagon with two sacks of rice and some cans of Chef Boyardee ravioli she found in the back room. She hadn't realized that Chef Boyardee was still a going concern, but the expiration dates were years away.

She had a new appreciation for preservatives.

A more careful canvass of the store yielded SpaghettiOs, stewed canned tomatoes, chicken soup, bottles of water, and a few packages of pasta shaped like bow ties.

She went back out into the light and sat on the stoop; she opened a package of Yum-Yums she had found near the cash register. They were past their expiration date, but they weren't nearly as old as the KreamKakes. Clare wolfed them down. She followed them with three Slim Jims and a piece of beef jerky, waited for nausea that didn't come, and then, despite their age, ate the KreamKakes too. She had always loved that creamy filling.

The sun was low in the sky by the time she pulled the wagon over to the big Fallon General Store, and she hesitated at the door.

She suddenly wasn't sure it was *that* silent anymore.

Clare stood still at the entrance. There was a quality to the silence that she did not like. The light inside the store was terribly dim. She had never realized how few windows most stores had, as if scenery might compete with the desire to shop.

She wished, again, that Bear hadn't gone off after the deer.

Clare stepped into the store, and when the floor creaked under her, she almost turned back. But then she caught sight of a section devoted to camping. She had left her flashlight at the cabin, so the first thing she picked up was a long heavy flashlight that took large batteries, which she found hanging in containers by the checkout. Then she walked through the store, bewildered by the number of things she was going to have to come back for—things that surely wouldn't fit in her little wagon: a tent, a backpack, dozens of packets of freeze-dried food, blankets and sweaters and warm clothes.

Just in case, she located the back door to the store. It was to the side of the changing room, and in the light of her flashlight she read the sign next to it: 'Emergency Exit—Alarm Will Sound.'

Clare thought not.

She put down the flashlight so she could use both hands, and soon she had the back door ajar.

In the clothing section, hurrying now, she pulled on a pair of jeans to see if they fit, listening to her surroundings all the time.

She had dropped a size. No surprise there.

From the corner of her eye, in the crepuscular light, she saw movement. She turned towards the front door and gripped her flashlight like a club.

She heard the sound of clothes whispering against each other, hangers clattering together. It was a casual, almost domestic sound, as if a shopper were sorting through the sale rack.

Clare's instinct was to stay low. She dared not call attention to herself by running for the back door. She began, as quietly as she could, to inch towards the front—only for her foot to slip on a blouse that was lying on the floor. She tried to catch herself as she went down by grabbing onto one of the clothes racks. The hangers above her jangled together merrily.

From her prone position Clare saw movement to her left. She scrambled to her feet. There was no more time to think—a figure with a pale blot of a face loomed up beside her. She swung the flashlight up over her head and brought it down as hard as she could.

"Ow!"

The 'ow' made her hesitate. Maybe she just wasn't all that eager to kill. There would be time to ponder the moment, the moment that was to determine the course of her entire life.

Instead of striking again, she lowered the flashlight and turned it on, thinking she could at least momentarily blind her adversary.

"Go away," she whispered. "Whatever you are—go away."

But she found she was facing a boy, a boy younger than she. He carried no marks of Pest. His face was deathly pale, his hair and eyebrows dark. He was squinting. Clare slowly lowered the flashlight.

"I'm just a kid," he said. And although he was still squinting, still partially blinded by the light, she thought she saw recognition dawn on his face.

"You're Clare Bodine," he said.

She nodded, incredulous; a moment later his name came to her.

"You're Jem Clearey," she said. "Ninth grade."

"You're the cheerleader," he said. There was disbelief in his voice. "You do those back flips."

"Chess club, right?"

"Right."

They looked at each other. Then, in the gathering gloom of the store, as the shadows outside grew longer, and the wind stirred up dust on the empty streets, fifteen-year-old Clare Bodine, the cheerleader, reached out and pulled thirteen-year-old Jem Clearey, member of the chess club, into her arms.

CHAPTER SEVEN
OLYMPIC GOLD

"I THOUGHT YOU were going to kill me," Clare said once they had disentangled themselves.

"Um. Me?" said Jem. "I don't have enough status to talk to you, much less kill you."

"Oh," said Clare. "That."

Clare pulled Michael's Varsity jacket closer around her.

"That," said Jem.

"I don't think any of that matters anymore." Clare remembered now that Jem's name had been in the newspaper when he had won the local chess tournament, and that he had gone on to some sort of national tournament. She remembered little else. Once she had run into him in the school hallway and had noticed his strange face, pale and thoughtful. Otherwise, he was a shadow in the background.

"You were a good cheerleader," Jem said. He was looking at her eyes.

"It's not a very helpful skill now, I guess." said Clare, looking down, embarrassed.

"I know what you mean. But I'm still carrying around a travel chess set."

"Just now I thought you were a Cured. That's why I tried to bash your head in."

"I'm really glad you missed."

"I bet your shoulder hurts."

"Yes."

Clare felt awkward. "I'm sorry I never knew you in school."

"The high school didn't have much time for ninth graders," said Jem. "And we didn't have much time for you, either, I guess. But it's hard not to remember a cheerleader."

"They made me a cheerleader because I can do back flips," she said. "But I read real good, too."

Jem laughed. "You're different close up."

She had liked being a cheerleader, though. It felt good to hurtle through the air. And, besides, her back flips made Laura Sparks—whose cartwheels were pitiful—so very jealous. Laura had once dropped her on purpose when they did the pyramid formation. After she had found out about all the phone calls from Michael.

And now all of that high school intrigue was over forever. All Clare had left of those intertwined relationships was Michael's jacket.

"What happened to you during Pest?" Jem asked.

"Everything."

"Yeah," said Jem. "Me, too."

They left the store, and Clare found herself blinking in the light. The town was no longer silent. Clare could hear laughter.

"What's that?" she asked.

"That's Mirri," said Jem. "She's at the playground. She's with me. So's Sarai—they're both little girls."

"I didn't know if there would be others or not," said Clare. "I only knew for sure that the Cured were out there somewhere."

"One of the Cured follows us sometimes," said Jem. "But she seems to be okay. Insane, yes, but not violent. We haven't seen any others. I try to be vigilant. You know. Watchful."

"I know what 'vigilant' means."

Jem looked embarrassed. "I forgot you read real good."

In the playground, Clare could see the two little girls. Two. Suddenly it was as if the whole world had been repopulated.

"The one pushing the swing," said Jem, "is Sarai. She's nine. Mirri's the little one with the bad haircut. She tried to do it herself. She's seven."

The older girl pushed the swing; the younger pumped her legs and yelled "Higher! Higher!" and laughed her uncanny laugh.

When Clare and Jem got closer, Clare noticed that there was something bizarre about the picture. Sarai wore a dress that reached to her calves, a pair of hiking boots and a sequined T-shirt. Mirri had on jeans, but over them she wore a frilly pink tutu. Both were crowned with tiaras.

"They like to dress up," said Jem. "But I figure there aren't any more fashion guidelines. I never understood what those guidelines were about, anyway."

"They were mostly about who was in and who was out," said Clare. "And we're all in now. Or out. I don't know."

Clare thought about what it must be like to take care of two people. She realized that she could barely take care of herself, although Bear had shaken her out of her lethargy. Yet Jem, at thirteen, had taken on these little girls. Sarai's dark hair was drawn back carefully into a braid, and her brown skin glowed against her pale shirt. Mirri jumped off the swing, her shaggy badly cut hair gleaming red-gold in the light. She was certainly cleaner than Clare.

The instant the girls saw Jem and Clare, they stopped playing.

"Jem?" Sarai asked. "Is she okay?"

"Yes."

"Her Pest rash isn't very bright," said Sarai, and Clare pulled Michael's jacket close around her again.

"I *like* my Pest rash," said Mirri. "It's kind of pretty. I've decided it's shaped like a fish. She looks old."

"I'm fifteen," Clare told them.

"This is Clare Bodine," said Jem. "She was at school with me. She's a cheerleader."

Clare felt herself blush.

"You don't need to be *embarrassed*," said Mirri. "I want to be a cheerleader when I grow up. Now I'm just a little kid."

"You'll be a kid for ages, Mirri," said Sarai. "I'll be a teenager a long time before you are."

"You won't be a teenager for years," said Mirri. "And by then Clare here will be *grownup*. If kids can live to be grownups."

"That's enough, Mirri," said Jem.

"It's okay," said Clare.

"I didn't mean to say you were going to be a grownup *soon*," said Mirri to Clare. "It's not as if you were *sixteen*. Fifteen isn't so much."

Jem sat on the curb near the swings. Mirri launched herself from the swing again and landed on her feet.

"I don't know how she does that," said Sarai admiringly. She and Mirri joined Jem on the curb. The four of them sat with their feet in the dusty street as the empty swings moved back and forth in the breeze. Jem idly started throwing pebbles and soon Mirri was doing it too. Sarai watched them intently.

"You're the first people I've seen since my parents died," said Clare. They all looked out at the silent town. The unkempt buildings loomed over the dusty street and here or there a door hung open or a sign had become detached from its moorings. Lawns were unmown and towering weeds were going to seed in a small graveyard next to the church. Grass was beginning to sprout up in the fissures in the street. Clare found herself thinking that wherever humans had left so much as a crevice, nature invaded.

In front of some of the houses, yellowed newspapers were piled in a heap. One door had a partial red 'X' on it, as if someone had made an effort to impose quarantine and then given up. Farther down the street was what looked like a small heap of clothes. Clare hoped it wasn't another body.

"Did you see the TV spot that the grownup made at the end?" asked Clare.

"I heard about it," said Jem.

"He said he had a cure," said Clare.

"Well," said Jem. "We've seen how cures work out." He turned and looked at her and then looked more closely. She knew it was her eyes. She moved uncomfortably.

"What if he was telling the truth?" she asked.

"I want to hope so," said Jem. "If there's no kind of cure at all, Pest will pick us off one by one as we get older. "

Clare pictured the emptied world. Everything would go eventually. The Golden Gate Bridge and the Eiffel Tower would join the pyramids and the Coliseum in the steady march towards ruin.

"There doesn't seem to be much point in anything," said Clare. "If this really is the end of the world."

Jem considered her words.

"There would be a point to a lot more things," he said, "if we could grow up."

"Maybe we'll make it."

"I wouldn't put any bets on turning twenty. Pest'll come."

"What about sixteen? Do you think I have a chance?"

Jem didn't automatically reassure her or tell her not to worry about it or promise to take care of her. She liked him for that. He said,

"I don't know."

As they sat on the curb in the rich evening light, their stories began to come.

"I knew Sarai before Pest," said Jem. "Our families were friends."

Sarai took up the story.

"Our families were close," she said. "Even though they were really different." When it was clear that Sarai and Jem weren't getting sick, their families moved in together so that the children could care for them more easily. The Cure had not yet been available.

"Thank goodness," said Sarai. "Because some of them might have become Cureds. Our own families."

Mirri threw a pebble into the street.

"I don't like this story," she said. Sarai put a hand on her shoulder.

"Moving in together seemed like the best plan," said Jem. "We couldn't know what would happen. That they would all die. Our parents. Our brothers and sisters."

"We didn't know anything that bad could happen," said Sarai.

When the house was finally silent, Jem told Clare, when all the others were dead, they had waited listlessly for Children's Services to arrive. But nobody came. Like Clare, after a while Jem and Sarai realized that there was no 'they' anymore. Jem and Sarai had stuffed two packs and two sets of bicycle saddlebags with clothes and supplies.

"But the most useful thing we brought is a can-opener," Sarai said. "And we almost forgot to bring that."

Then they had loaded their bicycles and slowly made their way out of the city and into the hills.

"We didn't see any other children," said Jem. "And we only saw one Cured. He was smashing every plate-glass window in a street of stores. He didn't notice us, and we just slipped by."

Clare listened with a kind of envy: these children had made plans. If her parents had died in the city, she might have been helpless. But Jem had taken charge. And Jem was only thirteen.

"We had to get out of there," Jem said. "It was only a matter of time before other diseases broke out. With all those bodies lying around."

Clare could feel Mirri getting restive as the story went on. Finally she broke in.

"I'm going to look in the store for some Pretty Ponies," she said. "I only have two Pretty Ponies, and they're both at the house."

Jem waited until Mirri was out of earshot.

"Her story is hard," he said.

"Tell it," said Sarai. "But before she gets back."

"Sarai and I found Mirri," said Jem. "She didn't talk much then."

Mirri's mother had come down with Pest first. She had gone to the hospital and never come back. Mirri's father bolted the door against the pandemic, but Pest found the rest of them anyway. By the third day, Mirri found herself locked in with her father's body and that of her older sister. Mirri's sister didn't have delayed onset Pest; she died of the disease in three long days, thus doing what

Mirri found unthinkable and unforgiveable—she left Mirri behind. By the time Jem and Sarai found Mirri, she had become too afraid to face the outside world. She preferred the reek of decay. She told them, through the closed window, that she was waiting for her turn to go dead.

Jem had forced the door with his hammer. Mirri was dehydrated. She stank. They cleaned her up and took her with them.

"And here we are," Sarai said. "What about you?"

But before Clare could begin, Mirri came running across the playground from the store, yelling. Jem looked alarmed and started up from the curb, but it was soon clear she was happy about something.

"Look what I found!" Mirri held up her arms. "I found these in the back of the store." She had a Pretty Pony in each hand.

The three of them settled down around Clare. Mirri clutched the Pretty Ponies. Her eyes were on Clare's face.

"Your eyes—" she started to say.

"Shush," said Jem. "Clare's going to tell her story."

"My mother was a painter," said Clare. She moved uneasily on the curb. She found it hard to talk about her mother. "But she died and my father married Marie, who's an interior decorator. Who *was* an interior decorator."

"What's an 'interior decorator'?" asked Mirri.

"Someone who decorates the inside of things, idgit," said Sarai.

"My father wrote books," Clare continued. "He won awards and stuff. The best book was called *Bridge Out Ahead*."

"I've read that," said Jem. "The end of it just about killed me."

"Happy stories just stop in the middle," said Clare. "That's what he used to say."

She told them about Michael, which didn't hold Mirri and Sarai's attention, although Jem listened carefully. Then she told them about Bear. Finally Clare told them about leaving Robin behind, and she felt grief well up inside her.

They did their best to comfort her, huddling close.

"My mother was a doctor, and my father was a sociologist," said Jem. "If my father had lived, I bet he would have studied everybody's reaction to Pest."

"There's nobody left to study," said Sarai.

"There's *us*," said Mirri.

Sarai's father had worked long hours at his grocery store, and her mother made Indian sweets for a bakery. Sarai's grandparents had all come from India.

"My mother had black hair that went down to her knees," said Sarai. "Really. Sometimes she would wear a sari."

Mirri's father was a fireman, according to Jem, but Mirri corrected him.

"A fire *fighter*," she said. "That's what he did. He fought fires. My mom took care of me and my sister, Liz." Mirri grew thoughtful; she let her Pretty Ponies fall into the dirt.

"You're with us now," said Jem. And he picked up the Pretty Ponies, dusted them off and made them gallop on the curb. By and by, Mirri took the ponies from him and started brushing her fingers through their pink and green polyester manes.

"I miss Liz," she said. Then she peered into Clare's face.

"Your eyes are very blue," she said factually. "That's what I was going to say when Jem shushed me."

Bear chose that moment to arrive. He bounded to Clare's side and then paused, as if waiting for instructions. She had a strong and uneasy feeling that he would have cheerfully torn the others' throats out if she had asked him to.

Jem, reacting to Bear's sudden appearance, pulled Mirri to her feet and gave her a push. Sarai was already running for the swings, and when she got there, she stood up on one of them. Mirri joined her. Only Jem didn't move.

"It's all right, Bear," said Clare. "Sit down. Now." He sat immediately, yellow eyes fixed on her. Bear's muzzle was tacky with blood, and some of it came off on Clare's arm as she scratched his ears.

Jem didn't move away but gently reached out his hand. Bear sniffed Jem and then, after a look at Clare, nuzzled his hand, leaving a smear of blood on his palm. Mirri, on the swing, began laughing, and Clare recognized the laughter of relief. Mirri pumped the swing up higher and higher and then leapt through the air, landing lightly on her feet.

"We're alive!" she cried. She threw her arms up in the air, as if she were a winning athlete. As if she'd won Olympic gold.

CHAPTER EIGHT
BONDS

THEY FINISHED SCAVENGING and sorted through the food that was left in the general store. Jem seemed uneasy and, every now and then, he stood and scanned the area.

"What are you looking for?" asked Clare.

"Cureds," said Jem. "They've had time to make their way here from the city; I don't want to be taken by surprise."

They divided up the supplies with Jem making sure that Clare got her share. Clare, for her part, found herself wondering what Michael would think if he saw her now, scrabbling for whatever food she could get, her long hair tangled into a rat's nest.

Jem put some last things into her little wagon: a small sack of flour ("it has weevils," he warned), some cans of soup, some withered potatoes. The wind had picked up, and fallen leaves danced in the street. After Jem helped Clare with her wagon, he showed her how to attach a tent and a sleeping bag to a backpack.

"I didn't think of you as the outdoors type," said Clare. "You know—chess club."

"My lore of the wilderness is mostly theory, not practice," said Jem. "And I watched one of my brothers. That helped."

Clare suddenly felt Bear come to attention by her side, and she realized something was wrong. There was a noise on the wind.

It was a peculiar sound, the sound of something being dragged through sand. It started and stopped. Clare reached for her heavy flashlight. At the edge of the playground, she saw the misshapen form of an adult. He was half naked. They heard a low moaning.

Sarai was incredulous. "I thought they were all dead."

"They are," said Jem. "It's a Cured. Don't move."

"He's already seen us," said Mirri.

The man began to make his way closer to them, and Clare could see the weeping sores on his face, the redness of the pustules on his neck.

The Cured looked up at them, his eyes almost closed by swollen tissue.

"It's *horrible*," said Mirri. "It's a *thing*."

"We have to get out of here," said Jem. "We need to get the supplies out too. If we can."

They hoisted their packs to their backs and pulled the wagons into the street. The Cured moved restlessly, and Clare saw something in his hand.

"He has a knife," she said.

"Leave the stuff," said Jem. "Let's get out of here."

But before they could move, the man was running. He was fast, and the distance was not great. Even so, Clare thought that she would have been able to outrun him—but Mirri and Sarai wouldn't have been able to keep up. And maybe Jem wouldn't have been able to either.

Jem grabbed Mirri and pushed her behind him, but Sarai was still out in front. There was no time to think, no time for Clare or Jem or even Bear to reach Sarai, no time to do anything but watch in horror as the Cured crashed into her and brought her down.

Clare saw the gleam of the knife as the man pushed it into Sarai's side.

"No," said Jem. "No."

Mirri slipped out from behind Jem and ran to Sarai.

"*No*," cried Jem again, but Mirri was already kneeling by Sarai.

The man yanked Mirri to her feet and held his knife to her throat. Sarai, at his feet, gave a thin cry.

At least, Clare thought, *Sarai's alive.*

A trail of blood began to trickle down Mirri's neck, and Clare had the weird feeling that she had seen this before. Déjà vu.

The Cured howled at them.

Clare looked down at Sarai and saw blood pulsing out of her side and opening out onto the dirt like a dark poppy.

Jem and Clare didn't dare move. Clare whispered "down" to Bear, but she could feel his desire to leap at the Cured. If only she could let him. If only the knife weren't at Mirri's throat.

"He's going to cut me," said Mirri softly. "I can tell."

The man spoke, and his voice was a croak, a rasp, a strangle of sound. Clare could barely make out the words.

"I'm going to kill her. I am. Going to."

And Clare knew that, knife or no knife, it was up to her and Bear, or it was over for Mirri and Sarai. Clare, without knowing precisely what she was doing, touched the dog. Bear stood and shook himself. She sent a command to him, and, as she felt Bear's response, she thought that this felt right. This was how it was supposed to be.

For one moment, Bear looked up at her with his strange yellow eyes. Then he leapt at the man, the knife, Mirri.

Clare would never be entirely sure of what happened next, but, in a moment, Mirri was free, and Bear and the man were tumbling over and over. Clare looked for the gleam of the knife, but she couldn't see it. Bear's mouth was closing over the man's throat. Then Clare stopped watching.

Bear loped back to Clare. There was no question that the man was dead.

Jem rushed to Sarai's side. Mirri stood weeping, and Clare walked over and put her arms around her. Faint moans came from Sarai, and, as Clare held Mirri close, she looked at the rich deep stain marking the earth.

Then the moaning stopped.

Clare was engulfed with misery and surprised at its depth. She hadn't thought she could feel much of anything anymore. There had been so much death.

Jem, who had been blocking Clare's view of Sarai, sat back.

Clare could see that he was holding the wound in Sarai's side closed. The blood stopped flowing quite so freely, and Sarai stirred. Mirri ran to her, and knelt in the dirt beside her friend.

"I thought she was dead," said Clare.

"She's not going to die," said Jem. "I need a needle and thread, alcohol and some matches."

"I'm on it," said Clare. She and Bear ran towards the store; behind her she could hear Jem soothing Sarai.

"You need to stay down," he said. "You're not going to die."

"I don't feel that good," said Sarai.

"You're going to be all right."

When Clare got back, Sarai was unconscious.

"She lost a lot of blood," said Jem, "before I could get pressure on the wound."

Clare looked down at Jem, who was pale and dirty, but who flushed under her gaze, even though she said nothing.

He sterilized the needle with the matches and the thread with rubbing alcohol from the pharmacy. As Clare watched, Jem sewed Sarai up quickly, before she regained consciousness.

"It's probably going to get infected," said Clare, "no matter how careful you are."

"Antibiotics," said Jem. "We'll get some at the pharmacy."

"How do you *know* this stuff?"

"My mother the doctor. She didn't want me to be helpless in an emergency."

"I don't know, Jem. I may have to get rid of my chess-nerd image of you."

And at that moment, Sarai opened her eyes.

"I don't feel so good," she said. But Jem smiled.

"It's going to be okay," he said.

By the time they found Sarai some juice from a 7-Eleven and some antibiotics from a pharmacy, the sun was almost gone. Clare shivered. Bear lay down as if he had no intention of leaving, but they would have to leave now, or it would be dark before she got back to the cabin. She knew that if one Cured had found his way into the hills, others would. She needed to fortify the house. Otherwise—well, otherwise the Cured would steal her food and kill her dog and murder her.

Clare began more and more to fear the long walk home to her lonely cabin, even with Bear to protect her.

"We should bury that man," said Mirri suddenly.

"We don't have time before dark," said Jem. "I'm sorry, Mirri. But he isn't one of ours."

Jem finished arranging the supplies and roped them down with a piece of elastic cord. Sarai was able to walk leaning on Jem. Clare watched them prepare to leave. There seemed to be nothing left to say. They stood in the dim light, and leaves fluttered orange and red in the wind. Clare looked at the children but didn't know how to ask.

"It's time to go," said Jem. He wiped his face, but the dirt only smeared across his cheeks and forehead. Then he looked at Clare and Bear, and it was suddenly very simple.

"I can pull your little wagon thing, if you want," he said. "Or you can do it yourself. It's not a long walk to our place."

"So can Clare be one of us?" asked Mirri.

"I think she already is," said Jem. "Okay, Clare?"

"Okay."

The wind ruffled Bear's fur. When Clare looked up, she saw that the night sky was full of stars.

MASTER

HE WOULD ALWAYS be a famous scientist. And the children would need a pediatrician. But he had re-named himself: now he was the Master.

The mansion that the Master had found was far to the north of the farmhouse where Jem, Clare, Sarai and Mirri lived. It was enormous—big enough to hold any number of the children that he imagined streaming towards him. They would have seen him on television, or heard his radio broadcast. Not all of them, of course, but if just a tiny fraction of those alive knew about him, if they were on their way, well, he would have a lot of work to do. They would be malnourished, possibly injured, perhaps carrying infections other than Pest. He would have to lay in broad spectrum antibiotics as well as bandages and vitamins, splints and latex gloves. And toys, of course. He would need toys.

But first he had to hang the art.

The Master had discovered a lot of art already in the mansion— even some sculptures—and he happily mounted his own art collection as soon as he moved in. So far it wasn't much of a collection, because he hadn't been able to take more than would fit into his van, but he had managed to liberate a large painting by John Singer Sargent when the panic over SitkaAZ13 had reached its peak. There were no guards at the museum, no one to sell him a ticket—and he had simply walked in and wrestled the large dark painting off the wall. He staggered under its weight as he manipulated the piece into his car. The canvas showed a dark interior with four children, one of them sitting on the floor.

He liked looking at them: four little girls. They didn't try to stare him down; they were alone in the unfurnished space around them—they weren't even playing with each other. He put the painting up in a comfortable room in the expansive basement of the mansion, and then he stood back and watched the four little girls carefully. There was, frankly, something a little odd about these painted children in their looming room. When he looked closely, he thought that there might be things hiding in the darkness at the edge of the canvas.

He couldn't rescue them from that darkness, of course. They had made it themselves.

The little girls looked out from the painting.

He wasn't just going to rely on television or on the radio broadcast; he would search for children as well. He knew there were children, now, still alive and immured in their houses, waiting out SitkaAZ13 while their families died around them. They would be waiting for someone.

Perhaps that's what Sargent's children were doing. Waiting.

He had left the radio broadcast on a loop. He didn't know how much good the television broadcasts had done—he had made them near the end, when most of the population would have been too sick to watch television. The newscasters had let him speak because he was the expert on SitkaAZ13, and he was acutely aware, even as he spoke into the camera, that most of the people in the room were already sick—the woman who read the news, who was waiting for her turn, was flushed and looked feverish. The man behind the camera sat down half way through.

But the light on the camera continued to glow red as he spoke.

And he kept looking at the light and talking to the children.

He knew everything about SitkaAZ13—what laymen called 'Pest.' He knew that the children who had survived so far weren't immune; the virus was simply lurking in their blood; they would grow into the disease. Adolescence had a little surprise for them.

Now, in the mansion, he stared at the children in the Sargent painting.

When the sun went down, he went outside. After climbing over a stone wall and brushing away the undergrowth that separated him from the forest, he went under the trees. The evening walk calmed his mind; he did not fear the Cured.

He was about to turn back when he heard a voice.

"Is anybody there?"

He stood, silent. It wasn't a Cured; he knew that from the perfect syntax of the sentence as well as by the tone. It was, he thought, a girl child.

"It's all right," he said and moved quietly between the trees until he could see her. She was dirty, and her hair was a dark nest of snarls. He had pictured something different when he had first heard her—smooth hair, wide blue eyes. Perhaps she would look different later, when she'd had a chance to clean up. But here was a start.

She began backing away from him.

"I thought you might be another kid," she said. "You're not a kid."

"And I'm not a Cured. I am, though, the master-of-the-situation." He had used the words so often on the broadcast that they came to him naturally. "You need to come with me. I can take care of you."

"I've been taking care of myself." But her voice said otherwise, and her cheeks were hollow, as if she hadn't eaten in a long time. Tear marks streaked the dirt on her face. She looked to be about twelve years old.

"I told you it's all right," he said. "I have food. I have water. Soon other children will come."

She didn't hesitate for very long.

They went back to the mansion together, and she ate his food. He liked watching her eat. He calculated how long it would take for her blood sugar to go up, and, sure enough, as it did she became more talkative. Her name was Britta and she had watched her whole family die.

He had watched people die—a lot of people—but after a while the deaths had become merely interesting. He hadn't liked the chaos, though. At the end the hospital had been mobbed, and he had been afraid of his own name.

"Why are you alive?" asked Britta. "Are you immune?"

"I cured myself."

"I thought I was the only one alive in the whole world. Except for the Cured. I waited with Mother's and Kevin's bodies for a long time." She stopped, and he didn't press her.

"You're alive," he said finally. "And we'll start there."

"There's no one left in Clarion," she said. "I walked around for a while, but there were only bodies. Then I got scared. I thought maybe I could build a tree house and live in the woods, but I just got lost, and it started getting cold. There weren't any berries to eat."

"Any Cured in Clarion?"

"One," said Britta. "He kept telling me to come closer. His face sagged down, and when I saw that, I ran."

"Very wise."

"You are the Master, aren't you? Of the situation? For real?"

He sat back in his chair. They were seated at the thick oak table in the kitchen, a table big enough to accommodate a large family. He thought that soon enough, as the children came, he would fill the places.

"Yes," he said. "I am the Master."

"I was worried you might be someone who hurts kids."

"Parents scare their children too much."

For being the first one to find him, the Master wanted to give Britta the most opulent bedroom in the mansion—the one with huge, gilt framed mirrors on the walls and oriental rugs on the floor and a bed with an intricately embroidered coverlet. But part of him knew that the room would be scary for her, and he wanted all the children to be comfortable with him. Respectful, but comfortable.

He finally gave her a small cozy room on the second floor, a room that overlooked the gardens that he meant to become lush and extravagant with flowers. Once there were other children, they would plant and reap and delight in excess of everything: food, flowers. They would raise domestic animals. He knew that children liked baby things. He would make sure that there would be ducklings and chicks. They wouldn't be able to resist ducklings.

That night, Britta let him tuck her in. Then he went outside to the perimeter of the estate. Britta hadn't wanted him to leave her alone in the house, but he knew it was possible the Cured she had seen in Clarion had followed her. If so, some clean up work needed to be done.

The air was cool on his face. He stared into the darkness and listened. The unmown grass was fragrant and the soft, and dewy heads of clover brushed his legs. Then he heard it—a low hooting sound, as if some night bird were calling to another.

The Cured was out there, but too far away for him to do anything about it. No matter. The Cured would soon come closer, and he would be ready.

He went back inside and up the stairs to check on Britta.

She lay on her side. The light from the kerosene lantern he held showed deep shadows around her eyes. He was about to close the door, but, in spite of the marks that exhaustion and fear and hunger had left on her, in spite of what must have been a deep fatigue, she woke up.

She didn't want to know where she was, or who he was, and she didn't ask for her parents.

"Is everything all right?" she asked.

"Yes."

"Leave the door open."

He did. When he checked back later, she was in a deep and lovely sleep.

He was still excited from the day. He picked up his baseball bat and took a chair—it looked like an antique, perhaps Louis Quatorze—and sat outside near the perimeter of the grounds.

He wanted to kill something.

The Cured hooted softly. It was a lonely sound.

When the Cure had started to go terribly wrong, he had feared that the unfortunate recipients of it might band together, but that didn't seem to be happening.

And one Cured, well, one Cured he could hunt down.

THE NEXT DAY, he and Britta took the truck that had been sitting, keys in the ignition, in the long drive of the estate. They didn't go to Clarion; he didn't want Britta reminded of the past. He would build society from the ground up, and that meant leaving the past behind.

So they went to Sennet, where there were very few bodies in the streets. Most people, it seemed, had been content to die at home. He kept watch for the Cured, baseball bat in hand, while Britta checked out stores and restaurants.

They finally found a warehouse of food. Britta spilled over with joy. He was less satisfied. The cartons all contained cans of soup—tomato, minestrone, beef with barley, mushroom. He didn't plan on feeding himself and the children on soup alone. The mansion needed luxuries, luxuries for the young children— candy bars and licorice and gum—and luxuries for himself and the older ones—caviar, paté, smoked oysters. His world needed to be enticing. Soup might get them through the winter, but soup wasn't interesting. And he wanted live animals to raise for food; he wanted chickens, pigs, sheep. He didn't fear butchering them; if there was anything he knew how to do well, it was how to wield a knife. And he knew anatomy.

The mansion had already been well stocked. He and Britta made trip after trip until the storeroom was full.

"We'll go back to Sennet tomorrow," he said to Britta.

"Don't we have enough for the winter already?" she asked.

"Are you doubting me?"

Britta hung her head.

"No, sir."

"It's all right," he said after a moment. "There *is* enough for us. But I think that soon there'll be more. More children."

That was the day that they found the farm. It stank of dead animals—they saw the carcasses of sheep and the bodies of two horses, now bloated and flyblown. But there were still chickens and ducks foraging in the farmyard, and it was Britta who spotted some sheep and a cow in a far meadow.

"They made it through," she said.

"We can get the chickens and ducks to settle in closer to home," he said. He looked at the stalls where the horses lay. "We need to get all the live animals away from this open graveyard. There's potential contagion here."

"Can't we bury the dead ones?" Britta asked.

"No."

"My parents didn't get buried." Britta seemed to wait for him to say something, but he was silent. "They're still in my house in Clarion. When they died, there was no one to call. I don't suppose—"

"No." He turned his back to her. Thinking ahead was the only way to survive. He supposed it must be hard for her to think of her parents rotting away, but they would as soon rot underground. As for the psychological trauma unburied parents might elicit, well, there weren't any more psychiatrists in the world. Britta would just have to get over it.

When they returned to the mansion, she somehow slipped away from him. The light was fading, and he was listening for the sound of the Cured when he realized that she was gone. He knew she wouldn't have left the grounds, but he was angry. Solitude was, in the world he was going to build, a luxury for the very few.

He found her in the grounds sitting on the edge of an old fountain. In the center of the basin, a naiad with a fish woven around her stood frozen, pouty lips open where the jet of water was meant to emerge.

"You shouldn't go out alone," he said. He was careful to sound calm. Reasonable.

"Let's go back to the house," she said quickly, and he tried to let it go.

But the anger remained. It needed an outlet.

That night he went hunting for the Cured that had followed her. He took the baseball bat and a gym bag. Sometimes rhymes got stuck in his head as he went on the hunt, and now he muttered to himself as he walked:

He left it dead, and with its head, he went galumphing back.

The soft hooting sound was much closer now, and he listened carefully to gauge the direction it was coming from as he ducked under the trees; twigs and leaves crackled under his feet as he went, and, shortly, the hooting stopped.

It went against instinct, but once he had gained a clearing he called out to the Cured.

"I'm waiting for you. Maybe I can help you." He put down the bat, hiding it in the long grass. "I mean you no harm." He had no way of knowing if his words would mean anything to the Cured, but he had seen cases in which some higher brain function remained. All of the Cured were, of course, insane. An unfortunate side-effect of the treatment. And the Cure had had so much potential.

He heard the soft sounds again, very near this time.

And then the sounds changed. The gentle hooting was gone.

He was almost taken by surprise when the Cured entered the clearing.

"Help," it said. Its hair was matted, and its face was disfigured by the thick scars and lesions of Pest. This one must have been in the intermediate stages when the Cure was administered.

"You don't need to live like this," the Master said.

"I need to eat," it said. "I hate everything." Then it took a breath and made the strange hooting noise again.

"I can take the hate away," the Master said. The Cured moved closer.

And the Master picked up the bat and started swinging.

THE MOON WAS high when he got back to the mansion.
He left it dead
He wiped the bat clean on the grass. He had already cleaned the hunting knife before sheathing it—scalpels, in his early experiments, had proved too small to be useful.
And with its head
He buried the full gym bag and then patted down the disturbed ground.
He went galumphing back.
Once in the house, he washed his hands and arms and face and cleaned under his fingernails. Then he went up to Britta's room.
She slept. Sound. Safe.

HE AND BRITTA worked hard the next day so that the mansion would be inviting when the other children came. They then spent the evening in his collection room in the basement. He thought that Britta looked a little like the girl wearing a pinafore standing in the background of the Sargent painting. Britta sat, looking tiny, in an overlarge armchair opposite him. She looked very alone.
"Britta?"
"Yes?"
"We're going to build a new world here. You'll lead it for me. You'll help me teach the other children, when they come."
"You're Master," she whispered, giving him, finally, the name.
He smiled at Britta, as if they now shared a secret.
"I'll keep you safe," he said.
Then the Master looked up at the painting of the four little girls. He tried to read the future in their faces, but the shadows around the glowing children only seemed to mock him.

CHAPTER NINE
THE FARMHOUSE

THEY MOVED SLOWLY, and Jem and Clare took turns helping Sarai, who, after some painkillers that Jem had found in the pharmacy, was both still in some pain and woozy from the drugs. When they reached the farmhouse that Jem, Mirri and Sarai had claimed as their own, it was full dark.

Once they had settled Sarai in bed, Clare collapsed on a sofa, Bear at her feet. She was too tired to worry about the Cured or the master-of-the-situation's cure or what was going to happen next. She noticed vaguely that the others slept in the same room, but before she could really take in the arrangements at the farmhouse, she was in a dreamless sleep.

In the morning, Mirri and Jem showed her around while Sarai slept; Sarai had a low fever, but there was no redness around the stitches, and she slept soundly.

"The penicillin should kick in and get rid of that low-grade fever," said Jem.

"Sure?"

"Sure. And if I'm wrong, we'll give her Cipro."

Clare didn't know what Cipro was, but her confidence in Jem had grown steadily. Sarai would be all right.

When they went outside, Bear gave Clare an almost begging look, and she released him to go and explore the area. Now in the full light of day, Clare could see that the farmhouse had a wide porch. A barn next to it was tilted at what seemed like an impossible angle, and its red paint was peeling in long and interesting looking strips. In front of the house, a flower garden bloomed with golden marigolds and red and orange zinnias; nearby, a stone wall overflowed with phlox no longer in bloom but still full of vigor. Nothing had been pruned or weeded.

"The vegetable garden's in back," said Jem.

"The garden's *work*," said Mirri. "But we'll take you scavenging. We break into all kinds of houses looking for food. That's *fun*. Except for the dead bodies."

Jem had a stick in his hand and was brushing the top of the grass with it. A grasshopper jumped out of the way, and he watched it go.

"Sometimes I can't believe the world is still working at all," Jem said. "Trees, grasshoppers, flowers. Pest hasn't touched them."

"If humans get going again," said Clare, "maybe we'll let everything thrive this time."

"And we'll have Peace on Earth," said Mirri, primly.

"'Peace on Earth,'" said Jem. "I don't know about Peace on Earth. But it's a nice day."

It *was* a nice day. Clare wondered how many nice days she had left; she thought about the messages broadcast by the man who called himself the master-of-the-situation. The Master. If he didn't have a cure, Sarai and Mirri would be, at the most, fourteen and twelve when Jem died. Clare would have died a few years earlier. If there were a cure, they needed to find it.

"We're not staying here forever," Mirri said as if reading her thoughts. "Jem says we're sinking into leth-ar-gy here. That's one of Sarai's vocab words. He also says that eventually we're going to run out of food. But Jem doesn't think we'll really need a cure for a while because he's only thirteen."

"I may be mistaken," said Jem. "We may need to move sooner than I thought." He glanced at Clare and then looked away.

"Well," said Mirri. "Clare's fifteen, and she's all right."

"She's all right *now*," said Jem.

Clare realized with a start that there was a woman in front of the barn, sitting on chair. Clare couldn't make out her face, but her clothes were a bright splotch of blue.

"It's the Cured-in-a-blue-dress," explained Mirri.

"A Cured?" Clare stopped walking.

"She's not like the other Cureds," said Mirri quickly.

"We've gotten used to this Cured," said Jem. "And so far, so good."

"Used to her?" asked Clare.

"She followed us here," said Mirri. "She doesn't attack. She's a *pacifist* Cured."

"She picked up our trail after we found Mirri," said Jem. "She doesn't seem to want to harm us. She never comes close, but she won't go away."

The woman in blue stood up, and even at that distance Clare thought she saw the marks of Pest. The woman's face looked like someone had put a thumb down and smeared it.

"She's kind of like one of the family," said Mirri.

"No," said Jem. "She's not."

Clare looked from Jem to Mirri. She had the feeling that they'd had this argument before.

"Aren't you at least a little afraid of her?" asked Clare.

"No," said Mirri.

As they got closer, Clare could see the woman's face more clearly. Her eyes and mouth had a beautiful shape, and Clare was strongly reminded of someone, but she couldn't quite pinpoint whom. The rest of her face was marred, and Clare recognized that the course of Pest had been arrested during the final stages. The thick ropes of scar tissue matted the woman's nose into her cheeks, and the marks of Pest on her neck were black. Her swollen knuckles had curled her hands into dirty claws.

Mirri stole a look at Clare's face.

"She won't hurt you," she said. "I *know* it. She's never tried to hurt any of us."

"You need to be careful," said Jem. "She's not a pet."

"I wasn't thinking of her as a *pet*," said Mirri.

It was at that moment that Bear rejoined them. He had the desiccated body of a long-dead squirrel in his mouth, and he dropped it at Clare's feet. He then looked up at her, tongue lolling out, as if waiting for approval.

"That's pretty disgusting," said Clare, but she stroked Bear's head as she spoke.

Bear snuffed the air and, in a moment, his body stiffened, and he made a move as if to lunge forward. Clare knew he had become aware of the Cured-in-a-blue-dress.

"*Grab* him," said Mirri. "He'll *hurt* her."

Clare knew she could never catch Bear if he went after the Cured-in-a-blue-dress, but, after his initial movement forward, he stopped. He let Clare put her arms around him. His ears were pricked forward, and he was alert, but he made no move to attack.

"He's not even growling," said Clare.

"That's because the Cured-in-a-blue-dress is *harmless*," said Mirri. "Dogs *know*."

Clare put a hand on Bear. He seemed relaxed. Perhaps Mirri was right.

Then Clare looked at the Cured-in-a-blue-dress. Oddly, the blue made her think of her mother. Not of Marie, her stepmother, but of her real mother, long dead. Clare remembered that they had buried her in a sky blue dress. Madonna blue.

They approached the barn, and the Cured-in-a-blue-dress got up and began to move away. She looked around urgently, as if for a place to escape. And then she ran past them and around the house.

"She isn't very stable," said Mirri. "That's the word Jem uses— 'stable.' Sometimes she does odd things. For no reason."

"She killed our only chicken," said Jem.

"You don't *know* that," said Mirri.

"But she didn't eat it," said Jem. "That's not very stable—she killed for no reason."

"Well, *we* ate it," said Mirri. "So it doesn't matter."

Clare, as she listened to Mirri, felt she needed to get some perspective on her situation. She thought simply that there were too many unknown quantities in her world now. She didn't really know Jem. Not really—not as she had known Robin. Mirri and Sarai were strangers. The Cured-in-a-blue-dress was a worry. And the Master was an enigma.

If only Michael were there, everything would be completely all right. He would know what to do. Sometimes she wanted him so much, she simply wished she could sit on the ground and put her head in her hands and rock back and forth until the want went away. And these children had never been part of her old world—even Jem had never been anywhere but on the periphery. She should be—what was the term Jem used? Vigilant.

But it then occurred to her that at some point she had already made up her mind: she trusted Jem. She trusted them all. Vigilance? It was already too late for that.

SARAI'S FEVER WAS gone that evening, and she was up on the sofa, reading, while Mirri and Jem showed Clare every corner of the house and attic before returning to the living room for dinner. The kerosene lantern shed a soft light, and what by day was, they assured her, a dingy wallpaper, looked a rich yellow with a golden inlaid pattern.

That night they lay on the floor of the living room, now covered in pillows, and ate out of cans and drank soda. Sarai moved gingerly, but she was clearly feeling better. Mirri seemed open and happy. She made a tower out of fruit cocktail tins in front of the blank television.

"I want to go explore east tomorrow," said Jem. "We haven't checked out that part of town."

"Okay." Mirri popped the top off another tin of fruit cocktail.

"I'm warning you about all that fruit, Mirri," said Jem. "It's going to bite you in the butt. No kidding."

"It's *really* good," she said.

"Mirri," warned Sarai. "Jem said."

"Yeah, but *you're* not the boss of me."

"But I am," said Jem. "And you're not having any more fruit cocktail after that tin. You'll get sick."

Mirri turned away and toyed with some of the cans, but she didn't eat any more fruit cocktail. She was smiling to herself, as if Jem had said something particularly reassuring. She obviously liked having Jem in charge.

Clare, meanwhile, was remembering her words to Bear about who was boss. It seemed strange to her now that there had ever been a time when they hadn't understood each other. She reached down and scratched him on the belly until he wriggled in contentment.

Without electricity, bedtime was early at the farm, as it had been for Clare at the cabin, but here they liked to use the kerosene lantern for an extra half an hour of light. They bolted the door against the night, and then Sarai and Mirri settled down for a game of Old Maid. Jem and Clare sat on the floor in the pool of light shed by the lamp and watched them.

"Whoever thought of the Cure," said Jem, "has a lot to answer for."

"At least they tried to stop Pest," said Clare.

"The Cure," said Jem with some contempt. "The doctors were just playing around to see what happened."

"Scientists worked on it, too. And epi—you know, the guys who work on epidemics. They helped develop the Cure."

"They didn't really know what they were doing," said Jem. "Doctors and scientists love messing around with plagues and cures. And where do you think Pest originated, anyway? Have you ever seen *28 Days Later*?"

"Your parents *never* let you see *28 Days Later*! My parents wouldn't let me see *28 Days Later*, and I'm fifteen."

"I was on a sleepover."

They were both suddenly reminded of how young they really were.

What hope could they have?

CLARE THOUGHT OF the last days of Pest, the screams in the night, the dead in the streets, her sojourns with Robin through Hell. The Cured had seemed to be everywhere in the city. She thought of a kiosk near her house that had carried the enormous sign: 'If you have any symptoms, see your doctor for the Cure.' Someone had spray-painted 'SYLVER' over it the night before they left the city.

Better to be dead than be a Cured. She thought of her father's lucid eyes as she brought him a glass of water on the day he died. She wouldn't wish the Cure on him—or on Marie, either.

Especially Marie.

She wouldn't have been safe from a Cured Marie.

The kerosene lantern was flickering, casting their shadows high up the walls. Clare looked at Jem's eyes. In the soft light, they were deep green and fringed with dark lashes like a pond fringed with reeds.

Mirri and Sarai bent over their card game. Clare, taller than Jem, tilted her head towards him as they spoke.

"Do you think the Cured have anything of themselves left?"

"I don't know," said Jem. "But something really terrible's happened to their minds."

"Maybe they're psychotic," said Sarai, looking up from the game. "Jeffrey Dahmer was psychotic. He ate people."

"The Cured-in-the-blue-dress, even though her mind is gone," said Jem, "hasn't tried to hurt any of us. Something about her's different from the other Cureds. As far as I can tell, the others are all violent."

"She likes us," said Mirri.

"I don't know if the Cured are capable of like," said Jem seriously.

Then it was time for bed. Mirri's pajamas had feet and were covered with unicorns and rainbows. Sarai wore sweatpants and a thin T-shirt with 'American Beauty' on it.

"I should change the dressing on your wound," said Jem to Sarai.

"I did it already," said Sarai. She was clearly proud of herself.

"And I helped her get undressed," said Mirri. "*And* I checked the bandage." Jem and Mirri then started clearing away the tins of fruit cocktail as Sarai curled up on the sofa and watched Clare unpacking more of her things.

Sarai explained to Clare that she, Jem and Mirri all slept in different beds in the same room. Jem looked up and watched Clare as Sarai spoke. When Clare caught his eye, he shrugged his shoulders. Clare felt very unsure of herself.

Sarai broke off and winced, as if in pain.

"Have you taken your antibiotics?" asked Clare.

"Jem already gave them to me. I'm not infected. He said."

"You have to keep taking them."

"I know. I actually feel pretty good." There was a silence. "You're not sleeping in here alone again, are you?" Sarai asked.

"I suppose Bear will keep me company."

"I get creeped out alone," said Sarai. "I don't know how you did it."

Clare thought of her night terrors at the cabin, of the heap of cans and the lack of a latrine.

"I didn't do so well," she said.

"Well, you're brave to sleep out here in this room all alone. I'd have nightmares. Actually, I do anyway, but Jem and Mirri are right there."

"I don't really know what I'm supposed to do," said Clare.

Sarai leaned in close to Clare and whispered, "Alone is scary. I always worry there are things in the shadows. And there's a bolt on the bedroom door to keep us safe. I wouldn't sleep out here if I were you."

"I'm sort of old to be sharing a room," said Clare. She was thinking of Jem. He wasn't that much younger than she was. He wasn't really a little boy.

"It's like a forever sleepover," said Sarai.

"Won't Jem mind?"

"He understands about the dark. About being scared."

So Clare moved her things into the bedroom, which was a cheerful mess of blankets and pillows. Jem's things tended to be royal blue; Sarai had found over a dozen bright hand-made quilts; Mirri had accumulated an impressive amount of bedclothes decorated with unicorns and horses. Clare put down a heaped up blanket for Bear at the foot of her bed. Jem looked away as she got under the covers and arranged the bedclothes they had given her – a pink cotton sheet, a lavender blanket. A deep blue quilt that smelled like the outdoors and damp grass. From the color, that would have been Jem's.

When they were finally in bed, they all said goodnight to each other.

"It's like *The Waltons*," said Clare sleepily.

"The *who*?" asked Mirri.

"Never mind," said Clare. "Part of the old world."

FIRST SHE HAD the old dream, the one that had kept coming back to her for years, in which someone she knew walked towards her in a garden. But this time the dream changed, and she was looking at three white vultures perched on the bedstead. Their wings were open as if they were drying them in the sun; except for their red wattled heads, the birds looked like white angels. The dream began to slip away, but not before one of the vultures tucked up its wings and lurched onto her chest.

"Sylver," said the vulture. "That's the true name."

The vulture moved closer to Clare's head and cocked its head to one side. Clare could see the word burning in front of her: SYLVER.

"Sylver," the white vulture said again, and then it leaned forward and plucked out her eye.

Clare awoke and, for a moment, didn't know where she was. Then she heard thunder and the sound of rain pelting against the window. She was in the farmhouse, and the room was a storm of blankets and comforters. Mirri and Sarai and Jem were deeply asleep and their measured breathing was in stark contrast to the cacophonous sounds of thunder and rain and the creaking house.

A flash of lightning lit up the room.

Clare got out of bed and made her way to the window. Below, the mounded rows in the vegetable garden looked like graves. The red and yellow tomatoes, large green zucchini, yellow squash and wrinkled red peppers had been swallowed by darkness. Lightning burst over the house, and she saw the figure of a woman in the center of the lawn. Clare waited for another flash, and, when it finally came, she half expected the garden to be empty; instead she saw the woman's pale, rain streaked face staring up at her.

Clare felt a hand on her arm. She almost screamed, and then she saw it was Mirri, her eyes blurry and vague with sleep.

"She's always there," murmured Mirri. "It's just the same."

"Let's get you to bed," said Clare.

Mirri went with her; once she was tucked in, Clare went back to her own bed, but not before checking that the door was bolted. For a long time, she lay awake.

In the morning, Mirri said nothing about the incident, and Clare was sure she had been sleepwalking.

"It looks like it rained in the night," said Jem when he woke up.

"Yes," said Clare. She thought of the vultures in her dream; she thought of the woman's face in the rain.

The real storm would come.

CHAPTER TEN
BIKES

SARAI HEALED QUICKLY and on one sunny day, while Bear slept in the sun, and Mirri drew unicorns in the dirt, Jem took out Sarai's stitches. Clare watched as he pulled gently and the stitches came undone like a zipper.

"Wow," said Clare.

"My mother the doctor."

"Still wow."

"She could put them in and take them out with one hand."

Now Sarai only needed a little Tylenol to help her sleep, which Clare gave her from her own supply.

"For headaches?" Jem asked her.

"Cramps."

Jem blushed.

Clare looked past Sarai and saw that the Cured-in-a-blue-dress was huddled next to the barn, gazing into the distance. From time to time Mirri, who was now drawing sad unicorns with sagging pockmarked faces, would turn and glance at her.

The birds were calling to each other. Pest had come, but nature went on. Fallon and the other towns and cities would slowly fail; rain and rot would bring down the buildings; creepers would cover the ruins. Nature would reassert itself until even the great highways were no more than paths through the wild. The era of the human race was over.

The Cured-in-a-blue-dress stood. Sarai and Mirri stopped playing and watched as she lurched around the side of the barn.

"What does she eat?" Sarai asked. "She comes and goes, but I never see her eat."

"I don't know," said Jem. "And I'm not sure I want to."

Food was a constant topic of conversation. Jem, Sarai and Mirri—and now Clare—worked constantly to maintain their supply. But three people, now four, went through a lot of food—and resources in Fallon were limited.

It seemed it was always time to scavenge.

They left the farmhouse early the day the stitches came out. Sarai and Mirri made sure that Clare had her own pair of rubber gloves, a kerchief for her mouth and Vick's VapoRub to smear under her nose.

"Our scavenging costumes," said Sarai.

In her few excursions alone, Clare had found foraging to be scary nasty work, often not worth the trip. In return for witnessing appalling horrors, Clare would get as little in return as a box of wormy cornflakes. Or everything would be covered in mold, or, in the refrigerator, she would find a mass of vegetables turned to a black soupy jello.

"Don't worry," said Mirri as they set out. "Jem keeps us out of the worst houses. He doesn't want us *desensitized*."

"I put that word on my vocab list," said Sarai.

"Jem does all the *really* nasty stuff," said Mirri. "He always goes into the houses first to see how much *decomp* there is. That's what he calls it. Decomp."

Clare thought, as she had before, that Jem was pretty tough for a chess player.

As they trundled onto the road with the wagons, Clare thought she saw movement out of the corner of her eye, but when she turned there was nothing. Sarai noticed the direction of her gaze.

"It's the Cured-in-a-blue-dress," said Sarai. "Sometimes she follows us."

The first house they approached had its curtains drawn. A lot of people, it seemed, had wanted to shut out the outside world as they died. Their houses were like tombs.

"I'll go with you, Jem," said Clare when they stopped.

"I've sort of gotten used to it," said Jem, "if you want to wait outside."

"How bad is it?"

"Well, put on your gloves, and we'll see."

"You think I should use the Vicks?"

"Yeah."

It was bad. The body of a young man lay half in and half out of the kitchen. He stank.

Then Clare saw movement.

"Jem. He's alive."

"No," Jem said. "It's the maggots. They can make a body look like it's moving."

"I feel a little sick."

"We'll keep the others out of here. It's always harder when the bodies aren't in bed. There's way too much to see."

But in many respects, the house was a winner. Someone had gone in for winter sports, and, besides ski equipment, they found down jackets, down vests, snow pants, neck warmers and woolen hats—some for children and some for adults.

"We'll take some of it now and come back for more later," Jem said.

"What if some of the children survived?"

"They didn't."

"You can't be sure."

"I checked when we first came in. They're in the back bedroom."

There wasn't much else of use in the house: a bottle of ketchup; some pickles; a jar of peanut butter.

The bodies in the second house they checked were also tucked away in a bedroom, and so Mirri and Sarai came in too, but there didn't seem to be much food.

"Look what *I* found," said Mirri when she came out of the pantry.

They looked at her armload of cans.

"It's *cherry pie filling*. Can you *believe* it?"

"Mirri—" Jem started to speak and then appeared to think better of it.

"Cherry pie filling is *good*. My mother used to let me eat it right out of the can. My mother—" Her eyes started to fill, and she looked down.

There was an awkward silence. It was Jem who broke it.

"I love cherry pie filling," he said.

Sarai just thumped Mirri on the back.

After they got back to the farm and stowed the food, Clare went down to the meadow, Bear at her heel. The soft afternoon light cast long shadows, and the smell of the grass was sweet. A movement caught Clare's eye, and she turned around in time to see the unmistakable figure of Mirri coming down the steps of the porch. Clare almost called to her before she noticed that Mirri had something in her hands. Mirri kept looking nervously over her shoulder at the house as she ran to the nearby copse of trees.

Clare slowly sat down next to Bear and buried her hand in his thick coat.

Mirri stood with her back against a tree, and Clare could now see that she was carrying a small basket.

There was a flicker of blue in the trees, moving rapidly among them. Mirri held out the basket stiffly, and the Cured-in-the-blue-dress took it from her. As she did, she hurriedly backed off, as if to run. But Mirri raised her hand, slowly and gently, and the Cured-in-the-blue-dress submitted, and came forward and let Mirri's hand rest on her shoulder.

The strange moment of intimacy over, the scared woman turned and ran, and the vivid blue of her dress flickered away between the trees.

Clare stayed still until Mirri had returned to the house.

When Clare herself returned, Mirri and Sarai were gathered around Jem, who had just returned from the local library with some kind of survivalist manual. On its cover a man dressed in camouflage held a gun in one hand and a dead turkey in the other.

"We'll have to read fast," Jem said. "It's due tomorrow."

"That's a joke, right?" said Sarai.

"Right," said Jem. "No librarian." He flipped through the pages. "There's an awful lot of stuff we don't need here. Where to get automatic weapons, for example. We'd probably shoot ourselves. What provisions to stock up on in anticipation of an emergency. It's a little late for that."

"*Anything* useful?" Mirri asked.

"Maybe. There's a section on gutting and preparing deer and wild fowl, as well as a section on finding edible mushrooms."

"Finding mushrooms sounds *fun*," said Mirri.

"The man on the cover does *not* look like a mushroom specialist," said Clare.

"You have no trust," said Jem.

Later Clare took the book from Jem, and she flipped through it. On the last page was a list of medications to stock up on, and someone had scrawled, right across the list, 'As many SYLVERs as you can get.'

AFTER LUNCH, MIRRI announced that she was going out. "I left a Pretty Pony where I was playing this morning."

"Take Bear," said Clare. But Bear would not leave her, and the image of Mirri using a little leash to try and drag along a determined dog more than double her size made Clare smile.

"I'll be okay," said Mirri.

Mirri came back half an hour later. Clare noticed that she did not have a Pretty Pony with her.

* * *

CLARE KEPT AN eye on Mirri the following day, but Mirri didn't attempt to slip away. Sarai and Clare went to work in the garden.

"Jem's in charge," said Sarai as they harvested tomatoes.

"Of course he's in charge."

"Even though he's younger than you are."

"Age has nothing to do with it." Clare really meant it. While she had wallowed in grief and self-pity at the cabin, Jem had saved and kept civilized two scared little girls.

As she picked tomatoes, she thought about how it had been before. The midnight runs to Pizza One with the cheerleading squad, where they would discuss the new cheer formation, or whether they should dress alike for a whole week, or if Hannah Preston had cheated on her boyfriend.

None of that mattered anymore.

And it occurred to her that maybe that was true for all of them. Each of them had a past that was moving, inexorably, to the vanishing point.

Later that morning, Clare, Bear padding behind her, found Mirri in the bedroom stuffing a blanket into a bag.

"What are you doing?" she asked mildly.

"Nothing."

"You're stuffing a blanket into a bag."

"So what?"

"I don't mean to sound like your mother; I was just curious."

"I *know* you're not my mother," said Mirri, and she dropped both bag and blanket and walked away.

Clare was sure the blanket wouldn't be there when she next went into the bedroom.

Back in the kitchen, Clare found Jem staring into a big cardboard box.

"Cheese Whiz," he said.

Clare peered in and counted. "Fifteen cans of Cheese Whiz."

"I don't remember finding this," said Jem.

"I did," said Clare. "Two houses ago."

"Cheese Whiz is disgusting."

"You're wrong. Cheese Whiz is good. We used to squirt it right into our mouths before a football game."

"That's just gross."

"Instant energy. Anyway, I bet you had a routine before a chess match."

"True. But it didn't involve ingesting cheese products."

Bear nudged at Clare for attention. "Sorry, Bear," she said, and scratched his ear.

"Is that dog of yours ever going to like me?" asked Jem.

"He's not a wag-tail kind of dog. But he hasn't taken your throat out yet. I think that's a good sign."

Sarai and Mirri burst into the kitchen.

"We were in the barn," said Sarai, "and we found bikes."

"There're a *bunch* of them," said Mirri.

"We're busy," said Jem.

"Don't be so grown *up*," Mirri said.

"There was a hand pump," said Sarai. "For the tires. We got one of the bikes ready. Mirri rode all around the barn. Until she fell off."

"I hit a *bump*. I didn't just fall off."

Jem sighed. "How are you on a bike, Clare? Can Cheese Whiz wait?"

Clare smiled. "I could live on a bike. And there's a dairy farm we could check out that's a short ride over."

"Then let's go," Jem said.

The bikes were behind an ancient horse cart. Sarai picked a green one; Mirri's was red. Jem oiled the chain of the blue bike he found and gave it to Clare with a smile before taking the last one, which was a battered silver.

Jem led the way down the path from the farm; Clare took up the rear; Bear loped along beside her. She looked behind and saw that the Cured-in-the-blue-dress had come out to the very edge of the meadow and was watching them. Her dress billowed like a sail.

It took them no time at all to leave Fallon behind. The rolling hills gave way to flatter terrain. Soon hay meadows alternated with overripe wheat fields. The heavy heads of wheat had spilled open, and Clare could see swaths in the fields where deer must have fed and slept.

They passed a field of withered, rag-brown corn, and they careened past a church and a series of small wooden crosses placed every quarter mile along the road. The first read 'GET,' the second, 'RIGHT,' the third, 'WITH,' and the fourth, 'GOD.'

As they sped downhill, the wind licked at the sweat on Clare's face. Bear's tongue lolled and his jaws were flecked with foam, but he still had no trouble keeping up with them. Up ahead, Jem had raised his arms and was peddling with his hands in the air. He shouted something before coming to a sudden halt. Sarai almost rammed into him; Mirri swerved off the road; Clare skidded to a stop.

They were beside a miniature golf course. It was overgrown, but all the main features were there: the windmill, the moat, the sand trap, the alligator pit.

It took them only a few minutes to break out the clubs and balls from behind a boarded-up counter. They weeded the course and then played a few rounds. And it didn't matter that the sails of the windmill didn't go around or that there wasn't any water in the moat or that the motorized alligators didn't snap at them. They laughed and made up rules, and when it was Mirri's turn and her ball almost made it to the hole, but instead hovered at the lip, Jem bent down and gently flicked it in.

Bear looked at Clare with his head cocked to one side.

"I would love to know what he's thinking," she said.

When they were ready to go, they carefully replaced the clubs and balls and then got back on their bikes.

"I wish we could do that every day," said Mirri.

"We'll come back," said Clare.

But they never did.

THE ROAD BECAME windy and lined with trees as they cycled up a gentle but long slope. Clare thought of the dairy farm ahead—the long, low milking sheds, the rambling farmhouse, the big barn.

For some reason, she felt uneasy.

When they reached the top of the slope, they stopped. The farm was spread out below them, but it had clearly been abandoned, probably sometime before Pest. The house was almost a complete ruin, and, even at that distance, Clare could see that the land had begun to reclaim the milking shed. The barn stood at an odd angle.

"Let's go back," Sarai said.

"Come *on*," said Mirri and hopped on her little red bicycle. "I just want to peek into the barn. Once." She started down the slope.

Clare looked up just as some clouds covered the sun.

"This is wrong," she said. And before Jem and Sarai could even get on their bikes, Clare was a blue streak rapidly gaining on Mirri. Bear was right behind her. They arrived at the farm in a dead heat. Clare reached out and took hold of Mirri's handlebars.

"Stop," she said.

Mirri smiled at her, and then the smile faded.

"Are you mad at me?"

"No. But let's wait for the others."

"You were really fast," Sarai said to Clare as she and Jem arrived.

"I forgot you're a powerhouse," said Jem. "I'm going to be very sore tomorrow."

The rotting barn loomed above them.

"Let's go in," said Mirri. Clare noticed that the sun was getting low in the sky; they were going to have to ride hard to get home before dark.

"I'll go first," said Clare. Jem made a move as if to preempt her and then stopped himself.

"Sorry," he said.

As Clare opened the door, Bear tried to block her with his body.

"Down and stay," she said, and he obeyed.

The light in the barn was dim, and the air was still. Some twenty-odd sacks hung from the rafters. Clare assumed for a second that she must be looking at some farm crop drying. Then her vision cleared.

"Let's get out of here," she said. "Now."

Sarai and Mirri hadn't had time to understand what they were seeing, but then Clare heard Jem suck in a breath.

"We'd better take a closer look," he said. "Sarai, Mirri, you wait for us outside." The girls did as he said without a challenge, but Clare saw Mirri look back over her shoulder. And she saw Mirri's expression change.

CLARE AND JEM walked among the hanging bodies. Men. Women. Girls. Boys. Some marked with Pest. Some not.

"What happened here?" asked Clare. She examined a corpse with paint splashes on its hands and clothes.

"I think they helped each other die," said Jem.

Clare raised her eyes. On the far wall someone had painted, in large scrawled letters, 'NO CURE.'

CHAPTER ELEVEN
THE GOLD HOUSE

Mirri and Sarai were unusually subdued for a few days, and they didn't want to go out on the bikes.

"I don't like *surprises*," said Mirri.

"Why don't we go to the yellow house?" asked Sarai. "There might be good stuff there." She turned to Clare to explain. "We passed this big yellow house coming in to Fallon, but we didn't stop."

"It wasn't yellow," said Mirri. "It was *gold*."

"Yellow," said Sarai.

"*Gold*," said Mirri. "With a front like a skull."

"A little scary."

"But *gold*."

"How about going now?" said Jem.

They tightened the wheels on their little wagons and set off for the gold (or yellow) house. They could really do with a fruitful scavenge—it seemed as if they had eaten almost everything in Fallon and were running out of places to explore for food.

Clare noticed that Mirri was looking towards the wood. As she followed Mirri's line of sight, she caught a flash of blue moving through the trees.

"Why is she following us?" asked Clare.

"She likes to be near us," Mirri said. "She doesn't mean any *harm*."

"Maybe. But we need to tell Jem she's here." As Clare did so, Mirri looked at her sorrowfully, as if she'd committed some kind of small betrayal.

The Cured-in-the-blue-dress came no closer, and they dropped the subject.

"I hope there's no one dead in the house," said Mirri as they rejoined the road.

"The dead won't bother you," Clare said.

"That's what Jem says. Right, Jem? It's not as if they went *walking*."

"They're re-incarnated." Sarai said. Then she frowned. "But that's hard to explain. My mother could explain it really well."

Mirri and Sarai now lagged behind Clare and Jem, who were trying to remember an old movie they had each seen.

"I don't remember the title," said Jem. "But it was about the Nazis. The Nazis took away this old professor for saying Aryan and non-Aryan blood was the same."

"I sort of remember. The professor had two sons, right? And one was sort of good and one was bad—but they were both Nazis."

"I don't know how you can be a sort-of-good Nazi. But I do remember that at the end Jimmy Stewart and what's-her-name try and ski across the border to escape."

"Right," said Clare. "Into Switzerland."

"Austria."

"Right. But they shoot her. Right?"

"Right. She dies," said Jem.

"I remember now. At the end, one of the brothers—"

"The sort-of-good Nazi brother—"

"Runs off into the snow. I actually cried at the end. The movie's ancient. I saw it on the Classic Movie Channel when I was supposed to be doing homework."

"And I thought you were a straight A student."

"Oh, I was."

They could see the house now. Clare, who had only heard the description, was taken aback.

"It really is yellow," she said. "Mirri had me convinced it was gold."

"It's gold when the light catches it," Jem said.

"All right. For Mirri we'll call it gold."

"See how it looks like a skull?" Mirri said.

Clare didn't like the house. She noted the configuration of the windows, and she understood why Mirri had said it looked like a skull. The gold house dwarfed its ruined garden, and time, Clare saw, was hard at work on the building. Morning glories curled up the banister leading to the porch; small plants were growing out of the gutters.

Then Clare looked away only to see that the Cured-in-a-blue-dress was no longer hiding but was standing in front of a tree. Jem saw her as well.

"She's never come so close," Jem said, and as he spoke the Cured-in-the-blue-dress slipped behind the tree and was gone.

"So much for that," said Sarai.

"It would be nice if she were gone for good," said Jem.

"No, it *wouldn't*," said Mirri.

They turned their attention to the house.

"Well," said Jem. "Here I go. I'll call to you if it's okay."

"If you think I'm letting you go in there without me and Bear, you're wrong." Clare said.

"It won't take me a minute to check it out."

"You need someone at your back. I don't like this place."

"All right. But not Sarai and Mirri."

Clare and Jem went in together, and Bear followed. For an instant, Clare thought of Michael. Michael would have *never* let her go in with him.

The door opened into a short hallway that led to a wide room where patterned blue wallpaper seemed to dance across the walls—in contrast to the slight odor of human decay. Everywhere there were display cases filled with butterflies. Each butterfly was transfixed by a pin that gleamed silver, as if a dot of mercury had fallen on its back. Wings glittered vermilion, orange, deep blue and green. Some of the butterflies had enormous shapes like eyes on their wings. Off the living room they discovered a study. The head of a doe sprouted out of the blue wallpaper above the desk. A buck with small antlers stared down at them glassily from another wall. Pairs of antlers hung above the fireplace.

"It's a deer mausoleum," said Jem.

"Let's find the kitchen," said Clare.

"And then the cellar. That's where they put the good stuff. Pretty often. You don't have to come."

"Forget it. I'm in."

The kitchen was filthy. Dirty broken dishes overflowed the sink and covered part of the floor. Bear started licking some brown stuff off a plate, and then turned away as if in disgust. Forks, knives and spoons looked as if they had been hurled at random.

Jem opened cupboards looking for food.

Cans. Huge bags of pasta. Flour, sugar, tea.

"I don't believe it," said Jem.

"Real food," said Clare.

Upstairs, in one of the bedrooms, they found a corpse lying with its arms crossed over its chest as if it had been posed. The other bedrooms were empty. Once downstairs again, Jem opened the door to the basement, and Clare used her flashlight to illuminate the steep stairs. A packed dirt floor was just visible at the bottom. The air was rank with decomposition, mildew, and a smell like rust.

"Something's dead down here," said Clare.

"I hope it's an animal. I don't think I'm up to another dead body right now."

Clare's flashlight lit up a corner of the cellar that was separated from the rest by a partition. Bear barked once.

Clare and Jem edged around the partition, and when they saw what was hanging there, they both stepped back quickly. Clare stumbled, and Jem caught her arm. She didn't want to look at the small heavy forms dangling from the ceiling. She remembered the bodies they had found swinging from the beams at the dairy farm.

Then Clare recognized what she was seeing.

Hams.

The hams hung in a row, eight of them, solemn and still as the corpses of infants. Clare touched the nearest one and it bumped its neighbor, and soon all of them were swaying back and forth.

Jem put his nose right up to one of the hams.

"They smell delicious," he said. Bear sat and looked up, his tongue lolling out. He looked as if he were grinning.

"Jem, look at this," said Clare.

The light from the flashlight had washed over an area of the cellar where the earth seemed to have been recently turned. The plot looked like a small grave.

Above them, they heard footsteps coming towards the cellar door. And then the slow creaking of floorboards stopped. The door began to close. Bear gave a low growl and leapt for the stairs, but Clare was there ahead of him. She took the steep steps two at a time, but she was still too late. The door grazed her outstretched fingers as it closed. On the other side, she heard someone fumbling with the lock.

It wasn't a time to speak or discuss or weigh options. Clare gathered herself together and crashed into the door.

When Clare hit, the door opened just enough for her to slip her hand into the gap before it slammed back onto her fingers. The pain was excruciating. Even so, she shut it out as she crashed into the door again. This time she heard the sound of wood splintering and the door flew open.

She found herself face to face with a Cured. He was a big man.

They stood there for a moment, neither one of them moving. And then he grabbed her, slammed the basement door behind her and bolted it, shutting in Jem and Bear. He dragged Clare to the kitchen, kicked her legs out from under her and pushed her to the floor. In a moment, he was on top of her. He was breathing heavily into her face, and his breath stank of the grave.

"I'm going to kill you," he said.

He started tearing at her clothes, ripping open her jacket and her shirt, revealing the Pest rash on her chest. She tried to push his hands away, but it was no good. As he fumbled with her clothes, Clare punched him with her good hand, hard. Her fist sank into his face as if into a sponge. She flipped the Cured over until his back was to the floor, and she was on top of him with a knee on his sternum.

She realized she was stronger than he was.

Go figure.

She stood up and kicked him in the side. Then Sarai and Mirri were in the house. Mirri ran to Clare, but Clare pushed her firmly away as the Cured slowly got to his feet. Clare kneed him in the groin. He curled into a ball and began to cry.

"What we need to do is tie him up," Clare said. "Mirri, get some cord. Sarai, get Jem and Bear out of the cellar."

For a brief second, Clare wished Michael were there to handle things, then she knelt down and twisted the Cured's arm behind his back before he could get back up. His hair fell back away from his face, and she saw an orange-colored patch behind his ear.

"Hurry, Mirri," she said. Then Sarai appeared at the top of the basement stairs with Jem. Bear was behind them.

Clare suddenly became aware that her blouse was torn open, but there was nothing she could do about it while holding down the Cured.

At that moment, Mirri appeared with a large ball of yellow nylon cord.

"Sarai, Mirri," said Clare, "tie him up. Can you help me, Jem?"

"*I'll* do the knots," said Mirri. "I got a badge in knots when I was a Brownie."

"I thought you told me you flunked out of Brownies," said Sarai.

"That was *after*."

"Will you hurry?" Clare shouted.

As soon as they had the man secured, Jem checked the bindings. Clare saw him looking at her, and then he hurriedly looked away. She quickly pulled her shirt closed.

"Did he hurt you?" asked Jem quietly.

"My hand," said Clare. "That's all. He shut the door on it." Jem came over to her and took her hand in his own.

"You'll need a splint."

"It'll be okay." Bear lunged over to Clare and nudged Jem away. He began licking her injured hand.

"He's jealous," said Jem.

"Yes," said Clare. "Well."

"I don't like the way that Cured's *looking* at us," Mirri said, glancing at Clare's attacker.

"I doubt he likes the way we're looking at him, either," Clare said. "We'll leave him here while we get all the food back to the house."

"Then what?" Sarai asked.

"Then I don't know."

"We have to hurry," said Mirri. "It's going to get dark soon, and I don't like the dark, and I don't want to be in the dark near *him*."

"He's tied up," said Clare.

"He's *spooky*," said Mirri.

There was no question that it was going to take more than one journey. Keeping together, they made two trips to the farmhouse, taking not only food supplies, but also blankets, some kerosene that Clare and Jem found in the cellar and the contents of the medicine cabinet—bandaids, surgical tape, cough syrup, Pepto-Bismol, and a bottle of prescription codeine. Clare took one of the pills, and in a little while the pain in her hand was reduced to a manageable ache.

The Cured lay and watched them as they came and went. He didn't struggle.

Clare thought of the body upstairs. She went over to the bound Cured and looked down at him.

"Who's that in the bed?"

"My wife."

"Is that a grave in the cellar?"

"It's the neighbor. He died of Pest. I didn't kill him." He smiled gently. "But I ate most of him."

"Instead of *ham*?" Mirri was incredulous.

"Go outside, Mirri," Clare said, turning to her.

As they approached the gold house on their final trip, Sarai and Mirri stopped chattering. Jem looked grim.

They entered the hallway and Bear's hackles rose.

The Cured was gone. The yellow cord lay in coils on the floor.

"I want to go home," Sarai said.

"It looks like he cut the rope," Jem said.

"He didn't have a knife," said Clare. "I'm sure of it."

"Let's get home," Jem said. "We'll be all right."

"We have Bear," said Sarai. "He's a secret weapon."

"From what happened in the house," said Jem wryly, "it would seem that our best secret weapon is Clare."

On the way back, they skirted the edge of the road, weaving in and out of the woods, and that's when Clare smelled it. Sweat, stink, something rancid.

"He's here," she said.

The sun was low now, and as the trees moved in the wind, their shadows flickered across the road.

"There," said Jem, pointing.

The Cured was slumped under a tree, unmoving. Clare went and stood right in front of him. Bear was by her side, but he was no longer bristling.

"He's dead." Clare looked into the damage of his face. The eyes were open, and the whites of his eyes were marked with pinpricks of blood.

"This is *really* creepy," said Mirri.

Jem had joined Clare. "Maybe he just died. Who knows how long the Cured can live?"

Clare leaned forward and touched the patch she had seen before. She gently pulled it off, making sure to use only her fingernails. It was the size of a quarter, and there was a trademark on it in tiny print: 'SYLVER.'

"Don't let it come in contact with your skin," said Jem.

"No," said Clare. "I don't think that'd be a good idea." She threw it next to the body.

"I REMEMBER SOMETHING more about that movie," said Clare later, as they were headed for home.

"What movie?" asked Jem.

"The one that had the two Nazi brothers in it. I remember that the woman skiing into Switzerland—"

"Austria."

"The woman skiing into Austria is called Freya."

"You're right," said Jem. "Freya. I would never have remembered that."

"But I still don't have the slightest idea of what the title might be."

"It doesn't matter."

"No," she said. "It doesn't."

They walked for a while in silence.

"You know, Clare," said Jem finally. "It's time to move on. It's time to find the Master. We can't wait until it's too late for you."

"I know."

But Clare was pre-occupied. She was still wondering about the title of the movie, and then she realized that Jem really was right. Like so many things, it didn't matter anymore. Perhaps it had never mattered—the idea that in the pre-Pest days she could have googled the title by typing in 'Nazi brothers Freya' seemed only decadent. The time to live fully in the new world had come. She remembered from English class, and she had been very good in English, that Faulkner had written that the past isn't dead; it isn't even past—but Faulkner had been wrong. Things past were best forgotten; they were engaged in the now; they were united in a fight against death; they were caught up in the mortal storm.

CHAPTER TWELVE
THE PIG

As THE DAYS slipped by, Clare's hand began to heal, the Cured-in-the-blue-dress began sleeping in the barn, and the first frost came. One morning they woke to see feathers of ice on the windowpanes. The greenish tomatoes that they hadn't yet picked hung limply from the vines. Clare noticed that Bear's coat had become thick and dense. And all around the house, leaves scudded in whirlwinds of color as the cold wind blew.

Jem talked about the master-of-the-situation, and all of them began to have a sense that their time at Fallon was drawing to a close. Scavenging had become a hard, desperate frustrating task.

There was nothing fun about Fallon anymore.

"You think it's time to leave," said Clare one bright cold day as Jem was slicing ham for lunch.

"Yes. It's time to think about how we're going to find this Master. If he's organized, he'll have food. And we have to get the cure. For you. And then for me."

"Before I met up with you," said Clare, "I kept hoping for an adult who would take care of everything. Now I'm not so sure that's a good idea."

"Clare, you still have the rash. *I* have the rash. We're *all* marked."

"I know."

"You're already fifteen."

"I don't think that's so old. Even for Pest."

"Besides. If we can stay with the Master, it might be a good thing." Jem cut the fat away from the ham slices as he spoke. "I don't want to settle into one place and eat everything that's there and then move on to a different place and eat everything's that's there and then—"

"I get the gist."

"The Master may have a place where we do more than just try and survive another day and search for food and go to sleep every night bone-tired."

"Yeah. But what do we do with all that free safe time?"

"Exist."

"That's it?"

"We could play a lot of chess."

"What about me?"

"You could write a book. Like your father."

He finished slicing the ham as Mirri and Sarai came into the kitchen. They sat at the counter and ate without taking off their jackets. The house was drafty, and the wind rattled the windows. Bear lay at Clare's feet and looked up as the ham was doled out.

"Give him a bit," said Clare. "That dry dog food we found is disgusting."

"Then you shouldn't eat it," said Jem.

"Seriously. He needs meat."

"Clare," said Jem very seriously, "we can't support him if he doesn't hunt."

"A little ham?"

Bear had not taken his eyes from Jem. Jem gave a slice of ham to Clare.

"You give it to him," Jem said. "With you, he's gentle. The last time I tried to give him a treat, he almost took my hand along with it."

Clare gave Bear the ham, and he nuzzled it out of her hand.

"That dog loves you," said Jem.

"I know."

Clare wondered how the Cured-in-a-blue-dress was coping out in the barn. She knew that Mirri had smuggled the pink sleeping bag out of their bedroom to her. How Jem managed not to notice was beyond Clare—he had noticed right away when she had put an extra comforter on her own bed. He had even said something about it, although she couldn't remember what.

Mirri and Sarai finished eating the ham using their fingers.

"Let's go find a house to break into," Sarai said.

Her suggestion met with instant approval. It had been a slow day, and they were bored.

"Maybe I can find some more Breyer horses," said Mirri. Mirri scavenged horses and unicorns, ranging from cheap plastic models as small as the tip of her little finger, to bronze sculptures heavy enough to bring down a strong Cured. Sarai collected children's books, which she would sometimes read aloud to Mirri. They were in the middle of *Tuck Everlasting* and Mirri was very doubtful about the way the plot was going.

"Eternal life is the *right* choice," she told Sarai. "And I plan on living forever *no matter what*."

Mirri and Sarai kept their collections by the side of their beds. Clare sometimes kept treats for Bear next to hers, but she had never seen much by Jem's, except for an earring that at first she thought must have belonged to his mother, but that turned out to be hers. He had found it on the floor.

Today, it was Mirri's turn to pick the house they were going to pillage. They walked into Fallon, and she chose one near the playground where they had all first met. Sarai heaved a rock through the windowpane.

"Maybe we're letting them run a little too wild," said Clare to Jem.

"Could be."

The Cured-in-the-blue-dress watched all this from the edge of the playground.

"Have you noticed how close she's getting to us?" said Jem.

"Yes. But Bear seems to think she's all right."

The house was empty of food. Bear sniffed around the kitchen and then lay down on the floor.

"*I'm* going to look at the garden," said Mirri. "Maybe there's fresh stuff."

"Wrong time of year," Jem said.

"Not for *pumpkins*. We could have pumpkin pie. My mother—" Mirri trailed off. She looked at each of them as if, for a moment, she didn't know where she was. Then she went out the door.

"*Jem!*" Mirri came running back a second later, barging into Sarai, who almost fell. "You're not going to believe this. I found a *pig*! There's a real live *pig* digging around in the garden. It's eating the squash."

They all went to see and, sure enough, there it was, a huge pink thing rooting through the garden.

"Let's catch it," said Jem.

Mirri, Sarai and Clare stayed in the garden while Jem went into the house to look for a rope. Clare kept one hand firmly entwined in Bear's fur. The dog was trembling with excitement, intent on the pig, and quietly and steadily drooling.

"I read somewhere," said Sarai, "that you can eat every part of a pig. Except the squeal. That's a joke, of course—about eating the squeal, I mean. Because of course you can't eat a squeal. A squeal's a sound."

"I don't want to try to eat a whole pig," said Mirri. "Especially this pig. I want a pet pig."

"What about bacon?" asked Sarai.

"I'd eat bacon," admitted Mirri.

"It's lucky I was raised Hindu," said Sarai. "We eat pork, but not beef. I bet my parents would relax the rules, though. If they were here."

"They wouldn't begrudge you a steak—if we could come up with one," said Clare.

"Well," said Sarai dubiously. "A steak. I don't know."

"What about you, Clare?" asked Mirri. "What can't you eat?"

"Supposedly no pork," said Clare. "But we ate it anyway. And we ate an unfortunate dessert called kugel."

"I eat anything," said Mirri.

Jem returned with the rope.

"Here we go," he said.

"I'm taking Bear inside," said Clare. "He's way too excited about the pig."

Jem nodded. The others were already approaching the big pink sow. Clare saw Sarai slip in the muddy garden and almost go down.

Inside the house, for a reason she couldn't articulate, Clare decided to go up the stairs. Bear was close by her side. At the top, there was a door on the right.

Clare opened the door. She saw a vase with a tangle of dead flowers in it. A gilded mirror. Part of a bed. She opened the door wider.

There was a dead little girl on the bed.

The girl carried no mark of Pest, but she was terribly wasted away, and her lips were cracked and parched. There was something odd about the shape of her legs under the covers. Clare lifted the sheets and saw that the girl was wearing leg braces. When she saw the crutches in a corner of the room, she realized that the girl had probably been left behind to die when everyone else was fleeing Pest. She may even have still been alive when Clare was in the Loskey cabin. Clare suddenly felt weak.

She heard footsteps on the stairs, and Jem entered the room.

"We've got the pig. Then we found Bear, but not you."

She watched him take in the scene. She heard yet more footsteps, and then saw Sarai and Mirri standing behind Jem.

There was a flutter of blue outside the door, and then it was gone.

"Someone left her. Just left her," Clare said. "And she didn't have Pest. We could have saved her. We could have—"

Jem pulled a sheet over the girl's face and put his arm around Clare.

"Let's go home. Come on, Clare."

"We could have done something."

"No. We couldn't have. We didn't know."

They went down the stairs, into the garden, and started herding the pig into the road.

"Do you like the pig?" Mirri asked Clare shyly. Clare was too shaken to answer her, but Sarai did.

"I like it," said Sarai. "It trundles along like a big pink barrel, don't you think, Clare?"

"We could call it 'Barrel,'" said Mirri. "Or maybe 'Wilbur.'"

When they got home, Sarai and Mirri went to pen up the pig while Jem took Clare into the bedroom.

"You need to lie down," he said. "I don't think you're okay yet. I'll be back in a few minutes. I just need to settle Mirri and Sarai and do something with that damn pig before your dog eats it."

"Okay."

"Don't faint on me."

"I'm not the fainting type."

He closed the door behind him. And standing there behind the door, half hidden in the murky light, was the Cured-in-a-blue-dress.

Clare was terrified.

"What are you doing here?" she asked.

The Cured-in-a-blue-dress seemed to be struggling. Her contorted face looked tortured as she worked her mouth.

"Watch Mirri," she said.

Clare stared at her.

"I know Mirri gives you food," Clare said. "I know you must care for her. We won't let anything happen to her."

"Promise." A muscle in the woman's forehead pulsed.

"I promise. Now please go away." But the Cured-in-a-blue-dress crept closer to her. "Don't hurt me," said Clare. The woman with the ravaged face shook her head, but Clare, truly rattled, began to plead. "Please keep back. Please go away."

"The bad man." The woman's voice was hoarse.

Somehow Clare knew immediately whom she was talking about. The Cured from the gold house.

"He's dead," said Clare.

The Cured-in-a-blue-dress reached over and put a hand on Clare's shoulder. She spoke softly and clearly.

"I killed him."

Then she slipped out of the room and was gone.

MASTER

The Master found it curious the things that children chose to travel with. They arrived at the mansion cold and starving—but among the cans of food and bits of blanket and clothing, they also had teddy bears and stuffed hippos and piglets and photographs of their parents and their brothers and sisters. They carried old newspaper clippings, and one of them had a ribbon from a horse show, and one of them had an old dog collar, and—this surprised the Master most of all—some of them carried their parents' wedding rings.

It was just junk, designed to pull them back into a world that was dead, that was no part of the living world he was building. So there were room checks. Children who had rid themselves of their personal effects received praise. The others—not.

The children came to him, but not as many as he had hoped. There weren't many people left, he reminded himself, child or Cured. But the Master wanted more children. He *needed* more children. So he would sometimes leave the charges he did have in the hands of Britta and Doug (the oldest boy of the arrivals), and he would go out looking for survivors. He had confidence in Britta. There wasn't much to Doug, but he listened to everything that Britta said, and that was good enough for the Master. Britta was sound to the core.

The Master's pack was heavy as he moved through the woods. It was filled with blankets, medicine and bandages, as well as enticements: bottles of juice, candy bars, stuffed animals—both pink and blue—and jewelry: gold necklaces, brooches studded with winking emeralds and rubies. It had been easier to break into jewelry stores than to find good-looking jewelry at a WalMart. He also carried plastic trucks and Star Wars figurines and a Cinderella Barbie with blue, blue eyes.

He shifted the pack. It wasn't easy to find children who had not yet grown into Pest, but it was of paramount importance. He would give them a life, and they—well, the right ones—would keep him cured. He knew that SitkaAZ13 hadn't given up on him yet, but the blood of the right kind of little girl would keep him alive. He was sure of it. But there were things one just didn't tell the children. Quite a number of things. Not until they were ready.

He was making an inventory of his supplies in his head when he heard the sound. He was caught off guard. Usually he was well aware of a child in his vicinity before he heard it. He could smell their youth, he really could, or maybe he could just smell a human smell—the same way he knew when an animal was near, and what kind. The sharp smell of fox; the benign scent of hay that belonged to deer; the diseased smell of the raccoon.

He moved closer until he could hear the low chant:

"We all fall down. We all fall down."

The child just kept chanting, in a low and monotonous tone, "We all fall down. We all fall down." The Master slipped off his pack and got down onto the leaf litter. The child was obviously young; he needed to see it.

He crept forward. If it were too young, or if it were on the verge of death, there was no point in taking it back with him. He crept forward. A low stone wall was between him and the child.

"We all fall down."

He slowly raised his head above the wall.

It was a girl child, foul with dirt that now offended his nose, her long hair slick with grease, her body rail thin. She must have been about eight. She was singing to the plastic head of a doll. Next to her was a stained sleeping bag covered with a pattern of carousel horses. A couple of plastic bags lay on top of it.

A little further on, he saw a body. Even at that distance, he could tell SitkaAZ13 had taken it. The smell of the body was sweet and strong.

The chanting went on. "We all fall down." She had her back to the body, and he didn't have to wonder why. Decay had already set in, and the corpse was rotting quickly, in the way that SitkaAZ13 corpses did. He understood that she probably couldn't bear to look at her companion, but he felt no empathy. He never did.

The Master picked up a pebble and threw it a short distance away from her.

She looked up

Cornflower blue eyes.

She was going to be very useful.

"Hey. Don't be afraid," he said.

At the sound of his voice she scrambled away, first towards the body, and then, as if surprised to find it dead, towards the woods.

He ran after her and caught her by the arms; she began to scream.

"I'm not a Cured," he said. "I'm all right. I'm here to bring you someplace safe. I'm here to bring you home."

She landed a good kick on his shin; he swore, but he held her tightly, and she began to settle down. He let her go, and she looked at him appraisingly.

"You're a grownup," she said.

"Yes."

"Why didn't anyone come before? Why didn't anyone come when Pest killed my parents and my brother?" A hank of hair had fallen into her face. He reached forward to pushed it back; she flinched, and then she let him touch her.

"It's been a busy time," he said.

"Yeah. I guess it has. Are you Child Services?"

"You could say that. You could say I'm all that's left of it."

She gestured towards the body. "Well, now we're going to have to do something about Luthe."

His full name had been Luther, she told the Master. They had only just met. She had seen that his face was flushed, but she hadn't expected him to die.

"He was nice," she said.

"Have some apple juice," said the Master. "You'll feel better."

He shuffled through his pack until he found two little boxes of apple juice. He could tell she was dehydrated.

They drank juice together solemnly. He gave her a choice of the toys in his pack, and she picked out the Princess Leia Star Wars figurine.

"I haven't had apple juice in forever," she said. She quietly began to cry.

"I have more apple juice," he said. "I have more everything at the mansion. There're animals, too. Ducks and baby ducks. We just found a nanny goat—she's very friendly; she'll nibble at your clothes. And there are children there who'll be happy to see you."

"I haven't seen any other children."

"There aren't many around."

"Luthe saw one."

"He did? How close? Where?"

"Near a cabin in the woods, not these woods, but far away. He saw a girl and a dog, but the dog was huge and black, and Luthe didn't like it."

"I don't know your name," said the Master.

"Eliza."

"Let's go, Eliza. Don't worry about any girls with black dogs. You'll be safe with me."

As they left the clearing, the Master heard the sound of a crow. He could smell it, too. He thought of Luthe's eyes. Crows always went for the soft parts first.

He began telling Eliza more about life at the mansion, and about Britta and Doug and the others. He kept her too busy to think about burying Luthe.

He took her hand.

"Time to go, my blue-eyed girl."

CHAPTER THIRTEEN
DARIAN

THEY HAD JUST finished breakfast, and the table was littered with the remains: three small boxes of cereal, two little white donuts, an empty bag of Cheetos, a bowl of oatmeal that Sarai had rejected. Jem surveyed the damage ruefully.

"I hope we don't get scurvy," he said.

"When we go to the next place," said Mirri, "we can look for vitamins."

They were almost completely packed and ready to go. There simply wasn't enough food in Fallon left to support all four of them for the long term. The pig was coming with them on the hoof.

Jem took the last donut. "We'd better feed the pig."

"It's Mirri's turn," said Sarai.

"Go on, Mirri," said Jem. "The stuff for the pig's in the bucket next to the kitchen door."

Mirri wrinkled her nose and hauled the bucket out the side door, slopping some of the leftovers on the floor.

"I'll get that later," she said. And then Mirri was gone for a long while.

"You think she's all right?" asked Clare. "Maybe Bear and I should go and take a look." But a moment later, Mirri walked back in the door.

"You took forever," Sarai said.

"Don't forget to wipe the floor," Jem said automatically.

Mirri was silent, and Jem looked up at her. She looked afraid.

"What is it?" asked Jem.

114

"The pig got out." Mirri started weeping big, wet little girl tears.

"What?" Jem was on his feet.

"The pig got out and it's all my *fault*." She hiccupped. "I opened the gate too wide."

"Honey," said Clare. "Stuff like this happens. We'll catch the pig."

"Let's go," said Jem. "Bear should be able to follow its scent. Bear won't kill the pig, will he, Clare?"

"No," said Clare. Doubtfully.

"The boy who was hanging around the pig pen said *he'd* help us, too," said Mirri. "So maybe it won't take so long."

"*What* boy?" asked Jem.

"*The* boy. The boy I *found*."

"Explain," Jem said.

"He was watching our pig."

It took a while to get the details out of Mirri. "He was eating cookies," she said, tearful again. "He offered me one, but I said 'no' because he was a stranger. Then I opened the gate, and the pig *slipped out*, right past both of us. The boy's already chasing it."

"All right," said Jem. "But I'm going after the pig alone. And if you argue, Clare, I'm just going to have to pull rank."

"You must be kidding," Clare said. "You must absolutely positively be joking."

"Someone needs to stay with the kids."

"You *are* joking."

"I'll take Bear."

"Bear won't listen to you. Without me, Bear probably *will* eat the pig. Or you."

Clare and Jem started the search at the pig pen. Bear knew the pig's scent, but, from his excitement, Clare was pretty sure he had picked up the boy's as well. Following both, they set off into the meadow. The Cured-in-a-blue-dress was by the barn, close enough that Clare could see her face, and, although it seemed an impossible emotion for a Cured, Clare thought she detected fear in those dark and shadowed eyes.

The boy and the pig had cut a wide swath through the long wheat-colored grass of the hay meadow. Clare felt the early morning dew soaking into her shoes and jeans as they ran. She could tell that Bear wanted to race ahead, but she kept him at close range. At the edge of the forest, they came to a place where the grass was flattened in a wide circle.

"It looks like deer spent the night here," said Clare.

"No," said Jem. "I don't think so. I think it looks like someone was wrestling with a pig."

"Are you scared?"

"I'm very highly nervous."

They finally found the boy sitting in front of a dilapidated woodshed deep in the forest. His clothes were torn, and there was mud on his face. He got to his feet. Bear rushed ahead of Clare, stopped only when she called him twice, and then howled.

"What's that about?" asked Jem.

Bear backed to Clare, fur raised, and she buried her hand deep in his pelt. "I don't know," she said.

The boy was calm. "The pig's inside," he said. "And I had a hell of time getting it there, I assure you. I assume it's Miriam's pig you're looking for."

"How do you know her name?" asked Jem.

"She told me, right before the pig made a dash for freedom."

He looked up at them as if he were seeing nothing new, as if he saw people every day. As if the world hadn't come to an end. His dark hair tumbled about his face; his mouth was wide and generous with a quirk at the corner, as if he found everything slightly humorous. And Clare stepped backward in something like horror.

The boy could have been Michael's brother.

The boy could have been Michael's twin.

Clare couldn't help herself. "Michael?"

"Darian. My name is Darian."

"Sorry," said Clare. "You look like someone I know. *Knew.*"

Jem looked up sharply.

"I'll help with the pig," said the boy.

Jem and Darian went into the shed. Clare heard a scuffle and a grunt and some mild swearing. Then Jem emerged, the rope securely around the pig's neck. The pig made a move to charge him, but Clare picked up a small branch and gave it a tap on the rump, and soon it was trotting along in front of them.

Clare now realized that Darian didn't really look all that much like Michael, not on closer inspection. It was as if Michael's features had been blurred. Darian was handsome enough, but his face was not as symmetrical as Michael's, and where Michael had occasionally been (Clare had to admit it) humorless, Darian didn't look like he took anything very seriously.

On the way back, the woods seemed oppressive. Clare kept Bear at heel. The air was still, and the freshness of the day had worn off.

When they returned to the meadow, the pig, in spite of its apparent desire for liberty, seemed content to return to its pen. Darian looked at it wistfully.

"It looks delicious," he said.

"We'll get you some food," said Jem.

"You're alone?" asked Clare.

"All alone."

"There're four of us," said Clare. "And a Cured. She's under our protection." Clare did not forget her debts.

"We haven't met any survivors," said Jem. "Except you."

"They're out there," said Darian. "But some of them are pretty beat up."

"And they all have the rash?" asked Jem.

"Oh yes. I saw one rash like a map of the world. Mine's pitiful in comparison. It doesn't look like a map of anything."

Clare looked at him carefully—the lock of hair that strayed into his face, his soft mouth. When she caught Jem watching her, she turned away.

ROBIN AND CLARE *sat in Clare's bedroom in a drift of homework papers.*

"I don't like Michael," Robin said, crumpling a page of algebra formulas.

"Everyone likes Michael," said Clare.

"Not me," said Robin

"He's not using me, if that's what you're thinking. Not that way."

"Which upsets you. Even though you know he's practically engaged to Laura. Red alert."

"He loves me. He just doesn't know it."

Robin tossed her civics book onto the floor.

"Come on," said Robin. "Let's get real for just a moment. He's like a vampire battening on to a victim. He will suck you emotionally dry. And then go back to Laura."

"He needs me as a friend."

"He's a vampire."

"Have you read Twilight?*"*

"Don't even go there."

Robin got up off of Clare's bed, picked up her civics book, and went home.

CLARE WONDERED, FOR just a moment, what Robin would have thought of Darian.

There was no sign of Mirri or Sarai when they reached the porch, Darian trailing slightly behind them. But when they opened the door, Sarai and Mirri almost fell out into their arms.

"We were *waiting* for you," said Mirri.

"Hello, Miriam," said Darian. "I caught your pig."

"We call her Mirri," said Jem.

"It's short for Miriam," said Mirri. Jem introduced Sarai.

They went into the kitchen, and Mirri and Sarai started to prepare Darian a plate of food. Sarai brought up some apples from the cellar; Mirri got out the jam jar and put a spoon next to it. Then she went into the pantry, stood on a chair and managed to lift down a ham. Mirri wrestled it to the big country kitchen table and started cutting slices.

"What else should I get?" asked Sarai.

"Open the can of pineapple rings," said Mirri. "My mother always put pineapple rings on ham."

Finally Darian sat and ate. Clare wondered how long he had been on his own.

"You've seen other children?" asked Jem.

"Some."

"Tell us about them."

"Well. The children I've met were mostly peculiar. Or pathetic."

"*We're* peculiar," said Mirri.

"You seem all right, though," said Darian. "Most of the children I've seen are seriously weirded out from the struggle to survive. I've watched them try to farm, a task at which they mostly fail, and I've watched them try to hunt, often badly, and I've watched them raid houses for food—which can't go on forever."

"So what's your strategy for getting by?" asked Jem.

"Until things get sorted out," said Darian, "I'm going to trade stories and news for what I need and then move on."

"You're a bard," said Clare. "Like Homer."

"Who?" Darian asked.

Clare narrowed her eyes.

Mirri was sitting close to Darian, and, while he was speaking, he absently began to finger a strand of her beautiful red-gold hair.

Clare glanced at Jem, and she could tell that he wanted to slap Darian's hand away.

And perhaps, if Jem had, everything would have turned out differently. They moved from the kitchen to the living room, where the dark television still sat prominently on its pedestal. Mirri grabbed a cushion and flopped onto her stomach and Sarai joined her. The wound in Sarai's side was now completely healed. Clare and Jem sat on the sagging sofa, leaving Darian the good armchair. He really looked an awful lot like Michael.

"Did you play football?" she asked him. "Before?" Jem gave her a look.

"Yeah," Darian said. "When I was a sophomore. Before I quit school."

"You quit school?"

"Yeah."

Clare didn't know anybody who had quit school. She wondered if that's why Darian seemed so much older than they were, almost an adult. And he looked as if he were only months away from Pest. Weeks even.

"How did you end up in Fallon?" asked Jem.

"I've ended up lots of places," said Darian. "And I plan to keep going. I heard all that rigmarole about everybody carrying Pest, but as far as I can make out, all Pest has done to the survivors is give them a rash. I'm eighteen and I feel fine. The Pest rash doesn't even itch. I've been on the road since I was fifteen, and I'm not stopping now."

"I'm fifteen," said Clare thoughtfully.

"Are you in charge?" asked the boy.

"Jem is," said Clare.

"Doesn't really matter. I just need a place for the night and someone to okay it."

"Can he stay?" Mirri asked, hopefully.

"Of course," said Jem. Clare looked down and found herself gazing into Bear's yellow diamond eyes. He knew something. He was telling her something. But she couldn't quite hear.

A little while later Darian opened his pack and unrolled a long piece of felt with pockets in it, of the sort that some people, Clare knew, used to store knives. But in each pocket he carried souvenirs of where he had been. He showed them a handful of gems that winked green and red in his palm, glossy rooster plumes of dark green-blue and red, five acorns in their brown caps, a small clay vase, the tail of a goat. Other pockets he didn't open. Mirri's eyes were fixed on the gems. He poured them into her hand.

"For you," he said. Then he looked at Sarai. "And for you." He gave her the glossy feathers.

"These look *awfully* valuable," said Mirri hesitatingly, as she turned the gems over and over in her hands.

"Nothing's valuable anymore," said Darian.

"We can't accept gifts from you," said Jem.

"Yes we *can*," said Mirri.

"Thank you," said Sarai to Darian.

"Consider it a return for your hospitality," said Darian.

As EVENING BEGAN to draw in, Darian told them of some of the survivors he'd encountered.

"Some of them have become very strange," he said. "There's one group of three that has a twelve-year-old girl in charge. She has the two others convinced that SitkaAZ13 is a demonstration of the wrath of God. She has a Bible, and whenever one of the two does something she thinks is wrong, she makes them wear a sign with a Bible verse on it. I didn't stay long.

"In another place, I found a kid crying over a dead horse. He'd killed it and then realized that almost all of the meat was going to go bad. No refrigerator."

"I'm sorry for the horse," said Mirri. "That's another thing you shouldn't eat—horses. You shouldn't eat people or horses."

"Have you ever met someone who eats people?" Darian smiled at her.

"Well," said Mirri. "Only one."

There was a pause.

"I don't think I can match that," said Darian. "I stayed with two members of a kind of goat clan for a while, but that didn't work out." Darian tilted his head and looked at Clare. His hair fell in his eyes, and he brushed it back. Michael again.

"And then there's the Master," Darian said.

He now had their complete attention.

"What do you know about the Master?" asked Jem.

"Supposedly he protects children from the Cured or whatever there is to be protected from, and they work for him. Or so I hear."

"That's feudalism," said Sarai. "We studied that in school. But there isn't any of it around anymore."

"We heard he has a cure for Pest," said Jem.

"Listen, kids," said Darian. "We don't have Pest. We're immune. The rest is just ridiculous—the Master's is just another place to go."

"Have you *been*?" asked Mirri.

"No," said Darian. "I've heard it's very nice, though. Like a summer camp. But I'm not a joiner."

"Where is it?" asked Jem.

"Near I-80 and Herne Wood. Don't you listen to your radio?"

"Not lately," said Jem. "Where do you come from originally?"

"I'd rather talk about what's happened since Pest," said Darian. "I like fresh starts."

Clare looked up at Jem and their eyes met in perfect understanding.

DARIAN SLEPT IN the living room in his own sleeping bag that night; he seemed to take it for granted that that was the way it would be, and Clare was glad. He seemed too old not to have his own room. He just said, "I'm sacking out here." And they watched him unpack his night things: kerosene lamp, sleeping bag, pillow. "Good night," he said. "Good night, Mirri."

"*I'm* his favorite," Mirri said as they went to their room and settled in to sleep. "And I *really* like him." Clare could barely see her face among all the stuffed animals she had scavenged.

"He likes you, too," said Jem. But Clare had trouble making out his tone.

Jem was usually the last one awake, but that night Clare outlasted him. She remembered the days when she had spent most nights wakeful. In many ways it seemed like a long time ago, but now she was unsettled with someone new in the house.

Clare found that she was watching Jem closely as he slept—his eyes, his mouth. He was a tidy sleeper. No drool, no snoring. Thirteen was a decent sort of age.

She wondered if Darian were awake.

Do you trust him? she asked herself. *Maybe. But I'm the oldest here except for Darian. I have to get this right.*

She pictured Darian sitting comfortably in their house, telling stories. But when she pictured him, she realized that she was picturing him with blood on his shirt. In her mind's eye, he was speaking, but as he spoke blood slowly saturated his shirt and began to drip onto the floor.

It was no fantasy; it was one of her pretty-good-guesses. And in that moment, she knew that Darian was going to die.

There was nothing to be done. Her pretty-good-guess didn't tell her what to do or where the danger to Darian might lie. She couldn't rescue him; she would only alarm him. And she didn't want to sound like the Oracle at Delphi, who, deep down, everyone believed was mad.

But maybe that hadn't been the Oracle's fault.

And later, when it was all over, Clare was to remember something she had forgotten about the Oracle at Delphi: that, while that prophetess spoke in riddles, her riddles always proved to contain the truth—but they were fragile, complicated braided truths, weavings waiting to be unraveled. And people were so impatient that they called the Oracle mad; they had no time to see the pattern, to follow the twists of the loom.

CHAPTER FOURTEEN
REDEMPTION

THEY WERE AWAKENED by Sarai, screaming for them from the yard.

"Darian's gone, and he took the pig." Her face was grey and marked with shock, her eyes, swollen and red. "And he peed on the ground right in front of me before he left. Right in front of me. There. By the door." As Clare looked, Bear trotted over to the damp spot, raised his leg and regained his territory.

Clare had failed; she had accepted Darian even though, in retrospect, there had been something off about him. His smile had been a little too wide. Yet there she had been, fearing for his safety and missing the danger he might pose to them all. It had never occurred to her—

"It's going to be okay," Jem said to Sarai.

"You shouldn't steal from people who give you food," said Sarai. "It's wrong. It's rude."

"We're going to get that pig," said Jem, and Clare could hear the anger in his voice. Darian had betrayed them, and the pig was the least of it.

"I'm telling you, he peed right in front of me," said Sarai. "Right there by the door. I saw his *thing*. He already had the pig; he told me to stay in the barn while he left; he told me to count to a hundred before telling, but I only got to seventy before I lost track."

"He only dared because he thinks we're kids," said Jem.

"We *are* kids," Clare said.

"Not in the post-Pest world," said Jem. "Not anymore."

"This isn't going to be easy," said Clare. "He has a head start. And he's strong."

"The pig will slow him down," said Jem.

"And you're our secret weapon, Clare," said Sarai. "Right?" Clare could not help but smile, and Jem laughed.

"Let's get our pig back," he said.

"Darian thinks he's a nacho man," said Sarai. "But he's *not*."

"Macho," murmured Clare. There was something emphatic about Sarai's words that reminded her of Mirri. And that's when she noticed that Mirri wasn't with them.

Mirri didn't come when they called. They looked in the bedroom to see if she were still sleeping, but her bed was empty.

"This isn't good," said Clare.

"I didn't see her when I came out," said Sarai. "I only saw the pig. And Darian. And his thing."

"Mirri goes into the meadow some mornings," said Jem. "She likes looking at the rabbits."

"Darian might have run into her," said Clare, "when he left with the pig."

"But I can't believe he'd hurt her," said Jem. "Or steal her away. She wouldn't go, for one thing."

Clare said nothing, but her thoughts were dark and bitter. Mirri would have trusted Darian because they had all trusted Darian. For her part, Clare had been making assumptions because Darian had looked so much like Michael. And it occurred to her that on some level she had assumed, too, that Pest had killed all the bad people—that they had only the Cured to fear. She had not imagined evil children. But she had been naïve; surely bad people had survived too. Bad *children*. Distorted children.

Clare had never realized how fragile, how tenuous her new life was.

Still. At any second Mirri might come up the path to the door of the house.

They searched the house and the barn.

Clare remembered Mirri saying "I'm his favorite," and, in looking back, she remembered Darian's hand touching Mirri's hair.

Clare remembered the vision of blood on Darian's shirt. Somehow she had got it all wrong. Darian wasn't the one to worry about; it was Mirri. They had to get her back.

Jem pulled his coat closely around him.

"Let's go," he said. "Bring Bear."

"Of course."

"And Sarai—go get the rope we used to bring the pig home."

Sarai came running back with the lead.

"Are you going to kill him?" Sarai asked.

Jem opened his mouth, but Clare forestalled him.

"No," she said.

"What if he's hurt Mirri?" asked Sarai.

"That would change things," said Clare.

"What about a gun?" asked Sarai. They both looked at her. Jem hesitated.

Then Clare spoke. "We don't need one."

SARAI SHOWED THEM the direction Darian had gone, and they followed his tracks and, more easily, those of the pig through the high grass in the meadow. When they came to the fence, the swath of broken plants widened and Clare made out a small footprint.

"Mirri," Clare said. "I'll bet she came here on her way back from a walk. I'll bet she was sitting here on the fence just in time for him to find her."

Neither of them spoke of why Darian might have taken her. In fact, that was a point on which they were never to be fully satisfied.

"Maybe," said Jem, "we should have listened to Sarai and brought a gun from town."

"It would've taken too long," said Clare. "And we don't know how to use a gun."

"I know how to use a gun," said Jem.

"No way."

They were over the fence now and casting about in the grass for signs of Darian, Mirri or the pig. It should have been easy, but the grass was tamped down in all directions.

It was Bear who found the way out of the tangle at the base of the fence.

For a while they followed the trail in silence. Clare was the first to break it. She had been trying to picture Jem with a gun.

"How do you know how to use a gun?"

"One of my brothers liked target shooting."

"Guns didn't help anyone against Pest."

"Darian isn't Pest."

"He's part of the post-Pest world, though," she said. "Your brother's world, the old world, where people used microwaves and cell phones and computers, is gone."

"Guns aren't gone. Although truthfully, I hate them." Jem smiled grimly. "I was never really much into what Sarai calls that nacho stuff."

It was hard going through the thick underbrush at the edge of the woods. Even Bear found negotiating the trail difficult.

They finally found Darian and Mirri in the late afternoon, in a small clearing ringed by a copse of trees. They weren't far from the road. Mirri lay by a small fire, her ankles bound. She was trying to crawl away from Darian, who stood over her. Her arms were scratched and her shirt was torn. She cried in a steady monotonous tone, as if she had been doing so for some time. When she managed to squirm a small distance from Darian, he reached down and pulled her back by the ankles. Her hair was snarled.

As Jem and Clare inched closer, Clare felt her stomach turn. The area before them looked and smelled like an abattoir. Blood spatter painted Darian's face and shirt. His hands were caked with blood. He held a long knife. On the edge of the camp, the pig's head, perched on a high tree stump, presided over the macabre scene. Off to one side was its body, gutted; organs and twisted intestines were heaped in a glistening, slick mass. For no reason that Clare could imagine, Darian had stabbed the rear of the pig again and again.

"It looks like Hell, Clare," whispered Jem.

"It looks like *Lord of the Flies*."

"Worse."

Jem moved forward, out from under the trees. "We've come for Mirri, Darian," he said. "You can keep the pig."

Darian was startled by the sound.

"There's nothing that you can do to me," Darian snorted. "If you try, I'll kill you. Better yet, I'll kill her." He yanked Mirri towards him by the rope and put a knife to her throat. Bear growled and Clare had to throw herself on him to stop him from going for Darian.

"Wait," she said. "Just wait."

"That's right," said Darian. "Keep the dog away, or I cut Mirri's throat, and we all get to watch her bleed out."

"And then Bear will take you down before your next breath," said Clare.

"I believe you," Darian said. "And you would be left with two bodies. Just leave us alone, and I'll leave you alone. You can have part of your pig, if that's what you're after." He seemed to think for a moment. "But I'll pick which part."

"We want Mirri," said Jem.

"Which part?" Darian waved the knife at them.

Clare sucked in her breath. Jem looked angrier than she had ever seen him.

"Just let her go," said Clare. "She'll only slow you down."

"I'm not planning on making her a traveling companion for long. If you like, I'll send her back to you in a few days."

For a moment there was no sound except that of Mirri weeping.

Then Clare saw Mirri look up and beyond Jem. Clare turned and did the same and saw that there was a terrible figure amongst the trees: a woman, her face convulsing uncontrollably. It was, unmistakably, the Cured-in-the-blue-dress, and she was coming up behind Jem.

"Jem!" Clare called, but he paid her no heed. All of his concentration was on Darian. Clare measured the distance between herself and the Cured-in-the-blue-dress, but before she could do anything, before she could hurl herself at this new threat, she saw Mirri's face transformed. She saw Mirri holding out her arms, not to her, not to Jem—but to the Cured-in-a-blue-dress. Mirri cried out.

"Mama!"

And the Cured-in-the-blue-dress left the shelter of the trees and threw herself, not at Jem, not at Clare, but at Darian.

When Mirri said "Mama," it all came together for Clare. Mirri stealing food. Mirri in the distance, meeting with the Cured-in-the-blue-dress. She remembered Mirri's survival story, as told by Jem: Mirri's mother had gone to the hospital, but she had never returned; Mirri's mother had become one of the Cured. She must have come back home to search for her daughter, found her with Sarai and Jem, and followed her ever since.

Mirri had never said a word because she would not, could not, betray her mother.

With a terrible strength Mirri's mother knocked over Darian and clawed at his face before locking her hands around his throat. The tip of something was protruding from the back of her dress, and Clare saw blood splattering Darian's shirt. But it wasn't his blood. Still the woman would not relinquish her grip. As Clare watched, unable to move, blood permeated the back of the blue dress in ring after pulsing ring, all emanating from the tip of what Clare now realized was Darian's knife.

But Mirri's mother didn't let go, not even when Darian ceased moving. Only when he had been still for a long time did she roll away and lie on her side, her breath noisy and strange, as if she were choking. Before Jem could reach her, her breathing stopped, and all that was left to hear was the sudden raucous noise of crows taking to the air.

"Mama." Mirri ran to her mother. After a time, Clare pulled Mirri away from her mother's side and took her into her arms.

"It's all right," she said, knowing that it would never be all right.

Jem pulled the knife out of Mirri's mother and managed to close her eyes. In death, she looked calm. Sane even. Clare thought that maybe she had been living just long enough to take care of her daughter one last time.

"She saved me," said Mirri.

"Of course she did," said Jem. "She gave you life twice." Clare just held Mirri close; she smelled like blood and fear. Bear nuzzled both of them. For the first time, he let Mirri stroke him.

Jem was checking Darian's body for a pulse, which they both knew he wouldn't find. Then he sat back, startled.

"Look," he said.

Leaning over Mirri's head, Clare looked. Jem had pulled away Darian's shirt, and she could see that there were pustules on his throat—very small ones, low down on his neck so that they hadn't been visible before. And behind his ear was a small orange patch with the tiny marking 'SYLVER' on it.

So, thought Clare, *this was why he kept his hair over his collar. He was covering up the unmistakable marks of Pest. He was a Cured all along.*

"We let him sleep in the house," said Clare.

"It doesn't bear thinking about," said Jem. Then he gently lifted the hair of the Cured-in-a-blue-dress so that Clare could see the patch behind her ear too.

"I thought the Cure was some kind of injection," said Clare. "But it's the patch-thing that keeps the disease from killing them."

"And that makes them crazy," said Jem.

"She never had a chance."

"Let's go. Sarai's waiting."

Mirri looked from Jem to Clare.

"Don't worry, honey," said Clare. "We'll come back. We'll bury the—your mother."

"Her name was Dinah," said Mirri.

"We'll bury Dinah," said Clare.

They walked back to the farmhouse slowly.

"Even after the Cure," said Mirri, "my mother didn't go bad."

And Clare thought for more than a moment of how Dinah must have struggled to hang on to that small vestige of sanity that said to her 'my child,' that small vestige of self, salvaged from the very brink of death and madness.

WILL, HANNAH, DANTE, TREY, ROGER

IN CALIFORNIA, IN the Great Northwest, in the Heartland, in New England, in points North, in points South, the ones who had not died of Pest, the very few children left in the world, woke up as if from a dream—and looked around—and some of them found a space to survive, and very many of them did not.

Will

IN LOVELL, POPULATION 1,257, only small children and the elderly were exempt from building the Wall. Will kept his distance from the Wall but tried to help by cooking dinner in the evening. The work exhausted his parents, so Will put together the meal for his mother and father and his baby sister, Jean. Jean was easy to feed—she would eat any kind of Gerber's as long as he started by feeding her the yellow smashed peaches. Will thought the yellow smashed peaches looked like something that came out of her diaper, but Jean slurped them up and left stains all over her bib. And his parents weren't picky about what he put on the table. They were just happy to find the food there at the end of the day.

No one worked anymore, except on the Wall. And at night the people of Lovell took turns acting as sentries. Those who lived outside the Wall had been given a choice at the very beginning— move in to the center of Lovell, or stay out for good. The sentries had orders to challenge anyone approaching; they were to turn back all strangers with one warning. After the warning, they were to shoot. If the person approaching were a neighbor, an old friend, a relative, he or she got three warnings instead of one. The sentries were posted in pairs.

"The Calder woman is one of the sentries tonight," said Will's father. He bit into a sandwich. "I can't picture her shooting anyone."

"You should see her at PTA meetings." Will's mother was picking the lettuce out of her sandwich.

Will hesitated; he didn't want to interrupt his parents, but they didn't seem to notice that Jean was falling asleep in her chair.

"I need some help," he said finally. "Because Jean needs to go to bed, and I can't lift her over the crib."

"I'll get her," said his father.

His mother gave Will a peculiar look.

"If something happens—" she started.

"I'll take care of Jean," said Will, not wanting to hear the rest of what she was going to say.

As WILL WENT to sleep that night—late, later than his parents, late enough that the moon had set—he thought about the Pest Wall. It was supposed to keep them safe. Walls kept things out. But his nine-year-old brain moved on a different plane than that of his parents: he knew about monsters under the bed; he knew about creatures with long fingers that lurked in the closet. He knew that there was no point in building a wall if the Thing were already inside. He knew, as he drifted into sleep, that it was already too late.

JEAN DIED LAST. Will had heard that most young children died directly of Pest, that very few were delayed onset. He held her and tried to feed her smashed peaches, but she wouldn't eat. Her face was no longer soft and round, but had been twisted by the torc of Pest into the face of a stranger. She died in his arms. He buried her in the back yard, next to the grave of Rosie, their dog. He scraped his hand on the handle of the shovel as he broke into the hard dirt, and for the first time in his life, he used a swear word.

His parents were too big and heavy to bury.

Now an orphan, Will wandered from house to house, eating what he could find, avoiding the places where the smell was too bad. Lovell was a ghost town. He was afraid almost all of the time—of the dead, of the black crows that seemed to be everywhere. He feared the silence of the night, and he feared the strange noises he occasionally heard. The scrape on his hand began to throb, and he felt it keeping time with his heart.

Eight days later, as he lay dying, feverish, his hand three times its normal size, he thought that Jean was snuggled in his arms, and that she wanted her smashed peaches. Her face was normal again, and he reached out to stroke it.

Hannah

THEY TOOK HER to the hospital when she first showed signs of Pest. There were about twenty other people in the waiting room. She couldn't tell what was wrong with most of them, but one man in a white T-shirt had blackened blood down his front, and a woman wearing pink glitter eye shadow held her arm at a strange angle. The nurse hurried Hannah deeper into the hospital right away when she saw the lesions on her face.

"You're lucky," said the doctor. "We just got the Cure in today. I've already treated over thirty people. I don't think we're going to have enough patches, but folks can always go to the city."

Once home, her parents tucked Hannah into bed. She rubbed the patch behind her ear thoughtfully.

"I think I feel better," she said.

"Don't touch the patch," said her mother. "Leave it alone."

Time passed, and the great dying began. Apparently, the Cure didn't work for most people. Hannah's parents went to the hospital for their own patches, but even with the patches, her father died two days after he first spiked a fever. Her mother had seemed all right, and then, a week after the death of Hannah's father, she came down to breakfast flushed and feverish. She insisted on cooking something for Hannah.

Hannah watched television and saw the stations turn to snow, one by one.

As she did, Hannah heard something fall in the kitchen. It might have been a pot or a pan, but the sound was really too soft and low for that.

Her attention was arrested by the television. One station was left, and it showed a man who claimed to have a different kind of cure. He was inviting children to go and see him.

Her mother hadn't made a noise since Hannah had heard the sound in the kitchen.

Maybe Hannah would go and get the new cure. This one was making her feel strange.

Later, she went into the kitchen.

Her mother was on the floor and didn't get up, and Hannah's world became even more crooked. Time passed. She couldn't remember things. Once Hannah woke up enough to look down at the food she was holding in her hands. Meat. Meat was good, but this was raw. Provenance unknown. She liked that word—provenance. It had been the hardest word on the last spelling test. But she didn't think there would ever be any more spelling tests.

One day she realized what it was she was feeling. It was a sensation of sinking back into herself, although what she found there was odd. She had not known herself, it seemed, at all. Now, pain was like an armchair. Hate, like a comfortable pillow.

Hannah was Cured.

Dante

KELLY HAD SAID Dante was timid, but that someday he would do some great good, and Kelly was his mother so she should know. Dante's father probably hadn't even noticed that his son was timid. He had moved away from Kansas, and he lived with a pretty woman Dante didn't like. His father probably knew what circle of Hell Dante—the Italian poet, not his eleven-year-old boy—condemned the forgetful to, but he forgot Dante's birthday anyway. His son's birthday. Not the poet's.

When Pest blossomed, his father didn't call them. Perhaps he was dead; perhaps he was busy nursing the pretty woman. Dante tried to call his father when Kelly got sick, but there was no answer. Kelly was too sick to drive, and the phone at the hospital was busy, so Dante walked across town to get there, fearing that he would return to find Kelly dead.

Lawrence, Kansas was dying in a civilized fashion. There had been no looters, as there had been in other areas, and people had diligently painted large X's on their doors when they had come down with Pest. As he walked, Dante passed X after X after X, and he wondered if there were still people walled up in the houses, or if they had finally run away, or if they had died, and, if they had died, if it had hurt.

It seemed to be hurting his mother. When Kelly could sleep, she moaned.

At the hospital, Dante couldn't even get in the front doors. People were milling around the main entrance; they looked the way lepers looked in the movies. They looked like Kelly.

When he got back home, Kelly died, and he sat and waited for something to happen. Then he sat some more and cried for a while. He ate crackers for dinner and wondered what he was supposed to do with his mother's body. He tried the telephone, but there was no longer any dial tone. All the television stations were off the air except for one that was broadcasting a rainbow pattern with the words PLEASE STAND BY on it.

Then he got up and went to the basement and got out an old radio that Kelly had given him when they spent one summer at the beach. He tuned to station after station, but all was static. He turned the volume way up, but there was still nothing. He was about to put it down when suddenly a station came in. It was so loud that he dropped the radio and cried out. Then he sat down and listened.

The broadcast he heard was on some kind of loop, and it was issuing an invitation—an invitation from a grownup who said he was master-of-the-situation. The man sounded calm.

Dante didn't think ahead when he made the decision; he didn't get a sleeping bag or tent, and he didn't load up on food. He figured, rather vaguely, that there would be a lot of well-stocked houses between Lawrence, Kansas and his destination. He unpinned his map of the United States from the wall in his room and prepared to set off down the street towards the road that led to the highway. The states looked small on the map, but he had a feeling he had a long way to go.

Dante went out the front door of his brick house and then turned around and locked it. He didn't miss his father, but he knew that he was locking Kelly away. Forever and ever and ever.

Then he set his foot upon the road.

Roger and Trey

TREY'S COLD WAS worse and they were out of DayQuil. It was that kind of morning.

And the snow kept blowing off the road. It was that kind of morning, too.

Trey wiped his nose on his parka. His mother would have hated that.

He stood on the road, worried about the snow. It had come early to Bailey, Colorado—but not in quantity enough to snowmobile down to the lower altitudes. As Trey watched, bare patches of black road emerged from the snow and then, as the wind became stronger, were covered up again. A snowmobile might hit the tarmac and flip without any warning at all.

Trey's nose wouldn't stop running. Usually he and Roger got colds at the same time, but this time Roger had been spared.

Trey was the older of the twins by twelve minutes. Roger had always been smaller and more vulnerable. He spent all his time reading or playing against himself at chess, but Trey never teased him. Trey admired the way his brother could concentrate, and he had been proud when Roger played chess in a national competition. Roger had quietly and efficiently put away almost all of his opponents. He had finally lost to a kid named Jem Clearey. The Clearey kid won the next few rounds, and then he lost too. Trey had been sorry. He felt that a kid who beat his brother should at least be the best in the nation.

Now Bailey, Colorado was like a mortuary; Colorado was given over to the Cured; it appeared that the whole nation was dead. This was no place for vulnerable people anymore—Trey was going to have to get Roger and himself out of the mess they were in.

When he opened the door to the house, the first thing he noticed was the warmth, the second was the smell of food.

"I found a can of Dinty Moore," said Roger from the kitchen.

"Thanks," said Trey. "There's still not enough snow on the road to get out of here." No need to speak. The silence was long. Then—

"We could ski," said Roger.

Trey walked into the kitchen, disconcerted.

"What about supplies?" asked Trey. "And wood? And sleeping bags and a tent? We can't just waltz down to Denver."

"Maybe we can."

"I'm the big brother. And I say we can't."

But they both knew that Trey, as always, would give way to Roger.

The first day they skied for six hours until the dark was on them, and they took shelter in an old lean-to that, at some point, had probably sheltered a horse. They doubled the sleeping bags and shared the warmth. Trey's cold was worse, and by midnight he started in with chills and fever.

"We've got to get off the mountain," said Roger. He had his arm around his brother, trying to stop him from shaking with cold.

They didn't ski far the next day. One moment they were careening down a steep hill, the next, Trey took a spectacular fall and lay shivering in the snow. His arm was broken; a tip of the bone poked through the skin.

Roger wrapped up the arm while Trey lay in a delirium of fever and pain.

"I can't move," said Trey.

"You can," said Roger. Roger half-dragged, half-walked his twin to a stand of pines that offered a little shelter. He put down sprays of fir to keep the sleeping bags off the ground.

Sometime in the night, Trey died.

Roger held Trey as Trey grew cold. The chill wind was coming in off the mountain. Roger decided to stay with Trey until sunrise, but when the sun had cleared the trees, Roger still hadn't left the sleeping bag. He was cold. The wind was bitter now. He was very cold.

PART TWO

CHAPTER FIFTEEN
THE LEAVING

DARK NIGHTS, AND a little snow. Winter coming. Time to move on. They were eating the last of the cans of Chef Boyardee that Clare had scavenged what seemed like years before. Nobody minded the idea of leaving anymore: Darian had poisoned the house, the meadow.

Still, inertia reigned. Finally Jem, with Clare's help, gathered all the backpacks and little wagons in the living room. But the packing effort was, at least at first, wildly unsuccessful. Sarai kept trying to hide a great heap of her books in her little pack. Jem would find them and fish some of them out. While Sarai took this like a stoic, Mirri became weepy when she found she couldn't take all of her Pretty Ponies and her Breyer horses and her unicorns. She wanted her whole collection.

"We have too much stuff holding us back as it is," said Jem reasonably.

"I love my stuff," said Mirri.

Clare watched the negotiations with Mirri and Sarai from a distance. They were still, when it came right down to it, Jem's little girls. Clare stared at the flames in the fireplace, and in the fire she saw one of her old dreams unfolding. She saw a young girl walking towards her out of the woods.

"Do you think there'll be a happy ending?" Mirri asked abruptly, startling Clare out of her reverie.

They all looked at Mirri.

"A happy ending to what?" asked Jem.

"To *us*."

"I don't know," said Clare, still feeling half asleep. "I don't even know what a happy ending would look like."

"Maybe this is it," said Sarai.

"We should finish packing," said Jem.

"We could just leave right now," said Clare. "If we had to."

"In an emergency," said Mirri, "we could leave *yesterday*."

Clare looked over at their handiwork. The wagons were full, but they hadn't loaded the packs, which were propped on the floor with open mouths.

They all took a break, and the break turned into a leisurely afternoon. Clare and Jem, both daunted by the idea of leaving, prepared for dinner. They picked weevils out of the flour so that they could make dumplings and float them in canned chicken broth. Jem began opening a jam jar so that they could each have a spoonful for dessert; he banged it against the floor to loosen the lid.

Clare thought of Michael. She wasn't sure anymore how he would have adapted to the post-Pest world.

Jem stopped trying to open the jam jar, and he stood up. He was as tall as Clare now. He would be fourteen soon.

"You know," said Clare thoughtfully, looking him over. "We might have been friends in high school, if I had known you."

"You? A cheerleader? I don't think so."

"Maybe not," Clare said. She thought for a moment. "My world was pretty small then. Cheerleader by day. Insomniac reader by night."

"You sleep now."

"Now it's safe."

Jem did not point out the absurdity of this. Instead he said, "You wouldn't have noticed a ninth grader."

"Well. You weren't invisible."

"You could have fooled me."

"And now my cheerleader glamour is gone."

"Naw."

They smiled at each other.

Sarai and Mirri came into the room with a pot full of markers and settled down to draw horses. Clare watched them closely.

"They take care of each other," she said to Jem.

"They're going to have to," said Jem grimly.

"Not if we get to the Master," said Clare. "Not if the Master has a cure."

"Not if that."

Mirri looked up for a moment from her drawing. "I hope you noticed Sarai," she said. "I combed out her hair, and I think she's *beautiful*."

Sarai's long hair fell in a sleek waterfall of black down her back.

"You do look beautiful," said Clare, and, for a moment, all her vague fears about the future vanished. "Really beautiful."

Time to go. Time to move on.

MASTER

THE MASTER GAVE ELIZA both Cinderella Barbie and Luke Skywalker for her birthday. She politely dressed and undressed Barbie a few times, but her main interest clearly lay in the Luke Skywalker figure. Britta and Doug gave her a comforter with dolphins on it. The others gave her various tokens: a bracelet, a packet of Gummi Bears, the Barrel of Monkeys game and a field guide to birds. Britta and Doug were in charge of making the cake, but first they had to prepare dinner. Eliza went to the kitchen with them: she loved them both.

The Master followed. He found he liked following Eliza, watching her discover the hidden recesses of the mansion, being there if anything frightened her, tucking her in, just as he did Britta, almost every night—when he wasn't away on his searches for other children. His searches would sometimes last for days.

"There's nothing like lamb stew on a cold night," he said as he poked around the dinner preparations. It was important to be able to do inanity. And he did inanity well—whenever he spoke, he made sure to appear very normal indeed.

"Did you figure out what killed the lamb?" Britta asked. They had found it dead in the field, its throat torn out.

"A wolf," he said. "Or a dog." But no dog had done this.

He had.

It was just one of those irresistible urges.

Somewhere behind the mansion the Master could hear the chugging of the generator. The oven was at just the right temperature, and Britta put in the cake. Eliza cut vegetables. A child named Dante was helping her. The Master was watching her handle the knife when it skittered off the potato she was holding and embedded itself deep in her hand.

Eliza made no sound. She pulled the knife out and the blood began to flow freely down her arm in a spiral of red against milk white.

"Put cold water on it," said Britta. She moved quickly, a dishcloth in her hand, but the Master got to Eliza first. What he felt was not an irresistible urge but the workings of cold calculation. The blood streaming out of Eliza's hand was enough to keep Pest at bay for six months—maybe more.

The Master was free of SitkaAZ13, oh yes, but as long as the disease was in the world, he needed—what to call it?—boosters.

Britta was the only one that the Master trusted with knowledge about the boosters. Boosters meant ingesting some blood from the right little girl. Boosters were Part One of the process that left him happy and healthy. Part Two was purely recreational. Britta didn't know about that. He cherished her ignorance.

Eliza bled.

The Master caught Britta's eye.

He suddenly turned away and pinned Eliza to the wall. Britta and Doug looked on as he bent down and licked the blood off her arm, moving his tongue right up into the wound.

Dante had stopped chopping vegetables, and he looked horrified, but Doug, without saying a word, went and stood against the door so none of the others could come in. Eliza was crying, but she did not scream.

The Master heard Britta as if from far away.

"You're lucky, Eliza," she said bitterly. "You're lucky. And you, Dante—if you ever say a word about this, I will kill you."

The Master knew that Dante would listen to Britta; all of the children did.

He released Eliza, expecting her to stay, somehow expecting her to go back to preparing the vegetables, but instead she stared for a moment at Britta, and then she pushed aside Doug and ran out the door. Dante began to follow, but Britta grabbed his arm.

"You won't tell," she said. "Ever."

"I won't," said Dante, his face white. "Not ever." Britta let him go. She turned to the Master. He smiled at her.

"They won't tell," Britta said. "Both Eliza and Dante are only ten. Children don't tell."

It was as if Britta could read his mind. She herself was only twelve, but she was mature for her age.

The Master then used his authoritative voice. He looked most carefully at Doug as he spoke. "My cure is in the blood," he said. "And without me, your new world would fall apart. It didn't hurt her at all."

"Is that what we do to be cured?" Doug asked.

"No," said the Master. "You have a different road. There's nothing children can do to keep SitkaAZ13 at bay. But here you have a life worth living."

"You could take some of my blood," said Britta to the Master. He could hear the hope in her voice.

"You don't have the right recessive genes." He deployed the scientific terms casually. His children believed in science. Luckily for him, however, they didn't understand it.

"You could try."

"It doesn't work that way," the Master said. "Go after Eliza, Britta. That's the best thing you can do for me."

He walked out of the kitchen and passed through the living room, where children of various ages were sorting through some new supplies. They stopped as he passed.

"Master, Master, Master," yelled a toddler.

"Leave him be unless he talks to you," a boy said to the toddler. "He's probably thinking. That's private."

"What are his thinks?" the toddler asked.

"Don't know."

"I hope he thinks about me."

"I bet he can make things happen by thinking," said one of the children.

The Master turned back to them.

"Thoughts are powerful," he said.

He went down into the basement and sat in his collection room. Lately the Sargent painting had begun to disturb him, and he had been seeing more shapes in the shadows, but this time what caught his attention was the crisp and dazzling white of the girl's pinafore as she stood, one foot in front of her, deliberate as a dancer.

This time he saw nothing in the background shadows.

All at once, he felt exhilarated. Maybe the blood from Eliza really had affected him, or maybe the pleasure of the act was healing in itself.

He waited for the house to settle into quietness before he went back upstairs again. As he turned left, into a corridor, he saw Britta and Doug come out of Greg's room.

Greg was eighteen. He was recovering from a bad case of food poisoning. SitkaAZ13 usually picked off children by seventeen, and the Master was watching Greg closely.

Britta's face lit up when she saw the Master.

"We were just reading to Greg," she said.

"*Children of the Corn,*" said Doug. "Greg picked it. It's scary."

"I'll check on him," said the Master. After Britta and Doug left, however, the Master didn't bother to open Greg's door. The Master gave Greg a month. Two at the outside. Then SitkaAZ13 would take him.

So it goes.

As he moved through the hallways, the house fell silent. He unlocked the door to the basement and went down the steps. Sitting under the Sargent painting, he pulled a large scrapbook towards him and started looking through the pages, stopping every now and then to examine a page more closely.

Eliza was ten. She would live for some years—if he let her—before she contracted StikaAZ13.

He flipped through the book.

To create a stable social order, he would have to make sure the children lived for as long as possible before SitkaAZ13 killed them. There needed to be a new generation. And he would live on and watch each generation grow. And every now and then, there would be—a booster.

He flipped through pages of the scrapbook.

A page. Another page.

A lock of blonde hair slipped out of the book and onto the floor. He didn't notice.

CHAPTER SIXTEEN
MEMENTOS

EVERY DAY JEM had tried to pick up a signal on the radio only to end up listening to static. But finally, early one morning, he found something. Two signals. Jem turned the volume up as far as it would go, and Clare, Mirri and Sarai—who had been sorting through all their belongings—stopped what they were doing and stood still, like startled rabbits.

"I am the master-of-the-situation," came the voice. "I can offer food, and friends and safety. I-80 at Herne Wood. I am the master-of-the-situation." The signal faded. Clare took the radio from Jem and moved the tuner from band to band. "I'm going now," came another voice, a whisper. "Good-bye." And that was all.

Jem looked stunned. Clare felt as if she were hearing the last words from the old world. That 'good-bye' shook her. She was never going to get her world back, not even if they were all cured, not even if she found some variety of happily-ever-after—although that did not seem very likely. Life was short in the new world. There was no time for happiness.

"Those were *last words*," said Mirri. "Weren't they, Clare?"

"Yes. They probably were."

"We leave tomorrow," Jem said. "We need to move fast. I-80 is pretty far." And Clare realized that he was looking at her, and that there was darkness in his green eyes.

As Clare and Jem finished filling the backpacks, Clare noticed that Mirri was restless.

"Do you think there's Heaven?" Mirri asked finally.

"I don't know," said Clare, startled.

"I don't think there's Heaven. In church they talked about it all the time, but—"

"But what?"

"I don't know. It's pretty hard to imagine. And I can imagine a *lot*."

Mirri started towards the front door, a Pretty Pony dangling from her hand by its mane.

"Where're you going?" Clare asked.

"The barn."

"Not alone."

"Yes alone. Please, Clare. I'm going to look at my mother's stuff. Before we leave."

"I'm coming with you," said Clare. "Sorry, Mirri."

Jem sighed. "Sarai and I'll come, too. It beats worrying."

In the barn they saw a small owl perched on a rafter, moving from foot to foot. Clare thought it looked like it was davening. Then the owl cocked its head and spit out a pellet that hit Jem on the side of the head.

"That hurt," said Jem mildly.

Sarai was already dissecting the furry pellet with a stick. "It's full of little bones."

"Mouse bones," said Jem, rubbing his head. "Probably."

The barn was vast. The lower half was cluttered with items that must have been accumulating for generations: fence-posts, old furniture, tools, a hay wagon. But all this was dwarfed by vast and empty space as the building soared up past the loft, past great old timbers, to the ancient roof.

They went past the broken furniture and over to the pink sleeping bag that Mirri's mother had used. Mirri's mother—Dinah—had made a sort of nest there. Clare pulled up the sleeping bag and underneath it she saw something she wasn't expecting.

The unicorn pen that Mirri thought she had lost. One of the tortoiseshell combs that Clare sometimes used to control her hair. Jem's pocket flashlight. She saw that there were other things there as well. Toys, bits of cloth, a pocketknife, a silver ring Clare thought she had misplaced.

"She was looking out for all of us," said Clare. "Not just Mirri. All of us."

They stood, mute.

Then, quietly, Mirri gathered up the little objects; Clare helped her. They walked back to the house.

Behind them the barn loomed like a cathedral.

CHAPTER SEVENTEEN
MOOSE

IT SNOWED IN the night, but not enough to keep them from leaving. In the morning, Mirri put some more rocks on her mother's grave. Jem carved all their initials on the inside of the front door. Clare caught Sarai putting some more books into her backpack, which were going to add substantially to the weight, but she said nothing, instead transferring them to her own when Sarai wasn't looking.

Right before they set out, Jem emptied Mirri's pack to see if anything could be discarded. He had worried that her pack was too heavy. What he discovered was that the bottom of Mirri's pack was filled with Pretty Ponies, her favorite unicorn footie pajamas, a copy of *The Secret Garden,* a seashell jigsaw puzzle and the Old Maid playing cards. Clare watched from the doorway, wondering how this was going to play out.

"Mirri," Jem said. "You know better. That space could be used for food."

"Don't you want me to have *any* stuff?"

Clare watched Jem debate with himself.

"All right," he said finally. "All right for now."

"Wuss," whispered Clare as he came over to her.

"You try saying 'no' to Mirri."

"Well," Clare said. "At least we have enough food to get to the next stop."

"I just hope we find fresh supplies along the way. I don't want us to get beriberi."

"You worry about everything."

"Or rickets."

"I *like* rickets," said Mirri. "They chirp like hoarse birds."

"That's *crickets*," said Sarai. "Rickets makes your legs fall off."

"No, it doesn't," said Jem. "Quit stalling and let's go."

Jem took the lead. At the end of the long driveway, he stood for a moment before turning left. They would pass through Fallon and then resupply themselves in the city, where it would be easy enough to pick up the I-80 to Herne Wood.

As they stepped onto the road, Jem abruptly laughed and said, "Well. Now we're off to see the Wizard."

"I just hope that he isn't a little man behind a big curtain," said Clare.

"The Master has to have the cure," said Jem. "Why wouldn't he have the cure?" Clare was going to respond lightly, and then she saw the grim resolution in Jem's dark green eyes.

Bear suddenly ran out ahead of them, snuffed at the air, and then fell back to Clare.

They passed the skeletonized remains of the Cured that Mirri's mother had killed. Now they were at the farthest point of their scavenging area.

They walked.

Shadows began to creep down the road in front of them, and when they found a house set back from the road and with no dead smell to it, they stopped for the night. Clare and Jem searched the house for signs of other occupants, but the place was empty. No dead. No Cured. No living children.

They made a big nest in the living room out of comforters and blankets, and, before the light was entirely gone, Clare got a fire going in the woodstove. She looked at their nest and suddenly felt bone-tired. Mirri looked unhappy.

"How're the feet?" Clare asked.

"Don't know," said Mirri. "I can't get my shoes off."

"That's not good." She saw that Mirri's ankles were swollen. "Does it hurt?"

"Yes," said Mirri. "It hurts like a *dog*."

Clare elevated Mirri's feet and massaged her ankles until the swelling started to dissipate.

The next morning, Mirri's feet showed minimal signs of swelling. They stopped early for lunch at a place where the road was bordered by trees. Under their shade, a light coating of snow covered the ground, and Clare thought she could make out deer tracks.

Bear went to investigate.

Jem shook out a tarp for them to sit on, set up the tiny camping stove and started heating up some Spam. Mirri lay on her back with her ankles in the air, just in case. Sarai read one of her precious books. Clare sat with Jem.

"You know what's weird?" she asked.

"What's weird?" He used his pocketknife to cut the Spam into small blocks.

"They're out there. Kids. If we survived, there have to be others. But where are they?"

Jem looked at her seriously. "They're hiding. Or making their way to the Master. Or maybe a lot of them just couldn't make it in the post-Pest world. Accidents happen all the time, and there aren't any more doctors."

Clare leaned against Jem. He was warm.

"God, I hate Spam," she said.

Bear loped towards them, and Clare started as she saw the trail of bright red blood he left in the snow. When he reached her, she searched through his fur for an open wound, but found nothing. His muzzle, however, was covered with clots of blood and tissue.

"It's not his blood," Jem said.

"Is he all *right*?" Mirri asked.

"He probably killed something," said Clare. "He has to eat, too."

"It looks like he killed something big," said Jem.

"Maybe a deer?" asked Clare.

"Maybe."

"I bet he couldn't eat a *whole deer*," said Mirri.

Clare and Jem looked at each other.

"Fresh meat," said Clare.

After putting away the food, they followed Bear's trail, the dots of bright blood stark against the white of the snow. Where the snow had melted, it was harder to follow the trail, but the further they got, the more blood marked the ground. Bear quietly followed Clare, who kept him close.

Soon they found the carcass. Bear had pulled out the entrails and gorged on the soft parts of the animal. The animal's fur was grey, and it had outlandish, peculiar antlers.

"What *is* that?" asked Mirri.

"It's a moose," said Jem. "And I have no idea how Bear brought it down."

"It's enormous," said Sarai.

"I suppose now we drag it with us," said Mirri. "But it seems kind of *big*."

"It's too big," said Jem. "We'll have to cut it up and take part of it. I brought a knife, but it's not very sharp." Jem studied the moose, and Bear watched him with his yellow diamond eyes.

"How do we get at the *steaks*?" Mirri asked.

"We need to pull back the pelt to get at the meat underneath," said Jem.

Clare looked at him as if he were speaking Esperanto.

"But first," he added. "We need to cut its throat to drain out any blood that might be pooling. Clare, why don't you take Mirri and Sarai someplace?"

"You've got to be *kidding*," said Mirri.

"I wouldn't miss this for the world," said Sarai.

"How do you know how to do all this?" asked Clare.

"I went hunting with my brother. Hated it. At the time, I wanted to throw up while he was dressing the kill. But this time it's different. *I'm* different."

Michael had always said that the school chess players, championships or no, were nerds, and that nerds didn't do anything physical. Like play football.

Clare wished Michael were here now to see this.

And then she realized, with some confusion, that this was a very different way of wanting Michael than anything she had felt before.

After he slit the throat of the moose, Jem slipped the knife between the pelt and the body.

"Now we all pull," he said, and, with some effort, the pelt began to peel away. When they were finally done, they had two haunches of moose and a slab of fatty meat from its chest. Crows watched them from the trees.

"Let's get out of here," said Jem. "I want to be settled in somewhere before dark."

The meat was heavy and bloody, and soon they were bloody too. Mirri pushed a strand of hair from her face and left a smear. Jem's shirt was soaked through, a solid red, and his hands were covered with drying blood. He tried to wipe them in the patches of snow, but that made them quickly numb and cold. Clare tried to warm his hands with her own, but it did nothing except smear the blood onto hers.

"There's something Lady Macbeth-ish about this," said Jem.

"Ninth grade is kind of young for *Macbeth*," said Clare. "I'm surprised."

"My mother used to read Shakespeare aloud to me at night when I was very small. She thought it would improve my mind."

"That must have been pretty dreary."

"It was absolutely terrifying. After *Macbeth* I slept under my bed for a week. I mean it."

"I was wondering," said Mirri. She stopped. She looked at what they had culled of the carcass as the others waited for her to go on. "Once *people* are dead, do they still *count*? Or are they just lost in a pile of bodies, in the thousands of bodies, in the millions of bodies?"

They stared at her.

"What I mean," she said, "is that we buried my mother and we remember her. But what about all the others? Are they just *nothing*?"

"I don't like the question," said Sarai.

"Nobody's nothing," said Clare. "Nobody. I mean it."

"How do you *know*?" asked Mirri.

"I just know."

As they were trudging back to the camp with the meat, they saw, half covered by leaf litter, the partially skeletonized body of a man. Clare stopped long enough to make a tiny cairn out of pebbles.

"Your thoughts?" asked Jem.

"That I could almost weep over the amount of meat we had to leave behind," said Clare, turning away from the cairn.

"I meant about the body." Jem seemed disturbed. "Because that's all it is. Just another body. Mirri's right. In the end, we're nobody." Clare put a hand on his shoulder, but it was Mirri who had the last word.

"I don't think that anymore," said Mirri. "You're forgetting, Jem. Clare said that *everybody* counts. Everybody. And Clare would know. Because she's Somebody."

CHAPTER EIGHTEEN
VISITORS

THE HOUSE WAS small and cozy. Outside, pumpkins rotted in the remains of a large garden, the black rinds caved in. Brown stalks of corn rustled in the rising wind. Mirri found one perfect cherry tomato that must have escaped the frost by being buried in leaves. She gave it to Sarai, who gave it to Jem, who gave it to Clare, who gave it back to Mirri, who popped it in her mouth.

This time they picked the smallest bedroom for their nest.

The other bedroom was occupied, but before they unpacked, Clare and Jem rolled the body into sheets, took it out back and sprinkled dirt on it. The ground was too hard for any real digging.

"It's too much like taking out the trash," Jem said.

"We can have a funeral," said Clare. "Mirri will love it."

And so they did. Mirri made up some tributes. Clare thought that it was not unlike allowing a small child to make a ceremony out of flushing a goldfish, but she kept those thoughts to herself. She had been the one to say it as they were walking through the woods: that body was Somebody.

Later that evening they had the moose steaks, and the steaks did not disappoint. They were gamey and strong, tough but delicious, and challenged the mouth in a way that food from a can never would.

"It's like eating Mother Nature," said Mirri.

"That's a really disturbing image," said Jem.

"I kind of know what she means," Clare said.

"Can I have some more?" asked Sarai.

Later that evening, Jem found a chess set. The board was outsized with large pawns and knights and kings and queens—pieces that fit nicely in the hand. The bishops all wore different frowns. The castles were many-turreted.

Jem challenged Clare. She sat down to play with great misgivings—Jem was, after all, on the chess team; he had almost won at the nationals and she doubted she could give him a good game. But when she moved her first piece, he looked up at her, startled and happy.

"The Fried Liver Attack!" he exclaimed. "This is going to be interesting. It's a gutsy move."

"Fried liver?"

"You haven't beaten me yet. Although this is going to keep me on my toes. Just let me think."

"I only made one move," said Clare.

He trounced her in four. The next game she moved a pawn, and, once again, he became animated.

"The Benko Gambit! You sure know how to start a game. You were holding back on me, weren't you?"

"No, I really wasn't."

"When Svein Johannessen made the Benko Gambit, Bobby Fischer declined—and I'm going to decline, too."

"I don't know what I'm doing. Really. I played Michael a few times, but he always beat me."

"Michael won?"

"Yes."

"Oh." Jem looked disappointed. "Maybe I should spot you a few pieces."

The others decided they wanted to play chess, too, but they finally went to bed after Sarai, checkmated in five moves by Mirri, threw the white king across the room, instantly beheading him.

As Clare began to doze off, she realized that it was snowing outside.

"Think the snow'll cause problems?" she asked Jem quietly.

"I guess we'll see," he said.

BUT THE NEXT morning, before they could leave, Noah, Rick and Tilda arrived on their doorstep. And then, sometime that night, Noah died.

THEY WATCHED THROUGH the side window as the three strangers came up to the front door and rang the doorbell. At the sound, Bear leapt to his feet and began barking at the door.

"Go to the bedroom," Jem said to Mirri and Sarai. "We'll call you when it's safe." He turned to Clare. "Do you think it's safe?"

"Don't know."

"Maybe we should have a gun."

"We have Bear. If we had a gun, we'd end up shooting ourselves by mistake."

They watched, half-hidden by the curtain, as the largest of the strangers began knocking lightly at the door.

"They're very polite," said Jem. "That's something."

"I'm going to open the door," said Clare. Bear stopped barking and walked with her, not at her heel, but with his head in front of her and with his teeth bared.

Clare pulled the door open, and three strangers dusted with snow filled the doorway. She felt Bear relax when he saw them. He even stretched his neck out over the threshold to sniff the smallest traveler who, Clare realized, was a little girl who must have been about Mirri's age. The tallest of them held out his hand to Clare.

Bear went back to attention.

The two boys seemed to be a year or two older than Clare. The one they learned later was named Rick carried a string of what looked like dried meat wound around his pack. He stared at Clare's face hard before he turned away and put down his pack.

The other boy, who was called Noah, carried the heaviest gear. He was loaded not only with a pack and sleeping bag, but a tent. Tilda, the little girl, carried a knapsack almost as big as herself. Clare doubted that they were related; Pest made new families.

It had stopped snowing but there were several inches on the ground. Still, Jem and Clare didn't invite them in, even as the introductions were made.

"We don't mean you any harm," said Noah once they had exchanged names. "Maybe you could tell your dog that. He's—large."

"He bites," said Clare.

That was when Tilda started crying.

"Hey," said Rick. "Just tell the dog to stand down."

Clare felt abashed. "All right."

"Klaatu Barada Nikto," said Jem to Bear in a stern tone. Clare stifled a laugh.

Tilda stopped crying and stared at him.

"What's that mean?" asked Noah.

"It's from an old movie," said Clare. "*The Day the Earth Stood Still*. The remake's awful, but the original's a real classic: in it—"

"It means that Clare won't let her dog hurt you if you're good guys," said Jem.

"We're law abiding," said Rick. "We don't even jaywalk."

"We won't stay long," said Noah. "We're headed south. For now." He spoke quickly.

Clare put her hand on Bear's head, and she felt him relax again. Jem's voice hadn't made him change his stance at all, but he was attuned to Clare's moods. She looked the travelers over one more time, slowly and carefully, then she opened the door wider and let them in. She saw Jem narrow his eyes as he watched Rick closely, and she wondered what that was about. Maybe later Jem would tell her.

They called Sarai and Mirri from the bedroom, and it was only minutes before Tilda went over to them, and the three began playing with Mirri's Pretty Ponies. Then Tilda looked up at Clare.

"Can we stay with you here tonight?" she asked in a quiet voice. "It's nice and warm in here."

"We wouldn't impose on you; we'd go in the morning," said Rick. "And we have some food we can share. If it's all right, Clare."

"Jem's the boss," said Clare.

Rick laughed as if someone had made a particularly funny joke. And Clare saw Jem narrow his eyes again. But all he said was:

"You can stay."

"We'll set up our little tent in here," said Rick. "It'll give us all a little privacy—plus, it's warm."

"I'll get you some food," said Jem.

"You won't *believe* what *we* had for dinner," said Mirri to the general company.

"But I bet you're going to like it," said Sarai.

Clare put her hand on Bear's head again, and he gave a great sigh as if he had been looking forward to putting his teeth into someone and had now lost the chance.

Jem cooked up steaks and heated up some tomato soup for the three.

"This is terrific," said Noah. "I mean it's really, really good. We're so tired of dried meat and flat bread, I can't tell you."

"I like flat bread," said Mirri.

"Maybe we could do some trading," Clare said. "We have a surplus of moose."

"You have a deal, young lady," said Rick.

Clare felt Jem bristle.

"'Young lady,'" Jem muttered. "Give me a break. She's almost as old as you are."

"I don't think she's quite my age yet," Rick said. "All right if I call you 'young lady,' Clare? I don't mean any harm."

"It's all right. But age doesn't matter any more. Here Jem's in charge."

Later, Clare and Jem snatched a moment to take Sarai and Mirri aside, to discuss the newcomers.

"They *seem* all right," said Jem.

"Bear gave them a good vetting," said Clare.

"Let's be clear," said Jem. "Bear's response was a little ambiguous, especially when they came to the door. But Rick's straightforward enough. Noah's something of an enigma."

"I *like* Tilda," said Mirri.

"You'd like anyone who played Pretty Ponies with you," said Sarai.

Meanwhile, Rick and Noah set up the tent in the living room. "The smaller space warms up fast," Noah explained when Clare, Jem, Sarai and Mirri came back out from the kitchen.

The atmosphere loosened up a little as they all sat by the fire together.

"Since Noah and Tilda and I met up," said Rick, "we've never stayed in one place for long."

"Our first place was good," said Jem. "But then we used up almost all the supplies in the area."

"Are you staying here for the winter?" asked Rick. "Because it doesn't look that way; it sort of looks like you're packing up."

"It does, doesn't it?" said Jem.

Tilda broke the tension with a massive yawn.

"I need to take off some layers," she said. "I think I'm starting to steam."

"Me too," said Noah.

"Just pile your stuff by the woodstove," said Jem. "It'll soon dry out."

Tilda started unwinding her scarf and took off her outer jacket.

"This takes a long time," she said. "I'm wearing about seven layers."

It was the most they had heard Tilda say so far.

Rick motioned to Clare. "Can I talk to you?" he asked. She looked over at Jem, Sarai and Mirri. Then she bent down and stroked Bear, who was lying at her feet. It was comforting how close he stayed to her. Always.

"All right," she said.

"Outside."

"Okay. But I'd really prefer it if Jem came, too."

"You're the oldest."

"That's not how it works here. Anything you tell me, I'll be telling Jem later. And if we go outside, my dog comes too."

"There's no need to be afraid," said Rick. "I promise."

"I'm not afraid."

Bear, who had been watching Clare the whole time, rose when she moved to the door.

"Clare?" asked Jem, when he saw where they were going.

"I'll be right back, Jem. Don't worry. Bear's coming." And Clare looked up at Rick, only to see that he had his eyes fixed on her.

"Don't stay out too long," said Jem. "It's cold."

The moon was a silver disc in the sky and the soft mounds of snow looked like graves in the dim light.

"Pest can't be very far away for you," said Rick, as the door closed behind them.

"Mirri and Sarai are far too young for Pest, and Jem's only thirteen." The words sounded odd in Clare's ears. She didn't think of Jem as thirteen.

"I meant you, not all of you. It's you I'm worried about."

"That's not your business."

"Jem can find a place and winter it out with Sarai and Mirri. But, if you like, you can come with us."

"South?"

"No. To the Master. You know about the Master?"

Clare looked at Rick with astonishment. "You lied to us about where you're going? What on earth for?"

"Noah and Tilda and I agreed on what we'd say if we met other children. We don't want hangers-on; we don't know what the Master's resources are."

"That's pretty cold."

"I know your friends would agree to let you come. Or at least they wouldn't stop you—not with Noah and me backing you up."

"Me. Without Jem."

"Pest *will* catch up with you," said Rick.

A light wind ruffled the tops of the snowdrifts and Clare pulled Michael's Varsity jacket closer around her.

"I want to go back in," she said.

"Jem has some years to go. You're running out of time."

"You seem to know a lot more about this than we do."

Rick lowered his voice. "Maybe you haven't heard yet, but the Master's broadcasting on a wider frequency now. He's setting up a new society, and he keeps saying that he has the real cure. He says the onset of Pest is between sixteen and eighteen. He's our chance. He's *your* chance."

"What's all this secret stuff about taking me out here to talk to me?"

"I like you."

Clare felt as if she were back in high school. "You're kidding."

"No. No, I'm not."

"You don't know me."

"I can see you in your eyes." He looked at her intently "They're very special."

"You can leave off with the 'eyes are the windows to the soul' crap."

"Are you and the boy lovers? Because if you are—"

Clare was suddenly, inexplicably angry. Bear seemed to feel her agitation, and he gave a low growl.

"Jem's thirteen," she said. "What do you think?"

"I think that I don't know."

"No. We aren't lovers. We're friends. Best friends. But that isn't your business, either."

"I just want you to get through to Master."

"You can stop talking now. I'm going in."

Bear almost herded her through the door in his apparent eagerness to get Clare inside. Rick followed. The frostiness between Rick and Clare was obvious, and Clare saw Jem watching her curiously.

When Rick and Noah and Tilda had all peeled out of their clothes and emerged from the tent in their sleepwear, the room began to smell of sweat and unwashed bodies. It was no worse than Clare, Jem, Sarai and Mirri smelled, but, Clare thought, it wasn't *their* sweat and unwashed bodies. Not that they didn't ever wash, but cold water baths tended to be cursory. Noah rubbed his neck.

"Let me see," said Jem.

"That's all right," said Noah. "It's just a stiff neck."

The three travelers disappeared into their tent.

The other four retreated into their bedroom. Clare and Jem decided to keep a watch, but Clare found it hard to stay awake. She went and sat on Jem's bed, and he climbed out of the covers and then draped a quilt around the two of them.

"It's strange to see other children," said Clare. "They're so normal."

"They're secretive."

"Maybe," said Clare. She thought of Rick. "Yeah, I guess they are."

"They don't quite seem like children to me. Except Tilda."

"What did you talk about while I was outside?" asked Clare.

"I played chess with Noah."

"Who won?"

"Please."

"Show off."

"What about Rick? What were you two talking about outside?"

Clare could hear the soft breathing of Sarai and Mirri.

"They know about the Master; they're keeping their destination a secret; they don't want what Rick called 'hangers-on.' And we talked about whether or not I'm close to the onset of Pest."

"You know you are."

"I'll be sixteen in the spring. But Noah and Rick look like they're almost eighteen."

"Let me guess. They don't want us, but Rick invited you to go with them."

"Well," said Clare. "Yeah. How did you know?"

"I saw the way he looked at you. What did he say when you turned him down?"

"Not much."

Jem was very quiet. It was too dark to see his face. As they sat on the bed, Clare knew that she would never tell Jem about Rick's question. Ever.

Time passed. It was warm under the quilt.

"Are you still awake?" Clare asked.

"Still awake. I'm thinking."

They huddled under the comforter. And, at some point, they both dozed off.

Clare awoke a few moments later to see Tilda standing at the foot of the bed. Bear was sitting up, alert, and then he did something very strange. He walked over to Tilda and nudged her.

"Noah won't move," said Tilda, putting her arms around Bear.

"What do you mean?" asked Clare.

"He's lying on Bunny, and he won't move." And Tilda just stood there, a darker part of darkness.

CHAPTER NINETEEN
A DEATH

"DID YOU WAKE up Rick?" asked Clare of the sibyl-like figure at the end of the bed.

"He's asleep," said Tilda. "But not as asleep as Noah. I can hear him breathing. Rick. Not Noah."

Jem was still leaning against Clare. He was sound asleep. It was chilly in the room, and, after lowering Jem to the bed, Clare covered him with another blanket. Hoping that there would be no need to wake him, she followed Tilda to the bright blue tent, which was outlined by the glow from the woodstove.

Tilda made a move to go in, but Clare stopped her.

"No, I'll go."

Clare only had to touch Noah's shoulder to know.

She left Tilda at the door of the tent and went to get Jem. When she entered the bedroom, it took a moment for her eyes to adjust to the darkness. Then she was by Jem's side, shaking his arm, telling him to wake up. His breathing and his warm flesh reassured her.

Life.

He stared at her, confused. Then, muddled by sleep, he reached out and pulled Clare to him. "Clare?"

"Bad news," she said.

"Clare! Are you all right?" He started to clamber out of bed. "Is it Sarai? Mirri?"

She could hear the others stirring.

"It's Noah. He's dead."

"Where's Rick?"

"Still asleep."

"How could he possibly sleep through someone dying?" asked Jem.

"I guess he was tired," said Clare.

"Where's Tilda?"

"I left her by the tent."

By then Sarai and Mirri were out of bed, and Jem explained to them what was happening. Mirri was out of the bedroom before Clare could make a move to stop her. Sarai followed. Tilda was standing in the dark, Bear by her side.

"What if Rick won't wake up either?" Tilda said.

"I'll wake him up, don't worry," Clare said. "You stay out here with Jem."

"Clare, do you want me to—" Jem started to say.

"No. It's okay." As Clare entered the tent, Bear gave a low whine and made as if to go with her, but she put him in a sit.

Clare tried not to look at Noah as she shook Rick gently awake. For a moment, she wished that Jem had come into the tent too. Rick must have been bone tired as it took her some time to rouse him. The tent was stuffy, and Clare smelled the underlying odor of death. When she finally made Rick understand what was happening, he brushed her aside and turned to Noah's body.

"Aw, damn."

Rick covered Noah's face with a blanket and, with Clare's help, carried him out of the tent.

They laid Noah in the center room. His body was red-gold in the light of dawn, but turned to greenish-blue as the sun rose higher in the sky.

"He knew it was coming," Rick said.

"Pest," said Clare.

"Yes," said Rick.

Now that she could see him more clearly, Clare could make out the pustules on Noah's throat and the lesions on his face.

Tilda turned away.

"Pest usually takes three days," said Clare. "And it's not usually so subtle. He didn't look sick at all last night."

"The stiff neck," said Jem.

"I thought Pest only got you when you were *old*," said Mirri. "Older than Noah, anyway."

"He was already seventeen," said Rick. "Although he was younger than I am."

"I'm sorry," said Clare.

"At least he didn't suffer," said Sarai.

"'At least he didn't suffer,'" said Rick, mocking Sarai. "'At least he didn't suffer.' He's *dead*. God."

Sarai looked stricken. Bear gave a low growl, but when Clare put her hand on his head, he stopped.

"We're *all* sorry," said Clare.

"You're all going to be where he is soon enough," Rick said. "She'll go first, though," he said, and looked at Clare.

"Hey!" said Jem.

"It's okay," said Clare.

"It's not," said Jem.

There was no doubt in Clare's mind that Bear was picking up on the tension; he stood stiffly between her and Rick.

Rick turned his back on them and began packing up the bright blue tent.

"That was a mean thing to say about Clare," said Mirri. "I didn't think you were *mean*."

Rick looked up at Mirri. "I'm sorry," he said. "I'm sorry about all of it, Clare. Jem."

"It's okay," said Clare, but Jem was silent.

Rick called Tilda. She came over to him right away, and he squatted down and took her by the shoulders.

"We have to move on now," he said. "We have to hurry south now so that I can keep taking care of you."

"Clare told me you're going to the Master," said Jem. "There's no need to keep up the going south lie. We most certainly won't be hangers on. You're free to get there first."

"If you know where I'm going, you should know that Clare ought to be coming with me. With us."

"That's Clare's choice."

"Stop talking about me as if I weren't here," said Clare. "It's annoying."

Tilda broke the tension. "I want Noah," she said.

"Noah's with the dead now," said Rick.

"Will he come back?"

"No, sweetie. He won't."

"Can they come with us, too?"

"It would be best if she came." Rick looked at Clare. He paused. "But they can all come if they like."

"Good of you," said Jem.

There was a glitter in Rick's eye that Clare didn't like, but then it was gone.

"Maybe Master can bring Noah back to life," said Tilda.

"There isn't a cure for death," said Rick. "We'll leave Noah's body here."

Jem nodded. Rick looked at him and sighed.

These are good people," he said finally to Tilda, "they'll help us bury Noah. And we won't forget him."

"Everyone counts," said Mirri. "And funerals are good."

THE GROUND WAS still hard with frost. They took Noah to the edge of the woods where they covered his body with earth as best they could before building a small cairn over him.

Tilda hugged each of them while Rick looked on. She made a move to hug Bear, but Clare said, "better not."

And then Bear surprised them all by padding over to Tilda and nuzzling her.

"Maybe we'll meet later," Rick said. He was looking at Clare again.

"Goodbye," said Jem.

"You know that it's time to go," said Rick. "For her. I wish you luck. I really do." He held out his hand to Jem, and, after a second, Jem took it.

"This is for you," he said to Clare and handed her a map. "The best way to get to I-80 and Herne Wood. To the place Master's talking about. I marked the trail."

Then Clare, Jem, Sarai and Mirri watched Rick and Tilda until they had climbed the rise behind the house and disappeared from sight.

"I didn't like Rick so much," said Jem. "But considering everything, he held up pretty well. He liked you, Clare."

"Maybe."

"Did you like him?"

Clare laughed.

CHAPTER TWENTY
JEM'S BIRTHDAY

THEY DIDN'T FINISH preparing for their departure until Rick and Tilda had a day's head start on them.

Clare returned from the washing line, where she had hung out their sleeping bags to air, to find Mirri in the center of the living room, drawing. Her picture showed a giant next to a globe of the world. He had shoveled children into his mouth; arms and legs dangled from his lips

"What's this?" Clare asked.

"I did *not* like Noah dying," Mirri said. "I had a bad dream. I drew it."

That night Clare and Jem waited for Sarai and Mirri to go to sleep before they crept from the room and went to sit by the woodstove. The glowing embers warmed their faces. Clare closed her eyes and imagined spring, her hands full of thyme and rosemary, and then a summer garden, where someone she trusted walked towards her under a cold moon.

"Rick was right, you know," said Jem. "It's only a matter of time before you grow into Pest."

Clare silently contemplated the winking coals as the fire began to die down. Then she sighed. "I'm just not that old."

Jem ignored her comment.

"When we go," he said. "We need to go at a faster pace. If Mirri and Sarai can."

"Mirri and Sarai would follow you at any pace. Anywhere."

"And you?" he asked.

"Yes."

"What's 'yes?'"

Clare smiled.

"You look like the Cheshire cat," said Jem. "And your answers are just as cryptic." Clare could tell he wasn't really troubled by her reply.

They sat by the woodstove companionably.

"My birthday's coming up," said Jem. "Soon, actually."

"You didn't tell me."

"It didn't seem like an auspicious occasion."

"Fourteen. You're catching up to me."

"When's your birthday?" asked Jem.

"May fourth."

"*Alice*. That sounds about right."

"What do you mean?"

"That's Alice Liddell's birthday—the girl who inspired *Alice's Adventures in Wonderland*."

"You know the weirdest things."

"I like Lewis Carroll. And we've certainly gone down the rabbit hole."

THE NEXT DAY they were up and on the road early. As they walked in the cool air of the morning, Mirri dropped back to flank Clare.

"Will we be together at Master's?" she asked.

"We'll stick together," said Clare, giving her backpack a hoist, "until world's end."

"The world's *already* ended. I just don't want us to come apart when we reach where we're going. So do you promise we'll always be together?"

Clare promised. Perhaps Clare should have considered the difficulties that might lie ahead of them, and perhaps she should have sensed the weight of the promise, but it didn't really matter. She would have promised anyway.

The next day it snowed lightly for a while before the snow turned to steady rain, which, while camped miserably under a lean-to, they tried to wait out. They set up the tent, but the rain dripped steadily onto the roof until it was saturated.

"And I didn't even keep the warranty," said Jem, but nobody laughed. Sarai was shivering, and Clare wrapped her in two sleeping bags. Sleep was sporadic that night.

The rain did not let up the following day, and they were becoming very tired, wet and quarrelsome when Mirri spotted a house amongst a copse of trees.

"We'll try it," said Jem.

The ceiling in the living room leaked, but the biggest bedroom was dry, and so they moved all the blankets and comforters and sleeping bags they could find inside it.

"Notice something?" Clare asked Jem.

"Yeah," said Jem. "No bodies."

"Nice change."

It was four in the afternoon. They all put on whatever dry clothes they could find and huddled together under the covers in the middle of the room. They finally slept soundly, lulled to sleep by their exhaustion and the murmur of the wind and rain.

And it rained.

When Clare woke up, it was still raining. She found herself curled around Sarai, who was holding on to Mirri for warmth. Jem's arm was around her waist. She tried to disengage herself without waking any one of them up. They didn't stir. They had slept through the late afternoon and the night.

Clare started making breakfast, and the rest of them soon came to the kitchen, drawn by the smell of hot food. Everybody's mood improved as they ate.

"Beans, beans," sang Mirri. "The musical fruit; the more you eat the more you toot!" Sarai giggled, and she wasn't usually a giggler.

"The more you eat," Sarai joined in, "the more you see that beans, beans are the fruit for me!" Mirri peered at Clare as if to see if she were shocked. Jem laughed.

"Let's do the cemetery song," said Sarai.

"That's the *best*," said Mirri.

Sarai began. "If you laugh when hearse goes by, you will be the next to die; they wrap you up in a bloody sheet—"

"And bury you a hundred feet deep."

"Chorus!"

"The worms go in, the worms go out. The worms play pinochle on your snout. Your stomach turns a ghastly green, and pus pours out like sour cream; you spread it on a piece of bread, and that's what you eat when you are dead."

"Second verse!"

"That's all right," said Jem. "We'll stick with the first verse."

"Do you know the one about diarrhea?" Sarai asked Mirri.

"*No*," said Mirri. "*Teach* me."

"Other room," said Clare.

They stayed in the house and spread their wet clothing across chairs to dry. And still it rained.

Clare and Jem started preparations for leaving, assuming that the rain had to give at some point. A plague and then a deluge. If there were a God, he had their attention.

The packing made Sarai and Mirri unhappy, but when Clare told them that it was Jem's birthday, the girls were ecstatic. Packing ceased.

Together they made a carrot cake—with flour, orange food coloring and a couple of very old carrots they found in the pantry. In the evening, they cooked it over the wood stove. It tasted terrible, but Jem loved it. Mirri handed him one of the two Breyer model horses she had hidden in her bag; Sarai gave him, very quietly, a locket with a wisp of her hair in it.

"So you won't forget me," she said. "Ever."

Clare herself had been carrying around a gift for Jem ever

since they had found the gold house. Luckily she had packed it in plastic so it had stayed dry. She had intended to give it to him earlier but had never found the right time.

"Let's go outdoors," Jem said once it had stopped raining. "You can't say 'no.' It's my birthday."

He took Clare by the hand, and they went out into the night. It was very cold. The stars were brilliant flecks of ice in the black sky.

"Here." Clare gave him the package under her arm. He opened it.

"*Peter Pan*," he said. "With illustrations by Arthur Rackham. This is amazing, Clare."

"Who knows?" said Clare. "Maybe you'll never grow up. Maybe you'll be fourteen forever. Maybe this is your last birthday."

Clare was sorry she'd said those words the moment they left her mouth. But they were already out there, and she knew no way to propitiate the gods of ill-wishing.

MASTER

THE MASTER PADDED DOWN the hall quietly. Eliza had been acting as if she feared him. She had given him her blood, and the act should have been a privilege for her. Eliza was lucky to be the right type. The completion of Part One: at its best, the act should be a duet. And even after Part Two, there would still be plenty of children like her to pair up, and those children would produce more with the recessive genes.

Britta, he knew, would have given anything to trade places with Eliza. Britta would have drained her own veins, if that were what it took to keep him happy and alive. For Britta, even Part Two, the recreation, would have been consensual.

In the basement, his scrapbook lay open to a blank page.

He stood in the dark hallway of the mansion, and in his hand was a pair of surgical scissors.

He went past what had been Greg's room. Britta and Doug had finally read Greg all of *The Stand* (Greg's choice) and a large portion of *Middlemarch* (Britta's choice) before SitkaAZ13 took him. Greg had died horribly, as if the disease were making up for the long reprieve it had given him. The Master let only Britta tend him; he didn't want his children to fear Pest. They were going to have to live their lives with Pest in their future, but the Master wanted them to get used to the idea gradually. There was nothing like denial.

Greg had almost made it to nineteen. Unheard of, really.

When the Master and all of his children had gathered together to bury Greg, the older children had looked restless. They were, the Master knew, waiting for him to say something about their cure. But the Master needed time, more time—time to train them. Their life with him would be good, rich and fulfilling. They would live well. But they would have to learn to accept that they would not live long.

The Master moved forward with confidence. He knew that the others were all outside looking at the newly hatched ducklings. The Master came down the corridor to Eliza's door. He fingered the scissors in his pocket.

He thought of the cellar. The open page waiting in his scrapbook. He could imagine the feel of the paper's grain under his fingers. Eliza would never feel the pain of SitkaAZ13. He wouldn't force her to live that long.

The Master didn't knock.

In Eliza's room the bedclothes were tangled. The window was open.

Eliza was gone.

He knew she wouldn't be back, and, in some ways, he was relieved—she had proved difficult; he wouldn't go after her. But he enjoyed picturing her struggling through the forest, growing weaker, becoming an easy target for a Cured. He thought of her death; he thought of it again and again and again.

Back in his cellar, he looked at the creamy page of the scrapbook. He decided to keep that particular page blank.

He hoped the birds got her eyes.

CHAPTER TWENTY-ONE
SHEBA

THE RAIN WAS depressing. They heard a crash outside the house and ran out only to find that the gutters had fallen. They may have been out-running death, but there seemed to be no way to outrun the persistent rain.

"There's something fundamentally optimistic about us," said Clare. "Instead of wintering over here, we're heading into the heart of winter and following an impromptu map made according to second-hand directions given to us by a man-boy whom we don't know whether or not to trust."

"Yeah," said Jem. "What could go wrong?"

"We're taking a chance."

"Everything's a chance," said Sarai softly.

But finally the rain stopped.

It was Mirri who discovered the horse. They were almost ready to leave when she ran into the house, wide-eyed and out of breath.

"I found a *horse*," she said, panting. "I ran all the way here. It's in the woods behind the house. It's *big*."

"Let's go take a look," said Clare.

"Are you sure it wasn't a deer?" asked Jem.

"It's a horse," said Mirri. "It's *much* bigger than a deer."

"Horses and deer look a little alike," said Jem.

"It's a *horse*. It doesn't look anything *like* a deer."

"All right," said Jem.

"The horse is going to *run away* while we're *talking*." Mirri danced from foot to foot with impatience.

"Let's go," said Clare.

"Maybe I could have it as a *pet*," said Mirri.

"We can't afford to have pets," said Jem. "Except Bear."

"Bear's not a pet," said Clare. They all looked at Bear, who was standing behind her. It was true that he did not, in fact, look like anyone's pet.

THE TREES GLITTERED in the sunlight. They startled a deer as they went through the meadow, and, for a moment, Clare thought it was the horse Mirri claimed to have seen. Then she saw it was too small and too fast and its tail flipped up, like a white flag. Bear wanted to spring after it, but Clare kept him by her side.

It was cold, and their breaths hung in the air. And that's how Clare first noticed the horse: as a plume of vapor coming and going a little beyond the first of the trees.

"It's just there," Clare said. "Before the old-growth forest."

"I don't see anything," said Sarai.

"There," said Mirri. "Can't you *see* him?"

The horse was now a brown blur among the trees.

"We're going to have to be really quiet," said Clare. "I'll see if I can get Bear to herd it towards us." Clare looked down at Bear, and he looked up at her with his yellow eyes. She was fairly sure that what he would really want to do was eat the horse.

Then the animal moved into clear view. Even at this distance, Clare could see that the beast was an old sway-backed country horse without an ounce of breeding in him. She thought he had probably been used for farm labor from the day he was born. He was like the big shaggy animals she had seen at horse-pulls at country fairs, except that he was now nothing but a walking set of bones in a hide.

"That horse doesn't look so good," said Sarai.

"We have to move slowly," Clare said.

The horse saw them, and its ears pricked forward. Then it took a step towards them.

Clare let Bear go, and he moved in a wide semi-circle in order to get behind the animal. He gave a low growl as he approached.

The horse spooked and leapt sideways with an agility that belied its condition. Clare called Bear back, and he came reluctantly.

"We're not going to catch it," said Sarai. She was biting her nails.

"Try clucking," suggested Jem.

Clare clucked.

"It's a she," said Sarai suddenly.

"How do you *know*?" asked Mirri.

"I looked."

Mirri looked at Sarai with newfound respect.

"I have an idea," Mirri then said, "give it some *food*."

"Excellent idea," Clare said to Mirri. "First get a rope. Then get us some of the carrots that we found in that bin."

("Not the carrots," hissed Jem. "We can eat the carrots."

"Yes, the carrots," Clare hissed back).

Clare told them to move back into the meadow. After Mirri came with the carrots and the rope, she obediently backed away as well.

"Horses are a girl thing," Jem said as he went into the meadow with Mirri.

"Coward," said Clare.

She stood quietly with her arms outstretched and the food in her hands.

The horse looked interested.

Clare gave a sigh, like the sound of a horse breathing.

The horse came a step closer. Then, abruptly, she came to Clare and, lowering her head, began to eat the carrots. Soon there were chunks of carrot and strands of horse saliva on Clare's hands. The horse breathed on her and then rubbed her huge head on Clare's shoulder. Clare patted the horse while slipping a rope around her neck.

"Well," said Jem as they walked back. "It looks like we have a horse. I notice that it's a wet horse. A smelly horse. But a horse nonetheless."

"We're *all* wet," said Clare. "And we all probably smell, too."

Once Clare had patted the horse some more and told her what a good horse she was, the animal became completely docile, as if this were what she had been waiting for. She shambled along with them, head thrust out a bit towards the carrots that Clare was carrying.

The rain began again.

Mirri couldn't stop looking at the horse.

"She's absolutely *beautiful*," she said.

Clare looked back. Every bone showed through fur that was, in places, matted and filthy. In other places, there was no fur at all where the horse had either rubbed it off or it had fallen out. She was knock-kneed and part of her tail was missing.

"Yes," said Clare. "She absolutely is."

"Useless, though," said Jem sadly.

"Nope," said Clare. "Now all we need is a harness and a cart, and scavenging will become much easier"

"You're brilliant, Clare," said Jem.

"Does that mean we're not going to *eat* it?" asked Mirri. "Because I don't want to do that."

"Can you seriously see one of us walking up to this docile creature and slitting her throat?" asked Clare.

Jem considered. "No. Actually, I can't." The rain stopped, and they took the horse into the nearest barn to feed and groom her. She shivered with pleasure as they brushed her fur. Clare named her Sheba. In a corner of the barn, near the horse box, hung an old mildewed harness that would do until they could find something better.

"We're lucky," said Clare.

"The whole thing's already written," said Sarai and nodded, sagely.

Throughout the exclamations and excitement, Sheba stood and chewed thoughtfully on moldy hay. She wasn't picky about her food. Clare looked her over. If they needed muscle, Sheba, once she had bulked up, would be able to provide it.

The next day, they found a horse cart in the third barn they searched.

It was time to get the harness onto Sheba and see if they could set her up in the traces. But it wasn't as easy as they had hoped it would be. Sheba was entirely cooperative and simply stood by the cart. She seemed to be waiting to be hitched up, but the harness was tangled, and it wasn't easy to figure out where all the bits of leather went.

Sheba became restless as morning passed into afternoon.

They paused for lunch.

"Well, we're not leaving today," said Clare.

"It's just a matter of patience," said Jem. "It's not as if we're trying to get the electricity on again, or restart a nuclear reactor. We're just trying to hitch up a horse; people did this for hundreds of years. It should be imprinted on our genes."

Clare made an effort to clean the harness and then, after lunch, they put it on the ground in the pattern that they felt it should go on the horse. This time the process went more smoothly. Mirri gave Sheba treats to keep her still. It took hours to get the harness hitched to the cart, but they were finished before dusk. By the time they were done, however, Mirri's treats were no longer keeping Sheba still, and she was pawing the ground and shaking her mane.

"That's about as annoyed as she gets," said Clare. "Personally, I'd be halfway to the meadow by now."

"I wonder what she thinks of us," said Mirri.

"She thinks we're idiots," said Clare.

"Now what?" asked Jem.

"Now we take it all off and do it again early tomorrow," said Clare.

There was a collective groan.

"And today and tomorrow we can load the wagon with what we'll need," said Jem.

Tomorrow, the real journey begins, thought Clare. *Tomorrow we set out on the final road.*

That night Clare lay awake for a while. In the bed next to hers, Jem was awake, too. He propped himself up on an elbow.

"I can't sleep," he said.

"Me neither."

"You can come in with me. If you like."

Clare sighed. "Yeah. Yeah, I probably would like." She got out of bed, crossed the room and crawled in with Jem. Bear followed her and lay down at the end of the bed.

"Chaperone," Jem said.

"Good night," said Clare softly.

"We'll be all right," said Jem.

Clare woke in the middle of the night. Jem was pressed tightly against her, his head buried in her neck. She slipped carefully out of his grasp and went back to her own bed, Bear padding along with her.

She was a little confused, but she couldn't stay awake long enough to figure out why. Jem was her best friend, and it made sense that they would find comfort in each other. Her love for Michael would have made of the gesture something very different. She would have given it a lot of thought before climbing into Michael's bed.

She went back to sleep easily now. Jem had said it, and, for the moment, she believed it—everything was going to be all right.

CHAPTER TWENTY-TWO
RAMAH

THE WAGON WAS loaded; Sheba was in the traces, and she took her first steps onto the road. Clare felt, for the first time, that they might make it to the Master's. Always before it had seemed like a game, but now things had changed. She thought of Noah's pale body then opened her coat and pulled down her shirt so that she could see her Pest rash. She thought of her father, unburied. And Marie. She thought of her real mother, whose death had seemed like the end of the world.

But it hadn't been. And Pest hadn't ended the world, either; the world was just taking a rest.

She touched her face and her neck. No pustules yet. If there were no cure, she might be able to get away with another year. Or two.

"What is it?" asked Jem beside her. "Are you all right?" Before Clare could speak, he felt her forehead; he touched her throat in the places the outbreak usually began.

"I don't have Pest," she said. "It's still just a rash."

"Don't scare me like that," said Jem.

THEY FINALLY JOINED the main highway. For the most part, they had taken back roads to avoid snarls of rotting metal.

That day the temperature went up, and the air was heavy with water that became neither rain nor snow. Mud was everywhere. Mud on their shoes. Mud on Sheba. Mirri had managed to get mud on her face and in her hair. Any attempts to wash her just seemed to spread it around.

Clare and Jem started arguing, and it seemed to Clare that they just couldn't stop. She didn't know why, but they were getting on each other's nerves.

"I'm telling you," said Jem, "that the mud sucks at the horseshoes. Mud can suck horseshoes right off the horse."

"You're not really an expert," she said. She even recognized her patented high-school cheerleader snotty tone, but she didn't seem to be able to stop herself.

"Common sense," said Jem. "Just putting two and two together. It's a chess thing."

"Do you think it's not my thing? Or am I not enough like that girl on the chess team—Rachel whatever—who has a face like a duck?"

"Where did *that* come from?"

Clare had no idea. She might have said she was sorry right then, but Jem's look was cold.

"Don't *argue*," said Mirri.

"I can't help it if Clare's decided to be a cheerleader today," said Jem.

"I'm a cheerleader every day."

"Condolences."

"Don't be so superior. You think cheerleaders are stupid, and that's stupid in itself."

"Yes. Laura Sparks was a real Einstein. And while we're at it, why don't you give that jacket a rest? Or maybe a wash?"

Fury consumed her. Clare turned and faced him, and she made every word count.

"Right now," she said. "I hate you."

He looked taken aback. "Well, I don't hate you."

"Do you think that means you win?" Clare raised her voice. "Do you think I care?"

At her tone, Bear turned towards Jem and growled softly.

Clare was immediately horrified. It was as if she had aimed a gun at her best friend.

*   *   *

LATER, THEY MADE camp in silence. They ate; they got into their sleeping bags. And the deep night stretched out in front of Clare. She kept picturing her anger—and Bear. Bear growling at Jem. She didn't sleep. Perhaps Jem slept, but she doubted it. He was too still, and his breathing wasn't regular.

Clare didn't understand her anger. Or his.

They broke camp in the early morning. Sarai and Mirri were already up when Jem and Clare woke.

"It's all *right*, you two," Mirri said.

"It's not," said Clare. She was, in fact, miserable. She felt locked into her mood, and it wasn't good.

"I have something I want to say," Mirri said.

"We discussed it," said Sarai.

"Here's what Sarai and I discussed," said Mirri. "Before you two got up. A long time ago, my parents had a big fight, and my mother said she wanted a divorce. My sister and I got *really* upset—just the way Sarai and I are upset now. But it was all okay. They went to see someone called a 'counselor' and told him all their problems, and then they were happy again."

"Tell them the rest," said Sarai.

"Well," said Mirri. "*We* think that *Sarai* should be the counselor, because she's older than I am, and *you* should talk it all over with her. Just pretend that she's a grownup and that you're married to each other."

To be spared that, they apologized.

"But," said Jem to Clare, "just to set the record straight, I was never remotely interested in Rachel Duckface. She didn't play good chess. Unlike Angela. Who, as you know, was lovely. And she knew what the Benko Gambit was."

The muddy road slowly grew a crust as the temperature plummeted, and Sheba's hooves made a crunching sound as she moved through the terrain. It began to snow.

With a powdering of white, the surroundings looked different; trees glittered against the grey backdrop. Clare felt as if she were awakening after a long sleep. She felt—better.

"It's good to be on the road," she said.

"Yeah," said Jem. "I was thinking that, too."

They settled into a rhythm of walking by Sheba and the loaded cart during the day, setting up camp at twilight, rising at dawn. They saw no one—neither delayed onset survivors nor the Cured. But the land was teeming with animals. Several deer, before scenting Bear, looked curiously at Sheba, and one of them took a step towards the horse before bounding away.

Bear kept himself well fed, and they sometimes shared his messy meals.

AND THEN THEY found a house that was unlike the others.

The house was set back from the road and looked closed and lonely, yet there was no snow on the path to the door.

"Somebody's here," Clare said.

"I bet it's not a Cured," said Jem. "I bet it's someone like us. I can't see any Cured shoveling snow."

They knocked at the door, and there was no answer. They tried the door, but it was locked.

"You know," said Clare. "I think I've been here before. A long time ago. Or something."

They moved back under the trees. They gave Sheba the feed bucket, but they didn't unload any of the camping equipment, and they didn't take off her harness. Jem was on edge; Sarai and Mirri were clearly nervous, but Clare felt a strange lassitude, and Bear lay down under a tree.

Ramah came out of the forest, not the house, and she looked like a figure out of a myth. Her hair scrolled down her back. She had a bow and a quiver of arrows slung over her shoulder, and she held a dead rabbit—its blood had trickled onto her hand.

Bear stood up, but he didn't growl.

Ramah was dressed strangely. She was wrapped against the cold not only with layers of clothing, but with the skins of some kind of animal as well. She looked gaunt and tired, but she didn't seem wary of them at all. As soon as she was close enough, she spoke.

"I'm Ramah. You're welcome here." She gestured at Clare. "Lift your hair."

"What's wrong with her hair?" asked Jem.

"I'm the only one with my hair down," said Clare. "Ramah can't see my neck."

"Why should she have to see your neck?" asked Jem.

"I have to know she's not a Cured," said Ramah. "I have to see that she isn't wearing the mark." Ramah stood, patiently, as if the world could wear down around her before she chose to move. She looked about ten years old.

Clare pulled her hair back. Then Ramah herself turned her own head from side to side. There were no marks on her neck.

"You can stay with us, if you like," said Ramah. "I don't have much food. This rabbit. Some cornmeal."

Mirri stared at the goatskins on Ramah's legs.

"Is that *fur*?" she asked.

Ramah smiled for the first time. "It's goat hair. Let's go in. You need to meet Bird Boy."

Ramah took them into the house. Coals in the fireplace were burning a hot deep red, and the over-all temperature was almost warm.

Clare sniffed at the air.

"You can probably smell the goat," said Ramah. "At least it isn't raining anymore—when the goat's wet, the house stinks."

"It's pretty strong *now*," said Mirri.

"Bird Boy?" Ramah called up the stairs. "We have visitors."

A moment later a boy came down the staircase. He had pheasant feathers in his hair and what looked like a necklace of crow feathers around his neck. His arms were raised as if he imagined they were wings, but he was making a considerable clumping noise as he descended. Even though Bear reacted with only mild curiosity, Jem pushed Clare roughly behind him. Sarai and Mirri were already near the front door.

"Hello," said the boy. As he lowered his arms, he looked much smaller. As Clare looked on in disbelief, Bird Boy knelt down and embraced Bear, who not only tolerated the attention, but licked the boy's face. Then Bear began the deep grumbling sound that to Clare meant he was utterly content. She didn't know what to make of it.

"It's just the two of us living here," said Ramah. "There are two Cureds somewhere nearby—they're very unstable."

"Very unstable," said Bird Boy, nodding and standing up.

"My dog," said Clare. "He's—he's not tame."

"Oh," said Bird Boy, and he got down and hugged Bear some more, until Bear was on his back, and Bird Boy was scratching his stomach.

"I guess Bird Boy's all right," said Jem.

Clare just watched. Bear had let no one but her touch him like that. She might have been jealous, but she sensed then, and she later knew it to be true, that Bird Boy communicated with Bear on an entirely different level than the rest of them. Their conversation took place on a wavelength that only the two of them could hear.

RAMAH HAD FALLEN in with Bird Boy when she was travelling. Where to, she didn't say, where from, she didn't say either.

"A Cured was going to hurt me," she said. "Bird Boy scared him. We ended up here."

"Not much food here anymore," said Bird Boy, looking away from them.

"We have goat milk," said Ramah. "But I have to leave some food out every day for the two Cured."

"Or they try to get into the house." Bird Boy nodded seriously.

"I want to show the goat," he added.

Bird Boy went deeper into the house and returned with a small brown and white goat that looked at them with its strange goat eyes.

"The goat stays inside unless I'm here," said Ramah. "Bird Boy used to act as goatherd, but he gets distracted."

"I do," said Bird Boy sadly.

Ramah looked around at them. "I'll cook the rabbit," she said.

Clare went out to the wagon and came back with ham and cold yams.

"Thank you. We're always hungry," said Ramah.

"Always," said Bird Boy. He filled his mouth with food.

"How old are you?" asked Clare.

"Ten," said Ramah. "I don't know how old Bird Boy is."

"I don't know how old Bird Boy is either," said Bird Boy.

"I would guess you're fourteen or fifteen," said Clare.

There was something oddly formal about Ramah. But Clare knew deep down to her core that Ramah would be straight with them. She was nothing like Darian, with his over-familiarity. If anything, Ramah had an air of being a little aloof.

Clare liked her.

Bird Boy, it seemed to Clare, was strange—but Clare trusted Bear's judgment absolutely. Something seemed to have happened to Bird Boy, but then something had happened to them all. There was no question in her mind as to whether or not he and Ramah would travel together. Pest created some bonds that couldn't be broken.

Clare's thoughts wandered as she and Ramah sat on the stoop and watched the goat pawing through the mud and snow for withered grass.

"Did you ever run across a boy named Darian?" Clare asked.

Ramah looked at Clare for a moment, as if sizing her up, then spoke.

"Darian was here," she said. "He killed two of our goats when we wouldn't let him in the house. We didn't dare go outside to get the bodies; we thought he'd left, but we weren't sure. The goats stank by the time we got to them."

"Did he hurt you?"

"He was afraid of Bird Boy. And..." she considered. "And I think he was afraid of me. So, no, he didn't try to hurt us."

"We welcomed him in with open arms," said Clare.

"He fooled me, too," said Ramah. "Until he slaughtered the goats. I would have let him in when he first got here, but Bird Boy wouldn't let me."

"Darian's dead now," said Clare.

Ramah said nothing.

Clare went indoors to find Jem. Mirri passed her on the way out, and Clare heard Ramah speaking to her.

"They're very close," said Ramah. "Clare and the boy."

"Of course," said Mirri. "*Anyone* can see that. And his name is Jem."

Clare found Jem in the living room. He was sitting on the stairs alone, and he looked unhappy.

"What is it?" asked Clare.

"I was just thinking—"

"What?"

"You seem so much older than I am these days. I'm never going to catch up."

"Really? I was thinking of how different fourteen is from thirteen."

"Yeah," said Jem. "Yeah, I guess it is."

RAMAH INVITED THEM to bring Sheba into the house for the night, in case the Cured came, but the horse refused to go near the door. Sheba was gentle and mild and soft-eyed, but she would not move. So, while Sarai and Mirri settled into Ramah's guest room, Clare and Jem, with Bear, made camp in the muddy snow.

Once Sheba was tethered and the tent was pitched, Jem and Clare looked at each other awkwardly. It felt odd without Mirri and Sarai there.

"You sleep first," Clare said to Jem. "I'll keep watch."

"Clare?"

"What is it?" she asked, but Jem was quiet for a long moment.

"Nothing," he said finally. "Let's check on Sheba."

The mare was asleep on her feet in the moonlight. Clare could see a star between her ears, and silver light seemed to run down her sides and pool around her hooves.

"It's as if she were made of light," said Clare.

"It's some kind of optical illusion," said Jem.

"You would say that," said Clare.

"No bickering."

"You know what?"

"What?"

"I've never hated you, either. Ever."

Jem looked at her, and the moonlight was in his hair too. Then Sheba moved a foreleg in her sleep, and more light seemed to pour down her in a steady rivulet.

So Clare was taken off guard when the attack began.

The faces of the two Cureds, a man and a woman, seemed to rush up into the firelight, but the light that made Sheba glow did not touch them.

"Go away," yelled Jem. As he scrambled to find the heavy flashlight, the man grabbed at Sheba. The woman laughed. Then she had Clare by the arm and was twisting it.

Bear took her down.

Clare grabbed Bear's back, not wanting to see her dog kill the woman, but then the man turned away from Sheba and attacked her. Clare fought back, and she was strong, but the man was stronger. He managed to get his hands around her throat.

It was all happening so fast, too fast. She saw Sheba, wide awake now, pulling back on her tether; she heard Jem shouting something; behind him, the door to the house opened and Ramah came running towards her; Bear was turning away from the woman, but it all seemed too late, too late. Clare pulled at the hands around her throat, but the man was strong and there were now large black patches swimming through her vision. Then there was more and more black and all the light seemed to be pouring away.

Jem reached her even before Bear did. She was so lightheaded that the thought seemed to register from far away: Jem was coming for her. And then she was breathing again and the black patches began to recede as Jem tore the Cured away from her. The Cured ran into the night. The woman Cured lay, unmoving, on the ground. And then Jem's arms were around Clare, and Clare was embarrassed because the tears were streaking down her face, and the moonlight was on Jem's face, just like the light that had made Sheba glow. Clare didn't hear Ramah, although she could see she was speaking.

"Jem," Clare said. And then the darkness took her.

CHAPTER TWENTY-THREE
THE VISION GARDEN

WHEN CLARE CAME to, they were still outside. Jem had his arm around her. "She's back," he said to the others. Mirri and Sarai clearly wanted a family hug, but Jem kept them at bay. "She looks kind of fragile."

The woman Cured was still alive, and they helped Ramah and Bird Boy tie her hands with duct tape. They couldn't bring themselves to hurt her. Not in cold blood. Not when she was so injured and bewildered; it wasn't her fault she was a Cured. Finally they managed to get her into the house. Clare came in leaning on Jem.

They dragged the woman to the sofa, tied her feet, and covered her with a blanket so she wouldn't get cold. Her scarred face was encrusted with blood. She lay there, helpless, unconscious, her thin hair spread out on the pillow.

Clare gently pulled away from Jem. Leaning down, she put her ear to the woman's mouth and, with her hand, tried to feel for a pulse.

"She's alive," said Clare.

"Did you think your dog would kill her?" asked Ramah.

"Yes," said Jem and Clare together.

Ramah fetched some towels, warm water and disinfectant. She washed away the blood from the woman's face and discovered puncture wounds on her neck, chest, and arms.

"Your dog missed the jugular by an inch," said Ramah.

"What's the juggler?" asked Mirri.

"Jugular," said Sarai. "It carries blood."

Mirri was impressed. "Your vocab list is working."

The Cured opened her eyes. One of them was half obscured by a flap of flesh, but they could see that the other was a deep brown. She moaned and moved into a corner of the sofa. As she did, her hair was pulled away from her neck, and they could all see the orange patch behind her ear.

"Tell us your name," said Jem.

"I want to kill you," said the Cured. "I could feed on you."

"She's decompensating," said Ramah.

"What does that *mean*?" asked Mirri.

"Even her craziness is breaking down."

"We need to look at the patch on her neck," said Jem.

Ramah brought some tweezers from the bathroom and a little plate from the kitchen. When she saw this, the Cured began to struggle, and Jem and Clare had to hold her down. Quickly, Ramah used the tweezers to peel off the patch. It was about the size of a quarter. She placed it on the plate.

"I see that one dead," said the Cured, pointing at Bird Boy.

Ramah pulled Bird Boy away from the Cured, and then sent him to play with Bear. Ramah, Clare and Jem bent over the plate and examined the patch. The sticky side was face up, grey and featureless. Ramah turned the patch over, and tiny letters at the edge were clearly visible. SYLVER. The patch was much thicker than Clare had thought it would be, about the size of two quarters pressed together.

"I wonder how it works," said Clare.

Mirri, Sarai and Bird Boy came over to look at the contents of the plate.

"I wish we knew what 'SYLVER' actually means," said Clare. "Before my family and I left the city, I saw 'SYLVER' spray painted on a notice about the Cure. I had thought the cure was an injection."

"I want to know why the patch isn't skin-colored," said Mirri.

"Why should it be?" asked Jem irritably.

"My father's was skin-colored."

Ramah looked at Mirri thoughtfully. The others stared.

"You said your father died of Pest," said Jem.

"He *did*," said Mirri. "But patches are how my father stopped *smoking*. He put on the patches and then he needed them less and less and then he didn't need them *at all*. He said the stuff on the patch was absorbed right through the skin. *Right through the skin.* I thought that was pretty amazing. He said I shouldn't touch them."

"A nicotine patch," said Jem.

"I guess," said Mirri. "Anyway, he hadn't smoked in over a *year* when Pest came."

"So," said Jem. "The Cure, the Cured, the nightmare, the insanity—they all come down to this little patch."

THE CURED, AFTER her lacerations had been treated, fell asleep on the sofa.

"I'll watch her," Jem told Clare. "You take care of yourself."

"You have the starting of a black eye," said Clare.

"Go look in the mirror. You're a bit disheveled yourself."

Ramah, Mirri and Sarai went with Clare into the bedroom. The mirror wasn't reassuring: Clare had cuts and bruises on her forehead and cheek, and her face and arms were streaked with mud.

"You should have told me how I looked," she said to Sarai and Mirri.

"We were busy discovering that the patch worked like a nicotine patch," said Sarai.

"That was *really* exciting," said Mirri. "And *I* had the clue."

"You should wash off that mud," said Sarai. "It's getting into the cuts."

"You look a little beat up," said Ramah.

Clare considered. Her whole body ached. "Yeah. I feel pretty beat up. But don't tell Jem. He worries about everything."

Ramah looked her up and down. "You must be cold. I'll get you some dry clothes."

"Look at your neck," said Sarai to Clare.

Clare looked in the mirror and saw deep bruises on her throat. They were in the shape of a pair of hands.

When Clare went back to the living room, Jem looked up at her anxiously. The tissue around his left eye was dark and swollen, and both eyes were deeply bloodshot. But when she smiled at him, relief lit up his eyes.

Clare and Jem sat together while the Cured slept. Mirri and Sarai, meanwhile, convinced Ramah to shed the goatskins, and then they took her to the bedroom and proceeded to dress her up. When they returned to the living room, Ramah was dressed in an ancient pair of jeans and—retrieved from a box in the attic—an old-fashioned print shift.

Ramah insisted on spreading the goatskins out to dry in the living room. At first the odor was simply appalling, but, as the skins dried, even Mirri stopped complaining. Clare didn't want Ramah to feel awkward so she said:

"Bear smells a little like that when he gets wet."

Meanwhile Mirri, seemingly intent on the makeover of Ramah, brushed her hair until it gleamed, long, light and wavy.

Ramah would have been, thought Clare, a good subject for a portrait.

Then the Cured woke up. She watched them intently as she chewed her nails.

"I can get you some water, if you want," Jem said to her.

"You're the dead one," she said.

Jem turned to Clare. Clare had tried to arrange a soft scarf around her throat to hide the bruises, but the material kept slipping down and revealing the marks.

"That must hurt," said Jem.

"Yeah," Clare admitted. "But it beats being pain-free and dead. Thanks, Jem."

He turned his head away. Ramah watched them, and Clare thought there was a bemused look in her eye.

And all the time, the Cured stared at them from the sofa.

"We're going to have to do something with her," said Clare. "Taking the patch off doesn't seem to have made any difference."

"It's only been a little while," said Jem.

"You want to eat me," said the Cured.

"I kind of think it's the other way around," said Jem. Ramah stood, watching.

"What are you going to do *now*?" Mirri asked Ramah. "There's still a Cured out there."

"I don't know what I'll do," said Ramah. "The same thing as before, I suppose. Wait out the winter with Bird Boy."

"I don't know how you've held on this long," said Jem.

"I didn't have any brothers or sisters. My parents were—distant. Coping with things is what I do. And Bird Boy is a great help."

"He seems strange."

"Does he?" asked Ramah.

Ramah's eyes were deep green. She looked at Clare and Jem until Clare began to feel uncomfortable.

"Why don't you come with us to the Master," said Mirri suddenly. "*Both* of you."

Ramah looked up at her sharply.

"That's a great idea," said Sarai.

"Jem?" asked Ramah. Her face had, for the first time since Clare had seen her, tensed up. It was hard for Clare to imagine Ramah being afraid of anything, but it was as if she were catching a glimpse of fear in Ramah's cool expression. "We wouldn't," Ramah said, "we wouldn't try and change anything."

"It's probably already written," said Sarai wisely.

"Whatever *that* means," said Mirri.

"Of course it's written," said Jem. He caught Clare's hand. "Right, Clare?"

"Right."

It was a moment that Clare was never to forget. She realized for the first time that maybe it was possible to form a new community as well as a new family.

"We would like to come," said Ramah. "It's kind of you to open your family to us."

Bird Boy made a sound like a dove.

And so then they were six.

IN THE EVENING, Sarai and Mirri huddled with Jem and Clare, as if to reassure themselves that all was well. When their eyes started to close, Jem sent them to bed. Ramah and Bird Boy, meanwhile, had gone outside to stand guard over Sheba, in case the other Cured came back. Bird Boy had Jem's hammer. Ramah had her bow and arrows and, much more practical at close range, an axe.

"She doesn't mess around," said Jem when Ramah and Bird Boy strode out the door. There was admiration in his voice, and Clare looked over at him thoughtfully.

A little while later, Clare checked on the Cured. And she discovered that sometime, while they had all been thinking and talking and planning, the Cured had quietly died. Perhaps the Cured had been more badly hurt than they had realized; perhaps she needed the patch to live; perhaps, simply, her time had come. That last thought scared Clare more than anything else.

THEY HITCHED UP Sheba in the dawn frost. Sarai and Mirri were both yawning. Clare's throat hurt, and she was still hoarse. Jem looked at her, concerned. Ramah and Bird Boy watched with great interest as they put the harness on Sheba.

"That must be complicated," said Bird Boy.

"You make it look easy," said Ramah.

"You have no idea," said Clare.

"I wonder what would happen if we used the Cured's patch on *ourselves*," said Mirri.

"Very bad things," said Ramah.

"There's nothing worse than being a Cured," announced Sarai.

"There's *Pest*," said Mirri.

"Pest is better than being a Cured," said Jem. And Ramah nodded her head in agreement.

"But then you'd be *dead*," said Mirri.

"Some things are worse than dead, Mirri," said Jem.

Ramah and Bird Boy went into the house to collect their bundles, leaving the four of them alone.

Mirri and Sarai looked at Jem anxiously.

"Now that you know Ramah," asked Mirri, "am I still your favorite?"

"That's not nice, Mirri," said Sarai. "What about me?"

"You and Sarai are both my favorites," said Jem. "And nothing's going to change that."

"What about Clare?" asked Sarai. "Is she your favorite, too?"

"Also," said Jem.

"It's different with *them*," said Mirri to Sarai. "*You* know."

They talked and waited for Ramah and Bird Boy. Finally Sarai and Mirri tired of the conversation, and went to the shed in the front yard.

It wasn't long before Jem and Clare heard a cry. Jem was in the yard in an instant, with Clare close behind him. Bear lolloped along by Clare's side; his ears were pricked forward, but he showed no signs of aggression. They burst into the shed.

Sarai and Mirri were squatting in front of an open trunk.

"What is it?" asked Jem. "Are you all right?"

"Board games!" said Sarai.

"They even have Chutes and Ladders," said Mirri happily. "I've been looking for Chutes and Ladders *everywhere*."

"Please don't yell like that again," said Jem. He left them setting up Chutes and Ladders and went back to the cart with Clare.

"They wear me out," said Jem.

"You love them," said Clare.

That evening on the trail again, this time with Ramah and Bird Boy and the goat, Clare took out her tablet of paper and sat for a long time looking at a blank page. She couldn't think of anything to write at all. Instead, she thought of sitting on the rock in the garden she had, half-awake, dreamt about. She hadn't told Jem about the aching sadness of the vision—an ache so deep that even its echo made her want to weep. She thought of how someone had walked towards her and how the pain had lessened. Then Clare looked up at the sliver of moon, and the sliver of moon, sailing in and out of the clouds, seemed to look back at her.

CHAPTER TWENTY-FOUR
WASTELAND

THEY CAME TO the place where the dirt track converged with the old highway to the city, the road that had been neglected ever since the new highway had been built. The new highway was a wide four-lane ribbon of asphalt with elegant clover leaves that provided exits and entrances: a transport system dotted with service areas and rest stops. But now the old way seemed the safer way. Once the only wide road in the area, now this highway was obscure, a place marked by decaying motels and abandoned gas stations. A wasteland, thought Clare.

Sheba took a step forward and paused as though surveying the way ahead before she pulled the wagon down onto the road.

"Not far to the city now," said Jem. "After that all we can do is go by Rick's map."

As they walked by the side of the cart, Bird Boy gave an occasional excited leap, which startled Sheba, though she soon enough grew used to it. The road—ill-maintained as it was, marked by pot holes and frost heaves and littered with empty, rotting cars—seemed full of promise.

They soon fell into an easy, steady pace. Jem handed Clare a Slim Jim. Mirri slipped her small warm hand into Clare's. Bird Boy sang a song about pretty little horses. And it occurred to Clare then that she might be perfectly content if they were never to reach the Master, if they were never to enter the city. She would be content to just walk—chewing a Slim Jim, talking with her friends—down the long road into forever.

But she still couldn't let go of the old world completely. Michael was part of the old world. She reached into her pocket and pulled out a folded piece of paper. She turned it over and over in her hands.

"What's that?" asked Jem.

"I found this poem in my pocket the other day."

"It looks like it went through the wash."

"It did. I meant to give it to Michael, but I never got round to it. It doesn't matter. He didn't like poetry."

"I'm sure he would have liked it." Jem was being his most polite. "Did you write it?"

"No."

"Poetry's a nice gift."

"Remember Robin?"

"The Robin everyone wondered why you bothered with? The National Merit Scholarship Finalist Robin?"

"Yes. Robin would say I tried too hard to please him."

"I wish I'd gotten to know Robin. We might've been friends."

"Oh, Jem."

"Why don't you stop waving it around and waste a little poetry on me? I like poetry." Jem took the piece of paper from her. "This isn't easy to read. What with going through the wash and all."

"I know."

"'I am half-sick of shadows.' I like *The Lady of Shalott*: 'she hath no loyal knight and true.'"

"That's not on there."

"No," said Jem. "But I like that part. What an optimist you were—giving poetry to Michael."

Clare found she wasn't angry. In fact, part of her wanted to laugh. Tennyson and Michael. Perhaps not.

The buildings that bordered the highway were broken and desolate. Gutters had pulled away from the side of one house; a tree had broken through the roof of another. They passed an old motel that had been left to rot long ago, after the road lost its traffic to the new highway. The walls in the front of the motel had fallen away, revealing old plumbing, some toilets, washed-out looking graffiti.

The sign in front of it still stood: 'Wayside Motel—No V ca cy.'

When they found a small farm with a barn set back between two houses, Clare urged Sheba off the road.

The farmhouse was small, but it had a large larder full of canned goods, as well as candles and matches and a stack of mousetraps. There were also mattresses and blankets and quilts and pillows in all the bedrooms. Curled up on one of the beds and partially under the covers was a small woman. Her eyes and mouth, or what was left of them, were frozen open.

"I still can't get used to it," said Clare.

"Come on," said Jem. "We'll seal off the room from the others. I love Mirri, but I don't think I could stand another funeral."

Outside, in a small corral, they found a horse carcass. There wasn't much horse left, just a sheeting of hide over bone.

"It had nowhere to go," said Jem.

"Poor thing," said Bird Boy. Bear went over and nuzzled Bird Boy before returning to Clare.

The loft of the barn was filled with hay, and Clare found the granary still dry and stocked with useable grain. The rest stop became a work stop, as they took corn, oats, horse nuggets and hay back to the cart. Ramah tested the horse nuggets on the goat, who found them very satisfactory. And Clare found some extra large bags of dog food to supplement Bear's hunting. On one trip, Bird Boy noticed a brood of chickens disappearing under the porch as he tried to approach.

"Pets?" asked Bird Boy hopefully.

"Sorry," said Jem. "Probably dinner."

"Okay. Can I have the feathers?"

"All yours. Once Clare catches them."

"Me?"

"Sure," said Jem. "I'm going to have fun watching you running down those chickens. And fun is hard to come by these days."

Ramah carefully and quickly wrung the necks of the chickens that Clare caught.

"Tonight's dinner," she said.

They put a bale of hay on the very back of the cart. The goat pulled at wisps of it as they moved on. The road had the same hypnotic effect on Clare as it had before. She felt as if she were shedding parts of herself as she walked—the cheerleader, the princess of the spring dance, the gymnast who practiced back flips on her front lawn. All aspects were peeling away to reveal a hard core of being that she wasn't sure she recognized.

On the next day they passed two derelict shacks half leaning against each other like a couple of drunks. The tin roofing was dark with rust and moss; the door of one shack opened into darkness, the door of the other was missing entirely, leaving a gap that reminded Clare of a mouth.

"They're a little creepy," said Clare.

"There's a fetid smell coming from them," said Ramah.

"'Fetid,'" said Clare. "That's one for Sarai's vocab list."

"We didn't have many books at my house," said Ramah. "One day I took to going through the dictionary."

"Was it fun?"

"No."

They began to continue to move on when Clare saw a movement from the corner of her eye.

"There's someone there," she said. "Should we hide?"

"Well," said Jem. "Horse. Goat. Dog. Six people. A large wagon. The hiding options are not good."

"I'm *scared*," said Mirri.

"Clare and Jem'll take care of us," said Sarai. "And Ramah, too. And I bet Bird Boy'll scare whoever's there."

"I'll try," said Bird Boy. He made a serious face but ended up smiling.

"The movement came from the second shack," said Clare.

"Whatever it is," said Ramah, "Bear's noticed it, too."

Clare looked at Bear and saw that he had come to attention. He was trembling as he focused on the window of the shack.

"It's not a Cured," said Clare. "Bear would be a lot more aggressive if it were. Particularly after the last attack."

Just then the dirty face of a young boy peeked out from an empty window frame.

"Don't come closer," he said in a small voice.

Bear began to bark; he wasn't growling, but even so, Clare could tell he was straining to be gone, to leap at the boy.

"Stay here," she said to Bear, and he lay down, still trembling.

"What are you doing there?" called out Clare.

"Hiding from you."

The boy came out of the shack. He was bundled up in clothes that were much too large for him, and he, or someone else, had tried to sew some kind of blanket onto the poncho that hung over his shoulders. The blanket was a lurid pink. There was straw in his hair. A little bit of snow fell from the roof onto his head.

He brushed the straw and snow out of his hair and rubbed quickly at his dirty face.

"Are you hungry?" asked Clare.

"Yes," he said.

He didn't move while she dug in her pack for some biscuits. When she held them out, he darted forward to take them.

"Do you have good water you can share?" he asked.

Ramah handed him her water bottle. Clare could tell he was trying not to drink it all, but he was eager, and some of it fell on his poncho as he lifted the bottle to his mouth.

"I've been melting snow before now," he explained. "It takes time. And it's not always clean."

"You haven't told us who you are," said Ramah.

"My name's Abel."

"I'm Clare," Clare said. Sarai and Mirri clambered out of the wagon, their fear gone. Abel's gloom, however, seemed to increase with the attention they paid to him.

"I'm actually doing fine," he said. Another dribble of snow fell onto his head.

Gillian Murray Kendall

"You don't have any food," said Ramah.

"I know. You don't need to harp on about it. Things are lousy enough as it is. If you want me to say 'thanks for the food,' then thanks for the food."

"Just skulking around that shack," said Clare, "isn't a good idea." She looked at him critically. He pulled at the shapeless poncho.

"I'm safe enough here."

"I doubt it."

"Hunger will get you," said Ramah. Her tone was neutral. "Or the Cured."

He brushed some more straw out of his hair and pulled at the pink poncho.

"I'm used to taking care of myself. Even before Pest."

"What about your parents?" asked Clare.

Abel's face darkened. "Don't ask. Pest was a good enough end for them." He then said, "wait a minute," and he went back into the shack before emerging a moment later.

"I needed my satchel. I've got canned sardines left," he said. "That's all. I was saving them for right before starvation. At least the satchel gets lighter the more I eat. I don't suppose you'd want to trade for anything?"

"We're okay."

"Well, let's go," said Abel. "This is all I have."

"You're coming with us?" asked Clare. She was taken aback. Jem lifted his eyebrows, but he said nothing.

"Yes," Abel answered. "No more skulking. You're right."

"You don't even know where we're going," said Jem.

"Okay. Where are you going?"

"We're going to the Master—the grownup with the cure to Pest," said Clare.

"Okay."

Clare and Jem exchanged a look.

"Maybe," Jem finally said. "Ramah?"

"We're building a new world," said Ramah. "We can't be too picky. But it's really your say—yours and Clare's."

"I'm good at not getting in the way," said Abel.

"We might regret this," said Jem softly.

Abel looked at them.

"He's not like Rick," said Clare. "Rick had some kind of an agenda. And he's certainly not like Darian." She hesitated. Abel spoke.

"Ready?" Abel said, hoisting his satchel.

And with that, as if it were taken for granted, Abel, with his pink poncho and dirty satchel, joined them on the journey to the Master.

"But please," he said to Clare as they started walking. "Tell your dog not to bite me. I've never seen a dog that big."

"He'll get used to you," said Clare. "Probably."

In the afternoon, the terrain got steeper. Even so, Ramah had taken the lead, and she didn't flag. She strode ahead briskly. Clare and the others were soon out of breath with trying to keep up. But nothing seemed to stop Abel from talking.

"This climb is too steep," he said.

"It's just a slope," said Clare. "Look at Ramah. She's not even breathing hard."

"My feet hurt."

Ramah waited for them patiently at the crest of the hill and then turned and continued. Once the road levelled out, Abel started telling Clare and Jem stories about himself. He didn't leave out any of the lurid details. In fact, he didn't seem to leave out anything at all.

"I used to like ghost stories," he said. "But now they're not scary anymore. Pest was scary. It was pretty gruesome watching my parents die. They howled and screamed, and when they *really* screamed, you know, like they meant it, I gave them water. Then Geordie, my brother, died, but I gave him all the water he wanted. And there were flies everywhere. I mean everywhere. And the *smell*!"

Ramah, who had let them catch up, heard the last part of this.

"We all have a version of that particular story," she said.

"You've never really told yours," Clare pointed out.

"No," said Ramah.

"Well, I haven't had a chance to tell mine to anyone," said Abel. "Anyway, the flies and the smell are what drove me out, right out of the town to those shacks. So now I'm alone. And there's no 'get me a beer,' or 'find your own dinner,' or 'go wash your brother.'"

"You've had a rough time," said Ramah.

"Yes. And I'm skipping over the part with the cigarette burns. And then the way they used to go after Geordie with the belt. When they were drunk, they would really lay into us. And then my father would beat up my mother. And then they would both fall asleep."

"That's horrible," said Clare.

"I suppose it was," said Abel. "I don't miss them. But I miss Geordie." He paused. "Sometimes I think that maybe even my parents didn't deserve Pest."

"There's nothing you could have done about it," said Clare.

"I could have given them more water."

"Maybe. But you didn't."

That evening Clare slipped away and dug her own hole near the latrine. She had her period, and she needed to bury the used tampons. Sometimes their lives seemed to revolve around little more than digging latrines, burying waste, finding water and food, keeping as clean as they could. Their bodies were needy little islands.

She was sorry she had been short with Abel. Having her period made her cranky.

She stood up only to find herself face-to-face with Bear, who must have followed her from camp. He turned as she turned, and they walked back together. He had her back. He would always have her back.

CHAPTER TWENTY-FIVE
PARTING WAYS

THE DREAM WAS very real.

In the city, the buildings had been eaten away and loomed over them like the skeletons of giants. She and Jem were surrounded by a horde of children.

Clare woke and sat bolt-upright in the darkness. They were camped somewhere beside the great road to the city.

As her dream faded, she rolled over to look at Sheba. Clare wondered if they would have made it even this far without the cart filled with food and warm clothing.

Soon the others were up, and they were on the road again, eating breakfast as they walked. True to her farm upbringing, Sheba had made no complaint about the journey so far, not even on the hills. When they came to really steep slopes, she kept on going even as her sides became slathered in sweat. Most of the time they walked to lighten her load. Bear loped along beside Sheba, who pointedly ignored him.

The route to the city was flanked by battered houses alternating with businesses that looked as if they had fallen on hard times long before Pest. Cars in various stages of decay had been abandoned in the streets.

"We could never have driven this," said Jem.

"Nobody's got a license," said Clare. And Ramah, who was usually reserved, laughed until she got the hiccups.

Later, as the rhythmic clip-clop of Sheba's hooves began to lull Clare towards sleep, she asked, "How long until we get there?"

"Another day," Jem said.

"Do you think everyone in the city's dead?" asked Clare.

"All the adults except the Cured. I would think the children that survived would have left by now. It'll be a ghost town."

They passed a boarded up Tastee Freeze, a derelict drive-in movie theater, a Big Boy with its signature sign planted head down in a parking lot.

The sordid little motels they passed began to make them uneasy.

"They look as though they're inviting us in," said Sarai uneasily.

"They want to chew us up," said Abel cheerfully.

"I don't like them," said Bird Boy. But Bird Boy was easily distracted, and Ramah found him the red feather of a cardinal, which he happily wove into his hair.

They made a strange caravan. Ramah, still looking like Diana with her bow and arrows, walked with Bird Boy, whose collection of feathers had grown until they protruded from his hair and decorated all his clothes. As Clare watched, Ramah found Bird Boy an acorn cap, which he put on her head like a tiny hat, and then laughed when it fell off. Mirri and Sarai stayed together and sometimes tried to play Hangman or even Old Maid while walking. Abel, who could not be persuaded to take off his pink poncho, walked alone. Clare and Jem stuck together. At one point Clare, suddenly curious, turned and spoke to Ramah.

"Can you actually use that bow and arrow?" she asked.

"Yes."

"Are you any good with it?"

"Yes."

Clare moved away from Jem and walked next to Ramah for a while.

"Did you know Bird Boy before Pest?" she asked.

"No."

"How did you find him?"

"He showed up in time."

"In time for what?"

"It doesn't really matter, does it? Not anymore."

It was like trying to make conversation with the Delphic oracle.

Then Bird Boy spoke abruptly. "Ramah is my parents. I don't have no others."

When they came to the junction with the main highway, they found a rest stop and decided that it was a perfectly decent place to make camp.

"We could go around the city," Clare said, while the others were setting up the tent.

"We're low on supplies, Clare," said Jem. "The cart wasn't full when we left, and there are seven to feed—and Sheba and the goat, too. Even Bear needs more food than he can hunt."

"We could load up at a town somewhere nearby."

"The city will have everything we could possibly want," said Jem. "There'll be warehouses of food, not to mention what we'll find stored up in restaurants and shops. We need to go in."

"All right."

"But I've been thinking," said Jem. "We don't *all* need to go. I can go alone with Sheba. You and the others can meet me on the other side."

A light breeze had picked up, and Clare felt cold. She could hear the sounds of the others as they finished putting up tents and as they got the fire started. She could hear Abel grumbling, and Sarai and Mirri chatting.

"You mean the two of us can go," said Clare.

"Clare—"

"Obviously I'm going with you."

"Clare—"

"If you leave without me, I'll just follow you."

Jem looked at her for a long time. "There's no point in arguing with you, is there?"

"No."

"All right. We go together and scavenge in the city as quickly and efficiently as possible. Then we meet the others on the other side. You're really up for that?"

"Yes."

"Plan?"

"Plan."

They went back to the campsite together. Ramah looked up at them. "I thought it would go that way," she said, as if she had heard the entire conversation. Then she went to the wagon and rummaged around until she had the map.

Ramah put her finger down on a green place marked 'National Park.'

"We'll meet you here," she said. "We'll wait until you come."

"We won't be long," said Clare. But what she really thought was that there were many ways to die in the post-Pest world. Except old age. That particular option seemed to be gone. She looked closely at Ramah. "But don't wait too long for us." She hesitated and then smiled. "We can always catch up with you."

"I understand what you're telling me," said Ramah.

"I knew you would," said Clare.

"There's something I won't do for you, though," said Ramah. "Sorry."

"What?" asked Clare.

"Tell the others."

That part didn't go very well.

Sarai, Mirri and Bird Boy cried themselves to sleep. Abel looked gloomier than ever.

And that night Clare imagined a different world, one in which she could grow old. And Jem would be there. And Sarai and Mirri and Ramah and Bird Boy and Abel. And others she couldn't yet see. Bear would be there too, and if Bear had to die first, he would do so curled up at her feet after having reached a ripe old age, toothless, maybe, but content.

She would give a lot for such a world.

And she did.

CHAPTER TWENTY-SIX
THE CARCASS OF THE CITY

THE GOODBYES WERE brief except for Mirri's. She walked with them for the first mile before turning back tearfully.

There was a rise and a dip in the road, and then Clare and Jem were alone together. The only sound was the steady clopping of Sheba's hooves.

"Do you think the others will run into any trouble?" asked Clare.

"No. Ramah will take care of them. In fact, this sort of has the feel of a vacation to it. Do you know what I mean?"

"Yeah. We left the kids with a sitter."

They proceeded down the central highway into the heart of the city. Clare remembered to look out for the spot where her family had stopped and taken a different car. Finally she saw it; the scene looked much smaller than she remembered.

They went over to the car together. When Clare got inside, she thought she could detect the scent she associated with her father. In the glove compartment she found the car registration, a triple A card and a bag of mints. The belongings they had decided they could do without were still lumped together in the backseat, moldering. Clare could make out a few items of her old clothes, including a white leotard she had sometimes worn to cheerleading practice. Somewhere in there, too, were her pom poms.

Imagine.

She couldn't bring herself to rifle through her old things.

"It all seems so long ago," she said.

Nature had been busy in the city. Parks, hotel courtyards, parking lots, had all begun to be taken over by the wild. Root systems were breaking up the sidewalks; vegetation burst through park fences, and everywhere there were birds. The windows of most of the stores had been smashed in, although sometimes it looked as if nothing had been taken. On the other hand, one jewelry store had been completely looted. Jem, curious, went into it.

"Almost everything's gone," he said when he came out. "But I found this." He handed her a gold ring. He must have noted her surprise, because he said, rather gruffly, "We're not engaged or anything."

Clare found a piece of string in her pocket and looped it through the ring. She then put it around her neck.

"Thanks," she said.

Later, after they managed to get out of the city, she began to think of the ring as a good-luck talisman and so began to wear it on her finger. The fit was right.

Jem and Clare spoke mostly in whispers. The city was huge around them. Bear seemed restless; he looked at Clare and gave a low whine.

"Go," she said, and Bear was a nimble black streak down the road.

"Would Bear stay if you asked him to?" asked Jem.

"Of course. Do you think I should? He's hungry; I thought he should look for food before nightfall."

"We might want him close. You know."

"Just in case."

"Yeah, just in case."

"We'll keep him with us when he comes back," said Clare.

But Bear wasn't with them when, soon after, they found a prime foraging place. Working in perfect synchrony, they loaded up sacks of flour, cornmeal and beans that they had found in the back of a Mexican restaurant. Jem heaved up a sack to Clare. Clare turned to secure it in the wagon when Sheba shied sideways. Clare, trying to keep her balance, turned towards Jem.

The attack took them by surprise.

Running towards them from the shadows of an alley came a group of children, all about eleven or twelve, all armed with sticks.

"Kill them! Kill them! Kill them!" the largest of them yelled. Before Clare could think about moving, she found herself alone in the wagon as Jem was pulled under the pack of wild children. Their hair was filthy and their clothes were little more than rags.

"Meat tonight," the largest boy screamed.

"Tork says 'meat tonight!'" said the others. They were jabbing at Jem with their sticks, ignoring Clare altogether. She didn't know if Tork meant they were going to eat Sheba or Jem. Perhaps he had plans to eat all of them. Jem was trying to shake them off. Clare took the spade they had found in a hardware store and jumped into the melee. Sheba, no longer held in place, started into a tentative lope before coming to a stop a few yards away. The one named Tork jabbed at Jem and opened an ugly wound on his face.

"I'll get you!" Clare yelled and swung the spade. With a dull thud, she connected with Tork's stomach. She then drove the flat of the blade into his face. Tork fell and didn't get up.

"Stop! Stop! Stop!" yelled one of the older girls. "Tork's down."

The children ceased fighting as suddenly as they had begun.

"That ain't fair," said one of them, addressing Clare.

"You were going to kill us," she said.

"Not for *real*. And now you kilt Tork."

"I don't think Tork's dead."

"Looks dead." But then Tork groaned.

Jem staggered to his feet. "We're just here to get supplies. We don't mean you any harm. And you can't eat our horse. Or us." He limped over to the wagon.

A girl with a dirty face and long tangled hair looked hard at them.

"Well, then," she said. "Welcome to the dark place. But you didn't start real good by playing for real."

"What's the dark place?" asked Jem.

"Here. All around you."

As they spoke, some of the others were giving Tork small slaps to raise him. One of the smaller children was stroking his arm. Tork seemed to be coming around.

"They won," the girl said to Tork casually, as soon as it was apparent that he was alive.

Tork sat up. His nose was skewed to one side, but he seemed otherwise undamaged. The girl with matted hair sat next to him and, without any preliminaries, snapped the nose more-or-less back into place.

"Thanks much," said Tork to the girl. He touched his nose gingerly and flinched. Then he looked at Jem. When he got to his feet, he staggered for a moment. Clare had, after all, swung the spade hard. She was surprised he could get up at all.

"Now what do we do?" asked Clare. "I don't want to fight again."

"Now we eat," said Tork, as if the answer were obvious.

And so they ended up down an alley in the children's homemade shelter.

"I kind of wish Bear had found us by now," said Clare. "It's getting late."

"He'll find us tomorrow, if not tonight," said Jem.

They left the cart at the end of the alley, brought Sheba to the shelter and tethered her outside.

"The Cured probably won't steal your wagon," said Tork. "They'd just tip it over."

Cardboard lined most of the shelter, and holes were plugged with plastic and pieces of metal and even the skins of cats, heads still on.

Tork saw Clare looking at the dead cats.

"They were stealing food from us," Tork said. "So we kilt them."

"I'm not sure we should have," said the girl. "The rats is worse."

"Get the jinormous pots, Myra," said Tork. "It's feast time."

And Clare realized that, despite the oddity of the situation, she was hungry.

The wild children used some of the supplies that Clare and Jem had found, but they took only what they needed. Soon they were cooking beans in a big pot over a fire and, in another pot, they had the makings of a cornmeal porridge.

Clare and Jem looked around the shelter, and they found that the wild pack of children didn't consist only of eleven and twelve year olds after all. The really young ones had stayed back in the sheltered alley. Most of them had runny noses; some had sores on their heads and faces.

"Your little ones look like they're ailing," said Clare.

"We do stuff for 'em," said Myra. "But the city is like a big dead thing, and the stench of it makes you sick. That's why we call it the dark place. Least the littles don't have Pest, and they don't have the fever."

"We seen Pest again, though," said Tork. "It ain't dead. Connor died of it. He was our leader then, but Pest got him. Not the fever—it was Pest."

"What's the fever?" asked Jem.

"You might see," said Tork. "It's not starvation we're dying of. It's fever what kills us."

"Maybe you should boil your water," Clare said thoughtfully. Myra and Tork just stared at her.

"Messing with the water won't stop fever," Tork said. "We think it comes from the bodies. The rotting gets up your nose and gives you fever."

"Why don't you leave the city?" asked Jem. "You could go anywhere."

"Maybe we could help you," said Clare.

Myra and Tork looked at them with something like pity.

"You're the ones needed to come here," Tork said.

*　　*　　*

WHEN THEY FINISHED dinner, they stacked the dirty dishes in a corner.

"Look at us gettin' along," said Tork. "Like fambly."

"Will you help us load the wagon with supplies?" asked Jem. "It'd sure make it go faster."

"Course," said Tork. "I ain't got no plans for tomorrow. You, Myra?"

"Nope."

"Not next day, neither," said Tork.

"Nope," said Myra.

Tork and Myra tended the fire and started banking it down for the night.

While Jem was feeding Sheba, Clare sat with a small boy called Stuffo on her lap, combing his hair with her fingers. He smelled as only an unwashed child can smell. While there was no stench, he exuded an unpleasant, greasy, over-ripe smell.

"Ouch," he said as her fingers snagged in his hair. "Too hard." But when Clare finally, in the dim light, noticed the nits in the hair, and when she thought she saw the quick movement of a full-grown louse, she declared the session over.

"You're done. Maybe I'll brush it out more later."

The children were readying for the night when Bear came loping down the alley. There was a general panic.

"It's okay," said Clare. "He's mine. His name's Bear."

When Bear nuzzled up to Clare, the children seemed to relax.

"He don't bite?" asked Tork.

Clare put her arm around the dog. "Apparently not today."

Tork did not look fully reassured.

"Well," said Myra. "Bring him in, then. It'll be all the warmer."

When Jem returned from feeding Sheba, he found Bear lying at Clare's feet. The children let Jem in before closing up the shelter. From the outside, Clare thought, it must now look like only so much refuse at the end of the alley.

The inside of the shelter was stuffy with a distinct odor of decay and unwashed humanity, but there was an air of safety and comfort there too. The little ones were already curled up in what looked like piles of rags.

"You can have Connor's bed," Myra said to Clare. "And you can sleep on the rag heap," she said to Jem. "It's comfortable."

"We'll just huddle up against the fire," said Jem. Clare was grateful. She couldn't have slept in the dead boy's bed.

"Well, that's all right," said Tork. "Myra and me share bedding too. S'warmer. And sometimes the little ones crawl in with us."

It seemed to Clare that in a world of grownups, Tork and Myra might have drowned in a sea of neglected children. Here, they seemed like the matriarch and the patriarch of a lost, but in its way noble, clan.

So Jem and Clare curled up close to the fire. Jem slept first. In his sleep, he cast a protective arm around her.

CHAPTER TWENTY-SEVEN
THE RUNNING OF THE DEER

MYRA WOKE UP Jem and Clare as she bent over them to get the fire going. Bear gave a sigh and got to his feet. Then he leaned down so that Clare could scratch his head.

"Sleep all right?" Jem asked Clare.

"I dreamed I was washing my hair," she said.

"It's still pretty clean from last time."

"This time I was washing it in hot water."

"Hedonist."

When Tork opened the shelter, the fresh air was like a gift, but the others seemed not to notice the difference. The smallest children split into two groups: one went with Tork and one with Myra. When they returned some minutes later, they looked quizzically at Jem and Clare.

"Well, aren't you going to go and do your business?" Myra asked.

"Go where?" asked Clare. "What business?"

Jem nudged her in the ribs.

"Bowel business," said Myra. "It's the rule: If you need to go, you need to check. If it's runny, you might be headed towards fever, and then you take the Pepto-Bismol."

"*You* ask them exactly where we're supposed to go," whispered Jem. "I am not going to discuss 'bowel business' with Myra and Tork."

"Well, Myra's right about checking if it's runny," said Clare. "That's a good idea."

"I am not discussing this with you, either."

Myra and Tork stood there looking at them patiently.

"Well, where do we go to do 'bowel business'?" Clare asked them.

"Anywhere not too close to the shelter, of course," said Tork. "We don't want poop near the shelter. That's messy. But go together—you never know what's out there. The Cured are always around. We seen wild dogs, too." Tork looked closely at Jem, as if assessing his ability to deal with wild dogs.

"You should of come with us," said Myra.

"If you see wild dogs," said Tork, "be careful. You don't want your dog tangling with them. Rabies. And don't leave fresh dead animals in the street. The rabies'll cook right out, and meat's always welcome."

Jem and Clare hurried out of the shelter.

"I miss Sarai and Mirri," said Clare. "And Ramah. All of them."

"I miss the latrine," said Jem. "Nobody ever has to do this in the movies."

No place seemed quite right, and they were getting farther from the alley.

"Jem," Clare said finally. "I just can't do this with you standing there."

"I'm glad you said that," said Jem. "We'll check out a perimeter and stay inside it. But not too close to each other. Bear should keep us safe."

ON THE WAY back, they caught sight of three dogs gnawing at the bones of what looked like a man. The largest dog looked up; the other two used the moment to drag their prize further away.

As Clare and Jem were about to turn into the alley leading to the shelter, the big dog snarled and began to run towards them. It didn't have Bear's bulk, but it was fast.

Bear collided with the dog in mid-air. The wild dog whined and tried to get away from Bear, but Bear had his teeth in the animal's throat. He shook the dog back and forth until Clare heard a crack that she was sure was the sound of the dog's spine breaking.

Bear finally dropped his kill.

"Bear seems to have one setting when he's annoyed," said Jem. His words were light, but he looked pale.

"That other dog would have been at our throats."

"I'm not complaining."

"How do you know if an animal has rabies?" Clare asked.

"You don't. Not without a lab. Check to see if Bear was bitten, or if he did all the biting."

"He seems clean. The blood on his coat isn't his."

"Try not to touch that blood."

The dead dog's teeth, bared in death, were still studded with flesh from the nearby corpse. Despite Tork's confidence that rabies cooked out, they left its carcass behind. The other two dogs had kept feeding throughout and displayed no interest in Clare or Jem.

When they got back to the shelter, Tork looked at them appraisingly.

"We should go on a romp," said Tork. "Before you leave."

"In the houses of the dead?" asked the little one called Leaf.

"In the houses of the dead," said Tork.

"Yes!" said Stuffo.

"What about the supplies?" asked Jem.

"The supplies," said Tork. "I think I'm tryin' to forget you're leavin'. But the houses of the dead are prime. We find all kinds of stuff in them. We found a music box with a dancing bear on it just a couple days ago. And a bunch of china statues—girls with sheep and princesses and stuff."

"They were seriously fun to smash," said Myra.

"Maybe next time," said Jem.

Tork perked up. "Next time," he said.

Clare and Jem followed the wild children to what they said was a prime warehouse for what Tork called "things you eat what don't go bad."

In a while, Clare noted that they seemed to be on the fringes of Chinatown. Huge Chinese letters, fallen from some of the buildings, lay in the street, and at one end of the road was a structure that looked like a pagoda.

"The warehouse's not too far from here," said Myra. "We should be able to fill up your wagon with stuff from there."

"We thought warehouses might have too much of one thing," said Jem. "Like a mountain of tires. Or a thousand pounds of beef jerky."

"This one's got everything," said Tork.

The day was warm. Myra helped Clare out of some of her warmer garments, and Jem went sleeveless. One of the children gave Clare some bangles, and soon she jingled as she walked.

"Almost there," announced Tork. "I'm sayin'—this warehouse is prime. You'll see."

And it was. They loaded the cart until the sun was high in the sky.

Afterwards they made their way back to the alley, joking and laughing, enjoying the unseasonably warm weather. They turned a corner.

And there was a deer standing utterly still, staring at them.

When it saw Sheba, it snuffed the air before giving a great leap and springing away. It ran down the center of the street. Clare couldn't hold Bear back. He ran, eating up the ground with his long stride.

Tork yelled "meat!" and the children grabbed their sticks out of the back of the wagon and gave chase.

"They don't have a chance of catching it," said Clare.

"Bear might," said Jem. They could hear shouts and hoots in the distance.

They waited. And then, not so very far away, they heard a huge crash, as if an enormous pane of glass had shattered. There was silence for a moment, and then howls from the children.

Minutes later, Myra came running up the street.

"You got one great dog," she said. "But we need the wagon."

"What happened?" asked Jem.

"I think Clare's dog scairt that deer almost out of his skin; he jumped through a store window, clear through, and then Tork cut its throat with a big piece of glass. Bear's eatin' his share. Very messy." She stopped, meditatively. "Tork cut himself on the glass too. There's blood everywhere."

Myra, Clare and Jem got up on the cart, and Myra guided them.

The wild pack was standing around the front of a store; shattered glass gleamed on the road. The deer lay on a display table, and blood dripped from its throat adding to the red pool already on the floor. Tork stood over the deer, a cloth, already soaked through with blood, wrapped around his hand.

"I should have put the cloth on my hand *before* I kilt the deer with that glass," he said.

But then they had their hands full, because Sheba, scenting blood, began backing away, and the cart began to twist sideways.

"Easy," Clare said. "Easy does it." She turned to the others. "If you want to load up the deer," she said, "you'll have to wipe off as much blood as you can."

"Okay," said Tork. "But first *I* got to stop bleeding. That glass just slices right through everything."

"Let me look," said Jem.

Clare couldn't see Tork's expression, but she heard Myra say, "Go on, let him look. He's no traitor."

Jem took Tork's hand in his own. The cut, Clare could see, was deep and gaping, and Jem bound it tight. "You'll carry the scar," he said. "And you need an antibiotic called penicillin. I'll get it for you at a pharmacy on the way back."

"Can you remember to take the medication ten days in a row?" asked Clare.

"I can do that," said Tork. "I've took medicine before. When I were little. My mom—" He fell silent.

They wiped as much blood as they could from the deer and then dragged it to the cart. Sheba was skittish, but didn't try to back away again.

"Meat tonight, meat tonight, meat tonight," the little ones sang.

"I am a *provider*!" yelled Tork. He waved his good hand in the air, his contemplative mood gone.

CLARE AND JEM got ready to leave early the next day, even though they had been up late feasting on venison. Myra stood and looked at them as they packed. Tork was crying.

They explained they had to rejoin their friends and about the quest for the Master.

"It's possible he's found a cure for Pest," said Jem. "And if he has, you'd all be safe. We could grow into one big family."

"If he has a cure, he has a price," said Tork. "Maybe we just ain't meant to grow up."

Clare put her arms around Myra and Tork, and suddenly it was a melee of hugs and tears.

"You belong here in the city, I guess," said Clare. "But we don't."

"You can come and join us whenever you want," said Jem. "I'll draw you a map before we leave."

"A map?" asked little Stuffo, as if Jem had casually mentioned building a surface-to-air missile.

"I can figure out a map, Stuffo," said Tork. Then he looked doubtfully at Jem. "But I would get Clare to help you make it if I was you. You know, so it's clear."

"You think Clare's more accurate?" asked Jem.

"She is with a shovel," said Tork, admiration in his voice.

It took Sheba a few moments to start moving. The wagon was loaded with as much as it could carry: flour, corn meal, cured meat, cheese, canned vegetables, sugar, salt, kerosene, batteries.

And then there was tea for Ramah, a feather mask from a costume shop for Bird Boy and model horses and books for Mirri and Sarai. It had taken Clare a while to find Abel a gift, but she had finally settled on a T-shirt that read: 'Happiness is a Rainbow.'

Sheba pulled into the harness with a will, and the cart slowly began to move. Clare and Jem walked beside the horse. The street they followed was broad and straight, and every time that Clare looked back, she could see the wild pack standing and watching them. Finally, as the road curved, Clare saw Tork and Myra put some young ones on their shoulders, and they all waved madly. Then they were gone.

AFTER BEING WITH the wild pack, the city was weirdly silent. On the flat, they found they could make good time. When they reached the hilly roads at the edge of the city, however, Sheba strained more and more at the harness. At the top of one of the hills, they had to stop to let Sheba rest and give her water. Going down was even harder than going up. Soon the terrain began to change. Brush grew into the road and there were houses instead of apartments, some of them perched precariously on the hills. As evening came in, they began to leave the houses behind. The road leveled out, and there were fewer obstacles.

Then suddenly Clare stopped walking.

"Jem," said Clare.

"What is it?"

"I don't feel very good."

Jem stepped back and looked at her. "What do you mean?"

"I feel weak, I have chills and my head aches."

"Why didn't you say so?"

"I just did."

Jem put his hand on her forehead.

"You're feverish," he said. Then he pulled her shirt away from her neck. He sighed with relief.

"No sign of Pest, though."

And then Clare was sick, right in front of Jem, right in a splotch of withered grass by the side of the road.

"Sorry," she said.

"We'll stop for the night. As long as it's not Pest, we can deal with it."

"Are you sure it's not Pest?"

"Sure."

"I can lie in the wagon, and we can keep moving."

Jem looked at her. "You'll puke on our provisions."

"Point taken."

Jem got her some water from a nearby stream, and then he unhitched Sheba, and they set up camp for the night. Jem boiled the water carefully before giving it to Clare.

"I'm going to hobble her and let her graze on the new grass for a bit," he said. He came over to Clare and gently brushed the hair back out of her face.

"I feel awful," said Clare.

"It isn't Pest," Jem repeated.

"Do you think it's the fever the wild pack talked about? That killed some of them?"

"You're not going to die. You didn't come through the first wave of Pest to die of some kind of stomach bug. I'll make you some soup. I'm betting that venison you were digging into at the feast last night was under-cooked."

"You're not sick."

"I didn't dig in with quite so much enthusiasm."

For the next few hours, Clare gave herself up to the fever and vomiting. Finally she slept for a little while.

"I feel better," she said when she woke.

"Really? You're the color of cheese."

"I'm not sure I'm ready for travel. Can we stay here tonight and start late tomorrow?"

"Sure."

Jem pulled the sleeping bags and mats out of the wagon; it was warm enough to sleep without the tent. Clare didn't feel like vomiting anymore, and when Jem put his hand on her forehead and then her throat, she didn't shiver.

"Your fever's broken," said Jem. "You're going to be fine."

"I told you I felt better."

"I'm glad it wasn't Pest," said Jem.

"I thought you were *certain* it wasn't Pest."

"Yeah, well. There wasn't much point in worrying you. I was worrying enough for both of us."

It took a while for Clare to get comfortable. First she burrowed deeply into the sleeping bag to stay warm. Then she overheated and tried lying halfway outside the bag, her arms behind her head.

"Are you through squirming?" asked Jem.

"Sorry."

She settled, and she realized how deeply tired she was. She looked up: the night was like velvet, and there was no moon.

Finally they lay side by side under the brilliantly starry sky.

"Jem?" Clare said.

"What?"

"I don't think there were ever this many stars before." She thought he would say something about the lack of air pollution or the clear air of the hills.

"Probably not," said Jem. "Probably not."

CHAPTER TWENTY-EIGHT
CHILDREN'S CHILDREN

THEY WALKED AND talked, and it was on that walk that she really began to know Jem. She was, in fact, so absorbed in their conversation that she didn't even particularly notice when they passed a body slouched by the side of the road. Both of them unconsciously gave it a wide berth. It was Bear who should have put Clare on the alert, but she was too busy listening to Jem to notice how he moved between her and the body, ears pricked, at the ready.

When the body lifted its head and stared at Clare with red-rimmed eyes, she had to stifle a scream.

"It's a Cured," said Jem quietly.

"Do we run?" asked Clare.

"We run."

Clare got Sheba into a shambling trot, but the Cured made no attempt to follow. He simply lowered his head again.

Sheba slowed to a walk. Jem put a hand on Clare's shoulder. "It's okay," he said. "Secretariat has out-run the Cured."

"He didn't look well," said Clare. "Maybe they're dying out."

"Even if they are, the world still won't be safe. As supplies get tight, we're going to have to do more than check behind people's ears before we trust them."

"You trusted Abel as quickly as I did. And Bird Boy. And Ramah."

"Ramah's pretty obviously all right."

"You have a crush on Ramah."

"Are you jealous?"

"Absolutely."

Clare smiled at Jem. And then it occurred to Clare that it was odd that the person she now trusted most in the world had been there in high school with her all along.

THAT NIGHT, CLARE was down in her dreams, struggling with something vast and evil, just as Beowulf had with Grendel, just as Perseus had with the sea monster, but she was only Clare and the thing was as large as the universe. She called out "Michael" and watched as the letters of his name trickled one by one into the void. She was suffocating and there was no one to rescue her.

Jem woke her up. They were squashed together in the tent that they had hastily put up the night before, when the weather had abruptly changed, and it had started to drizzle.

"You were having a bad dream," said Jem.

"Sorry if I woke you," she said.

"Clare—"

"What?"

"It's morning. Almost. And I have to go pee. That's all. I'll be right back."

Clare rolled up her sleeping bag. She had to pee, too. When they had all been travelling together it had astonished her how much waste four—and then six—people could produce. She didn't know why the old world hadn't been swimming—everywhere and all the time—in crap. Maybe it had been.

She put her rolled sleeping bag in the back of the tent. She had grown a little shy of Jem since he had turned fourteen. Thirteen, to her, didn't really seem to count. But fourteen—she thought back to the night she had curled up in Jem's bed with him, and it seemed long ago. It felt as if they had been a lot younger then. She remembered how warm he had been. His arms around her. And yet it had been odd being curled up together by the fire when they were staying with Tork and Myra. It was odd now, sleeping side-by-side—even if they were kept apart by separate sleeping bags. She couldn't say that such physical proximity was unpleasant—she was too close to Jem for that. But odd.

Jem and Clare sat in the warmth of the tent and ate granola bars. The flap was open, and they gazed out at a world that was rapidly being overtaken by nature.

"What flavor's yours?" asked Clare as she chewed.

"Don't talk with your mouth full," said Jem. "Chocolate banana."

"Chocolate banana granola?"

"Yeah."

"That's disgusting."

They finished eating. Clare pulled her knees up to her chin and wrapped her arms around her legs.

"You look like you're trying to disappear," said Jem.

"I wouldn't leave you alone. Otherwise, *poof.*"

Later, they passed farms and fields, and stopped at one horse farm to replenish the feed they'd already given to Sheba. The barn was silent, and the air was still. They found the granary with no difficulty, but not without first having to pass the body of a man hanging from a beam. A chair was overturned beneath him. Jem righted the chair, and they moved on.

WHEN THE FIRST three stars had appeared in the sky, they came across two delayed-onset children—a boy and a girl. They sat on a porch. They were, at first, so still that Clare and Jem almost went right by them. When one of them moved, even Sheba shied. And then the boy spoke.

"You're not Cured, are you?" The boy who spoke was maybe as old as seventeen.

"They're way too organized to be Cured, Sam," said the girl. "And they've got a horse. And a dog. I've never seen a Cured with animals."

Clare tried not to stare at the girl. Her shirt was cut low enough that Clare could see the dappling of the Pest rash, but that wasn't what caught her eye. The girl looked to be about fourteen. And she was very obviously pregnant.

She saw Clare looking at her.

"Two months to go," she said, and she actually smiled. "The baby's not Sam's—we got together after Pest. But he's going to be the father. I'm Becca."

Becca heaved herself out of chair with the help of Sam, who carefully took her arm.

"I'll get started on dinner," said Sam. "We have enough for all of us. For tonight, anyway. We don't get many visitors."

"We don't get *any* visitors," said Becca. "I hope you'll stay for the night?"

Becca spoke tentatively, and Clare suddenly realized that she was shy.

"We'd love to," said Jem. He and Clare exchanged a look.

"But after tonight," said Clare, "we're headed towards a place that may have the cure, and we're moving fast. Would you like to join with us? It's not just Jem and me. We're meeting up with others. You could come."

Both Sam and Becca smiled.

"That's kind," said Sam.

"But we're not going anywhere until after the baby," Becca said.

"It's still wonderful that you've found your way to us," said Sam. "I'll just go out back and send a chicken to its doom. Chicken's good for Becca. We found a book on what to expect when you're expecting, and it was pretty firm on what to eat."

They ate together in a small dining room. The wallpaper had a pattern of alternating daisies and cornflowers. Sam and Becca provided dinner—the chicken, potatoes, beets. In exchange, Jem and Clare gave them a bag of beans and some fine flour. Jem helped carry everything to the table, while Sam set out the dishes. Jem treated Becca as if she might break.

Sam and pregnant Becca. They would have to live a lifetime in a couple of years. Or less. And then, Clare thought, Becca would need to find another, younger, child to mother her child.

That night Clare and Jem shared the only other bedroom in the house. Jem slept in a sleeping bag on the floor. Clare had won the bed after a coin toss. But after Clare heard Jem tossing and turning on the hardwood floor, she pulled back the covers, pointedly. He climbed in next to her, sleeping bag and all. It had felt more odd to Clare having him on the floor than having him in the bed.

"Good night," she said.

"Good night," said Jem. There was a pause.

"What's going to happen to Becca?" Clare whispered to Jem.

"She'll do the best she can."

"But Sam must be only a few months from Pest. Maybe a year."

"I know."

"And Becca's just a baby herself."

"Go to sleep. You'll feel better. All this whispering is worse than my sister's slumber parties."

They hitched up Sheba at dawn. Bear stayed close to Clare.

"You really won't come with us?" Clare asked Sam and Becca.

"Becca and I are fine," said Sam. "We're going to be fine." And he put a hand on her round belly.

"You really could come with us to the Master's," said Clare. "Think of the difference it would make to your baby if there were a real cure."

"If Pest comes, it comes," said Sam. "But I don't really think it's going to come. We have to be immune, or we would be dead by now, don't you think?"

"Actually, Sam," said Clare. "I don't think so. I *don't* think we're immune."

He smiled at her indulgently. "Don't worry so much," he said. "I'm going to be here, and I'm going to take excellent care of

Becca both before and after the baby comes. I won't let her down by dying."

"Oh, Sam," said Clare.

But he just smiled and put his hand on her shoulder, as if to comfort her.

Clare could hear Becca saying goodbye to Jem. Becca laughed. "He's kicking," she said. "Want to feel?"

Jem put his hand on her belly gently. "Wow. When my cousin was going to have a baby, it never kicked this much. This is great."

Becca looked pleased. Sam went back to the porch, but Becca lingered.

"If you find the cure for Pest," she said to Jem, "come back."

"Why don't you let me show you our route?" Jem said to her. He pulled out the map, and they bent their heads together over it. Sam didn't seem interested.

Then it was time to move on. "Come and find us if you need to," said Jem.

"I will," said Becca. Then she paused. "*We* will."

"THEY DON'T BELIEVE they're infected," said Clare when the old farmhouse was behind them.

"*She* does," said Jem. "I can tell."

"Maybe they'll follow us."

"Strange to think about. A baby, I mean. I guess it's all starting over again. Still. Fourteen years old. My age."

"When you put it that way, it's kind of scary."

Jem seemed thoughtful, even sad, as they walked, and Clare saw him looking at her from time to time. She looked away. There were no words, but she understood.

The terrain had leveled out, and Sheba didn't have to work as hard. Her ears flicked back and forth as though she were listening to something none of them could hear.

MASTER

"I want to hunt them Cured, too," said Charlie.

"You haven't even been debriefed yet," said the Master. "You haven't met the other children properly. We need to know you before you go on this hunt."

"I bet I'd be good at killing them Cured. Undo me now."

"Debrief you."

"That. Then we'll hunt them Cured."

They had begun to sight the Cured more and more frequently. The Cured had pilfered from their stores, and one of them had approached a toddler, Ryan. Ryan was unhurt, but the Master thought it was just a matter of time before one of the children was taken or killed. All the children wanted to help with the hunt, although they had no real idea of what he had in mind. But this Charlie seemed like a canny child. A child who might prove useful. What in the Master's youth had been called a Forward Child. He was a new arrival, but he was eager, very eager.

"Give me the details of your past," said the Master. He sat back, prepared to hear yet another version of what was essentially the same story. Mother dead. Father dead. Sisters dead. Brothers dead. He had felt for a while now that debriefings were unnecessary, but he wanted to appear concerned, fatherly—and very much in charge. Besides, there was always the chance that he would hear something important. Because something was nagging at him; it was as if he had forgotten something; it was as if there were something he should know, but didn't, or something that was coming that he should be aware of. That unsettling feeling sometimes made him roam the woods at night. Then he would return, powerful in the thought that he was the most frightening thing out there.

"I come from the city," Charlie said.

"Go on. You're the first to come from the city."

"I heared you on radio, and I dint want to die of Pest."

"Quite right," said the Master. "Are there others coming?"

"Don't think so. There's kids there right enough. There's Tork and Myra who runs everybody. They ain't coming. But I dint want to get run by no kids anymore. Or get Pest, like the Connor kid did."

"One of them died?"

"Yeah."

"They should all have come with you."

"They likes it free," said Charlie. "They wouldn't have no room for grownups."

"You need to work on your grammar."

"Don't care, and I'm guessing you don't care neither. Not really."

"*Either*. Don't care *either*. And you're right. I don't."

"You're after something."

"But not anything you can think of. That's the beauty of it."

Charlie smiled. Maybe he understood more than the Master had thought. There it was again—a Forward Child.

The Master and Charlie were in the library with the overstuffed furniture and the ebony paneling. The room smelled like old furniture polish and the dust of a thousand books. Books lined an entire wall. The Master had investigated most of them. There were field guides to birds, plants, animals. Classics were displayed in old leather Victorian bindings. This was where Britta and Doug had found *David Copperfield* and *Middlemarch*. Britta was in a corner now, reading *Emma*. The Master didn't care what Britta overheard: Britta was to be trusted absolutely.

He liked to debrief the children here. He found that the room overawed them. Of course, they were always even more overawed by him.

The Master considered Charlie. He liked the idea of him, and the news about the children left in the city was useful. Those children would swell his numbers and, once at the mansion, they would soon fit in—and would then pose no outside threat to his authority. There would be useful ones among them—ones carrying those lovely recessive genes. And he could always use more children to tend the farm and clean the fountain and beat the dirt out of the tapestries that hung in some of the rooms. He wondered, since the offer of a cure from SitkaAZ13 hadn't been enough to bring them, what kind of incentive he could offer to these city children. Perhaps they would simply tire of playing at being adults.

He looked closely at Charlie, who was disheveled and needed a bath.

"Did they try and stop you from coming here?" the Master asked.

"Naw. They don't care none what a kid do. I could even have left more early and come with the ones what passed through. The girl what had the dog. And that boy what scairt me. But I thought they wasn't right for me. Thought they'd be here before me, though."

"Things happen," said the Master, wondering what might have happened.

"Things does. And them two made things happen."

"It's too bad you couldn't all come." The Master's thoughts were half with Charlie and half on the upcoming hunt.

"I almost dint come at all. And I tell you—I dint want to go with that girl and dog. That dog were scary. I nairt seen a dog so big."

The Master discounted some of what the children told him and sometimes—not often, but sometimes—by so doing he missed crucial bits of information—bits of information that could have changed everything.

This was one of those times. He simply didn't think much more about the boy and the girl and the dog. If they were coming to him, he would watch for them. That's all. After all, a girl. One never knew. He might need to find out a little more about her.

But had he drawn Charlie out on the subject, the entire trajectory of events might have been changed. He would have moved more quickly. And if he hadn't managed to get the girl to come with him alone, he would have been at the mansion when she arrived with the others.

"I'm glad you decided to join us," the Master said to Charlie. He decided that Charlie would, after all, be an appropriate participant in the hunt and sent him to the kitchen to get something to eat. Charlie may have had shallow brown eyes, but he had his uses too.

DOUG, CHARLIE AND Dante were the children who finally set out with the Master to hunt the Cured.

The going was hard at first. The Cured retreated in front of them, and soon they found themselves stumbling through the razor-sharp head-high grasses at the edge of a marsh. The Master could see the deserted nests of red-winged blackbirds, and he thought to himself that the marsh would be teeming with life come the spring.

As a child, he had once killed some songbirds and nailed them to the garage door. His ferocious blue-eyed Mama had hit him, and he had never done it again. Now he found he looked forward to seeing the black and red birds building their nests, keeping their tasty little eggs warm.

His mother had been wrong. There was nothing the matter with him.

They found the first Cured in the sparse trees, and he went down without a fight. One minute he was alive, the next, the Master had killed him. The Master itched to open his bag and take out his supplies and take off the creature's head.

But not, he finally thought, in front of the children.

They went deeper into the marsh. It was Dante who brought the second Cured to bay. By the time the Master caught up to them, this Cured had his back to a tree, and Dante faced it with his long knife pointed at the creature's throat. Doug and Charlie were nowhere to be seen, but the Master could hear sounds in the underbrush further on.

"Go ahead," said the Master.

Dante breathed heavily. The Cured was cringing, pale as a corpse; mucus came from its mouth and trailed into the scraggle of hair on its face. It was pathetic. The Master saw Dante hesitate. He started to lower the knife, and then he looked the Master full in the face.

"What if it has a soul?" he asked.

The Master didn't have time to answer because, at that moment, Doug and Charlie arrived. In a moment, the Cured was on the ground holding its hands in front of its face—but what Charlie lacked in grammar, he certainly made up for in enthusiasm. Doug and Dante did nothing; the coup de grace belonged to Charlie. The Cured died fast. But the Master was worried.

A soul?

It had never in a million years occurred to the Master that someone could entertain the idea of believing in the soul. A *soul*. It was far worse than believing in God; it was destructive; it was a kind of blasphemy. Surely children were taught better these days. Belief in a soul wasn't—scientific. He would have to watch Dante.

Now there was one Cured to go. A small one. Female. New to the territory. It was the Master who saw its trail, and he rushed ahead of the others even though he was soon out of breath. He didn't want to give Dante another chance to ask questions. Questions undermined authority, and authority was something he had sought all his life, attained, reveled in. He had been a leader in his field, a recognized pioneer who had, right before SitkaAZ13 rendered such things meaningless, received the MacArthur Fellowship. But this would convey nothing to the majority of the children. He had to earn his authority in other ways now.

He caught up with the small Cured at the top of a rise. It cowered against a stiff thicket of thorny bushes, and there were scrapes and tears on its arms from trying to get through them. Its face was in shadow, and its long hair covered its neck.

But he didn't have to look for the patch beneath her hair to know immediately that she wasn't actually a Cured at all. She was a healthy delayed onset child. He wondered about her mental stability—after all, she could have come to the mansion anytime; she must have seen the other children in the courtyard when she came up to the perimeter. He examined her more closely. She appeared to be all bones; a tangle of long hair covered her face. Then she reached out a hand and pushed back her hair to reveal strange wide eyes.

"Eliza," the Master said. "So here you are."

She didn't try to stop him as he leaned forward and gently put his hands over her mouth and nose.

She struggled, but only a little.

By the time the others arrived, she was unrecognizable.

The three they had hunted were dead. Charlie let out a whoop. Doug looked relieved.

Dante turned away.

CHAPTER TWENTY-NINE
SNOW

THEY TOOK THE turnoff for the reservoir and were at the water's edge almost immediately. A few ducks swam close to the shore, and a blue heron stood in the shallows. The water stretched beyond them, winking brightly like cut glass.

"I had no idea it would be so big," said Clare.

"The question is—where are the others?"

As they gazed out over the lake, there was a shout, and a small creature seemed to detach itself from a nearby wall.

It was Mirri.

She hugged Clare and gave a howl of victory before bursting into laughter. Then she hugged Jem for a long, long time.

Mirri led them into camp, where Sarai ran to them and clung first to Jem and then to Clare. Ramah stood and gave one of her rare smiles.

For Clare, seeing them all was as if the world had been born anew.

Bird Boy's greeting was exuberant. He danced around them and then hugged them until he started shedding feathers. Bear rubbed up against him and began the job of licking him all over.

"I thought you two were probably dead," Abel said, looking on happily.

Bear stayed close to Clare after greeting Bird Boy, and she noticed that the cold light of his yellow eyes had been replaced with a golden warmth.

It was later, as Clare and Jem were resting, and the others were putting together dinner, that Bird Boy approached them; he seemed profoundly uncomfortable.

"I'm supposed to talk to you," he said.

Clare drew back, fearing something awful had happened in their absence, and that the others hadn't wanted to break the news right away.

"What is it?" asked Jem.

"I'm supposed to tell you that you two stink."

"What?" blurted Clare. "After all we've been through—"

Bird Boy looked abashed, but Ramah stepped over to them to help him out.

"You're pretty ripe," she said. "To be truthful."

"Sarai used the word 'stink,'" said Bird Boy. "Abel's heated some water for you to wash with."

His tone was so mild that Jem and Clare couldn't take offence.

"We might have known," Jem said to Clare. "Sam and Becca must have noticed."

"If they did," said Clare, "they were very polite about it."

"Goats in the rain smell worse," said Ramah. "But goats are supposed to smell like goats. So it's not so bad. You two—well."

"All *right*," said Jem. "Bring on the water."

"Ramah also wants to boil your clothes," said Bird Boy.

Jem and Clare sheepishly went and began the process of re-civilizing themselves. After washing, Clare sat while Bird Boy combed through the mats in her hair.

"Whoo," he said. "There's some things here that'll have to come out."

Head lice. Jem and Clare both had head lice—and Clare remembered how she had seen nits while brushing Stuffo's hair. Ramah at least knew a cure for head lice: she soaked both of their heads with kerosene, let it set, and then washed it out. But she couldn't wash out the smell, and, for a long time, Jem and Clare left a wake of kerosene fumes behind them.

Finally they were ready for dinner. They all sat while Ramah ladled out venison stew, and Bird Boy pulled apart flat bread so that everyone had a hunk.

"Mirri and Sarai have something for you," said Ramah.

"What is it?" asked Jem.

"This," said Sarai. She and Mirri took out two wreaths from behind their backs and crowned Jem and Clare.

"Return the conquering heroes," said Ramah. All of them began stomping their feet and clapping their hands, and Bird Boy made loud whooping noises. Abel cheered. Jem grinned. But Clare couldn't help it: she burst into tears.

AT FIRST CLARE FELT that she wanted to stay and rest for a long time, but, really, when it came to it, leaving wasn't that difficult. Ramah had kept everything in readiness for departure, and they were excited about reaching the Master's.

"We're so very close to the cure," Jem said to Clare. "Sometimes I can't bear it."

"You're worried something might happen before we get there."

"Yes."

"I'm worried enough about it on my own. Don't add."

He didn't mention it again, but sometimes she caught him glancing at her, and there was anxiety in those muddy green eyes.

Sheba drew the wagon down the middle of the road. Runoff from a thaw had undermined the edges of the tarmac, making it dangerously unstable. Their second day back on the road, the temperature dropped. The grey sky lowered over them; Clare couldn't remember ever seeing clouds that looked so close to the earth. Soon snow came down in thick beautiful flakes that trapped themselves in her eyelashes and hair.

"We're going to have a snow day," said Mirri. But Clare moved closer to Jem.

"I don't like the way this looks," she said. "Those clouds are packed with snow." She was about to suggest setting up camp, when the wind picked up, and the flakes began to fly in their faces and make forward motion difficult.

And then the storm began in earnest.

In another twenty minutes, they were all holding onto the wagon for support.

And ten minutes after that, they were in the middle of a whiteout. Sheba came to a halt. Clare could see nothing except the part of the wagon she was holding. Moving up the wagon to get to Sheba's head, Clare found herself knocking into Jem.

"We have to keep Sheba going," he said.

"I'm on it."

The wind whipped the snow into her face, and her cheeks and nose were freezing. She called out to the others, but her words disappeared into the wind. She felt her way to Sheba's head and tried to pull her forward, but Sheba had lost momentum, and the wagon wouldn't move. Finally, Clare smacked Sheba on the rump. Sheba shied away for a moment and then strained to get the cart going. They were moving, but Clare had no idea where; she could only hope that they wouldn't go off the road or overturn the wagon in a ditch. They crawled across the landscape. Clare moved back along the wagon until she was with Jem again.

"We're going to have to stop and get them all under the wagon," she said. "There's nowhere to go. I can't see anything."

"Okay, gather them up."

At first, being under the wagon was a warm haven. They could see and hear again. Steam rose from their clothes as they huddled together, but soon the chill set in.

"I'm *cold*," said Mirri.

"We're going to freeze," said Abel. "I've seen stuff like this on television. Hypothermia sets in and then, after a while, you think you're warm. And then you die. You can tell when hypothermia's started, because you start to shiver. I'm shivering now. For example."

"We're not going to freeze," said Ramah with perfect calm.

"I *feel* like I'm freezing," said Mirri. "Why *won't* we?"

"Because if this doesn't let up very soon, we're going to drag the tarps down here," said Ramah. "Then we're going to drag out the sleeping bags and put them on the tarps and the other tarps over the sleeping bags. Then we're going to take our clothes off and crawl in, two to a bag. And we're going to release Sheba so she can find shelter."

"That's brilliant," said Jem.

"Do we really have to take our clothes off?" asked Abel.

"Yes," said Ramah. She looked at Bird Boy. "Including feathers. But don't forget to drag your clothes in with you, or they'll freeze."

The snow did not let up. Jem and Clare and Ramah went out from under the wagon and faced the blizzard. In a moment, Sheba was free. Clare gave her a tap to let her know she could go. As they heaved the tarps and the sleeping bags out of the wagon and to the ground, Sarai pulled them under the wagon.

"I'll get in with Mirri," said Clare to Ramah. "You share with Sarai."

Jem, on the other side of the wagon, was trying to zip two sleeping bags together. Abel and Bird Boy were fumbling at the zipper in an effort to help him.

"My hands are so cold," Jem said. "But we need room for three. Or someone's going to freeze."

"Use my back," said Clare.

"What?"

"Warm up your hands on my back. Hurry."

Jem's hands, Clare thought, well, Jem's hands were, not surprisingly, like ice. And they were larger than she expected, so that she gasped as he touched her.

"Sorry," he said.

And then he had turned from her and managed to zip the sleeping bags up. Sarai and Ramah were already in one sleeping bag, and Clare couldn't help but notice, as they had gotten in, how small and thin Ramah was. Then Mirri was in the other sleeping bag waiting for Clare, and Clare shed her clothes.

The sleeping bag was like a frozen block of fabric, and Mirri was all elbows and knees as she squirmed to get warm. Jem, Abel and Bird Boy were packed together in the double sleeping bag.

"How're you doing over there?" asked Jem.

"Peachy," said Clare. She was beginning to warm up. It helped that Bear was lying at the end of the sleeping bag.

"Peachy," echoed Mirri who, to Clare's relief, had stopped wriggling.

"Also peachy," said Sarai.

"I'm warm," said Ramah.

"I bet this is going to get *really* boring," said Mirri. Then she added,

"You have bigger boobs than I thought, Clare."

Jem laughed.

The storm went on for hours. Snow drifted around the wagon's wheels.

And then, as abruptly as it had started, the storm let up.

Clare felt as if she were in an ice cave. Not just icicles, but thin sheets of ice extended from the wagon to the ground. Beyond the sheets of ice were mounds of snow, so that sound was curiously muffled.

"How many snowflakes make a snow drift?" asked Sarai.

"A million," said Mirri.

They scrambled into their clothes while still in the sleeping bags. The sun was blinding as it glittered off the blanketed landscape. As they emerged from under the wagon, the snow came up to Clare's knees. The wagon now looked like part of the landscape, a mound among trees.

"I don't think we're on the road anymore," said Clare.

"We're lost," said Abel.

"The road can't be *far*," said Mirri.

"We need Sheba," said Ramah.

"We need the snow to melt," said Jem.

"Aren't you going to say anything?" Clare asked Bird Boy.

"No." He shook his head and the frozen feathers in his hair clinked together. They waded through the snow to the trees, where the snow wasn't so deep, although the sides of the trees were spattered with white. There were no tracks of any kind; if Sheba had been there, it had been before the snow got deep.

They spread out a little and kept walking. Soon the exertion had warmed Clare to the extent that she took off her outer jacket. Then she noticed an odd thing. Jem had his coat off, too. And Bird Boy was in his shirtsleeves.

They weren't warm solely because of the exertion. They were warm because the day was warm. Clare realized that she could hear the music of a thaw everywhere—the sound of water dripping, trickling, moving, flowing. And then she walked out of the wood and found herself standing on a patch with no snow at all on it, and before her was an open meadow. At the far end of the meadow, cropping the newly exposed grass, was Sheba.

Clare looked over her shoulder at the snowdrifts behind her.

"That was a *very* local storm," said Jem.

"It ends here," said Clare. "Who knows how far the storm reached in the other direction?"

The song of running water continued. Clare could hear snow plopping off the trees behind her.

"We'll get Sheba," said Mirri and started pulling Sarai by the hand.

"Well," said Clare. "Jem said we needed the snow to melt. It's melting."

"It'll take days for this amount of snow to melt," said Abel. "Weeks."

But he was wrong. By the time they caught Sheba it was easy to get to the wagon, and the snow that had seemed knee deep was now up to their ankles. By the time they had hitched up Sheba, they were squelching in grass and mud as rivulets of water ran over their shoes.

"It's *magic*," said Mirri.

"It's a meteorological finger," said Jem.

"What's that?"

"It's a place where the weather is different from anything around it."

"That *definitely* sounds like magic."

They hadn't strayed far from the road during the storm, and they must have made some forward progress as well, because all the landmarks looked different. Around the stump of a tree, tiny purple flowers were opening. A little way into the wood, Clare saw a bank of snowdrops. There was a slight rise in front of them, but after her rest, Sheba had no trouble pulling the wagon. When they reached the top, the whole countryside was spread out before them.

There were meadows and copses of trees and streams.

"It looks like the chess board in *Alice Through the Looking Glass*," said Jem.

"Do you know *everything* to do with chess, Jem?" asked Mirri.

"I'm a chess bore. I could talk about it for hours and hours and hours."

"But you don't," said Clare.

"I don't."

"See that house off the road?" said Clare. "We could go there to get dry, get some rest."

"We should just push through until we get to Master's," said Jem. "We can't afford to stop for every little thing, Clare."

"Everyone's tired," said Clare.

"I'm thinking of you."

"We wouldn't stay long."

"Let's do what Clare says," said Ramah. "I don't think we should arrive at Master's looking too needy. It puts us at a disadvantage."

Jem looked dubious.

"She's right," said Clare.

They made their way to the house. It had only one inhabitant, a man, dead, seated in a chair in the kitchen. Ramah dragged him out into the back garden, chair and all.

The real problem was where to sleep. It was easy enough to find a place for Sheba. They cleared out a potting shed, put a rope across the front where the door had been, blanketed Sheba and put her in. But when it came to the rest of them, things were more complicated. Clare, Jem, Sarai and Mirri were used to sleeping in the same room. Ramah was used to solitude. Bird Boy and Abel were going to share a room, but then, at the last minute, they all dragged mattresses into one bedroom. It seemed unlikely that there would be any Cured in such a rural area, but they felt safer together.

Before she went to bed, Clare gave Mirri and Sarai a kiss on the cheek. After a moment's thought, she gave Ramah a kiss, too. Then she kissed Bird Boy and Abel. She was about to crawl into bed, but, as if in an afterthought, she went over and kissed Jem. He kissed her back.

CHAPTER THIRTY
THE SWAMP

THE WHOLE AREA was dotted with fields and farms made fertile by the ancient soil left by what was now a small non descript river. Jem found a pair of binoculars in the house and he spent part of the morning scanning the countryside.

"You should do something useful," said Clare. "Feed Sheba. Help unload some of the supplies for breakfast or lunch or whatever meal it's time for."

"I'm thawing out my toes," he said, and continued to scan. Then he suddenly stopped.

"Look at this," he said. "Above the white house by the trees." Clare took the binoculars and gasped.

"Those are *sheep*," she said.

"And cows," added Jem.

"And *cows*," she said.

"You sound like Mirri. There's got to be someone there caring for them, and a Cured couldn't do it. A Cured might slaughter them, but I can't picture one taking care of anything."

At first, except for Ramah, the others didn't believe Clare and Jem. Abel was sure that they were seeing white boulders. But he was silenced when he looked through the binoculars and actually saw the boulders moving.

"We should go over there now," said Jem. "After all, it's on our way. And there could well be other children."

"Let's *stay* there for a while," said Mirri. "We can make friends with the children. And we can make friends with the *sheep*. Then we can herd the sheep to Master's. It'll be a *gift*, and—"

"You don't understand," said Jem. "We really don't know how much time we have before Pest comes. We're not *staying* anywhere."

But, as it turned out, it was very hard to leave.

They repacked the supplies they had taken from the cart, hitched up Sheba and set off, the horse swishing her tail discontentedly. Clare and Bear walked in front with Jem, who was carrying his hammer.

"Is this going to be *scary*?" asked Mirri.

"No," said Clare. "I've got a good feeling about this."

It took them the better part of the morning to get there. The house was a large ramshackle farmhouse with a barn in the back; the pasturage was huge.

"There's a *lamb* on that hill," said Mirri. Any fears she might have had vanished.

Jem knocked at the front door.

Nobody answered. Jem opened the door, and the familiar smell of something or someone rotting curled around them.

They found the body in one of the downstairs bedrooms. It was that of a young man, eighteen or maybe nineteen years old. There was no question as to how he had died: his neck was black and bloated with Pest; his face was contorted, and its skin was mottled and marked with open sores. Someone had pulled the sheet up to his chin and tucked the ends of the comforter under the bed. Someone had cared for this boy. Clare thought of her dead father.

And she was fairly certain, despite the distorted face, who the boy was, and who had cared for him. She pulled the sheet down a little and looked at the clothes to make sure.

"It's Rick," she said.

"Oh *no*," said Mirri. "Where's *Tilda*?"

Clare explained to the others about the visit of Rick and Noah and Tilda.

"He knew he was pushing his time," said Clare. "I don't understand why he's here."

"He was stupid," said Jem. "He should have pushed on to Master's."

"That's harsh," said Clare.

"It's not harsh," said Jem. "Rick knew better—he was right there when Noah died, and Noah was just a little older than *you*, Clare. We should be back on the road tomorrow."

"Maybe," said Clare.

"What we need right *now*," said Mirri, "is to have a *funeral*."

BEFORE THEY BURIED Rick, they stabled Sheba in the barn and searched the house for Tilda, in case she had heard them come in and was hiding. The house was like a rabbit warren, with passageways and unexpected rooms and additions to the original building. In the attic, a fine coat of dust covered the floor and motes danced in a beam of light that came in through a grubby window. Mirri opened a box on top of one of the trunks. It was filled with gold Krugerrands that she let slip between her fingers, laughing as they fell to the floor in a glittering drift of gold.

"Can I *have* them?" asked Mirri.

"Yes," said Jem.

"I want to be *rich*."

"You are rich," said Clare.

Mirri gave her a look. "Don't sound grownup. I mean rich with *money*."

Bird Boy opened one of the trunks and pulled out a pink feather boa.

"This color is wrong for feathers," he said. "Unless its flamencos."

"Flamingoes," Ramah said absently. She put the boa around his neck while she ferreted around some more in the trunk.

"Clothes," she said. "Shoes, photographs, papers. These things look as if they've been here a hundred years."

"What if the house's haunted?" asked Abel.

"It's not haunted," said Clare.

"I like it," said Bird Boy.

Next they explored the outbuildings beyond the barn, but there was still no sign of Tilda. Someone had left rabbit hutches open, but the rabbits were still there, feeding off the pellets in their bowls. Chickens and ducks had been released from their coops, but it looked as if they wouldn't be hard to round up. In the pasture, the cows, along with two calves, came right up to them, and Clare saw why. Their udders were swollen with milk.

"Anyone here know how to milk a cow?" asked Jem.

"Actually," said Clare. "I do."

"Get out of here."

THEY BURIED RICK in a shallow grave—the frozen ground wasn't far under the surface, making deep digging impossible. As they had with Noah, they put rocks over the freshly turned earth so that it wouldn't be disturbed.

Then Clare walked with Jem to the upper pasture, and they spoke together for a long time.

When they returned, Sarai came running for them.

"I couldn't find anyone," she said. "It's Mirri. You have to hurry."

"Mirri?" said Jem sharply. "What's the matter?"

"She's stuck in some kind of quicksand by the pond. We have to hurry."

Jem was the first to reach Mirri, even though Clare was usually faster. He waded into the mire and stopped when he could reach out and take Mirri's hands. Despite her shrieks, and Sarai's dire predictions, the marsh gave Mirri up easily.

"It's not quicksand," Jem explained when he and Mirri were on the bank again. "It's wet mud, but not, I think, deep enough to swallow you up. We won't, however, try the experiment." The swamp issued a few anaerobic burps, and the smell was a good old-fashioned stink, an innocent odor of fish and rotting vegetable matter. Clare breathed it in deeply. At spas, she knew, people paid for stinks like these.

But as they started back to the house, Mirri stopped and turned a white face to Jem.

"Something's *moving* on me," she said.

"Are you sure?" asked Jem.

"Where?" asked Clare.

Mirri patted her blouse, looking scared.

"I've got *lumps*," she said. "On my stomach. D'you think they're *death* lumps?"

"No, Mirri," said Clare. "I am sure you do not have death lumps."

"But there are *lumps* on my *stomach*. I'm probably *dying*."

Jem bent over Mirri and then stood in surprise. "Come here, Clare," he said. "There really are lumps."

Clare lifted Mirri's shirt. There were seven large black slippery objects on Mirri's stomach. They were the size of banana slugs. Her torso looked like a road map of blood.

"Leeches," said Clare.

"Don't try and pull them off," Jem said. "I bet Ramah will know what to do."

They ran back to the house where Ramah, who had been wondering where they all were, took in the situation.

"Salt," she said. Soon she was back with a box of iodized salt, which Jem poured liberally on the leeches. Clare told Mirri to close her eyes, worried that she might be queasy.

But it was Sarai who fainted. "I feel hot," she said and slumped to the floor.

"Put her head between her knees," Ramah said. "So her head's below her heart."

Then, as Sarai groggily came to, Ramah returned to Mirri. She and Clare brushed off the leeches, now loosened by the salt.

"They're gone," Clare said to Mirri. "They're all gone."

"How did you know about using the salt?" Jem asked Ramah.

"In *The African Queen* that's how Katherine Hepburn gets the leeches off Humphrey Bogart. It's the only movie I've seen."

"What about *SpongeBob SquarePants*?" asked Sarai. "Have you seen *SpongeBob SquarePants*?"

"No."

Sarai looked at Ramah as if she were from another planet.

Jem got the Bactine and some gauze and cleaned out the round mouth-wounds left by the leeches as best he could.

"There," he said to Mirri. "You're all set."

Mirri was irrepressible once more, and she went with Clare and Bear when they went out to the barn to feed the cows. The cows were contentedly chewing their hay, and Clare pulled the great barn door closed to keep out the sharp wind before turning to Mirri.

When she did, she noticed that Mirri seemed different somehow. She looked, in a way that Clare could not have quantified, healthier.

"Those leeches were *gross*," said Mirri.

"How do you feel now?" asked Clare.

"Actually," said Mirri. "I feel really good. In fact, I feel *terrific*. It's strange, but I don't remember feeling this good in a long time. I feel like I've been half *dead* for all these months. D'you know what I mean?"

But Clare didn't. Although, when it came right down to it, she couldn't remember the last time she'd been in the mood to do a cartwheel or a handspring or a back flip.

"I feel *alive*," said Mirri.

"You're absolutely glowing," said Clare.

PART THREE

CHAPTER THIRTY-ONE
LEAVING THYME HOUSE

LATER THAT EVENING Tilda walked out of the woods near the pond, pale, thin and wraithlike, like the spirit of a tree out of some old story. She had grown taller, and to Clare she seemed a lot older.

"I heard you come in," said Tilda. "But when I saw him"—she indicated Bird Boy—"I thought he might be a Cured."

Bird Boy gazed at her mildly. "Not a Cured," he said.

"Rick died four days ago," Tilda continued. "I tucked him in. For the long night. We didn't want to leave this place, and then it was too late. You'll see—life here is good. But you have to remember to leave. I saw Mirri and Sarai in the garden just now and decided to come and see them. In case they needed help. In case you and Jem were dead."

"Not dead," said Bird Boy. He looked upset.

"We're all right," said Clare. "For now."

"We're going to Master's," said Jem.

"That's what Rick said," said Tilda sadly.

They ate together and then went through the ritual of picking a bedroom. They moved in the mattresses, sleeping bags, comforters, sheets and pillows and unloaded a stock of the food supplies. Tilda made it clear she would be more than happy to sleep in the same room with them that night.

While the others went to help Tilda round up the chickens and ducks she had released when she saw them coming to the farm ("I didn't know who you were or how you'd treat them—I thought I should let them go"), Jem put the two packs he and Clare had been carrying against the wall.

Ramah was watching carefully.

Jem didn't seem to notice her gaze as he set about putting more food and fresh clothes in the knapsacks, but Clare found that she couldn't look Ramah in the eye.

"Were you thinking of leaving without me?" Ramah asked quietly.

Jem didn't look up. "Yes," he said. "You have more time than we do. And I'm not letting Clare go to Master's alone."

"When do you plan to go?" she asked. Jem still didn't look up.

"The day after tomorrow," said Clare. "We want to help you settle in. But Jem and I agree that we should check Master's place out before you and the others go. We know nothing about the set-up there. You'll stay and take care of the others until we come back for you. It won't be long, Ramah, and this looks like a good place; you'll all thrive here."

"The others will be all right without me," said Ramah. "Bird Boy would die for them." And she put her pack next to theirs, along with her bow.

"We don't know that Master is safe," said Jem. "The fewer who go, the better."

"We thought that two would be best," said Clare. "And we're the ones who most need the cure."

"I see," said Ramah. She was adding flat bread to her pack.

"You're not invited," Jem said quietly.

"You'll need me," said Ramah. "More than they'll need me here. I know it."

"I'm sorry, Ramah," said Jem. "We're the oldest. It's our risk to take."

Ramah sat back on her heels. "It's not the way it's supposed to happen," she said unhappily. "I'm supposed to go with you. I've dreamt it. It's not like the old days, when dreams didn't mean anything. You're going to need me before the end."

It was, perhaps, the longest speech Clare had heard from Ramah.

Clare had been dreaming, too. She dreamed of the flood of gold coins cascading out of the box and onto the floor of the attic. In the dream, Clare could pick them up, and they were like warm suns in the palm of her hand. They were so real that they were like the promise of a return.

Perhaps they should listen to Ramah's dreams.

As Clare was taking the radio to put into her pack, she turned it on. It was tuned to the Master's frequency.

"I am the master-of-the-situation. If you are alive, you are a child, and when you come of age, you will die of Pest. This is what the Pest rash means. But I can cure you. Come to me. North of Herne Wood near route I-80. North of Herne Wood near route I-80. I am the only adult left. I am the master-of-the-situation. If you are alive—"

The message cycled on and on. Clare turned the radio off. She realized that she had come to a decision.

"All right," she said to Ramah abruptly. "Come with us."

"Clare," protested Jem.

"When," asked Clare, "has Ramah ever wanted anything that wasn't good for us?"

JEM AND CLARE and Ramah woke early the next morning so that they would have the full day to help the others set out a routine for running the farm. And Clare took some time off to walk through the meadow that surrounded the garden and to sit on the big rock in its center. In the kitchen garden then she saw that herbs were already coming up—oregano, basil, mint, thyme. Perhaps it was a little early, but then the farm seemed to have its own weather patterns, and the days had been temperate and inviting. The earth was warm. Clare was glad that she and Jem were coming back, if only to get the others. Maybe, after the cure, they could come back to stay. She decided to call the house 'Thyme House.' The others followed her lead that day and called it Thyme House too. They named the house as if they could all stay there always, as if Clare and Jem weren't leaving the next day, as if there were no possibility of darkness waiting in the future.

Clare and Bear and Sarai took Bird Boy fishing on that last day. It seemed a good skill to have. Bird Boy caught an eighteen-inch trout in the deep pool by the creek, but he couldn't bring himself to kill it. It was Sarai who took it from him and hit it with a rock.

"It's dinner," she said.

"It was alive." Bird Boy was sheepish. He watched as Clare used her scaling knife to gut the fish. Bear ate the innards and then went to put his head in Bird Boy's lap. "You smell," said Bird Boy. But Bear didn't move, and soon Bird Boy was stroking him.

That evening, before eating Bird Boy's trout, Clare and Jem went back to the pond and sat and watched the ducks dipping their bills into the water for duckweed. Only when Clare saw Jem frowning at her did she remember they were going to leave the next day for the Master's.

Time's winged chariot hurrying near.

Tilda, who had spent some time at Thyme House, knew how to care for the animals. And Clare found packets of seeds in the house—tomatoes, peas, peppers, corn, squash, radishes—and left them with Sarai after telling her what to do and when to plant.

"You and Mirri manage the garden," she said. "And Tilda can help, too."

"But you'll be back *soon*," said Mirri.

"You'll be fine," Clare said. Mirri looked at her pleadingly. "And you're right. We'll be back soon."

Abel, astonishingly, turned out to be good at milking cows, once Clare showed him how. She was always to remember him sitting on a cow stool, the top of his head not even reaching the flank of the cow as he milked in a steady rhythm.

"Make sure they share tasks," Jem told Bird Boy.

And Clare saw Ramah take Bird Boy aside. Clare listened hard, wondering what Ramah would say, not minding the fact of the eavesdropping in the least.

"I'll be back," Ramah said to Bird Boy.

"You'll be back," said Bird Boy, but he didn't look convinced.

"Until then," she said. "You have to watch over all of them."

"Watch over them."

"If we don't come back—"

"You said that first. That you'd be back."

"If I'm wrong, don't go straight to Master. Find out about him."

"Okay."

"I love you, Bird Boy." Bird Boy was weeping.

Clare and Jem and Ramah set out the next morning after frightened goodbyes and frantic well-wishing—and with Mirri's last-minute gift of one of Sheba's spare horse-shoes. They would miss Sheba, but they were moving fast overland now, so that soon they would be at the Master's.

They left on May third, the day before Clare's sixteenth birthday.

They walked miles through hypnotically swishing waist-high grass. Maybe Clare was still in a kind of dream, or maybe neither Ramah nor Jem were there to steady her at the crucial second. But one moment she was crossing a stream on a fallen tree, and the next she slipped on the moss, her ankle gave out, and she fell. On her way down, she hit her head on a boulder in the water.

JEM DRAGGED HER out of the water and onto the bank, and, she was to remember vaguely later, pressed down on the wound on her head while swearing fluently, which was unlike Jem. She had swallowed water, and she was sick, and her head ached—and she wanted to sleep, but Jem wouldn't let her. She could feel that Ramah was there, too. But then even Jem couldn't keep her awake.

She didn't remember anything for some time after that. When she woke up, she was leaning against Jem, and he had his arms around her.

"Look at all that blood," Clare said. "Such a lot of it," she observed. "Where did it come from?"

"You," said Jem.

Clare lay down again.

Not much later, Jem leaned over her. "I think you have a concussion," he said. Clare was vaguely aware that Jem and Ramah had made camp, but, really, all she wanted to do was sleep. Jem kept rousing her back into consciousness, and she supposed he was worried about the concussion, but mostly she was annoyed at being awakened. The next afternoon she woke with a terrific headache and an ankle that looked like a puffball mushroom, only bigger.

The others were speaking as if she were still asleep.

"It looks broken," said Jem anxiously.

"It's just going to have to heal itself," said Ramah. "You can make a crutch to help her."

"We could go back," said Jem.

"No," said Ramah. "We have to get there. Pain is better than Pest."

"You think she's that close?"

"I dreamed something last night," said Ramah.

"What did you dream?"

"That we can't go back. For us it's only forward."

"That doesn't sound like dream-vision stuff. That sounds practical."

"Who says dream-visions aren't practical?" asked Ramah.

Ramah was sponging Clare's ankle with cool water from the stream when Clare finally opened her eyes. When she did, their eyes met.

"I can keep going," Clare said.

"How's your ankle?" Jem asked quickly.

"It hurts."

"You're sixteen now," he said. "You slept through your birthday."

"They aren't something to celebrate anymore."

Jem gave her some pills from the codeine they had liberated from the gold house, but Clare didn't like the feeling they gave her.

"The pills help the ankle," she said, "but they make me feel as if I have cotton wool in my head."

"Don't be such a baby. You're just lucky I managed to fish you out."

"Thank you," said Clare. She hadn't thought any thanks were needed. Of course Jem had saved her life. Of course.

THAT NIGHT CLARE dreamed of Robin. Robin was saying to her, very earnestly, "It's not Michael, Clare. It's not Michael at all. Wake up."

Clare woke up. The tent was dark and still except for the soft sound of breathing, but she could make out Jem's form near her. She knew that the dream-Robin was trying to tell her something, but she wasn't sure what. Something about Michael. She hugged his varsity jacket to her. She had thought her heart was a shrine, and all of that, but sometimes Michael seemed a world and a lifetime away. Lazily she wondered what it was she was supposed to wake up to. Jem murmured in his sleep, and Clare kept very quiet.

Whatever it meant, Clare couldn't say the dream had been a nightmare— not at all. And it had been nice to see Robin again.

CHAPTER THIRTY-TWO
TEMPTATION

By day, Clare limped and leaned heavily on the crutch Jem made for her. When she slept, she made sure to keep her ankle elevated and this, thankfully, alleviated much of the swelling. They decided then that it was sprained not broken. After a while, the days became easier. Though Clare was punishing her ankle, it was getting better in spite of her.

As Clare healed, their resolution became more firm: they were going to reach the Master's; they were going to get the cure if there was a cure to be had, and they were going to take it back to Thyme House.

One evening, while Ramah was collecting wood for a fire, Clare and Jem sat on a boulder near the copse of trees they were camped under. A sea of ferns spread out from the rock. The moon glowed on the ferns, and the wind rippled through them. It looked as if a giant hand were stroking fur against the nap.

"You miss Thyme House," said Jem.

"Don't you?" asked Clare.

"Some. But we're together. And that's good."

Clare dipped her feet into the ferns as if testing the waters of the ocean. The leaves tickled her legs. "I feel like we met a long time ago," said Clare. "Like we've been friends forever."

"You should have seen yourself when we first met. You looked like death. No offense, but you smelled a little like death, too."

"I was a mess. Now I'm not such a mess, but I can't walk without a stick."

"Now you smell like rosemary and mint. Like the herb garden at Thyme House."

"Beats death."

Jem got down off the rock and gave his hand to Clare to help her down. The grass beyond the ferns was damp, and they walked through it back to the camp, where Ramah was waiting for them.

The next day dawned bright and glorious, and, as they walked, Bear rushed into the grass ahead of her, flushed a pheasant out of the underbrush and went streaking after it.

"Good news," said Clare. "Nobody's here to shoot the pheasant."

"Bad news?" asked Jem.

"I think it's going to be Bear's lunch." But, to her surprise, the pheasant took quickly to the sky, leaving Bear behind, a black dot against the ripe gold landscape.

When they reached a hill, conversation stopped for a while. A butterfly alighted on Ramah's pack. Bear panted, his pink and black tongue lolling. The light flickered through the trees.

Clare thought of Thyme House, and she thought of the deep past, when she had been needy and lonely. Such a very long time ago.

That day they camped away from the road in the center of a ring of trees. Small yellow flowers glowed against the moss at the base of the trees and reminded Clare of the gold coins they'd found in the attic of Thyme House. As evening came in, they built a small fire, for comfort as much as for anything else, because the nights were no longer so cold. Clare heated up some food, and they all ate well. Then the three of them crawled into the tent, as, overhead, the Big Bear, the Little Bear, Gemini and Virgo wheeled in the sky.

CLARE WOKE IN the dark with a start. Bear was asleep at her feet. She carefully unzipped the flap and looked out, and at once Bear was up and by her side, but Clare stopped him with a gesture. Deep in his throat, he growled.

She saw the figure of a man sitting by the fire. He was warming his hands, and, as the orange coals flared up, she could see he was smiling. He didn't behave like a Cured, but he was old. Clare thought that maybe he was fifty—more than twenty years older than any age a delayed-onset could hope to reach. She was glad Bear was with her. His reaction was the only thing that made her think she probably wasn't dreaming the man. Even so, she wasn't certain. She could, after all, be dreaming Bear too.

Clare looked from Bear to the man, then she sent Bear to the end of the sleeping bag and whispered "down." After all, if she so much as breathed distress he would come crashing through the tent's netting to save her. She went outside as quietly as she could.

"I was waiting for you to wake up," he said. "Your dog wouldn't come over and keep me company."

"He doesn't like strangers," said Clare.

"He didn't mind my watching you make camp. He didn't give me away, and I think that's a good sign, don't you?"

"I don't know. I don't know what you might have done to him."

"You think I drugged your dog? You think I hypnotized your dog? I've always gotten along well with dogs. And other animals. As long as they understand the rules."

"I should wake the others." Clare wondered why she hadn't done so already. She almost called Bear right then, but the man was so very old. She wanted to hear his story.

"But I want to meet *you*," he said. It was as if he could read her mind. Clare went out and sat on the ground across the fire from what was surely the oldest man in the world. His face bore no signs of Pest, but it was a worn face; it was a face, Clare thought, that had seen many things. He wore jeans and a shirt that was buttoned up tightly against the cool night air.

"Why me?" asked Clare.

"I've heard of you and your dog. I received a full description," he said. "One of my children talked about you."

"You have children?"

"Have you been travelling long?" he asked. And Clare didn't mind the change in direction the conversation was taking. Rather than hear his story, she found herself wanting to tell him everything. But somehow she didn't think that telling him would be a good idea.

Bear, she noted, had left the end of her sleeping bag and was standing at the flap of the tent. His eyes glowed in the firelight.

"A lot of things have happened," she said. "We've been different places."

"What place are you thinking about now?"

"Home."

"Thyme House," he said.

"How did you know?"

"I heard you talking as you were setting up camp."

"You eavesdropped."

"I consider these woods mine. So I suppose the conversations in them are mine, too."

"What about you? Who are you?"

"A traveler. And I've got something to offer you."

"I don't think that's true."

"As we speak, the Cured are moving into the countryside and destroying what they find. Your Thyme House will eventually perish, long before the time comes when the patches fail and the Cured die."

"You know about the patches?"

"Of course. I know about a lot of things. But here's my offer: I know that if you come with me, tonight, now, we *will* get the real cure, and you *will* see Thyme House again."

"I'd have to talk it over with the others."

"I don't mean the others. I'm not interested in the others, although you can give them the cure if you want. Just come with me and everything will be all right."

Everything will be all right. When Clare had been a child, her real mother had always told her that. But then her mother had died.

"And if I don't come with you?"

"Then we'll meet later, anyway," he said finally.

Clare thought of what would happen if she left now, in the night. Jem and Ramah would wait for her as she had once waited for Robin. "How do you know that everything will turn out all right if I come with you?"

"You'll have to trust me."

"I need to get my pack out of the tent."

"No," he said. "Leave your pack. You need to come with me now."

"Not without Bear," she said, and suddenly she became acutely aware that they had somehow moved from a discussion of whether or not she would leave (how did they get there?) to a discussion of what she could take with her.

"All right," he said. "The dog can come."

"You're not a Cured?"

"I'm not."

"Are you the Master?"

"Of course I'm the Master."

At that moment, Jem called out in his sleep, "Clare."

His voice brought her back to the moment. The fire was almost out; the glamour that had hung around the man was gone.

At that moment his game seemed perfectly obvious to her.

"I won't make them wait for me; I won't scare them like that," she said.

The man stood. From the opening of the tent, Bear growled, an echo to Clare's thoughts.

"You've made an interesting choice," said the man as he moved towards the trees. And then he was out of sight.

Clare sat by the embers. The memory of the man was fast disappearing into the world of dreams.

But the dream had been a strong one, and she realized that the apparition had been infinitely more powerful than she was. But she thought she had finally won their little game. It was true that the stranger was older, stronger, and, perhaps, wiser. But then she remembered in some corner of her mind that the battle is not always to the strong, nor the race to the swift. Time and chance come along and screw with everything.

CHAPTER THIRTY-THREE
HEAVEN

THEY KNEW THEY were close when they reached the gardens— beautiful gardens that seemed to serve no useful purpose whatsoever. A profusion of flowers tumbled together in a jumble of colors—Clare made out yellow daffodils and purple irises. There were no vegetables, no herbs and no weeds. Not one.

Following the path, they turned a corner to see a child not far from them chopping at the dirt with a hoe. Nearby, they spotted two more children trying to pull along a goat. The goat head-butted the girl leading it, and she turned and smacked it on the rump.

"Children," said Clare. "I can't believe they're real."

The goat head-butted the girl again, and she let out a cry.

"They're real," said Jem.

At that moment, the children with the goat stopped and stared, and the child with a hoe stood and looked at them.

"Let's talk to the one with the hoe first," said Ramah. "The ones with the goat look older."

"Maybe we should talk to the older ones first," said Jem.

"No." Ramah was seldom this firm.

"Why?"

"Little kids aren't as easy to brainwash as adolescents," she said. "The Emperor's New Clothes. And all that."

"You know about some weird things, Ramah," said Jem.

As they approached the little boy, he raised his hoe, alarmed.

"You can put down your hoe," said Jem. "We're not Cured."

The boy's look of fear was replaced by a sheepish grin.

"Sorry," he said. "In that case, I'm supposed to say that you're welcome here and to go ahead to Master."

"Where is the Master?" asked Clare.

"Just keep going. Straight ahead, beyond Britta and Doug—the ones wrestling the goat, you'll come to the gate."

"Who are you?" asked Clare.

"My name's Dante."

"Like the poet?"

"Like the poet. My father's choice." He leaned forward to rest on his hoe, and Clare could see the sprinkling of red freckles on his chest.

"You still have the Pest rash," she said. "Does it stay even after the cure?"

"I'm not cured yet," said Dante before turning away from them.

The older children struggling with the goat barely acknowledged them.

"We'll see you inside," said the one Dante had called Britta, and then she got behind the goat and started to push. Doug got in front and pulled. The goat didn't move.

"Try scratching it under the chin for a while," said Ramah.

"Thanks," said Doug and then ignored her advice.

Clare, Jem and Ramah walked on.

"Dante seemed nice," said Clare finally.

"The word 'nice' doesn't mean anything," said Jem.

"Well. The two with the goat *didn't* seem particularly nice."

"Point taken."

"So I can use the word 'nice?'"

"No."

"Sorry to interrupt," said Ramah. "But we need a plan."

"We don't get separated," said Jem. "We act all innocent."

"We *are* all innocent," said Ramah. "That's what bothers me."

Then the gate was in front of them, set in a formidable wall of stone. Jem gave it a push, and it swung open.

Inside, the landscape was lush. The thick grass was carefully clipped. There was a pond with a fountain bubbling in the center. Three ducks waddled over the grass, and a peacock cocked its head at a peahen and spread his tail. Clare thought of Bird Boy: he would have been ecstatic.

The peacock saw them and screeched.

Beyond the rolling lush lawns and gardens stood a mansion, its windows glittering in the sun. Someone, apparently, had decided to build an English manor in the rural United States.

"This makes Thyme House look like a run-down farm," said Clare.

"Thyme House *is* a run-down farm," said Jem. "But we still love it."

Clare had expected something quite different. She had pictured children fighting for survival, scavenging and hoarding food, not weeding ornamental gardens. This looked like nothing less than Paradise.

She idly wondered about the location of the snake. But mostly she was thinking about whether or not there might be warm water for bathing. She had a momentary fantasy about washing her hair in a hot shower.

They turned a corner, and Clare was startled. She automatically took Jem's hand. There must have been twenty-five children in front of her—and they were actually playing. A game of foursquare was going on in the corner of the courtyard; two small children were chalking out a place for hopscotch; other games involved a lot of running and some hiding and much laughter.

When the children in the courtyard caught sight of them, they began to crowd around. Most of them were younger than Ramah. Where Clare could see throat or chest, she saw the Pest rash.

"New ones!"

"You're welcome here."

"Someone get Britta."

"What's it like out there now?" asked a girl, but she was shushed.

An unnaturally beautiful little girl with a heart-shaped face and a long braid reached out and touched Ramah, who drew back.

"Sorry," the little girl said. "But we haven't had new ones in a while."

At that moment, Britta and Doug, along with the goat, arrived out of breath. The effect was instantaneous. The children stopped playing.

"It's still recess," said a wispy little girl. "You said we could play."

"It's all right," said Doug. "But one of you get the goat back to the barn."

Britta looked at Jem, Ramah and Clare as if she found them less than interesting. Clare stood up straight and let go of Jem's hand. Letting go, she realized how hard she had been holding on to him.

"You seem to be in charge," said Jem.

"Until Master's back," said Britta.

Doug, oddly, eagerly, looked hard at Clare.

"You're staring, Doug," said Britta. She sounded haughty. "It's rude." Clare rather hoped that the goat had kicked her.

"It looks like you came just in time," said one of the younger ones. She tossed her head, and her tight braid flipped onto her shoulder. Clare was suddenly reminded of Laura Sparks, Michael's girlfriend from long ago. She also noted how very clean the group of the Master's children looked. There were a lot of shiny faces and a lot of just-washed hair. The fantasy of a hot shower returned. Then Dante came in the gate, still carrying his hoe. His shirt was smudged with soil and pollen and grass stains, and his face was dirty. He smiled at them, but Britta snapped at him.

"Go get cleaned up. You're filthy." Dante fled.

Then Britta led them into the mansion. "We'll give you your rooms now," she said. "Work assignments come whenever Master gets back. We'll heat water for you—we only take two bucket hot showers here usually, but I'm going to tell Fran to give you three buckets. You look like you need it."

"A hot shower," said Clare.

"Don't get ready to sell your soul yet," said Jem.

"Finally," said Britta, "don't go prowling about on your own. You'll just get lost."

"No prowling," said Jem.

"You're part of the Ingathering now," said Britta. "That's a good thing."

"'Ingathering,'" murmured Ramah.

"When Master gets back, he'll have a few questions for you. But while he's gone, I sort you out. I find out who you are, or were, and then I decide how you'll fit in."

Clare raised an eyebrow at Jem. Ramah sighed.

While they waited for Fran, Britta questioned them, and the story of their journey began to emerge. Clare noticed how careful Jem was to leave certain things out. He never mentioned Mirri and Sarai. He even left out Sheba.

The rooms were the real issue. Britta insisted that they be separated.

"Just during sleeping hours," said Doug. He glanced at Britta, and she nodded.

"I don't think so," said Clare.

"The rules of Ingathering are for everyone," said Britta.

"'Ingathering' again," said Ramah under her breath.

"You need us." Britta's tone was icy.

"You need us, too," said Ramah. "I just haven't figured out why."

"I don't know, Britta," said Doug. "What harm could it do if they share a room?"

"We're not having sex," Ramah said coolly. "If that's the problem."

Clare was embarrassed, and Jem blushed so very deeply that she worried for a moment that he was ill.

"It isn't worth arguing," said Britta. "Doug, get Fran and tell her to hurry. She'll get them settled. We have to monitor the others."

"'Monitor,'" sighed Ramah.

When Fran arrived, Clare saw that she was the sharp-faced girl who had reminded her of Laura Sparks.

"Put them in the tapestry room on the second floor," said Britta. "It's plenty big for three. But no dog."

"That won't work," said Clare.

Bear walked up to Britta, and Britta backed up very quickly as he tried to sniff her.

"Then take the dog," she said. "But Master'll want it leashed."

Fran led them up a staircase with a peculiar banister: at its base, the wood was sculpted into a leering gargoyle; at the top, it ended in the face of a man with vines coming out of his mouth.

"The green man," said Clare.

Fran took them part way down a long hall.

"Here you are," she said. "Get settled in and get cleaned up. The bathroom's first door on the left. Come down in a couple of hours for dinner, if not before. Everyone's going to want to hear your story." Then she left.

Forty minutes later, the three of them were clean and warm. The hot three-bucket shower had been magnificent, and Clare had washed her hair with real shampoo.

They explored their room. Two tapestries hung on the wall. The titles were underneath: 'Diana and the Hunt' and 'A Royal Picnic.' Clare looked closely at the Diana, but she seemed a little solid for the part. Ramah would have been an infinitely better model for the weaver.

Jem lifted the tapestries and looked behind.

"This isn't *The Secret Garden*," said Clare. "You're not going to find a door."

"Maybe not," said Jem. "But you do have to admit, this place looks like something out of *The Secret Garden*."

There was a big four-poster bed with a canopy and a smaller bed with a sleigh headboard on which was painted a tiny sailing ship in a stormy sea. They were near the top of the house, and the window looked out over a great green lawn.

"Let's take a look around before we go down," said Jem.

"I think that counts as prowling," Clare said.

"Yes. Let's prowl. If we run into Britta, we'll say we're lost."

"I vote for prowling, too," said Ramah.

"I just hope we don't find anything awful," said Clare, "before I have another shower."

They wandered down the hallways and tried the doors they came to. All were unlocked. Most of them led to bedrooms of no interest.

"They're not big on personal belongings," said Ramah. "Have you noticed? No photos. No jewelry."

While they were exploring the upper rooms, they ran into Dante. His hair was wet, and he had changed his clothes.

"Hello," he said. "I'm clean."

"We're looking for skeletons in closets," said Jem.

"You won't find any," said Dante. He hesitated. "But can I help you look? Britta never lets us poke around."

They found linen closets, and closets filled with mops and brooms, and chests full of blankets and quilts and rooms full of old pieces of furniture. One room had a sewing machine in it with a supply of sewing equipment: scissors, straight pins, bobbins, knitting needles and plenty of things that Clare couldn't put a name to.

"Kelly would have loved this," said Dante. "Kelly was my mother. She knew how to sew. She made quilts."

They tried more doors, but, except for the occasional tapestry or painting, the rooms were uniformly dull.

"Ramah's right," said Jem. "There should be more personal stuff. I thought the house would be full of stuffed animals and mementos of parents and things like that."

"'The old world's gone,'" said Dante. "'The past is dead.'"

"You're quoting someone," said Clare.

"Master."

"Look," said Clare. "We just want to get the cure and leave. That's all. We want to go home."

"You'll have to talk to Master," said Dante.

THE UPPER FLOORS of the house were light and airy. Clare could smell beeswax and polish and pine. The atmosphere was hushed.

"Let's keep prowling," said Jem.

Finally they found a door that was locked. It was low and uninviting and painted an ugly yellow.

"Maybe we shouldn't do this," said Dante. He suddenly seemed nervous, less confident, younger.

Jem pushed at the door, but it didn't give way. Ramah finally spoke up.

"I'm going back to the sewing room," she said. "It has what I need."

Ramah returned and picked the lock neatly with a bent pin and a narrow knitting needle. Clare had the curious sensation that they were doing something very much against the will of the place itself. The corridors didn't seem so airy now; the house seemed to close around them.

Then the door swung open.

"That's excellent," said Clare to Ramah. "Any other special skills?"

"Oh, yes."

Windows lined one side of the room, and the light was so bright that they had to squint. Jem quickly closed the door behind them. From the windows, they could see the Master's entire domain— from the fountain in the courtyard to a small pond behind the gardens. Beyond that were rolling hills. On the floor of the room, piles of books had apparently spilled over from a small bookcase.

Clare leafed through them. Some of the titles were familiar to her: *Great Expectations*, *Lolita*, *The Screwtape Letters*. Then there were textbooks on medicine and psychology. She opened one of the medical texts and found that, at the top of the first page, someone had written 'SYLVER.' She showed the others.

"That's what's written on the Cure patch," said Jem to Dante. "What's it doing here?"

But Dante didn't know.

At the other end of the room was a wooden angel that looked as if it had stepped out of the fourteenth century. The angel's face was painted, and the rest was covered with gilt. It stood with wings folded, as if it had been caught at a moment of rest. At the foot of the angel was a small box.

"Maybe we shouldn't have come in here," said Dante.

Ramah, with one finger, lifted the lid.

Photographs.

There were hundreds of them, and all of them were of children. Some of the children were in a playground; they were caught forever in a moment on the teeter-totter, frozen going down slides, stopped in the arc of a swing. Ramah examined one carefully.

"It's a close-up," she said. "But these children aren't looking into the camera."

Jem shuffled through the photographs again, taking a moment to look at each one. Then he put them down.

"What?" asked Clare.

"It's just that they all have blue eyes," said Jem. "The photographs focus on their eyes. Sometimes the eyes are all you can see clearly."

"I don't like this," said Ramah.

Clare, still under the influence of the hot shower, wasn't ready to be suspicious yet.

"They're just photographs," she said.

Dante nodded in agreement.

Then Clare turned away and found herself staring into the eyes of the angel. The eyes had been painted a pale blue. They gazed out at the room as if nothing in the world could disturb the angel's rest, as if everything in the universe had been weighed and measured and dismissed. At the base of the statue was the word 'SYLVER.' Clare couldn't understand the expression on the angel's face at first, and then she realized that it was all in those eyes: blank, flat, perfectly indifferent. There was no room in those eyes for sentiment or affection or love.

She had found the snake.

CHAPTER THIRTY-FOUR
HELL

INITIALLY THERE WERE four tables at dinner, but Doug and Britta found another for Jem, Clare and Ramah. Bear went under the table and lay down. Dante, as soon as he entered the room, came and sat with them. Each of the other tables was headed by an older child. Clare picked up a fork and put it down again when she noticed that nobody had begun eating. Then Britta delivered the observation: "We are Master's children," to which all the others replied, "Each of us is his."

"Creepy," Ramah whispered.

"But grammatically correct," said Clare.

"I hope the Master has the cure," said Jem. "Because this is over the top, and I want to go home."

They ate pasta and salad. Bear slept at Clare's feet after refusing the scraps that she tried to give him. He was going to have to go hunting soon. As the meal began to draw to a close, Clare said, "I need to let Bear out."

"I'll tell Britta," said Dante. He returned a moment later. "It's okay," he said. "I get to be your escort."

"Do you check with her about everything?" Jem asked.

"Only when Master's not here."

"You don't look very happy," said Clare.

"She's kind of bossy."

Outside, the sun was setting. The evening air was cool. The moon, almost full, was rising; it looked enormous, as if it were resting on top of the trees. The night scent from the garden filled the air, and Clare noticed a bed of strange white flowers, wide open as if they were soaking up the moonlight.

"I spent a lot of nights like this hiding from the Cured," said Dante. "I was always afraid they'd find me in the moonlight."

"Where do you come from?" asked Ramah.

"Half way across the country. I walked here, mostly. The Cured were everywhere in the cities. I didn't sleep much. Not really."

"Maybe you should go inside," said Clare.

"No. I'll wait. I *like* you."

As soon as Clare gave Bear the signal, he galloped through the lush grass, perhaps in pursuit of a rabbit, or following the scent of a pheasant, or, Clare thought, just for the joy of it. Then, out of nowhere, a long wail split open the night. Bear raced to Clare's side. Then Jem was at her other side with Ramah close behind.

"It's a Cured," said Dante. "Master got rid of three of them, but now two more are in the territory. Sometimes, at night, they come right up to the perimeter. We don't see them during the day."

"Do they speak to you?" asked Clare. She thought of Dinah.

"They make noises. That's all."

When they re-entered the dining hall, all faces turned to them.

"Tell us your story," said one of the younger girls. And so Jem did, embellishing where it seemed harmless and still leaving out significant pieces of information.

"Tell us about before Pest," said a small boy with deep brown eyes.

"Don't you remember?" asked Clare, but he shook his head.

And so Clare talked about her life before Pest. The children were especially excited to learn that Clare had been a cheerleader, and they pulled back the tables so that she could do a cartwheel. Her ankle felt fine, so she did a back flip as well.

"Lordy," said Jem when she was done. "It's like being at a pep rally."

"Did you have pom-poms?" asked a young girl.

Clare assured them that she had had pom-poms.

Jem laughed.

It was late before Britta and Doug sent the children to their rooms. Clare felt a hand on her arm as one of the children passed by on her way to bed.

"I wanted to make sure you're real," she said.

Clare, Jem and Ramah went back to the tapestry room and started getting ready for the night. Clare and Ramah would share the big bed.

There was a scratching noise at the door. Jem opened it, and Dante entered the room and stood awkwardly. Jem motioned him to the small bed.

Dante sat and looked profoundly uncomfortable.

"I've been holding back," he said finally.

"Spit it out," said Clare. Bear padded over to her and sat at her feet.

"Master will want you to stay." Dante looked unhappy.

"There's something else too," said Ramah. "Isn't there?"

"This place is a sanctuary. It's the only loving home any of us is ever likely to see. You can't forget that."

"You must be leaving out something pretty bad," observed Ramah.

"It's just that the way things work here might sound peculiar to a newcomer."

"Try us," said Jem.

Dante looked troubled. "Being cured isn't the main point," he said. "Master's cured, of course. And he'll cure those who are close to Pest. At least," Dante hesitated, "he promises that. To the new children."

"Just how many children has he actually cured?" asked Ramah.

"Actually," said Dante. "None. He has another, bigger project."

"A project bigger than the cure for Pest?" Clare sounded doubtful.

"I don't think you three are going to like this."

"We're waiting," said Clare.

Dante stood up and walked to the window. He turned back to them, his face miserable.

"Don't get mad," he said.

"No guarantees," said Ramah.

Dante crossed the room and sat on the little bed again. He looked down at his hands.

"Master's going to start the world over again," said Dante. "He's going to match us up—the special ones, anyway—and then—and then we'll have babies. And then we'll fill the gaps that Pest has left."

Clare looked at Dante, appalled.

"He calls it his 'brave new world.' That's from *The Tempest*. By William Shakespeare."

"That's very edifying," said Clare. "Thank you."

"We're not sure who he's going to match first," Dante said. He looked at their expressions. "It's not weird. Not when you think about it. No weirder than Pest."

"And what does the Master get out of this?" asked Ramah.

"He gets what we all get," said Dante quietly. "A world with people in it. He thinks we don't have the luxury—that's what he said, the 'luxury'—of waiting until we've grown up to start the world over. Sometimes, to those of us who've been here a while, he stops talking about the cure."

"That's—" Jem seemed at a loss for words.

"That's interesting," said Ramah. "Even though it's not quite what I thought was going on here. Still."

"I hope you'll decide to stay on," said Dante hopefully.

Clare didn't know how to convey to him that their staying under those circumstances was an impossibility beyond impossibilities.

"I should just set Bear on you," she said finally.

"No," he said. "Please don't."

"We need to look around some more," Jem said. "This place has secrets. Like those photographs."

"We've looked at the upper floors," said Clare. There was a silence.

"Do you have a basement?" asked Ramah.

Dante blanched.

Clare thought of the basement of the gold house that they had explored in Fallon. Of the terrible smell of decay underlying everything. Of descents into Hell.

"What's the matter?" Jem asked Dante.

"We're not allowed in the basement."

"Make an exception."

"There aren't any. Exceptions."

"Dante," said Clare. "We're just going to go, anyway. You're only making it more appealing."

"I'll ask Britta if it's all right," said Dante, and he hurriedly left the room.

"Seems like Britta's very much in charge here," said Jem.

"I don't like her," said Clare.

"She can't handle a goat," said Ramah.

"A brave new world," said Clare. "I don't think Dante's read as much as he thinks he has."

"It's a cult," said Ramah abruptly.

"You think?" asked Jem.

"Yes."

"Whatever it is," said Clare, "when Master's away, Britta's the head of it. I think we need to get out of here."

"We need the cure," said Jem firmly. He didn't look at Clare as he spoke, but she knew: he was thinking of her.

"If he has the cure," said Ramah. And she was only stating what Clare was already thinking.

The three of them sat in the darkness on the big bed.

Clare looked out the window. The moon had cleared the trees and now cast giant shadows onto the lawn.

"I could stay here," she said, "and you two could go back to Thyme House."

There was a moment's silence, and then Ramah laughed. "I can just see you matched to Doug."

Jem was not amused. "We're not leaving you."

"Ramah, at least, should go back," said Clare.

"I don't think so," said Ramah. "Cults are interesting."

There was a knock at the door. It was Dante again.

"Britta says that, when Master's come back, you can do all the exploring you want."

"I bet you don't even like Britta," said Clare.

Dante looked startled. "That's not the point." But when he said it, Clare thought that some small thing had given way inside of him. Clare felt that they had begun to slip into Dante's psyche, and that if he spent just a little more time with them, they could open him like an oyster.

"Do you want to come with us or not?" asked Jem.

"Yes," said Dante meekly. "I do."

CLARE SLIPPED DOWN a staircase, opened a door and let Bear loose in the compound. For what they were planning, Bear was likely to be a liability rather than an asset. Jem took the heavy flashlight from his bag.

No one was roaming the halls; they could hear the sounds of snoring and the rustling of bedclothes and mutterings of uneasy sleep, but everything else was silent. Even the Cured had given up wailing. Dante took them to the door to the basement. The door had a small jagged mouth for a Yale key.

"I can't pick this," said Ramah. Jem leaned forward and turned the handle, and the door swung open.

It was a deep basement. The passage was narrow, and they had to go single file. Clare didn't count the stairs, but before they came to the bottom, her ankle had begun to hurt. She'd already put a lot of stress on it, but it wasn't just her ankle; she ached all over. And she had a headache behind her eyes.

"This is it," said Jem, and stopped. Clare, behind him on the stairs, started to fall forward and almost knocked him over.

"Easy," said Jem.

"Flashlight out of my eyes, please," said Clare. "My headache's bad enough."

Finally they all huddled together at the end of a long, wide hallway. Clare felt air coming from under the nearest door.

"This is a lot more scary than I imagined," whispered Dante. "I didn't picture the dark."

"Nobody pictures the dark," said Ramah. "That's the nature of dark."

Jem stepped up to the door. As he did, it slowly swung open, and cool air rushed out into the hall.

The room was filled with naked dolls. And gazing at them were hundreds and hundreds of small eyes. Some of the dolls with porcelain heads had fallen on the floor and smashed open like vandalized Halloween pumpkins. In places, there were dolls altogether without eyes, as if a rapacious crow had plucked them out. It was a flesh-colored wall embedded with a thousand sightless blue eyes.

Jem, Ramah and Dante automatically looked at Clare.

"Maybe you should go back," said Jem.

"No," said Clare.

"They all have blue eyes," said Ramah.

"All the children in those pictures we found had blue eyes, too," said Jem. "Remember? I remember I noticed because—because I noticed."

"It doesn't mean anything," said Clare uneasily.

"It does," said Jem. "I think it means that, for some reason, Master is obsessed with blue-eyed children. But none of those children in the photographs had eyes that were a really deep blue." He lifted his gaze and looked her in the face. "Not blue and dark as the wine dark sea. Not like yours, Clare."

CHAPTER THIRTY-FIVE
PEST

DARK AS THE wine dark sea.

It was true that her eyes were very blue—a strange deep blue. People noticed; Mirri had noticed that first day.

"I don't understand," said Clare. "What do you think the Master does? Collect children with blue eyes?"

"Even that angel upstairs had blue eyes," said Jem. "And those dolls. Keeping those dolls around just isn't normal."

"Master liked Eliza's blue eyes," Dante said. "But she disappeared. We're not supposed to mention her name anymore. Master likes his blue-eyed children best, though—he talks about their recessive genes."

"But what does he have in mind?" asked Clare.

"It's a cult," said Ramah. "People in cults don't think analytically. Not in a way that's easy to follow. Usually any logic there is circles back to who's got power."

"You know a lot about it," said Dante.

"Yes," said Ramah.

They moved out of the doll room into the hallway. Yellow light spilled out into the darkness from under a far door, and they could see a shadow moving back and forth, back and forth.

"I'm scared," said Dante.

"That makes sense," said Ramah.

The movement stopped. Jem took Clare's hand.

"It knows we're here," he said.

"Why did you have to say 'it'?" whispered Dante.

The door opened, and light poured into the hallway.

A figure stood silhouetted in the doorway. The man was big, much bigger and taller than any of them, although Clare realized that they weren't used to adults anymore. She had guessed, on the night in the woods, that he was fifty or so, and she saw that she had probably been right. But she hadn't noticed then that his face had smile lines around his eyes and mouth. It was a soft face, gentle and inviting.

"It's Master," said Dante, with relief and anxiety mixed in his voice.

"It's you," said Clare to the man, and Jem and Ramah and Dante looked at her, startled.

"It would have been less complicated if you had come with me then," said the Master to Clare.

Clare couldn't think how it could possibly have been simpler if she had left in the night with the Master, but then the pain in her head had spread to her neck, and she couldn't think very well. She only knew that the Master was the adult, and she didn't have to be responsible anymore. This was the moment she had been waiting for since she had watched her father and stepmother die. The Master would care for them all; he would give them the cure; they would go home. It would be as he had said: everything would be all right.

But she had discovered in all her time with the others, and even before, that things happen. That just when it seems that you're sitting safely beside the great road, you find that you're actually smack in the middle, where the traffic is.

The Master stepped aside to let them into the room.

"Jem," she murmured.

"Clare?"

"I don't feel so good."

The room that the Master led them into was one of light and shadow. Hurricane lanterns illuminated high ceilings and walls filled with niches. Everywhere they looked there were paintings and statues and tapestries. A large painting with four children in it dominated the room.

"It's not hard to collect art anymore," said the Master, as they looked around wonderingly.

"This is beautiful," said Ramah.

"Clare needs to sit down," said Jem.

"You should all sit down," said the Master. "And tell me why you're down here."

"We were exploring," said Dante. "We weren't prowling. They wanted to explore. And I'm sorry. I'm sorry I went with them."

Ramah cast Dante a look of utter contempt.

"We passed the room full of dolls," said Jem. "We didn't like them." The Master laughed.

"I found them when I first came to Haven," he said. "Which is what I call this place. I should get rid of them. I suspect they were a child's toys."

All the 'I's strung together in his sentences annoyed Clare, but she was finding it hard to focus.

"This wasn't always your home?" she asked.

"Oh, no," said the Master. "I lived and worked in the city, but after Pest I needed a place where I could offer help to the survivors I found."

"That's very good of you," said Jem. Clare recognized his tone; Jem did not like the Master.

"But we're not really survivors in the long run," said Ramah. "Pest'll eventually get us. True?"

"True," said the Master. "The rash indicates the presence of Pest. You may notice it in other ways as well. Perhaps, without even realizing it, you're becoming more lethargic. Maybe you don't really feel all that well. The symptoms depend on the child."

Clare certainly wasn't feeling very well at all. But she suddenly found herself remembering Mirri saying, "I feel *terrific*."

"And you have the cure," said Jem.

"I do," said the Master.

"And you're going to cure us all," said Jem.

"I am. But you have to wait here until you're on the very cusp of Pest. I can't cure you before that. And my price for the cure is fair—you need to help me rebuild the world."

"We heard about that," said Jem sharply.

"Careful," said Ramah quietly.

"We heard you want to pair us up as if we were sheep or cattle."

"Sheep and cattle don't pair off," murmured Ramah.

"I don't think you understand," said the Master. "Let's go upstairs. We can talk more there. Nobody has to be part of the new world if they don't want to be, and I allow personal preferences. I could match up you two, for example." He nodded at Clare and Jem. "If you want."

Jem looked away.

"That's just wrong," said Clare. "Personal preferences or not."

The Master's eye lingered on Clare for a long moment.

"Come with me," he said. "I'm upsetting you, and I don't mean to." Holding a hurricane lamp, he ushered them out of the room. Then he held up the light and gazed into Clare's eyes.

"Really remarkable," he said.

On their way to the stairs, they passed the doll room again. Clare felt cool air brush her cheeks, and she shivered.

The Master walked in front of them with the lantern, and his long shadow covered them all as they went up the stairs. He turned down a hallway and then went up another flight to reach the airy regions of the central house. Behind her, Clare could hear Dante whispering apologies to Ramah. And Jem—Jem was at her elbow, as if he knew how tired she was and was ready to steady her if she stumbled.

They passed a window, and Clare thought she detected the first light of dawn on the horizon. Finally the Master stopped in front of a door they had not seen before.

"Dante," said the Master. "You go to bed. When it's time for breakfast, tell them all I'm back."

Dante turned and left.

The Master used a heavy key to unlock the door.

This room was the mirror opposite of the room in the basement. Big windows let in the weak light of dawn; the furniture was spare. There were two Madonnas on the wall and what looked like several portraits, although it was still too dark to tell. But there was nothing like the riot of color and form they had seen below.

"This is my special collection," said the Master.

"I want to go home," Clare said. Her voice was weak. She swayed on her feet, and Jem put his arm around her waist to steady her.

"You want to go back to Thyme House," said the Master. "Yes, I know. You want the cure, and you want to desert us, too. But we can bring your friends at Thyme House here. We can make them part of this larger family, and they'll be safe. I'll care for you all until you're older."

"We could go back and forth between here and Thyme House," said Jem. "We could come and visit when the time for the cure comes."

"Maybe," said the Master. "But maybe you think so because you're so very young. Maybe what you want isn't what you need."

Clare did not want to move to Haven. Yet she heard something in the voice of the Master that made her believe that maybe what he said was true—maybe what she wanted wasn't what she needed. She glanced at Jem.

"We're doing pretty well," said Jem. "We just need a cure."

"It isn't that easy," said the Master.

Of course not, thought Clare. Nothing had been easy, not since Pest. She missed the before time—the hours gossiping on the phone with Robin; the number of back flips she could do; Reading *King Lear* in the middle of the night. Or reading *The Hunger Games* as Chupi pecked at the margins. Or *Jane Eyre* for the millionth time. And talking with Michael. It seemed as if she hadn't thought of Michael in a long while.

"Who are you?" Jem asked the Master. "What were you before Pest?"

Clare wasn't listening. She was drifting on a flow of her own thoughts. She looked at the paintings. One showed two adults in a house, the woman knitting. Outside on the lawn stood a child, but she wasn't playing with her toys, she was standing by what looked like a pet sheep and looking away with her ice-blue eyes. The eye-color looked as if it had been added to the painting. And the shadows around the toys were all wrong, as if she were in a different world than the adults. The plate screwed into the frame was blurry to Clare, but she stared at it until the words became clear. 'Mourning Picture. Smith College Art Museum.'

Clare turned her attention to the Master again.

"I was and am a doctor," said the Master. "A pediatrician, originally. There's a certain irony there, don't you think? But at the end I was a research scientist. And I think it's safe to say that I know more about Pest than anyone living or dead. I was close to a cure before Pest shut everything down. A real cure. My name is Doctor Andrew Sylver."

"The patches on the Cured," said Jem, after a pause. "'SYLVER.'"

"Yes."

"You made those people insane."

"Yes. But not on purpose, of course. The side-effects are unfortunate, but soon enough there'll be no Cured in the world—the patches were only ever designed to last a year, while we developed a real cure."

"Can't you cure the Cured as well?" asked Jem.

"Well, no," said the Master. "No. Their madness is too far advanced. Their brains are like, well, like cheese."

Clare seemed to rise to the surface for a moment, out of the tide of her thoughts.

"Why blue eyes?" she asked.

"I love my blue-eyed children," said the Master. He shook his head as if bemused, and his hair fell back from his neck.

"You're wearing a patch," said Ramah.

"I had to endure the Cure, yes," he said quickly. "I needed the Cure to gain the time to find a real cure. Which I have."

Clare didn't think this was a good time to point out that the patch had made him insane.

She slid quietly to the floor. Such weakness. And nothing to be done.

Almost immediately, she could feel Jem's arms around her, pulling her up onto his lap. Then he was unbuttoning the top buttons on her shirt, and she could feel his cool hands on her burning neck.

He was so gentle, so tender. She was grieved for him when she felt him touch the telltale blisters that she had discovered less than an hour before.

"Pest," he said softly.

"I'm sorry," said Clare.

And it occurred to her, now that it was too late, that she loved Jem, and that she had loved him for a long time. Knowing she loved him was like knowing her heart was still beating. Clare would have given a lot to have the time to talk about it with him, not least because he was her best friend. And Clare wanted to explain to him how he had saved her from the danger of her silly, selfish self.

She closed her eyes and as she did she felt something wet on her face. Someone was crying.

CHAPTER THIRTY-SIX
ASHES, ASHES

CLARE CAME OUT of her delirium to find that they were back in their bedroom. She stared up at 'Diana and the Hunt' and 'The Royal Picnic.' She turned her head then and saw Ramah and Jem by the bed, watching her.

"She's coming out of it," said Ramah.

"For now," said Jem bitterly.

Clare propped herself up on her elbows.

"I feel better," she said hoarsely.

"I'm glad," said Ramah. Jem was silent. Clare looked at him.

"It's the kind of feel-good that comes before the final relapse," said Clare. "Isn't it?"

"Yes," said Jem, finally. "It is." This time Ramah was silent.

"I guess it won't be long, then. I don't even get three days." She touched her face with her hand and felt the lesions on her skin, especially around her eyes and mouth. Soon she wouldn't be able to speak.

"I guess I'm pretty ugly," she said.

"Not to me," said Jem.

"The Master brought us here and left," said Ramah. "He says he's going to announce that you have Pest. He wants to show you to the children; he wants to scare them. We don't know where Bear is. Still in the compound, maybe."

"I wouldn't have minded," Clare said.

"What?" asked Jem.

"Being matched with you. I wouldn't have minded."

"We can talk about that later. You've been delirious."

"There is no later."

Clare thought of the first time she had seen Sarai and Mirri and Jem. She had thought of Jem as a little kid. She remembered further back, to the cabin she had lived in, first with Chupi and then alone, to the stag in the cabbages, to Bear's breath on her face.

"I don't want to die here," said Clare.

"Clare," said Jem.

"I'm so sorry I didn't see it before."

"Didn't see what?"

"I'm glad, Clare," said Ramah drily, "that you've started to realize the obvious, but we are still, as always, deeply in need of a plan."

At that moment, the door opened. Clare was expecting the Master, but it was a very small and frightened looking Dante. He took one look at Clare's face and stepped backward. A very pissed-off looking Ramah caught his arm.

"I don't think so," she said.

"Don't hurt me."

"Then do something useful."

He paused. "What do you want me to do?"

"I want you to tell us everything. I want you to explain why Master isn't rushing in here and trying to cure Clare."

"I'm really sorry," said Dante, and he burst into tears. Ramah took him by the shoulders and shook until he stopped.

"Explain. Now."

"Master doesn't really have a cure."

"Then why are you all here?" asked Jem. "What's the *point* of all this?"

"Master cares for us. He takes good care of us; he can't help it that when we get older the Pest blooms, and then we die. But we don't tell children about that when they first come in. They get used to it here, and then they stay. And it's a *haven* here. You've *seen* the outside world. What difference does it make if there's no cure?"

"A lot," said Jem. "It makes a lot of difference."

"That's why he wants to match up children so young," said Dante.

"So that, when there're enough of us, we can breed a new, young world. He's going to be careful who he selects; he wants survivors."

"Blue-eyed survivors," gasped Clare.

"You know an awful lot," said Ramah to Dante.

"I'm not *stupid*," said Dante.

"You're stupid and spineless," said Ramah.

Clare was impressed. Not much got to Ramah.

"I listen to things," said Dante. "And Master tells the kids who've been here awhile some of the facts. Not the facts about the blood; I figured a lot of that out on my own. From what Britta told me."

"What are you talking about?" asked Jem. "What about the blood? What blood?"

Dante cringed. "He likes it. Blood. From the blue-eyed ones. I saw him with Eliza once; she'd cut her hand in the kitchen."

"You are *kidding* me," said Jem.

"He kills them, doesn't he?" said Ramah.

"Yes," whispered Dante.

"I can't believe Britta told you this," said Jem.

"Master trusts her absolutely completely totally—and she'd do anything for him. But she still told me a lot; see, she likes me. And she shows off."

"Both you and Britta have brown eyes," said Clare thoughtfully.

"Yeah," said Dante. "Master'll never match us up. Thankfully. Britta likes me, but I don't like Britta."

"Lordy," said Clare. "It's like high school."

"Tell us what you know," said Jem.

"The blue-eyed girl children are different," said Dante. "Master told Britta that their recessive gene blood keeps him alive, but that, as a cure, it won't work on children. Just on him."

"He drinks their blood?" said Jem. "He kills them because they have blue eyes?"

"Not all of them," said Dante. "Some live. He wants to match them up. Until there are as many blue-eyed children as he needs. It's *scientific*."

"And you believe his little excuse for murder." Ramah's contempt was crushing.

"Well, he's alive," said Dante.

"He's alive because he's a Cured, you idiot," said Ramah. "He wears the patch. That blue-eyed-blood-is-a-cure stuff is nonsense. He just likes killing blue-eyed children."

"I bet he's obsessed with Clare," said Dante. "I bet Clare's eyes are in a different category from anything he's ever, ever seen. I mean, who's seen a blue like that? They're—"

"Shut up," said Jem.

"It's a good life here. Even for the blue-eyed ones. For a while."

"No," Jem said. "It's not."

"We need Bear," Clare said. It was bizarre to feel so normal when she knew she was dying. The relapse was in the shadows, waiting, but she still had a little time.

"Britta locked your dog in the courtyard," said Dante.

"Is there anything else you're forgetting to tell us?" asked Ramah. "Because it would give me great pleasure to hit you."

"I'm sorry, Ramah. I'll do whatever you want."

"Go and find out what the Master's up to," said Ramah. "Then come back. Quickly." Dante left the room, but not without casting a curious glance at Clare.

"Your eyes are really blue," he said. "I'm sorry you have Pest."

"Get out of here," said Jem.

Nobody said anything as he left. Finally Clare broke the silence.

"He's sweet on you, Ramah."

"He's an idiot."

"He's still sweet on you. Really. Trust me. In high school I was an expert."

"I'm ten."

"So's he. But maybe he can get you and Jem out of here."

"You're not going to die alone in this place, Clare," said Jem.

Now that Clare was sitting up, she could see the yard outside the window. Doug and a girl with dark curly hair looked like they were trying to erect a tire swing. A girl with a braid was jumping rope. Clare could just hear the girl singing and jumping to the rhythm of the song

"Ring around a rosy
A pocket full of posies
Ashes, ashes, we all fall down."

Britta walked into the bedroom. Clare started to get up, but the movement brought on the full weight of Pest. The fever and the pain began to settle over her again, and she was suddenly blanketed in agony. Jem eased her back down on the bed.

Ashes, ashes.

"Master's coming," Britta said. She looked at Clare. "You don't know how much I wish I had your eyes. Maybe I could pay him back then."

"What on earth do you think you owe Master?" Ramah asked Britta.

"I owe Master everything."

"I'm not going to let him murder Clare," said Jem. "It's not going to happen."

"She's dying anyway," said Britta. "She's not going to walk out of here. And we're going to show her to the other children. They can see what disobedience to the Master looks like."

Clare felt Jem's hand on her head as he smoothed back her hair. She wished she could see him, but her eyes were almost swollen shut.

"I'm taking her home," he said.

"It's over, Jem," said Clare.

Clare knew she was growing weaker. She had to get Jem and Ramah back to Thyme House, but there was only one way, and that way was very bitter.

Clare abruptly pushed herself off the bed. She almost fell, but she knocked away Jem's hand. Then she was on her feet and moving, unsteadily, towards the door. She found it hard to see her way.

"No," said Jem. "Don't do this."

"I'm going to Master," said Clare. "Thyme House is for you and Ramah and the others."

Clare reached the door. Then she was teetering at the top of the stairs. Jem reached her and took her arm, but she shook free of him. The Master, now visible at the bottom of the stairs, began to bound up. A moment later Clare was in the Master's arms, her face cradled against his chest.

"I've got you," said the Master quietly.

"It's not supposed to be this way," Jem said.

"This is exactly how it's supposed to be," said the Master.

Then, with what effort she could, Clare reached up and clawed at the Master's shirt, just enough to open it so that they could all see his Pest rash and the Cured patch.

"He's made it all up about the blood of blue-eyed children being a cure for him," she said. "He just likes killing."

"You can't do this," said Jem, and Clare didn't know if he were speaking to her or to the Master.

"Britta," said the Master slowly, "I'm not done with these house guests. You and Doug get Jem and Ramah nicely tied up, will you? They should co-operate; if they don't, I can make the end unpleasant for their friend."

"Let Jem and Ramah go," said Clare. "That's why I came to you now. So you'd let them go."

"Didn't work out, did it?" said the Master.

Then the Master looked down into Clare's eyes, and she could see her newly misshapen face reflected in the washed out blue of his eyes.

How do you like your blue eyed boy Death, she thought. *ee cummings*, she thought. *no caps.*

INTERLUDE

There was a flash of light that seared through Clare's brain. The flash lit up her whole mind and burned it and left her weak and panting. A familiar voice was yelling something about convulsions.

Clare roused herself. Before the final sleep, she must tell Jem how she loved him. With a cure, there might have been a full lifetime in which to do it. Now she wished only for a week, a day, an hour. But you can't always get what you want. You can't always get what you want. And sometimes, even if you try, you can't get what you need.

CHAPTER THIRTY-SEVEN
JOURNEYS END

CLARE SLEPT FOR a while in the Master's arms. She couldn't help it. When she awoke, she was in the collection room in the basement, lying on a cot. The light in the room was bright; hurricane lanterns were everywhere, and the tapestries, paintings and statues stood out sharply. She saw that Ramah's bow and quiver were on the large table, and she wondered if Ramah had tried to threaten the Master.

Then she saw Ramah and Jem. Their backs were against the wall, and their arms and legs were bound. Their mouths were sealed with silver tape. Jem had a black eye and a large scratch across his cheek. There was no sign of Bear.

Jem struggled in his bonds when he saw she was awake. The Master looked at him dispassionately.

"I'm killing Clare first, and then I'm killing you," he said. "For purely practical reasons. But as Shakespeare says, 'journeys finish when lovers meet.'"

"'Journeys end in lovers meeting,'" said Clare. "*Twelfth Night.* You got it wrong. Asshole."

Clare watched as the Master turned away from Jem and Ramah. And then all of his attention was on her.

"I want to look into your eyes while I do it," he said. And then he was kneeling in front of her. "They are so very blue. I've never seen eyes like yours—not in thirty years of looking. Maybe yours won't fade at the end." And she saw that he had a knife in his hand.

She tried to swallow, but her throat was too swollen. She tried to think of something she could say to stop him, but a high-pitched whine in her ears kept her from being able to think. She hoped that Jem and Ramah would somehow get away—they were strong and filled with ingenuity. Surely they would.

"I need to drink the blood before you die," the Master said. "That's Part One; I have to do that. Then I'm going to kill you. That's Part Two, that's recreation, but I have to do it, too." He sounded apologetic. Then his knife was under her ear. She felt a trickle of blood run down her neck as the cold metal touched her. The Master leaned down and licked it up.

Despite the tape on his mouth, Clare thought she could hear Jem scream. Or maybe she just knew he was screaming, swearing, struggling.

Pain. Life. Love. It was all about to end.

And then there was a huge clatter, and the door to the collection room burst open. Clare had trouble distinguishing the shapes that rushed in, and when she could, she thought at first she must be hallucinating. But not after one of them spoke.

"What are you *doing*?" asked Mirri. "Let her *go*."

CHAPTER THIRTY-EIGHT
WHAT HAPPENED NEXT

THE MASTER LEAPT TO his feet in surprise, lowered his knife and simply stared. They were all there.

"I think we'd better knock him over," said Bird Boy.

"Let's all jump on him," said Tilda.

"Watch out for that knife," said Abel.

The Master looked down at his hand, as if he were surprised to find a knife still there.

Meanwhile, Sarai walked over to Ramah and Jem and pulled the tape off their mouths.

"Get Clare away from Master," gasped Jem.

Clare listened to the disorganized clamor of voices with joy. And then she realized that she had a chance, weak as she was, to make things a little more difficult for the Master. The cot she was lying on wasn't quite flush with the wall. As the Master faced the children from Thyme House, Clare tried to move towards the gap. Movement was agony—as she pushed herself back from the lip of the cot, she felt as if her skin were being scraped from her body.

The Master turned for a moment and saw what she was doing, and when he did, as she pushed herself into the gap, he opened his mouth in a wide smile. She saw all his madness revealed in that smile, and then the smile grew.

Clare fell.

The fall to the floor was painful, but she didn't care. Now the Master stood in front of the cot, and she was behind it.

And then, at the back of the room, Clare saw Bear. The enormous dog had his hackles up and was growling softly.

Bear's first leap took him halfway across the room. His paws scrabbled on the floor as he landed and, for a moment, he lost his footing. Then he was up. Mirri was in his way, but with his bulk he pushed her aside.

Now he was facing the Master.

But the Master did not look afraid; he didn't even look angry. He shouted out and then filled the room with his weird laughter. The Master pulled up the flimsy cot she had been lying on and held it out like a shield.

Bear lunged forward, shattering the wooden frame of the cot and then leaping through it as if it were a hoop at the circus. The Master fell back against the wall. With one hand, the Master somehow managed to take Bear by the throat and hold him off. With the other, he stabbed at the dog.

Bear yelped, but he did not fall back.

"Somebody get us loose," said Jem.

"Can't you see?" said Mirri. "We're *busy*."

There was a noise in the hallway, and then Dante was with them.

"Untie us," said Jem. "Hurry."

Bear yelped again, and then he twisted in the air and broke the Master's grip. Now he was snarling. A spray of blood spattered the floor and wall, and Clare felt the droplets on her face. Clare didn't know if the blood were the Master's or Bear's, but she thought she knew what would come next: Bear would tear out the Master's throat. But Bear was off-balance, and the Master fell back against a tapestry, still living, still breathing.

And then, in an instant, the Master was gone.

BEAR CRAWLED TO Clare and, as they lay there, he licked her pitifully changed face. Jem, newly freed by Dante, ran to them both.

"Save Bear," said Clare. Jem ran his hands over the dog without once taking his eyes from Clare. Bear heaved himself to his feet, shook off Jem, and started licking Clare again.

"Bear'll heal," said Jem. He sat down next to Clare and took her hand.

Meanwhile, Bird Boy pulled down the tapestry to reveal a door. Abel tried it. It was locked, and, like the door to the basement, it took a Yale key.

"Damn," said Ramah.

"*Ramah*," said Mirri. "You *never* swear."

"He got away," said Ramah.

"Or *we* got away from *him*," said Mirri.

"Clare's not in good shape," said Jem. He squeezed her hand. "We need to get her to Thyme House. I want to get her to Thyme House. Once we're there—" He broke off.

Once they were there, Clare thought, she would be able to die quietly, with all of them around her. With Jem beside her. And maybe, if he were there with her, she could die without fear. Was that too much to hope for?

It seemed that it was.

Clare watched their faces change as each of them—Mirri, Sarai, Abel, Bird Boy, Tilda—took in her appearance. She saw shock, anger, fear, and, in Mirri's face, a kind of triumph that she did not understand. But in Jem's face, she saw only a deep anguish and defeat.

"Hurry, Mirri," said Sarai.

"I'm *hurrying*," said Mirri. "She looks *terrible*." And Mirri was suddenly fumbling with a box. She opened it and reached in without hesitation, but—

"This is *so* gross," she said.

Then she was applying leeches to Clare's arms and chest.

For the first few moments, Clare felt nothing, and then there was a tingling sensation. She realized that Jem had his arm around her. But memories crowded out the present. She saw into her deep past. She saw her own real mother dancing with her in the kitchen; Robin's face as they bicycled down the dark streets; her father walking away from the wreck on the highway; the first earth she had shoveled on Noah's body. The memories came faster and faster. And then she was two beings: an almost-grown who was no more than a small reflection in Jem's eye, and, at the same time, an infant, far, far away and long ago.

Clare came back to the present. She watched the leeches impartially as blood oozed out from around the places they had embedded their mouths.

"I was starting to wonder about those leeches," Clare murmured.

"Mirri's been feeling so terrific, you see," said Sarai.

"And no more rash." Bird Boy nodded sagely. "Not after the leeches." He unzipped his sweatshirt and obligingly showed his chest, which was free of any mark. "So we came."

"I'm not going to die?"

"No," said Mirri and Sarai and Bird Boy and Tilda and Abel. "You're not."

"I feel strange. But not bad. Good."

Jem tightened his arm around her.

Clare lifted her hand, meaning to touch his face, but she couldn't seem to find him in the dim light.

DARK TIME PASSED before Clare stirred in Jem's arms again. He helped her sit up.

"I feel better," she said. "Better than the last time I felt better."

"The Pest welts are already going down," said Mirri. "I can't tell you how *awful* you looked."

"Then don't," said Jem.

"We came as fast as we could," said Tilda quietly. And Clare saw that they all looked very dirty and very tired—there were deep circles under Sarai's eyes.

"We didn't sleep *at all*," said Mirri.

"*You* slept, Mirri," said Abel. "Bird Boy carried you for hours."

"She was tired," said Bird Boy.

"We are *so glad* you're not dead," said Mirri.

"How did you find us?" asked Ramah. "This place is a labyrinth."

"I was talking to Britta and Doug," said Dante, "when your friends arrived. Clare's dog knew them right away, and I brought them here."

"Thanks," said Ramah to Dante. "You came through."

Dante looked down, but he was smiling.

And then they were all chattering, like the ragtag band of ill-disciplined almost feral children that they were. They weren't particularly clean, like the Master's children. But, thought Clare, they had come through. They had pulled together. They knew what love was.

"I hate to interrupt all this," said Ramah finally, "as I always seem to do, but the Master's still out there. Somewhere between us and home."

"And what about his children?" asked Dante. "You can't just leave them. Us."

It occurred to Clare that, always and already and forever, everything was complicated.

She looked around. The Master's collection room looked completely different to the last time she had seen it. It was just a room with some paintings and statues, its mystery gone. She liked one of the paintings: children in a looming room.

"That's a Sargent," she said.

"You're wandering," said Jem.

"Maybe," said Clare. "It's kind of hard to focus."

"But we have to," said Ramah.

"Master must be somewhere close," Dante said. "He wouldn't leave his stuff behind. He likes his stuff."

They searched the room. Mirri kept trying to use a plastic wand with sparkles in it as a divining rod.

"What are we looking *for*?" she asked.

"Don't know," said Bird Boy. The feathers in his hair bobbled as he spoke.

"Better look at this," said Dante. He held up two enormous scrapbooks. The first was packed with newspaper articles and magazine clippings about Pest, often accompanied by a photograph of 'Doctor Andrew Sylver.' It was the Master. In a number of articles, he was quoted as saying not to panic, that a cure and a vaccine were imminent—that the cure might be something as simple and painless as a patch, like the ones people used to stop smoking.

In all of the pictures, even in one about the stages of Pest, he was smiling.

The other album was very different. The early pages also contained newspaper articles, but these were widely dated, and were all pre-Pest and all were all about missing children.

"Read the names," said Clare.

Ramah and Mirri took turns.

"Samantha Eckert."

"Elizabeth Mendel."

"Martina Hans."

"Sally Long."

Ramah looked up from the book. "That's a lot of children. Even for a serial killer."

"You think he *killed* them?" asked Mirri.

"I do."

"What kind of world do you come from?" Jem asked Ramah. She ignored his question.

"He has packets of hair next to the articles," said Ramah.

"What for?" asked Bird Boy.

"A collection," said Ramah.

"So these were his victims," said Jem. "In the pre-Pest days."

"There're probably others," Ramah said. Ramah slid the book over to Jem and Clare.

On one page, the Master had pasted in the side of a milk carton. On it was depicted one Andrea Laughlin, who had been eight years old, with blonde hair and blue eyes. The grainy photograph looked up at them. At the bottom of the page was a little glassine envelope, like the kind stamp collectors use. Only this one contained a lock of very blonde hair.

Clare felt sick.

The rest of the album was post-Pest and contained no articles at all. Instead, the Master headed the few used pages with a name, followed by a description below. There was a complete entry for Eliza.

The elect of the Master's blue-eyed girls had probably never had much of a chance. Of course, none of them had ever had much of a chance, really. All the roads had been hard roads.

"The leeches come off now," said Mirri. "They'll've done their work." She heated a metal pen in the hurricane lantern and poked the leeches, after which she peeled them off, one by one. "*Yuck*," she said as the leeches curled in her hand. Then she put them back in their little box.

"We still have to get back to Thyme House," Clare said. "And I suppose we have to do something to help Master's children."

"As soon as you're ready, we'll go," said Mirri. "That is, as soon as we find a way *out*. Those *awful* children locked the door behind us."

"I heard them piling up stuff behind it, too," said Abel, mournfully.

"I don't see why we have to help them," said Mirri. "I really don't like that bossy one. And they haven't helped us *at all*."

"We can't just leave them," said Clare, wishing very much that they could.

As they walked into the hall, the hurricane lantern she was holding cast huge shadows before them. She leaned on Jem, but instead of keeping up with the others, the two of them lagged behind.

"The swelling's going down," said Jem. Clare felt her face, and it was true. Some of the marks of Pest were still there, but her skin was mostly smooth.

"Jem," said Clare. "I have something I have to say to you."

"Clare," said Jem. "If it's about gratitude or eternal friendship, I don't want to hear it."

"I love you, Jem. I've loved you for a long time, only I didn't really know it. Not at first."

"I'm glad you figured it out," said Jem finally. "As for me, I've loved you since we first met."

"That's not true."

"Look down at the ring on your finger."

Then Jem leaned down and kissed her.

"I suppose any sane adults would say we're too young to know what we feel," said Clare.

"There aren't any sane adults. And I know exactly what I feel."

Then he slipped his arm around her back and pulled her to him and kissed her some more.

CHAPTER THIRTY-NINE
GETTING AWAY

RAMAH HAD NO trouble unlocking the door that opened onto the hallway that led to the stairs, but behind it was a mound of boxes and chests and furniture and mattresses blocking the way out. Two chairs fell off the mound and landed at Abel's feet. Clare couldn't see beyond the barricade, but she could hear the Master's children clearly.

"We want Clare's body," said a thin voice. "The others need to see what happens if you turn your back on Master."

"That's the snotty one," said Mirri.

"Britta," said Dante.

"Whoever. She doesn't seem too upset about Clare, even though she thinks that Clare's a body now. I mean a *dead* one."

"I don't think Master's with them," said Sarai. "He's probably hiding."

"Why would he hide?" asked Dante. "I don't understand."

"Because we're scary," said Bird Boy. "And we're not afraid of him."

Clare looked at the bunch of them. Bird Boy had sewn more feathers into his clothes, or what was left of his clothes. Mirri wore rabbit fur attached to the back of her shirt like a small cape, and she had her plastic wand at the ready, as did Tilda. Sarai was resplendent in a sequined T-shirt that spelled out 'DANGEROUS.' Her jeans were rolled at the bottom to reveal a flannel unicorn-print lining. Abel looked as if he were dressed in the colorful rags of a deeply disturbed person. And she loved them. And she loved Jem with all her heart. It was odd to think that there was a time when that fact wasn't obvious to her. Poor shallow Clare. She was gone now, forever.

They were gradually dismantling the mound that blocked the doorway.

"If we tell them we have the cure," said Sarai, "maybe they'll help us out."

"You have to pretend you don't know the cure," said Ramah. "All of you. Leave it to Clare and Jem and me."

They pulled more things from the pile only finally to face a wall of cedar chests and old steamer trunks. Abel sighed. "His children have been busy," he said.

"We have to find him and stop him," said Jem. "He has a taste for killing."

"We could bonk him on the head," said Bird Boy cheerfully.

"You can't even bonk a trout on the head," said Sarai.

Then they heard Britta's voice again. "We'll clear the door and let you through one by one," she said. "But we want the body first."

They ignored her. Jem and Bird Boy hauled a chest down; a mattress behind it collapsed onto them.

"We should explore the other rooms," said Ramah. "There may be all kinds of exits that don't involve coming face-to-face with that awful Britta."

"I don't understand," said Dante. "You all don't seem panicked at all, but we're trapped in here. There may be no way out. Master may just let us die down here. This could be *it*. This could be the end."

They all stared at Dante.

"I'm not sure what you mean by 'it,'" said Ramah. "Or what this could be the end of."

"Right now, we're just locked in," said Abel. "That's not very scary. Even for me."

Mirri walked over and put her hand on Dante's arm. "We've been through a *lot*. Being locked in is the *least* of it. Trust us.

Fresh air soon."

Fresh air.

"The doll room," said Clare. "I could feel the air moving in there—it had to be coming from somewhere."

They took three of the hurricane lanterns and hurried down the hall. Jem held Clare's free hand. With the strength of the lights, the scene in the doll room was even more disturbing. One shelf was nothing but a row of heads;, the hair very crudely chopped away from the faces. Mirri lifted her lantern and they saw, in the corner, a sparkling pile of blue. The eyes themselves.

"This is just *evil*," said Mirri.

Clare took the lead with Jem right behind her. She slipped behind the bookcase of dolls and found herself next to the foundation of the building. Just above her head was a window. The bottom of the window was flush against the grass at the edge of the courtyard. Air was seeping through a gap between the top of the window and the casing. But the window, like the doors, was locked, and the lock seemed to have been painted over. Jem couldn't prize it open.

"Ramah?" he asked. "Do your skills reach to jammed locks?"

Ramah moved over to him and examined the window. Then she pulled down one of the frail-looking curtains, wrapped it around her hand and smashed in the glass.

"There," she said.

They used a tapestry to cover the glass so that they could crawl out without cutting themselves. Jem gave Clare a leg up, and she was through. One by one, with Jem pushing from below, Clare hauled the little ones up and out. Lastly, she gave Jem her hand, and a moment later, he was out. They emerged into the courtyard, into the twilight.

It looked nothing like Clare remembered it. Now, in the evening light, everything looked washed out, the flowers unnatural in their regular rows. In the meadow beyond the walls, Clare could see sheep, and even they looked flat, as if they were pasted onto the grass.

All the false flashy beauty of the place had fallen away.

Bear pushed up under Clare's hand, and she stroked his head.

"Let's get *out* of here," said Mirri.

"What about Master's children?" asked Dante. "The older ones are on the cusp of Pest."

"I don't feel any great love for Britta or her little followers right now," said Jem.

"But I don't suppose we can just leave them to grow into Pest." Clare sighed.

Jem put his arm around Clare's waist.

"Something's changed between those two," said Mirri to Sarai.

"It's what we talked about, I bet," said Sarai. "They must've finally figured it out."

Clare, when she was to look back later, was to wish those moments had no end. She stood with Jem, remembering how he had kissed her, how she had kissed him back, and thinking ahead to the infinity of time before them. She could see that Ramah looked worried, and Dante was frightened, but she couldn't feel anything but joy, and not just the joy of being at that moment with Jem, but the joy of being with Jem in the years that suddenly and miraculously had opened out before them all.

But something had to be done about the Master and the Master's children. Clare couldn't help but think that it would be so much easier just to leave the children. She didn't want to take them in at Thyme House, even temporarily. Another thought occurred to her.

"What if the Cured have overrun Thyme House," said Clare, "while we're here?"

"We didn't leave Thyme House *empty*," said Mirri. "We left Sam and Becca there—you remember, *pregnant* Becca. They showed up right before we left. They looked just the way you described them. Not that you needed to describe much about Becca. She's *huge*."

"Sam and Becca," said Jem. "I'm glad."

"We put the leeches on them," said Mirri. "For Sam it was *just in time*. He already had the marks on his neck. Becca cried until he was better."

And that's when Britta and Doug and several of the others came out of the Master's mansion and walked down the steps into the courtyard.

When Britta saw Clare, she stopped.

"You should be dead," she said. "This isn't possible."

"Actually, I feel pretty good." And it was true, Clare did feel pretty good—more than pretty good. She felt terrific. She felt as if all her senses had come alive. "You can be cured, too," Clare said. "You don't need Master. The blue-eyed ones don't need to die."

"Master's building a new world," said Britta. "And he's said there is no cure. You're just some weird lucky exception. And the blue-eyed ones he takes would die anyway—just like the rest of us."

"Their sacrifice builds community," said Doug.

"Ignorance is strength," muttered Ramah.

"Come with us," said Jem. "There're better places to be. You don't need Master."

"Nothing you can say makes any difference to us," said Britta.

"I weren't nothin' before Master," said Charlie.

"That's right, Charlie," said Doug.

"And I seen that girl what has the dog before," said Charlie. "In the dark place. Her and the boy. Them two makes things happen. Them two is—" Charlie seemed to reach down deep into his vocabulary—"perilous."

Then Clare heard a quick intake of breath. She turned and looked. On the path that led to the gate was the Master. He was striding towards them. And he was smiling.

There was a sudden tussle as Jem tried to push Clare behind him, and Clare tried to push Jem behind her. Clare was still weak; Jem won. The Master couldn't see her as he greeted them.

"Hello," said the Master. His smile was so broad that he was absolutely beaming. He turned to his children. "I believe our guests are just leaving," he said.

Perhaps he really had intended for them to leave. Perhaps not. Clare was never to know. He pushed Jem aside suddenly, and as soon as he saw her smooth and glowing face, he ceased to smile. The change was as sudden as snakebite.

"You're alive," he said.

"Yes," said Clare.

He stared at her neck. "No more marks of Pest. And no patch. I guess you're not leaving after all, Clare."

"We're going home," said Jem. "*All* of us. And I think that these other children are going to come, too."

The Master sighed. Clare thought that he probably preferred the anonymous blue-eyed children in the photographs he kept in his secret box to the living, breathing riddles that lived with him.

"You have a real cure, Clare," said the Master. "Give me the cure, and I'll let you go."

"Your world's over," said Clare.

"Do you know why they call me 'Master' instead of 'Doctor Sylver'?"

Abel spoke up. "Because it sounds really scary?"

Dr. Sylver frowned. "Because since Pest, I've shaped everything the way I want it. The world is mine, and I can make what I like of it."

"No," said Clare. "You can't."

"You're just an ignorant little girl who's out of her depth," said Dr. Sylver. "You've happened on a cure for Pest, and you have the eyes I've been waiting for my whole life. I want it. And I want you."

"Not happening," said Jem.

"Yes. It is."

"Do you really think we're going to let that happen?" said Jem.

And that's when the Master pulled out the gun. "If you don't give me the cure," said the Master, "I'll shoot. It's very simple."

"It is simple," said Clare. "If you shoot me, I won't be able to tell you what it is."

"Oh I won't shoot *you*," he said. "I'll shoot your little friends." There was a moment of silence.

Then he lifted the gun and shot Jem.

Blood and flesh exploded from Jem's shoulder. Clare caught him as he fell, and they slid to the ground together. Ramah ran to them. In the horror, Clare could find only two words.

"Get him," she said to Bear.

CHAPTER FORTY
RAMAH'S ARROW

JEM WAS BLEEDING. Clare ripped off part of her shirt and pressed it into the wound, and the cloth was scarlet almost immediately.

Clare felt rather than saw Bear begin what would almost certainly be the last action in his life. Then she looked up, because she was responsible for the great animal, and if Bear didn't make it all the way to the Master, if he were shot down, she should have to watch.

Bear hurtled towards the Master. Clare could only hope that he would somehow survive long enough to reach him.

Then Clare heard someone shout out "NO!" and Bird Boy was running, running so hard that none of them had a chance to try and stop him. And Bird Boy, Clare realized, wasn't running toward the Master; he was running towards Bear. He collided with Bear as the Master fired.

Bird Boy went down, shot in the chest.

Less than a moment later, Clare heard a resonating singing sound.

And then Doctor Sylver, the Master, the tempter, the ghoul, the murderer, fell, an arrow through his eye.

Ramah lowered her bow.

As RAMAH RAN to Bird Boy, Clare pressed her shirt harder into Jem's wound and put Jem's hand over it. Ramah cradled Bird Boy in her arms.

"Help me," Ramah said quietly.

"I have to get to Bird Boy," Jem whispered.

"You can't move," said Clare. "You'll bleed out."

But she couldn't stop him. Jem got to his hands and knees and, painfully, began to crawl. Clare would have carried him if she could have. As it was, she got him half upright, and he leaned on her until she was taking almost all his weight. In this way, slowly, Jem made his way to Bird Boy.

"Save him, Jem," said Ramah. "There's so much blood. So much."

Clare let Jem down next to Bird Boy. Bird Boy's chest had been torn open by the bullet. His face was spattered with blood, and Jem wiped it off. He tried to put his hands on Bird Boy's chest, but, as Ramah had said, the blood was everywhere.

"Ramah?" Bird Boy called for her even though she was right there.

"I'm here. You're going to be all right. You're going to be—"

He took her hand and pressed it to his cheek.

"Ramah," he said. And then he died.

"No," said Ramah. And then, more softly, "Stay here, Bird Boy. Stay here." But Bird Boy wouldn't stay.

All the children except Britta stayed well back from the Master. She approached him, but as if she were terrified; she crawled on her hands and knees until she was next to him. His breathing was harsh and deep, stertorous, and Clare knew he was dying. Blood flowed in a torrent down his face, and as he convulsed, some of it scattered into the air. Britta was speckled with blood. She tried to cradle his head in her arms, but it kept lolling to one side. Blood was everywhere. It was almost enough, Clare was to think later, almost enough. But not quite.

Mirri didn't move, but she looked at Ramah and Bird Boy. Her cheeks were wet. Her nose was running, and she wiped it with a sleeve.

"Why didn't Bird Boy *stay*?" Mirri whispered to Clare.

"He just couldn't," said Clare. Jem was unconscious now. She knew he was fighting for his life.

"Is Jem going to leave too?" asked Mirri fearfully, and it was the first day they had met all over again, and Mirri was just a little girl who had seen too much death.

"I don't know, honey," said Clare. She put an arm around Ramah, who was weeping silently over Bird Boy's body. "I just don't know."

The Master writhed on the ground, and the sounds he made were obscene. He tore at the the arrow, although it was all too late. Where his eye had been was now no more than a pulp of flesh and blood. Britta backed away from him with a kind of horror. He turned on his side, and then he lay quietly in the stillness of death.

Bear sat back on his haunches, lifted his head and howled at the sky.

"I wish Master were deader," said Mirri.

"He's dead enough," said Clare.

And Ramah wept.

CHAPTER FORTY-ONE
IN THE MEADOW

SOME OF THE children took over houses near Thyme House, but many of them, especially the young ones, brought sleeping bags and stayed with Clare and the others. They all doted on Becca's baby girl. Becca had named her 'Little Clare.' After a long and, to the children, scary labor, Clare had delivered the baby. Clare had remained serenely confident throughout, which lent strength to Becca.

"I'm beginning to feel like a matriarch," Clare said after it was all over.

"That's how they're beginning to think of you," said Ramah.

"Charlie and Dante should be back with Tork and Myra and the others soon," said Clare. "I think they'll come to us. I really think they will. But I don't know where we're going to put them."

"I think we're going to have to build on an addition," said Ramah. "Because Thyme House is now, officially, full."

"If they come," said Clare, "they're going to make life interesting."

Most of the children moved into the houses and cabins spread widely in the farm area. But Lee, a doctor's son, and Sharon, who was good with mechanical things, and Dante, and even Britta, stayed with them at Thyme House. Britta seemed oddly lost, and she tended to wait until Ramah or one of the little ones told her what to do. At first Clare only spoke to Britta when she had to, and she only allowed her in the house at Ramah's insistence.

"She's damaged goods," said Clare.

"We're all damaged goods," said Ramah. And Clare knew better than to try to win an argument with Ramah.

Tomorrow they were to talk about starting a school, and maybe beginning an apprentice system of study.

As they went their ways to bed, Clare remembered the early days with Jem and Sarai and Mirri. Pest had left them with only fragments of a world, but they had made a family.

Clare woke up in the night. Gently she slipped out from under Jem's arm. She left him and Sarai and Mirri asleep, passed through the center room and quietly stepped over the sleeping children there. Outside, the meadow was flooded with moonlight. Pale moonflowers were open, and Clare breathed in their heavy scent. She walked through the garden until she came to the rock in the center.

The moon was full. Clare climbed up onto the rock and sat for a long time. Bird Boy would have liked to have seen how it all turned out, she thought. Bird Boy should not have died. He should not have died and broken Ramah's heart. The moon was beautiful and cold. At midnight, Jem found her, and they went back into the house together.

THE END

Gillian Murray Kendall is a Full Professor at Smith College, where she specializes in Shakespeare and non-Shakespearean Renaissance Drama. She has two children, Sasha and Gabriel, and lives in Northampton, Massachusetts with her husband, biologist Robert Dorit. Gillian likes all gardens, dark and light.

ACKNOWLEDGEMENTS

A special thank you to Richard Curtis, agent *extraordinaire*, whose close reading helped me remove some of the darker jumble of the manuscript of *The Garden of Darkness*. Thank you, Richard, for being such a superb agent, indefatigable on the matter of placing a manuscript, tolerant of my exhilaration when it was placed and indescribably supportive. Thank you, too, for your great sense of humor.

It also gives me real pleasure to thank James Gunn, whose generosity of spirit brought Richard Curtis into my literary life. A luminary in the realm of science fiction, Jim promptly answered my first email to him and has warmly supported this book ever since.

To go back more years than I care to remember, I owe a deep debt of gratitude to Alec Shane, who, at the very beginning, plucked my manuscript from a slush pile, brushed it off and said something like "hmmm." Alec gave my manuscript its first serious critical reading. And its second. And its third. And, without wilting, staunch to the end, its fourth. Without Alec's sharp eye and guiding intelligence, *The Garden of Darkness* would never have seen light. Thanks, Alec.

Thank you also to the team at Rebellion/Ravenstone. Jonathan Oliver was always a pleasure to work with, and I can't imagine a better editor. His suggestions were always acute; he's a superb reader, and we bonded over commas. Ben Smith deserves a thank you for seeing this through and Michael Molcher a medal for his work on publicity. Luke Preece delivered, as promised, a superb cover. I'm so glad for the blue-greens, and the crows and the size of the dog. In short, for all of it.

Smith College has been my academic home for many years. I am grateful to Marilyn Schuster, who understands the importance of sabbaticals. Many colleagues have given me their support over the years, particularly Bill Oram (with his enthusiasm), Nancy Bradbury (who believed that it would happen) and Naomi Miller (fellow author and Shakespearean).

I am indebted to Jane Yolen, who helped me not only in my role as new author, but also in my life as an English professor at Smith College. Thanks, Jane, for your kindness and support. Jessica Brody is a good friend as well as a wonderful writer. Caroline Kendall Orszak, a marvelous reader, made me cut three chapters (yes, it had to be done), and is also my sister. Robert N. Watson is a dear friend and a supportive colleague who has guided me for years and years and years. My participation in the Stanford Creative Writing Workshop, set me on this path, and among many marvelous and influential writers in that program two faculty members deserve my special thanks: Nancy Packer and Robert Stone. Nancy Packer taught me from the sentence up (and I was married from her house), while Robert Stone, who can't possibly remember me, once said, after reading one of my short stories, "If you can write an ending like this, you can be a writer."

Thanks to Mimi, sometimes known as Irene Dorit—a wondrous mother-in-law—and to Murray Dorit, whose memory remains. A particular thanks to my parents, Carol Kendall and Paul Murray Kendall—both no longer with us—who were both writers. My mother wrote children's books—one a Newbery honor book; my father was a distinguished historian who wrote, among many other things, the definitive biographies of Richard III and Louis XI. They encouraged my imagination and my voice from the outset, and for that—among many other things—I thank them. I've already thanked my sister, but that was for her skills as a reader; here I thank her for being my big sister. Finally, thank you to my two boys, Sasha and Gabriel, and to my husband, Rob Dorit, who did everything.

Gillian Murray Kendall